Babe thought he had done all the right things. He works a respectable job, owns his own home, pays his taxes, and throws jury duty summonses in the trash just like every other fellow American. He even stays faithful to his promiscuous boyfriend. But even through all of the right things, he is unsatisfied with his life.

Chance, an Eminem wannabe, drops his pants low and listens to hip hop to show his alliance with Black culture, but Babe has to learn to accept him as more than the "W" word: a wigger.

Alise and her special-needs son, Rueben, have been evicted and reduced to living in a car when her husband runs out on them. They now have to rebuild their lives after losing all their earthly possessions.

Babe finds that Alise and Chance may represent an opportunity for a fresh start as they navigate the intricacies of race relations, working class disillusionment, and mental health.

A BLIND EYE

David Jackson Ambrose

A NineStar Press Publication

www.ninestarpress.com

A Blind Eye

Printed in the USA

ISBN: 978-1-64890-248-2

First Edition, April, 2021

Also available in eBook, ISBN: 978-1-64890-247-5

CONTENT WARNING:

This book contains sexually explicit content, which may only be suitable for mature readers, depictions of bullying, violent acts against gay men, domestic violence, police violence, dialogue/words that may be offensive, ableism, abuse, bullying, cheating, death, eating disorder, fat phobia, graphic violence, grief, homophobia, bi-phobia, abduction, murder, past trauma, and stalking.

Prologue/Epilogue

The headlines dropped early one cold November morning.

The headlines did what headlines are designed to do. Carefully, or perhaps carelessly, curated word selection designed to capture the attention of the busy commuter on their way to work.

"Homosexual House of Horrors."

"Crack Baby Chained in Basement."

"Welfare Queen Kidnapping."

The headlines generated public interest. Sold papers to interested readers.

But newspapers had two different types of readers.

General readership, drawn to the words like flies drawn to shit, were lured by the specter of filthy children handcuffed in dank basements. Titillated by images of lecherous pedophiles, oversexed drug addicts focused on their next fix more than child supervision.

Wiser folk, like the residents of Norristown, where the supposed event took place, knew better. Those folk knew to wait for the local papers. Grassroots periodicals like the *Tribune* had long been the go-to source for events as they truly happened, rather than the nationals, which picked up a few morsels of truth and inserted the rest of their stories based upon whatever political zeitgeist was at play during that particular era.

For this era, the post-Reagan Clinton age, despite slogans of a more liberal, African American friendly president, the zeitgeist included fables of rabid teens randomly running through parks assaulting innocent joggers, Black women with wombs like breeding farms, lavish lifestyles of lobster dinners and Cadillacs funded through welfare entitlements, skeletal ghouls roaming the night in search of drugs cooked down to minuscule white crystals, and inner cities: a mythic imaginarium created by white flight—barbaric microcosms within the city proper where crime and vice ruled over morality and decency.

For those in the know, the smaller subsection of the population, those who were not white, there was a bit more involved with getting to the root of the advertised story. For those people, after reading the *true* story, they obtained the key words, the catch phrases, along with the names of the parties involved when available. Most times, if those involved in the crime were African American, names *would* be available; if the names had been omitted, one could safely assume the perpetrators were not Black.

This article, this story, was an anomaly in that the monikered *welfare queen* was unnamed. The absence of her name, age, and photo was curious.

Taking those keywords, nonwhite citizens would then piece together the actual story. Men would head to the barbershops. Women would schedule appointments with their hairdressers. The righteous would pull out their most ostentatious hats and head to the next church meeting. Men who loved men would wait until sundown to gather in the park below the county courthouse. Women who loved women would call around, find out where the week's tonk or pitty pat game was being held.

In these places, as in generations past, the story beneath the story would be extrapolated. The wheat separated from the chaff.

They all knew the house on Leviticus Street had to be the *house of horrors*. That place had been a refuge for *those people* for as long as Miss Rock had owned property in Norristown. That it was a house of horrors was subject to opinion, and to some, it was that simply for being there. While they had never heard that particular name, they were familiar with other names cast at the house with laughter or with derision.

Freak.

Funny. He/She.

Sugar in the tank.

Queer.

Those were the kind words. There were others, used by less kind people.

Most even knew already who the participants to the story were most likely to be simply by the association with that house. The quandary arose from the other participants, the outsiders. The baby, who was not a baby, and this queen, who did not descend from royalty—no one had heard of these people before. Who were they?

Chapter One

Babe & Chance

The Lark Bar was a decaying local dive on the edge of town. It was the only gay bar that did not require a trek into Philadelphia proper. His nerves were too frazzled for a long drive, but he felt like he would go mad if he sat waiting around in that empty house one second longer.

He waited as the bartender casually, deliberately served every other patron before pretending to notice him standing at the end of the bar, his sleekly muscled arm held aloft like some rare tropical bird, signaling with the only lure that outweighed racism; the cold hard cash held in his fist.

Babe pondered the subtle ways prejudice played out in small-town gay bars versus the clubs in the city. In the city, you were denied entry, waiting while burly doormen examined your photo ID as if the secrets of the universe might be found within. You tamped down on your slowly mounting fury as inebriated white fag hags were nodded past, screeching in your ear as they obliviously bumped into you along the way.

Here, no one carded you on the street. Because they could not run the risk of a public confrontation. The Lark Bar was tolerated, not welcomed, by the conservative county commissioners, bureaucrats, and taxpayers. Bringing undue attention and police involvement were verboten.

He leaned forward and mouthed *Grand Marnier, rocks* and floated a ten-dollar bill onto the damp bartop, noting the derision scouring the attendant's face before he turned and plunged a tumbler into a mound of ice. Babe knew that look. He had seen that same expression all through his childhood in the white suburbs of Upper Merion. The expression was designed to remind him that he was a pretender, that he did not belong; his delusions of grandeur had been noted and silently challenged.

Babe acknowledged maybe this time it was true. Ordering a beer would have been a more financially responsible choice. Especially if he planned to follow through on the thing he had vowed to do not more than thirty minutes before, storming out the house in search of a drink to bolster his resolve. But he had to let these gatekeepers know he wasn't an outsider begging for the scraps of their acceptance. So he ordered top shelf, even when his budget indicated well options would have been the smarter choice.

He tipped 20 percent because he knew they expected nothing. He was aware of the stereotype of Black people being poor tippers. That was another irony that struck him. White servers didn't seem to grasp that they were poorly tipped because they served poorly. He overtipped even after being made to wait until all other patrons were served. He ignored abrupt behavior and belittling expressions.

He counted out the change handed back to him, peeled off the proper percentage and threw it dismissively onto the bar, turning his back before the bartender could also deliberately ignore the tip, and leaned back with his elbows on the ledge behind him.

The hypervigilant jukebox playlist was another harbinger of the gradations of exclusion. Philly DJs played the current Black divas but remixed and diluted bass, lifted treble, and quickened bpms until most remnants of Africa were obscured to an acceptable approximation of *pop* (read: non-Black). Here, in the city perimeter, the only divas of color were Diana Ross and the Pointer Sisters fighting amongst a plethora of Patsy Cline, Celine Dion, and Barbara Streisand.

But here, in this small, dark space, with its abysmal checkerboard dancefloor off by the fire escape at the back, only occasionally populated for a rousing two step, and the echoing wail of canned music with its lone, weak strobe waving across dusty walls, the desire of lonely men was far more palpable than hidden amidst the revelry of big-city dance palaces.

It was bleakly evident in every wizened, mustachioed gaze glancing from hooded eyes. It was signaled in the way conversation momentarily froze as he passed, and the tremulous, trepidatious smiles Babe was too distracted to notice.

Babe crossed the peeling linoleum dancefloor to the seating area sectioned off by an ornate metal railing with steps going down like a cockpit. Sitting at the table by the wall furthest to the back, Babe set down his drink with shaking hands. He found this space, away from lustful consideration, with 8x10s of golden age Hollywood stars lining concrete walls somewhat comfortable. The scent of lemon wood polish merged with the orange blossom wafting from his glass. Even through his distraction, he was able to appreciate the gleam emanating from the wood floor beneath his unlaced Timberlands.

If they would tear up that awful linoleum on the dancefloor and show off the natural-random-width wood flooring beneath, he speculated, this place might not be as pathetic as it was. But, he realized, appealing to people like him with his mass of thick dreadlocks and tight wife beater, was most likely not part of the demographic the business model would have been designed to attract.

A loud, braying laugh cut through the din of a Tammy Wynette song. Peering through the smoke, Babe recognized the boy wavering at the bar. Pale and thin, basking in the attention of sad, old men, vaingloriously accepting drink after proffered drink, he swayed and bobbed from one torso to the other like a badminton birdie being hit between two opponents. Babe had occasionally seen him during the course of running errands, grocery shopping, or driving his friend Ricky down to the city to cop. The wan, pale boy always seemed to be sitting out on the cement stoop of a narrow two-story row house on Airy Street, no matter the time of day, in weather both clement and inclement. Ricky would point at the boy as they passed, cackling derisively.

"What?" Babe would ask, looking briefly at the boy as they roared past in a cloud of gas fumes and pumped-up mixtape bass.

Ricky pointed a pudgy manicured finger at the boy slouched on the stoop, wearing sagging jeans and Timberlands with his thin purple hair woven into sloppy wide cornrows.

"Would you look at that mess over there? Who did that head like that? These wiggers always be getting the whole shit wrong, chile. Especially the sissies."

Then, as now, Babe didn't find anything terribly wrong about how the guy was dressed. He didn't find anything even notable about it. He didn't see how wearing baggy jeans or oversized T-shirts denoted someone aping Black culture. Everybody wore big jeans. He admitted the braids were kind of bad, but he had seen worse.

As time passed, Purple Braids meandered from one patron to another until he gradually made his way back to the one most willing to pay for his drinks. Babe tried to remember how often men had offered to buy drinks for him. He could count on one hand. At some point, the man and Purple Braids began to nuzzle, then kiss, which turned to rather passionate demonstrations until the bartender drifted over and mouthed something to them while bobbing his head jerkily.

The two of them stumbled toward the vestibule where the restrooms were, giggling as they went. As they passed into the narrow passageway, Purple Braids looked through into the seating area, briefly locking eyes with Babe before the man fell back into the swinging doors, pulling the boy with him. Babe wondered if Purple Braids had the secret to happiness. He wondered if he should have spent his twenties fucking random men in public stalls, sowing his wild oats, so to speak. Maybe if he had spent more time single, he might have been less inclined to blindly tolerate infidelity.

He took his empty glass to the bar and waited, and waited, and waited, his arm once again lifted to signal, this time holding the empty glass aloft. He had met Matthew when he was eighteen and had been involved with only him for the past thirteen years. He nodded in confirmation to the bartender's silent communication asking if he wanted the same drink as before. Clearly, if the man remembered what he had ordered, Babe couldn't have been as forgetful as the man wanted him to feel.

Babe pondered if he had spent more time sowing his wild oats as they say, he might have a stronger sense of confidence that would have immediately faced the infidelity in his relationship from the very start—first, as Matthew had slept with girls while coming to terms with his sexuality, then with the supervisor at his part-time night job. Babe blamed himself for the infidelity. He had practically forced Matthew to get a second job. He had wanted to buy a house, and he stressed that they would be able to save up money for a down payment if they both found second jobs. But really, he had never intended to get a second job himself. He had a good salary. Matthew had been earning much less than he had, and so he searched the want ads and called to make an appointment for Matthew for a nighttime cleaning job. This was where he had met Darrell. And what had started as a casual friendship, propelled by their mutual appreciation for weed, morphed to more than casual, then moved to cocaine use.

Babe took his fresh tumbler of amber liquid back to his spot at the back. He wasn't certain when that cocaine use had become dependence. Nor was he certain when the friendship had become sexual. But when Matthew stopped coming home after the end of his shift and started stumbling in at daybreak, just in time to shower and change for his full-time job as a line cook for Quaker Chemical, Babe steadfastly ignored the thoughts that clouded every waking moment.

He had not been able to ignore the paraphernalia he pulled from Matthew's pockets when he sorted their clothes for laundry. The whispers through town about Darrell being a crack user turned out to be true, and unless Matthew was holding Darrell's works for safekeeping, it was clear he was not using it by himself.

As he had sat in that empty, lonely house another night, angrily digging the tears from his eyes with the heels of his hands, Babe had vowed this would be the last time. When Matthew came home, when he eventually came home, Babe planned to tell him this was the end. He didn't want to live this way any longer.

He looked up as the doors to the men's room banged open. The man lurched out, tightening his belt, and walked toward Babe, up onto the dance floor, then exited out the back door through the fire exit. Purple Braids sauntered out, smoothing his unsmoothable braids and walking in the opposite direction before circling back toward the seating area then patting exaggeratedly at his pockets. He approached the faded cigarette machine, slipped in coins, and banged on the top to help a pack dislodge more quickly. He looked covertly over his shoulder.

Babe rolled his eyes and groaned as Purple Braids drew close. He did not need nor want the attention.

Chance swayed as if a breeze had swept through the building. "Hey".

Babe nodded.

"Need some company?"

"No."

The boy nodded as he approached then pulled out the other chair. He struggled to remove the cellophane wrapping, tore back the gold seal, and gripped the butt of a cigarette, and clutched it between two fingers. His fingernails were long and dirty ovals. He raised a brow.

"Mind if I smoke?"

"Yes."

"I recognize you from town. Driving around in that dope-ass SUV with the booming system. Surprised to see you up in here."

"Why is that?"

His laugh came a few beats after his mouth splayed open, showing even, terribly white teeth. "Come on, man. You know they don't like us in here. If I had a car like you do, I'd damn sure be in the city instead of this hillbilly paradise."

Babe stared across the room.

"It's total bullshit. I've been coming here since I was fifteen. They never card me. Not once. And there ain't never no niggahs in here. People here make it clear who they want and who they don't. Well, wait. There used to be this old Black drag queen that came here every fucking night. Some old dairy queen. Thought she owned the place. She used to get them to card me. Didn't want anybody in here that might take away from her options, I guess. Shit, I wasn't no competition. I like Black guys."

Babe wondered if he was supposed to be impressed. He peered at him, his eyes burning from carcinogenic byproduct. "And how old are you now?"

"Huh?"

"You said you've been coming here since you were fifteen. So how old are you now?"

Chance peered around the room conspiratorially before turning back and whispering, "Twenty."

Babe laughed against his will before Purple Braids swiftly held a finger to his lips and shushed him.

"Well, listen, this is Bridgeport. You gotta expect you find some racism—" Babe paused pointedly for emphasis. "—for people...like us."

He agreed. "The whole town is full of racist assed wops and cops. They act like this raggedy assed town is someplace anybody wants to be."

"This is the last place on earth anybody would want to be. You come here if your car is broken down, or you are low on cash. This is where old faggots come to die. You know, the old leather-queen crowd. Seeing a Tom of Finland sketch when they squint at their reflections in these dim lights, but they're really closer to a dirty old mop when the lights come up."

"So is your car broken down? I was gonna ask you for a ride."

"What? No it's not."

"Well you can't be broke. You have a rich old white fag taking care of you."

Babe took a swallow of his drink. "Yeah, okay."

"That ride you got cost a grip, I know. Them subwoofers alone would pay my rent for four months." He closed his eyes, seemingly seduced by the smell of Babe's breath—menthol and Grand Marnier. He reached across the table, offering his hand. "Name's Chance."

Babe paused a beat as he decided whether or not to further engage. His good manners outweighed his judgement, and he took the damp hand into a firm grip. "Babe."

Chance wrinkled a brow. "You're shitting me, right? I mean, yeah, agreed and everything, but nobody is named Babe."

He laughed, "Well somebody is."

Chance's cordiality made a slight swerve to a more sedate demeanor, the lids of his eyes lowering as he leered at Babe, who struggled to keep his scorn hidden from view.

"So, how about it, then?"

"How about what?"

"You said your car is here. Want to give me a ride home?"

"I'm not heading out anytime soon. Sorry."

He huffed in exasperation, "Come on, man. Don't you know I'm not really looking for a ride?"

"So, what are you looking for, then?"

"A *ride*." He made an emphatic leer at the last word.

Babe laughed. "I'm good."

Chance sat, staring at him, undeterred by the rebuff.

Babe asked, "Do you even live by yourself?"

"We can't go to your place? Oh, yeah. You live with that sugar daddy. We can hit up a hotel, right? He didn't give you a black card? If not, you ain't running the game right."

Babe, growing weary of the interplay, huffed abruptly. "I'm not sure what you're referring to, but my personal situation has nothing to do with you. You and me will not be getting into anything at this time or any other time. I do have a partner, though nothing like what you're talking about, but I would think you should be satiated at the present time since you just finished up with one of these sad old men you were talking about."

Babe's laughter pelted from his mouth, brief, staccato, and unkind. Chance stood abruptly, causing the table to topple toward Babe, who reached out to either side to keep it steady while deliberately avoiding making eye contact.

"Fuck you, then."

He wasn't sure because there was a sudden bomast of Celine Dion yelling from the nearby speaker, but Babe thought he might have heard the word *nigger*. While he couldn't be certain, it caused him to laugh even louder. It had been such a long time since he'd been called that word, it struck him as unexpected, and that made it even more funny to him. That he would not have expected it and the unimaginativeness of the word. He just couldn't stop laughing.

He laughed at the broad, retreating back and narrow waist as Chance strode angrily toward the bar. He was large of bone, despite his thin frame, with gangly arms and wide hands, boasting outsized knuckles. Babe's mother had always called those sorts of disparatcly proportioned figures "peasant bodies." Babe chuckled in agreement.

He tossed back the remains of his drink. Sitting in this sad, unwelcome place was doing no good to his wounded psyche. As he stood to take his glass back to the bar through the vestibule doorway, he saw the front door slam open as two men entered on a wave of loud, deeply booming voices. He froze, peering through the haze with dread, before sinking wearily back to his seat.

At the bar, Chance cocked his head around excitedly. The two men were a complement of light and dark. One was sinewy and lean, sporting a modified hightop and skin so dark it absorbed the light around him. The other one was the color of toasted almond, thin like a reed but with the wide shouldered stance of a former football player. His height was emphasized by the outdated hightop fade rising alongside well-shaped ears that stood out from his strong neck like two cups. Blue Jordache jeans fit his well-formed legs flatteringly, but rose an unfashionable inch above the ankle of his Converse hightop sneakers.

Chance walked toward them as Babe whispered his name with dread.

"Matthew."

Chapter Two

The Confrontation

It was clear to Babe that their evening of drinking had started earlier.

Their slurred voices rode above the jukebox music, making his stomach churn with discomfort.

Before landing at the Lark Bar, Babe had driven the perimeter where Darrell's apartment was, searching for Matthew's low, white Supra along the curb, circling in increasingly wider circumference before consigning himself to the probability that the two of them were somewhere in Philadelphia. It had never occurred to him they would end up here, at the end of the universe, just as he had.

The two of them passed a conspiratorial look when Chance approached, parting like the Red Sea to allow him to rest between them. Babe observed from his darkened space with sickening dread, immobile and disassociated. This game had gotten old. Two summers past when he had found out, Matthew had promised it had been a one-time fluke, encouraged by disinhibition encouraged by too much liquor. He swore it would never happen again. Babe had chosen to believe him. Believing a lie was an easier option than paying a mortgage by oneself, easier than thinking he was no longer the object of Matthew's desire. But when the late nights once again turned to no shows, he had known why.

He wondered if the less than fluid body language was due to the liquor Chance had imbibed or just youthful inexperience. Even from his distance, Babe was able to read the minute signals the two men gave each other, so it had to be glaringly obvious up close. He considered the possibility that Chance might be deliberately ignoring those signals. The wide flashing smiles, the hand gestures ordering more drinks, followed by hands grazing shoulders, then belt buckles, heads lowered to allow lips to murmur into ears all sickened him, but he sat there immobile in his rage, unable to move.

He worked on a confrontation scenario where he would storm across the room, do a full out passive aggressive Bette Davis in *Beyond the Forest*. Let his eyes sweep melodramatically from one to the other and bark out a withering bon mot, "I thought I smelled failure and delusion! What a big disappointment. Make that an average sized one." Or maybe he could go all Cher in *Moonstruck*; storm over, gasp in surprise before slapping the dogfuck out of Matthew and yelp, "Snap out of it!"

Instead, he sat there. Time melted the ice in his glass to water. The ancient ritual played out before him, and he did nothing. They walked around to the vestibule toward the restrooms, oblivious of his presence except for Chance, who briefly, triumphantly glared in his direction as they hurtled into the men's room.

Racism would not permit this act of spontaneity. The bartender walked out from his post and over to the restrooms. Babe couldn't hear above Peggy Lee's self-aware warbling, but he could read the tension in the man's facial expression, note the vein throbbing in his neck as he stood at the doorway, speaking animatedly into the interior. The three figures walked out. He could hear Matthew's familiar slurred base as they stormed past the man, walked around and passed the bar area amidst the gaping stares of titillated patrons, and out through the back fire exit. Babe hunched down in his seat, certain he would be spotted, but the power of ethanol always outweighed Matthew's powers of perception.

Babe sighed in relief. His big confrontation had been delayed. He didn't know how long he sat there staring into his empty glass, finally drinking the dregs that had melded with melted ice, ignoring the blatant stare across the room he knew meant it was either time to renew his drink order or stop taking up space.

He slowly rose and walked out through the strobes, not taking his glass to the bar—fuck him—heading down the fire escape to the dimly lit parking lot. The sole source of light sat on the far end of the parking area, abutting an alley that ran past, leading to the subsidized apartments further down the road. The reek of garbage wafted on the air from the sanitation company further down the road, causing Babe to crinkle his nose in displeasure.

There was no sign of Matthew or his Supra. He sighed, imagining they had driven back into Norristown to Darrell's house. He considered driving there himself, but the five-story walk up had no doorbell, requiring visitors to shout the name of their intended party. He did not see himself screaming on the streets of Norristown while his man obliviously fornicated several stories above him.

Babe had parked beyond the lot, hiding his jeep behind the hulk of a dumpster. He wasn't sure why he had hidden his car, other than not wanting anyone to know he had been reduced to this, lurking in small-town watering holes. As he passed the trashcans at the landing of the fire escape, movement caught his peripheral vision. He turned, and there they were.

The sublevels of the bar housed rooms for let, and there was a narrow passageway leading from the entrance of the rented rooms that bled out to the street in front of the building. There, three dark forms undulated, separating then merging, then separating again in a microcosm of illicit, wet sounds and pixels of light from the glare of the streetlight beyond. Babe walked back toward the passageway, his eyes adjusting to make logic of the rapidly shifting shapes before him.

His heart thumped the dull sound of blood into his ears. His breath thickened in his lungs as he struggled to remain calm, tried to collect his thoughts, and draw in even breaths. He heard his shoes crunching on the gravel and the whispered drone of alcohol-fueled instructions merge with wet, sickeningly familiar sounds.

The tableau before him was not what he had expected. His first, uncontrollable response was an acknowledgement of the aesthetic beauty of the bodies before him, and how lovely the combination of dark blended with gold and creamy white in a whorl of complimentary shades. Beyond that, he was shocked at the positioning. He had expected to find Chance on his knees. Instead, Matthew was positioned there, emitting loud, embarrassingly amateurish slurping sounds. Fury replaced shock. He would have preferred to find his boyfriend at least fucking a young wigger twink rather than this. He would have preferred Matthew to be in either of the other two positions.

Babe leaned against the wall and folded his arms across his chest. His calm pose belied the condition of his soul. Involved as they were, they were unaware of his presence until he spoke, low and sultry. "You might need some K-Y to help with that, Darrell."

Darrell turned his entire body toward the voice, the dick in his hand pointing pallidly toward him.

"Ever since you first fucked my boyfriend, I wondered what it was. If maybe the dick was better. Now I see—"

Babe wasn't able to finish his sentence. Chance gave a yelp of surprise as Matthew pushed past him, charging toward Babe with an angry snarl. "You sneaky bitch! What are you doing out here? Trolling for dick?"

He collided into Babe, and both slammed into the cement wall. Babe stiffened his arms in front of him and pushed Matthew off. Darrell staggered forward and swung a fist at Babe but missed.

"What the fuck?" Confusedly, Chance yanked up his pants, lunged forward, and grabbed at Darrell's torso. He was able to gain control of him because Darrell had not bothered to pull up his pants.

As Matthew scrambled to throttle Babe, they fell to the ground with Babe on top. He sat on Matthew and screamed, "You're done. We are done. Don't even bother to come back for your shit. I don't want to see you again."

"That's my house too. I ain't going nowhere."

"You go stay with your buddy, there. I'm sick of this." He jabbed an angry, accusing finger toward Darrell.

Darrell yanked free of Chance's grip and pulled up his pants, then came forward and put a hand on Matthew's shoulder. Matthew angrily pulled free. "The fuck off me, man!"

"Come on. You can stay at my place. Y'all can talk it out in a couple days. Y'all too mad right now."

Babe laughed and stood up. "Nobody mad. Couple of days my ass. This is a done deal. Finally."

Police sirens wailed dimly, getting louder. A head laden with a neon scarf corralling big pink curlers bobbled out of a low window. "I called the cops! You assholes better clear out of here!"

Matthew and Darrell walked out through the vestibule toward the front of the building, teetering unsteadily. Babe's heart lurched at the sight. He scanned the ground near his feet for a rock to throw at them, forcing himself to calm down when Chance put a tentative hand on his shoulder.

"You okay?"

Too numb to speak, Babe shook his head. If he tried to formulate words or thoughts, he would dissolve into a thousand pieces.

"I didn't know, man. You know? I never would have rolled out if I hadda— "

"Don't sweat it. I was waiting for my chance anyway. You did me a favor."

"I mean it, though. My bad, man."

Babe managed a raspy, "Yeah."

"So, it's really a wrap? Just like that? You seriously going to end it on a humbug, no preamble?"

Babe barked in derision, "Oh there's been plenty of preamble. Believe that." He dusted off the dirt on his pants and turned to head toward his car.

Chance tightened his belt and hopped behind him across the lot. "Hey, man. No offense or nothing, think you could give me a ride home? I don't know if those lunatics might circle back."

He kept walking toward his Jeep, signaling for Chance to follow.

Babe fired the ignition and backed out of the space. Chance, energized by the proceedings, rambled constantly.

"Wow, man. That was intense, yo. Like, why didn't you flatten dude? I mean, he's been fucking your man, right? He had a beat down coming, you ask me."

"If the recent scenario is any indication, I'm not sure he was capable of doing much fucking. And if he deserved a beat down, then wouldn't you deserve one too?"

Chance laughed appreciatively. "I'm glad he couldn't get it up. I really wasn't too keen on getting plowed in an alley."

Babe rolled his eyes. "Seriously? You didn't seem to be averse to it."

Chance held onto the door strap as the vehicle careened out into the main street. They zoomed past Darrell and Matthew walking along Dekalb Street toward Matthew's car. They both jumped reflexively as a loud warped metallic sound erupted on one side of the Jeep.

"No way, man. Did they throw a brick at your shit? That's some shit. Ain't it? You caught *him* fucking, but he's the one that's pissed off?"

Babe tamped down on the accelerator, his blood boiling. Chance's constant droning was fast becoming annoying. The quicker he got rid of him, the better he would feel. He needed to be alone to process everything that had just taken place.

Chance went on obliviously. "Just like when you rolled up on us. I thought he'd be all 'Bay, I'm so sorry. Bay they raping me, I didn't want to do this.' Or even 'Bay, what you talking about? This really ain't me you see fucking this niggah' cause you *know* cheating-ass negros be lyin' they ass off.' Man, one time I was messing around with this slut puppy, right. I took him over to the Lark, and some fish was there, so dude was all embarrassed about being spooked at a gay spot, right, so he was trying to fuck her right in front of my face! I mean, I know he wasn't my man or nothing, but damn, right in front of me? And then, I gets home, right, and don't you know his dumb ass gone come following me still trying to fuck? Crazy!"

Babe turned on Oak Street. "You're on Airy, right?"

Chance paused. "Yeah. How you know that? Hold up, I thought we was going to go to your place, no?"

"No."

"Well, come on. You don't want to hang?" Chance's voice became strangely husky, a drunken approximation of sultriness.

"Not really. I'm kind of out of it. What's happened is a lot to process."

He put his hand on Babe's leg and began to meander it up his thigh. "Yeah. I get that. You don't need to be alone, though, at a time like this. Let's just chill. No pressure. Just a chill night."

Babe hoped he kept his face devoid of a smirk as he jammed on the brakes and the Jeep careened to a sudden halt. He grabbed Chance's hand and gently moved it back toward his own lap.

"No," he laughed despite being puzzled by Chance's behavior. He was also puzzled about why he was suddenly angry with him about his part in the night's events even though he knew Purple Braids had not done anything intentionally hurtful to him. "Thanks. But I'm good."

Chance would not be dissuaded. He slit his eyes and pursed his lips in what Babe assumed was a barbaric approximation of allure. Babe leaned forward. Chance closed his eyes and puckered. Babe reached over, opened the door, and nudged him out.

"Thanks for your help, man. You're trashed. Go sleep it off."

Chance struggled to gain footing as he tumbled out of the Jeep. He glared across the leather seats, sputtering incredulously.

"What? You trying to decide whether you should call me a nigger again? If it will make you feel better, go ahead."

Chance glared angrily, hands on his hips, seemingly at a loss for words. The door opened behind him, and a woman swore at him to bring his ass in the house as Babe skidded loudly into gear and sped off.

Chapter Three

Vacancy

Immediate availability
cozy 1 bdrm - 1st flr. apartment
quiet building
$500 pr mnth.
(sec. 8 welcome) inquire within

Leviticus Street sat on a shady pocket of Norristown's West End. At the end of the block sat what had once been a robust elementary school, named after a racist president. In the early part of the twentieth century, its classrooms were filled with the well-fed children of factory and mill workers from the steel mills, cigar factories, and corsetieres of the surrounding areas. The grand houses on Leviticus Street once lodged large families with spacious kitchens where housewives baked pound cakes and roasted chickens. Dark cavernous basements housed washrooms offering a cool reprieve on hot summer days, its ceilings strung with wire to hang unmentionables. Spacious backyards offered a breeze, rippling damp uniforms and brickyard aprons drying on clotheslines as toddlers played hide-and-seek amongst the billowing sheets.

As the century waned, those large homes lost their luster. Children grew into disenfranchised adults, moving far away from factories reeking of working-class ideals into more affluent suburbs abutting business parks and tech firms. Newly minted suburbanites obliviously ignored dwindling warehouse jobs in favor of rapidly expanding information industries, chasing jobs in America's booming global industries.

Enterprising families left behind, unable to secure a way out, rented out rooms vacated by their disenfranchised children in an effort to supplement diminished coffers. Other families finally relented, selling to those previously forbidden access: —African Americans, who excitedly moved in, cashing in on an illusion of status and prosperity the West End no longer had.

Upwardly mobile African Americans, armed with better job opportunities of the information age even in the face of discrimination, surged from the east to the west side. But by then the once grand homes had become a shadow of their former glory. The once spacious rooms were paneled over, hardwood floors covered with cheaper, easy to replace low nap carpeting. Staircases were divided with particle board to deconstruct single family homes into apartments and rooming houses.

Avaricious real estate agents convinced the German, the Italian, and the Jewish old guard to sell low, terrified them with tales of white flight and encroaching populations of a darker hue. Fearing they might be left behind, they relinquished their homes to the young Black professionals eager to own a space of their own.

It was the cavernous, Victorianesque-styled house on Leviticus Street with the large porch that wrapped around the front like a protective arm Babe and Matthew had been drawn to. The property had been hacked into two units, cheaply installed drywall creating two abodes from one. This added to its allure as Babe had read an article in *Black Enterprise* magazine about smart homeownership and multiple streams of revenue via rental property.

His mother had scoffed at the idea of any home in Norristown being a sound investment, fixing her withering glare at him, saying little; relying on the power a few well-placed phrases had always been the most effective method for controlling Babe's actions. This time, he had ignored her, allowing the simple lure of the slightly askew Adirondack chairs, the brilliant green of the philodendron bursting from a blue clay pot, and the homey feeling of the looped pull on the shade on the front door to telegraph a message of home he was not getting from the cramped apartment at the rear of a podiatrists office he and Matthew had been sharing at the time (not to mention the five-hundred-dollar rental unit that would pay nearly half their mortgage).

Babe ignored the slightly disreputable feel, ignored his misgivings. It felt safe. The houses were mostly clustered, but still felt scattershot. There was an alley splitting the block in half, allowing sanitation trucks access to rear alleys where trash was set to the curb for pickup.

The farthest end of the street offered a laundromat at one corner and an antiques store at the other.

On warm summer nights, Miss Imogene Vant would pull a lawn chair out onto the sidewalk and string the chord from her small TV through a window so she could watch *Knots Landing* reruns. Or she would drag out her rusty grill and burn a few franks while she helped Angela Fletcher solve the newest mystery on *Murder, She Wrote*.

Babe was always horrified at such rampant displays of trailer park behavior outside the confines of a trailer park, but on his way back from picking up his order of broccoli chicken from Number 92 Kitchen, across from the laundromat, he couldn't help but rest a hand on her shoulder and *tsk-tsk* along at Abby Ewing and Valene's shenanigans.

Miss Imogene's constant sidewalk presence, while somewhat alarming to him, was also a comfort in the absence of home alarm systems. Miss Vant observed all activity within the eyesight of her windowpane.

Across the alley from Miss Vant lived the only Latino family on the block (but Babe believed they were passing themselves off as Italian). A small, bronzed woman of indeterminate age lived with her three sons in one of the few houses still intact, unblemished by subdivision and room letting, having managed to avoid the ravages of Reaganomics, recessions, and great depressions of the last century. Babe was grateful one of those sons had little use for blinds, offering vicarious views of him masturbating fitfully on a bed of artfully rumpled sheets most every evening. He watched along, sighing languidly at his windowpane, imagining guttural grunts while watching the tendons in his thighs tighten and his broad feet arch against the headboard.

The vacancy sign Babe had posted in the front window of the first-floor apartment of his duplex was the same advertisement that had been in the local paper. There had been a few curious inquiries, callers asking inane questions about whether utilities were included with the listed rental price or if the apartment came with cable. After a month had gone by with no serious offers, Babe was starting to panic.

For the first two weeks after the dust up at the Lark Bar, Matthew had been respectfully absent, allowing Babe the solitude he had asked for. Babe assumed those two weeks had passed with Matthew and Darrell reveling in the novelty of uninterrupted drug use. Knowing what a mean drunk he could be, Babe knew it would only be so long before Darrell tired of living with him. By the third week, Matthew had begun stopping by uninvited, letting himself into their apartment with his key, making hollow promises of loyalty when sober and threats of violent acts when not.

Babe had managed to keep him at bay for an additional two weeks, but by the end of the month, with no prospects for the rental property he needed to bolster the mortgage payment, he began to reluctantly reconsider whether he might be able to tolerate staying with Matthew. He was terrified of defaulting on his loan and being put out on the streets or worse, needing to ask his parents for help.

When Alise knocked on the door to inquire as to whether the apartment was still available, Babe sighed in relief, praying a solution to his dilemma was personified by the short, stout woman standing on the porch threshold. She adjusted the strap of her vinyl shoulder bag across her bosom, sweating in the heat of high noon.

"It is." He grinned as he did a quick perusal. Her home-dyed auburn hair was styled in a beveled angle that swept down across one darkly rimmed eye. The darkness of her lipstain and her make-up made her light skin seem even lighter with just a slight hint of coloring on her plush, freckled cheeks and the tips of the ears peeping through the hair tucked behind them. She wore large gold-hoop earrings that Babe gauged to be real. "Would you like to take a look?"

She beamed happily. "If I could, that would be great. I just happened to drive past when I was taking my car to the mechanic and saw the sign."

He stepped back, waving her into the narrow vestibule. There were two doors at the opposite end of the short hallway, numbered one and two. The door to number one stood slightly ajar.

Babe pressed himself against the wall to allow her to get by him. She appeared to be assessing the width of the space as she approached the door. She wore snug denims and a plain violet shirt, but he noticed her ballet flats were made of good leather, pressed into oval shapes by her plump feet.

"It's a one-bedroom unit, but there's plenty of space."

They walked into the darkened living room where two tall windows faced the alley of the house next door. The beige, low-nap carpet was lined with fresh vacuum tracks, leading into the bedroom, which faced the front of the house, boasting the huge, bowed window looking out onto the shaded porch where they had just been standing.

Babe continued nervously, anxiously, "The one drawback is that the bedroom is at the front, so you hear all the traffic from the street and also my comings and goings."

"Oh? You live here too? How's the landlord? Is he on top of fixing things when they break down?"

Babe bit back his annoyance. Why was it, he wondered, that people were so quick to assume that the landlord had to be some cranky old white man. Even his own kind presumed that Black people didn't have shit.

"That's me," he said through clenched teeth. "I'm the landlord."

"Oh, but that's wonderful. I would feel much safer, being a woman alone, knowing the landlord is only steps away."

Alise walked out of the bedroom, across to the rear of the house, into the narrow kitchen with a meager gas stove and a heavy, midcentury porcelain sink. "Y'all take Section 8?"

Babe now gave her a more critical, discerning once-over. "Section 8? Yes, we do."

He was partly leery. Section 8, government-assisted subsidized rental payments, usually indicated the grantee was unemployed. He didn't like the idea of someone sitting around the house all day, running up the water and heating bills, watching his every coming and going. But he also considered the reliability it promised. Payments would always be on time.

Alise said, "I just got approved by the assistance office. It's just for four fifty though."

"Well, the rent's five...so..."

Babe did an inward eye roll. *So this bitch doesn't have a job and doesn't have enough to pay the rent.* He imagined her sitting around on her big ass all day long, frying chicken necks and fatback.

"I could front you the extra fifty, if you okay with that?"

So now she wanted him to break the damn law. What she was proposing was what was known in the Black community as *the hook up*. But it was illegal. You were supposed to take whatever amount had been determined by the waiver, and the tenant was required to find an apartment that was within the range of that waiver. But what the fuck. He figured people like him, like her, sometimes had to rely on these intricate subterfuges to navigate in the grossly uneven playing field of Black/white relations just to get a leg up and stay afloat when it seemed that everything was stacked to make survival far more difficult than it was for others.

Alise briefly checked the tiny bathroom at the very back of the house, which, in a previous life when the building had been one full living abode, had been the shed. She turned around to re-enter the kitchen which had no dishwasher, nor microwave.

"Oh, there's a basement?"

The knowledge of a basement perked her up. Babe nodded and opened the door leading down to the cool sublevel.

"It's not finished or anything. But there's a washer and dryer hookup. If you bring one of your own, I'd have to charge an extra ten dollars for water usage." Babe knew if she brought her own appliances, he would not be responsible to pay for repairs.

"This is a lovely apartment, Mr...?"

He smiled. "Perry. Balthazar Perry. Thank you."

"This porch is perfect. I can sit out here in the evenings and read my Bible. And there is the Church of the Holy Redeemer right up the street."

"You go to that church? That's Presbyterian, isn't it?"

Alise shook her head. "I'm AME. But I like being in walking distance to a house of worship. It keeps my spirit grounded."

Babe bit back the urge to shout a facetious, *won't He do it?* He needed the tenant as much as she needed him. It wouldn't be smart to mock her, at least not if she might be able to tell he was mocking her. Removing all expression from his face, he tried to channel an expression of devotion. A mousy, Bible-thumping holy roller with a Section 8 voucher was as close to a sure thing as he could hope for.

"Tell you what I'll give you the extra fifty for first, last and security right now. That's one fifty. Then all I need to work on is getting you a check for what the agency will pay you. If you can tell them you're charging me four fifty, we can hook up the rest between us, right? How's that sound?"

"Ok. I have one question. You're getting Section 8, right? So how will you be able to pay the extra money?"

"Oh, that won't be a problem. I'm an RN. I can always pick up hours through my agency. I've taken some time off. My husband recently passed. Well, it's been a few years now, but still, I've needed more down time to get myself together from all that."

He nodded. "Oh, I feel you. I'm so sorry for your loss. Getting back on your feet after you've experienced such a terrible event takes time getting used to."

"Oh. I'm glad he's gone. The motherfucker was cheating around on me from day one. Probably since the honeymoon. At least I don't have to lay eyes on the bastard."

Babe commiserated. How nice it would be to have no worries about randomly coming across Matthew in his day-to-day travels. He briefly reveled in the image of an Amtrak Zephyr plowing into Matthew's unfashionably clothed body.

"You know what? I have a feeling about you. I think we might be kindred spirits. At least we seem to be at similar places in our lives. Let's do this. When did you want to move in?"

Alise grinned effusively. "As soon as possible."

"Well, let's get this paperwork taken care of, and you can move in as soon as everything clears."

He extended his hand, and Alise shook it, the two of them smiling broadly.

After having her fill out the rental application form he had bought from Staples, he showed her out, then breathed a sigh of relief. His money problems were solved.

He had never had any intention to run a credit check on the woman. He didn't have money to spare for that. He and Matthew had rented out the apartment many times during the four-year time span since they purchased the duplex. They never bothered with credit checks. Babe relied on instinct. Instinct was the asset he relied on through a childhood fraught with dangerous potential virtually unscathed, and so he had continued to use it through his formative years as his primary means for decision making.

As he walked into the living room of his upper-level apartment, he examined Alise's looping swirls on the signature of her hastily completed application form. He had read somewhere a hard right slant in handwriting indicated a reliable personality, committed to tasks and directness. His impromptu handwriting analysis led him to believe Alise was a dependable person, who would pay her rent promptly. He would give her a call tomorrow. He tossed the earnest money she had offered onto the large green-tinted-glass tabletop in front of the low-slung red leather sofa, and giving a shout of relief, Babe had a vague sense of unease from the beginning. He admittedly sensed something off-kilter, something more than the bureaucratic lie of a payment discrepancy. That, in and of itself, was no big deal. He sensed something else, some other thing lurking beneath the surface that he couldn't put his finger on. What he didn't know, could not have known then was how many branches the lie would sprout.

Chapter Four

The Cat and the Fox

Sitting on the carpeted steps leading to the covered hot tub, Rueben rooted in his pocket for his bag of Twizzlers. His heart skipped when he counted only four ribbons left. He mushed them into one branch and hastily chewed off a big hunk.

A white Persian cat mewled and rubbed against his bare feet. He picked her up and rubbed her against his cheek, now sticky with candy. Pretzel, their wizened dachshund, yipped for attention. Rueben scolded him for being jealous and rifled fingertips through his stiffened coat.

Although it was midday, all the blinds in the house were drawn, casting every room in gray shadow. A dark pallor fell upon bare surfaces of empty rooms, spaces where furniture had previously sat now reflected a paler spot on the carpet as a reminder of what was no longer there. Even out here, on the sunporch at the rear of the house, most light was missing. When the destroyers had swooped in, tossing and pillaging every item they lay their gloves on, the white witch, with her tightly pulled back hair and pointy red talons, had demanded the blinds be left in place.

Mama had stormed the white witch's heels, beseeching her to be kind. To give them an extra week. But the white witch had continued to breech each room, acting as though Mama wasn't even there, her cold blue eyes darting hither and yon, assessing each and every item, approving a few old, heavy pieces of furniture she treasured, shaking her head at most other items.

Mama had instructed him to gather up all the photos in their dusty frames. To take them from every table and mantel then put them into his big canvas duffel bag. But he had not had to collect them from tables. The destroyers had pillaged, hoisted items and carried them out of the house, throwing the pictures to the soiled carpet littered with dog excrement and other unidentifiable detritus. Most of the photos were of Papa and Baby Boy, taken long ago before Rueben was here.

He wished Papa was with them now. This wouldn't be happening if Papa were here.

Crunching sounds like glass being crushed underfoot erupted the silence. It came from the outermost area past the kitchen. He clutched the duffel to his chest. His heart battered excitedly. He reached into the bag and grabbed the muzzle, quickly placing it over Pretzel's snout, so he wouldn't bark. He picked up Puff Puff, who mewled in resistance as he clasped her a little too strongly to his chest. There was nowhere to hide. The furniture had all been taken out by brusque, efficient men wearing baggy tan uniforms with white nametags.

He remembered earlier times. Resting his head on Mama's lap as she read his nightly bedtime story. He remembered the story of *The Cat and the Fox*.

Once a Cat and a Fox were traveling together. As they went along, picking up provisions on the way—a stray mouse here, a fat chicken there— they began an argument to while away the time between bites. And as usually happens when comrades argue, the talk began to get personal.

"You think you are extremely clever, don't you?" said the Fox. "Do you pretend to know more than I? Why, I know a whole sackful of tricks!"

"Well," retorted the Cat, "I admit I know one trick only, but that one, let me tell you, is worth a thousand of yours!"

Just then, close by, they heard a hunter's horn and the yelping of a pack of hounds. In an instant the Cat was up a tree, hiding among the leaves.

"This is my trick," he called to the Fox. "Now let me see what yours are worth."

But the Fox had so many plans for escape he could not decide which one to try first. He dodged here and there with the hounds at his heels. He doubled on his tracks; he ran at top speed; he entered a dozen burrows—but all in vain. The hounds caught him, and soon put an end to the boaster and all his tricks.

(Aesop)

There were footsteps on the stairs outside the sunroom. Perhaps it was Mama. She had promised to only be gone for a little while. But she had scolded him to stay hidden inside where it was warm and not show himself to anyone until she returned. It had been much longer than he had expected.

His belly growled through lunch time. He ate the last of the ramen noodle packs he'd had nestled in the bag next to the pictures of Papa and Baby Boy. His teeth crunched satisfyingly on what remained of the dehydrated noodles while his head pounded after he had sprinkled the contents of the silver packet on the back of his tongue. The way the golden powder felt as it landed made him imagine sea urchins resting on a sponge in the ocean.

He wondered why Mama called Baby Boy, Baby Boy when he was older than Rueben. He imagined Baby Boy sitting there in the sunroom with him. Mama said Baby Boy was smart and handsome. Mama said he would shout the answers from the lesson books before she even finished the questions. Whenever Reuben got the answers wrong, she'd frown and tell him Baby Boy had never gotten the answers wrong. He had always made proper use of his time for studying.

Rueben imagined Baby Boy would be like the fox. He'd have so many ideas in his head he wouldn't know which one was best. He'd ask Rueben, his eyes wide with fright, what to do, and like that cat in the story, Rueben would use the one trick he knew best. He would hide.

He scanned the room once more before hoisting his bag over his shoulder and standing with Puff Puff in the crook of his arm. He pushed back the heavily padded hot tub cover, sweat beading his brow from the exertion. He threw the bag inside and climbed in after, dropping the empty Twizzler wrapping on the landing. He whispered urgently to Pretzel, who jumped up the stairs to the hot tub, and Rueben scooped him up and pulled him in with him.

Once all were tucked safely inside, he grasped the strap and drew it back across the lip of the tub, enveloping the three in darkness.

Chapter Five

Shopping While Black

The next time Babe saw Purple Braids, his hair was deep burgundy, buzzed close on the sides with stiffly gelled curls standing at least two full inches above his head.

As he pulled his Jeep up to the curb, he groaned with trepidation as Chance slouched against the brick wall of a consignment shop. Babe locked up and walked swiftly toward the liquor store, keeping his head down, hoping to go unnoticed. No such luck.

"Yo, my man!" he yelled out, dipping toward him with a swagger.

"Hey."

"You headed to the state store? I need you to do me this solid."

Babe cut him off in midsentence. "I don't have any money."

"You think I'm out here panhandling?" Chance scoffed. "I don't need your money. Look, can you get me a pint of MD? I got the money, but they carding."

Babe looked at the outstretched hand holding balled up dollar bills with derision. "MD? What's that?"

"What! You don't know about Mad Dog? Where you been?"

"Evidently, I've been places where beverages are not named after rabid animals."

"Huh?"

"Nothing." He took the money from him slowly, then patronizingly smoothed them from their balled-up state as he stared at him contemptuously. "Mad Dog it is. And how appropriate, might I add."

"Oh, you got jokes." Chance was right on his heels.

Babe stopped short. "You're coming with me?"

He shrugged. "Why not? I'm not busy."

Chance held the door open for him as he bowed low and waved a hand in front of him into the cool of the store.

"Listen, about the other night. Sorry about my behavior. I was really fucked up. I would never have acted like that in my right mind."

"Sure, you would." As they passed the bank of registers at the front of the store, a salesman immediately exited the cashier area and approached them.

"Can I help you with anything?"

"We good," Chance flagged him then kept talking to Babe. "You think I just act like a dick when I get turned down? I'm not that hard up."

"Where would this, MD, was it, be found? Would that be in imported wines?" They walked down one aisle, "I do think that's the way all you guys act when you get shot down because your ego can't understand, not everybody wants a piece of that rock."

Chance blinked back being offended. "But hey, that's not me though. I'm not some white guy from the burbs trying to bed a Black man for the night so I can tell my friends all about it. I practically been raised by Black people. My best friends are Black. I went to Norristown High. What's blacker than that?"

Babe scoffed, "My mistake then. I didn't know you were so Black adjacent."

Spotting the desired bottle on a low, dusty shelf, Chance lunged forward with a grunt of pleasure, grabbed it, then quickly handed it to Babe when he noticed the salesman shadowing them one aisle over as he pretended to straighten a shelf.

The salesman peered over the gleaming bottletops, "That is on special today, 20 percent off. I can take that up to the front for you."

Babe walked down another row of bottles, passing the man as if he hadn't heard him. Chance looked at the salesman and then at Babe in confusion before following him. The salesman sidled up a different aisle and quickly headed in their direction.

"So what you looking for? You one of them fancy shits, I bet. You looking for that Hypnotiq?" Chance picked up an ornate bottle and held it up to the light to see the colors dance. "My moms and her old man be getting amped on that shit twenty-four seven, so that kind of turns me off drinking a lot. They be getting it in. Then they want to fight and shit, and it comes down to me and my sister to break shit up and clean up the mess. There's nothing pretty about two drunk niggahs trying to have an intellectual conversation, and don't nobody know what they're saying."

Babe snorted. "Tell me about it. Do me a favor, right? You need to ease up on that *nigger* shit. You're going to end up getting youself fucked up if you say that to the wrong person. You might think it makes you down or whatever, or shows how you were 'practically raised by Black people,' but I promise you, that's not what people are thinking."

Noticing the shadow behind them, Babe turned to the salesman, who faced the shelf behind them and slid bottles to and fro. "Excuse me, I'm looking for a new cognac I saw an ad for. It's blended with passionfruit. Alize, maybe?"

The salesman smiled, his lips curving overtly, "Oh, I think you mean All Leeze. It's pronounced Ah Leeze."

He huffed in annoyance. "Do you have it?"

The man nodded in consent, walking closer. "You have I.D. with you? I'll have to verify you are legally able to purchase these products."

Chance barked, "Would he be in here if he was illegal, man? What a stupid ass thing to say."

"Hey, I'm just doing my job."

Babe grimly reached behind him, pulled out his wallet, then freed his license and held it out. The man took the card, peered at it intensely, then held it up to the light and turned it slightly back and forth. Chance moved closer and yanked it from his hands before giving it back to Babe. The salesman harrumphed disconcertedly before he guided them further down the aisle and stooped to retrieve the slim frosted bottle. Chance tried to yank the bottle from him, but the man pulled back and turned away from them.

"I can take this to the front and ring you up when you're ready."

Babe followed with a chuckle, removing a twenty-dollar bill from his wallet and waving away Chance's attempts to give him back the formerly balled up bills, recently pressed into a semblance of order right before they entered the store.

He stood with his arms folded as the man took the twenty and held it up to the light for scrutiny, squinting wordlessly. Then, he grabbed a marker from the countertop and ran the tip across the serial numbers with a nod of satisfaction as the color stayed true.

"What is all that about, my man?" Chance barked. "You scrutinizing that note like it's Monopoly money. This is actual legal tender, you know. Our money spends just like yours."

The man looked toward the Black man standing in the security booth, then turned and placed the bottles in a bag. "Thank you, sir. Have a pleasant rest of your day."

"Get fucked," Chance mumbled, snatching the bag from the counter and following Babe to the curb.

"What the fuck was that about?" he peered at Babe, handing him the bag as they approached the Jeep. "First I thought it was my imagination, dude was trailing us like we was breadcrumbs on Hansel and Gretel's trail, but when he tried that 'it's pronounced All Leez' bullshit, I knew that idiot was full of shit."

Babe laughed, reaching into the bag to hand over the smaller bag to Chance. "I thought he was right. What do I know? I'm not French."

"That shit don't bother you? He was an asshole."

"If I let myself be bothered by that, I wouldn't even be able to come out my house. That shit happens every day. You should know this, you being practically Black, and everything." Babe shook his head in regret. "That man was so anxious to put me in my place that he fucking lied? Lied about how to pronounce Alize? That defies all logical thought, so I don't even think about it because it's not rational."

"Fuck that peckerwood."

Babe doubled over, leaning on the car with laughter. "Peckerwood? Where the hell did you get that from? I haven't heard that word anywhere but blaxploitation movies."

Chance laughed grudgingly. "My mom's old man calls white people peckerwoods every day, all day. This is the first time I understand it though."

Babe climbed into his car, leaving the door ajar. "Thanks for having my back, Malcolm X, but the revolution will not be televised."

"That's not Malcolm, that's Gil Scott Heron."

Babe paused, then gunned the engine, nodding appreciatively. "Okay. You know a little something. You have to change your mind before you change the way you live. I'll see you around."

Chance bobbed his head, stepping back from the curb as the Jeep pulled out.

Babe drove down to the light before the idea struck him, and he peeled off up a nearby alley to circle the block. He spotted Chance bobbing not too far from where they had been before. He shouted out the window, "Get in. I don't want you drinking on the street like a commoner."

Chance hoisted himself up onto the seats. "What makes you think I was going to drink on the street?"

Babe smirked. "I feel like I know you. I can take you home."

"Thanks, but who says I was going home? I try to stay away from there until it's time to bring it on down to sleep."

The car veered around a corner with a loud screech and tossed Chance against the door. "You trying to kill me? Speed limit's twenty-five."

Babe screeched to a halt. "You want to drive?"

"Wha...?"

Babe climbed out, leaving the car idling as he ran around to Chance's side. "Come on, get in the driver's side."

His eyes bulged in disbelief, "You serious? How you know I have a license?"

Chance slid across the seats onto the seat warm with Babe's body heat.

"I don't know that you don't, do I? Let's go. Airy Street."

Chance cranked up the music before gunning the engine and peeling away from the curb as a group of onlookers gaped and CeCe Penniston blared from the speakers.

Babe shouted over the din. "I came back because I wanted to ask you if you're looking for a place to stay?"

Chance eased his pressure from the gas pedal, slowing the car down to a crawl, and turned the volume back down. "Say what?"

"You said your folks argue all the time, and you have a sister. I'm thinking it's pretty crowded where you are, and I'm looking for a roommate to help with my bills. You might have heard that I'm newly single."

They were both silent for a stretch, both lost in thought. Babe knew the modest two-story houses on the street where Chance lived were small. He imagined him in a cramped dirt-floor basement, dust permeating his clothes and his ridiculously colored hair.

"I been looking for a spot for a while, now. Man, I have to turn my shoes over to pour out the dirt before I put them on. Staying in that basement is like a troll living under a bridge."

"Well I'm not saying you're not a troll."

He laughed. "Fuck you."

I have a two-floor apartment right around the corner from here. In fact, if you want to come take a look at it. I stay on the top floor. I have an empty room on the first floor, private, right off the bathroom. Same floor as the kitchen and living room. There's no dining room."

"Dining room. Man, we ain't had a dining room ever since we moved to Norristown. Them houses on Violet, Airy, they must have been slave quarters or something. Ain't no room to even scratch your ass. But how you know I can afford it? You don't even know if I got a job."

"I'll charge you two-fifty. Anybody can pay that, it's only fifty a week."

"Niggah, you can't add. That ain't fifty a week."

"That's the thing we are going to have to come to an agreement on though. That niggah shit is done."

"You right, I got you."

"And you do have a job, don't you."

"Yeah, man. I been working since I was sixteen, yo. You think a broke bitch can walk around dressed like this?"

"Salvation Army chic can be done just by trolling the drop box on Markley Street. And we already established you live like a troll."

"Like I said before, man, fuck you."

Chapter Six

Curbside

The grey Silverado sat idled at the curb in front of what they had formerly known to be Alise's house. The elderly white couple sitting within peered at the mounds of discarded furniture, swollen black trash bags, and split open cardboard boxes spilled across the expanse of land in front of the porch with dismay. Mitch scratched his head through a tattered baseball cap and whistled.

"Look at all this shit, Pegs. They seriously did it, just tossed all her stuff out here like this in broad daylight."

Mitch's wife, Peggy Ann, reached a thin hand out to clutch her husband's flannel covered forearm.

"She's coming right on our tail, Mitch," she whispered. "She's going to have a conniption when she sees this!"

They looked out the driver's side window as the taxi shuttled past. The back door of the cab flung open before the vehicle made a full stop, and Alise hurtled from inside. Two lean young boys climbed through the teetering debris at the curb, picking through the remains, tossing things into a red wagon.

Mitch sighed in exasperation, hearing the muffled sound of Alise cursing. "What the blazes is all this shit?"

Peggy Ann gasped in horror. "Now you watch that language, Mitch Dorrance."

"Don't start up with me, Peggy Ann. I told you I didn't want to be involved in this mess from the first."

Peggy Ann shushed him while opening the door. Her flowered dress tangled between her knees as she exited. "Well what did you expect me to do? All her belongings put out on the sidewalk like she's an animal. It's just plain wrong. Is that how a woman of the church is expected to act? Just put the woman out on the curb like garbage?"

Mitch turned off the engine. "And you running to take her in. So she can spend the next ten years filling up our house with more garbage. I don't think so. Let's load as much of this shit on board as we can, and be done with her. I'm only doing one trip Pegs. God's honest. That's it. What y'all can't fit won't get got."

"There's no need for you to be using the Lord's name in vain."

"She did bring this on herself, you know."

Peggy Ann shushed him and slammed the door. "Come on, now. Before the neighbors get hold of the police. I don't need to have the church throwing our names into no gossip about dust ups on the street,"

He grunted in exertion, hoisting himself from the warmth of his seat and out toward the agitated voices at the curb. He passed behind the rear of the cab as the driver climbed out and used a hand to shield his eyes at the tableau playing out before him. He chuckled a low "*what the fuck*" and rested his other hand on his hip.

Peggy Ann approached Alise, who was sobbing and grabbing broken lamps from the wagon, mumbling incoherently. Peggy Ann recognized the boys from the neighborhood, knew their parents as parishioners at their church. She shooed them off with scandalized admonishments and hints of phone calls to their parents. She grabbed a box from one of the boys walking past.

"This is private property!" Alise cried. "You get out of here before I call the cops on your ass."

Peggy Ann absently massaged Alise's shoulder. Alise shrugged her off and dropped to her knees to open the just rescued box, inventorying its contents in a frenzy.

"Call the cops," one of the boys remarked, "They'll cite your ass before they do anything to us."

The other boy chuckled. "If it's out on the curb, it must be for trash pickup."

Alise raised a savage middle finger at them as they jumped on their bikes and pedaled away, dragging the wagon noisily behind.

Noticing the shifting curtains on the windows of the houses across the street, Peggy Ann tried to calm Alise, whose voice was rising tremulously as she berated the boys' fast receding backsides. Mitch approached as they sped away, hitching his belt awkwardly. He spat on the pavement, ignoring his wife's reproachful stare. "Where's the boy?"

"Maybe inside. Can you go around the back, through the sunroom, and see if it's unlocked? All the locks were changed when she came by with the moving crew. They just left us out here on the sidewalk like we was just a piece of the furniture. No offer to take us to a hotel. No storage unit. No money to get us through. Nothing."

"You expected she would give you a hotel and storage unit? You been given an eviction notice. They don't give you a warm handoff when you get evicted."

Peggy Ann glared at him pointedly.

He walked off toward the back of the house, cursing under his breath.

Peggy Ann smoothed Alise's hair making consoling noises.

The taxi driver walked up, scratching his head in perplexity. "Lady, I need to be paid. Five bucks."

"I need you still on the clock. I'm going to need your cab to help load up these boxes. How much is it going to cost to get to Norristown? Plus, I'll give you one hundred for your time."

The driver added up the mileage from Oaks to Norristown, along with the promise of one hundred dollars. He weighed the likelihood of her having money on the ready for an impromptu move with all her belongings stacked out on the curb.

"Imma need cash up front."

"No problem."

Peggy Ann watched in disgust at the lascivious expression that flashed across the driver's face when Alise reached into her ample cleavage and came out with a thick roll of cash before speaking to her in a placating tone.

"I'll go see if I can help Mitch get in through the back. You know he's not the most patient man in the world. Why don't you start going through this stuff and loading what you can sweetie? We can only load up one time and I'm not sure how much we're going to be able to fit in the truck."

Out back, Peggy Ann walked up the wooden steps to the deck. Mitch was noisily jerking the handle of the glass door, leading to the sunroom.

"Locked," he said definitively.

Peggy Ann approached and examined the frame around the door, bending to remove the metal rod lodged in the ledge. Mitch harrumphed and slid the door open.

"You'd think the boy would've heard all the commotion and come on out, wouldn't you?"

Peggy Ann conceded. "You'd think he'd come running out in his drawers, just like he'd do on any other day. Maybe he was scared, sweetie. This is a lot for the poor boy to have to go through."

They entered the darkened room, Mitch grumbling under his breath. "Smells like ten months of get back in here. Jesus."

"What is ten months of get back, I've always wanted to know. And what does it smell like?"

"Like this."

"Where d'you think he'd be? Maybe upstairs in his room?"

"You and I both know he's wherever the food's at, so let's just go on through this other door, provided that one's not locked, and check under the cabinets. I tell you this, wherever this smell gets strongest, is more'n likely where we'll find him."

"He's just a child, Mitch."

"He smells like a full-grown man. And he eats like one. That boy is surely as big around the waist as me, Pegs, and you know it."

She conceded. "But it's a parent's job to show children the right way, poor thing. And with her husband dying so unexpectedly there was no man to guide him."

"You don't need no man to tell you not to eat twenty-four seven—cheese cubes, tater tots, and chicken nuggets."

"I should have kept my mouth shut. You wouldn't know any of this if I hadn't told you. I'm no gossip."

"I might not have known, but everybody in the church talks about how she has the boy running around the front yard in his skivvies like he's a toddler."

She shushed him. "Now that's enough, Mitch! Do you know anything about trauma? How it affects a woman to lose a loved one? Someone you love so much and expect to be with you the rest of your life? Lord knows how she's survived."

"With the church's money, is how. Using up every ounce of sympathy and damn near all the available money too. You know we used to give to several needy families every year, not just one. This woman has been draining everybody's sympathies for way too long now, to say nothing about our pockets. This eviction is the culmination of everyone being fed up with kowtowing to Miss Alise Norwood and her fat ass kid!"

Mitch was cut off when they heard the rasp of the sliding door opening. Alise walked through, her eyes darting nervously around the perimeter of the room.

"Okay, not much of the big furniture is left. She had her movers take most of my good antiques. I need help getting the bed and TVs onto the truck. I can take many of the boxes in the cab. Come on out, Bookums."

The large boy ambled clumsily from the hot tub and struggled to raise his feet over the rim before reaching back to lift out his miniature menagerie.

"I stayed hid, just like you said."

Alise walked over into the softness of his bulk. "That's Mama's good boy."

Peggy Ann marveled that the boy, not yet even an adolescent, was larger than his mother. One was the mirror image of the other, both round but sturdy: Alise, pale and freckled, and Rueben, a rich mocha with wooly hair spreading around his shoulders like a lion's mane. Peggy looked at the boy's hands as he hugged his mother. His abnormally small fingers reminded her of overstuffed sausage casings, plump and narrowing at the tips.

Alise grasped Rueben's shoulders and moved him to arm's length, staring into his eyes. "Okay, Boo, we got to get all our stuff packed up into Mr. Mitch's truck. I found us a place. We got to get moving!"

He rushed back to the hot tub and grabbed his duffle. "I'm ready."

Chapter Seven

Leviticus Street

Next to the house of masturbating Latin boys stood the near-derelict parking lot abutting what had once been the administration building of Andrew Jackson Elementary School. It now sat mostly empty but allowed for supplemental parking for the other houses on the block. The squat, two-story building was now a senior center, providing day activities for the people that had once built and populated this block.

A red Honda Accord hatchback puttered into the lot, moving to the rear, which was lit by a lone streetlamp. Alise backed the car up against the fence, facing the house across the street. At this time of evening, the porch was cast in shadow, illuminated by lamps from the houses on both sides.

"Well, Ruebs. That's it."

"That's it?" He frowned. "It's small."

Alise grunted around the cigarette jammed in her mouth. She reached across him and struggled to wind down the window, hoping the cross breeze would cut down on the smell of the bags of moldering food behind them, along with animal scent and sweating young boy.

"It's really nice inside. Wait 'til you see it. It's got a really good basement for Puff Puff and Pretzel to play in and a nice back porch where we can play Chinese checkers and read our Bible.

"Can I go see it, now?"

"We have to wait, sweetie. The people need to send the check for the down payment before we can move in."

He huffed. "We got to sleep in the car, still? Can't we stay with Miss Peggy Ann? They got a nice big house."

Alise had known Mitch would be furious when he found out all of the things they had packed into the vehicles would not be going along to Norristown, but would be stored for an unspecified period in their garage. But Peggy Ann really called the shots in that house. As much as she called the shots, however, she had not been able to convince Mitch to allow them to stay for a few days.

The car was even more cramped with the dog and cat, even though they were small.

"Listen, it's late now. Time to go to sleep."

Rueben turned the knob on the side of his seat, reclining the chair as far back as space would allow.

Puff Puff mewed and leaped on his belly. Rueben laughed at the unexpectedness of it.

"Can I have some Oreos?"

Her voice became stern. "Just two. And get me one too."

A White Supra drove onto the lot, rumbling menacingly as it moved along the perimeter. Alise dimmed her beams as the car slowed to a stop in front of her for a second, growled to life, and roared out of the parking lot.

"Who was that?"

"Don't know."

"Nice car." He handed her a cookie and reached a fist toward his face. Alise's hand quickly flashed out and grabbed his wrist. She grabbed the fistful of cookies from his hand.

"I said two cookies!" She threw the other cookies out the window.

"Sorry. Mama, I miss our house."

"I know you do."

"Why can't you use the money for this house and pay for our old house? All our stuff is there. It's gonna be gone forever."

She sighed, trying to tamp down on the anger beginning to surge in her chest. "It doesn't work like that. The white queen wanted us out. You know how mean she was. Did you forget? How you had to hide whenever she came around."

"No."

Alise struggled around behind the seat and came forth with a thin blanket with cracker particles and dog hair clinging like pine needles. She placed this over the boy, and he reached below his seat and took the cushion Pretzel had been resting on for his head. "Mama, can you tell me a story?"

"What do you want to hear?"

He shook his head. "Anything."

"Okay. Let's see. There once lived a town mouse in a great big city with a nice big house. The town mouse once visited a relative who lived in the country. For lunch the country mouse served wheat stalks, roots, and acorns with a dash of cold water for drink."

Rueben laughed and frowned. "Roots and wheat stalks? Who wants to eat roots and wheat stalks, Mom?"

"Do you want to hear the story or not?

"Okay, sorry."

"So, anyway, the town mouse ate very sparingly, nibbling a little of this and a little of that, and by her manner, making it very plain, she ate the simple food only to be polite."

"I wouldn't even be trying to be polite."

"After the meal, the friends had a long talk, or rather the town mouse talked about her grand life in the city while the country mouse listened. They then went to bed in a cozy nest in the hedgerow and slept in quiet and comfort until the morning. In her sleep, the country mouse dreamed she was a town mouse with all the luxuries and delights of city life her friend had described for her. So, the next day when the town mouse asked the country mouse to go home with her to the city, she gladly said yes.

"When they reached the mansion where the town mouse lived, they found on the table in the dining room the leavings of a very fine banquet. There were sweetmeats—"

Rueben snickered. "Sweetmeats? That sounds whack."

"Where'd you learn that ghetto talk? You don't talk like that around me. You leave that right where you got it."

He huffed. "Mom. They say that on SpongeBob."

"Well, you leave it on SpongeBob. I'm not raising SpongeBob. Okay. How 'bout this? On the table was some macaroni and cheese, candied yams, mashed potatoes and gravy, and fried chicken with fresh made lemonade."

"Now that's what I'm talking about!"

"So SpongeBob says 'now that's what I'm talking about'?"

Rueben rolled his eyes.

"Then, just as the country mouse was about to nibble a big old chunk of sweet potato pie, she heard a cat mewing loudly as it scratched at the door."

As if on cue, Puff Puff lifted her head from the comfort of Rueben's belly and meowed loudly. Both mother and son laughed and commended Puff Puff for her contribution to the story.

"In great fear the mice scurried to a hiding place where they lay quite still for a long time, hardly daring to breathe.

"When at last they ventured back to the feast, the door opened suddenly, and in came the servants to clear the table, followed by the house dog.

"The country mouse stopped in the town mouse's den only long enough to pick up her carpet bag and umbrella.

"'You may have luxuries and dainties I have not,' she said as she hurried away. 'But I prefer my plain food and simple life in the country with the peace and security that go with it.'"

Rueben struggled to keep his eyelids from drooping as he stifled a yawn. "So what's the moral to the story?"

Alise rubbed his beautifully sprawling hair, fanning over the seat. "You tell me."

He sat up and began to sing. "Don't go chasing waterfalls. Please stick to the rivers and the lakes that you're used to."

She punched him playfully. "Smartass."

"Goodnight."

"Night, sweetie."

"Mama?"

"Hmmm?"

"You think Papa and Baby Boy would like our new house if they was here?"

A light flickered in the uppermost window at the front of the house, wavering like a lonely firefly as she softly lied, "Oh yes, pumpkin. This time things are going to be so much better than before. Promise. No more white queen. 'Member how mean she was? The nasty way she would to talk to me? This time we have a Black king. And he's going to be way better than before."

Ruben's steady clotted breathing signaled he had fallen asleep. Relieved, she grabbed her purse and clambered out of the car, quietly closing the door after Pretzel jumped down to the blacktop. He followed her back toward the fence and loudly relieved himself onto a patch of ivy.

Alise leaned her butt onto the fence and shuffled around in her purse for a lighter, lit a Newport, then dragged hungrily. This was her first cigarette in over an hour, and as the smoke filled her lungs, it was like the filling of a void in her soul.

The filling of a void helped. But it was insignificant in the face of the tremendous physical loss she had suffered. Leaving the evidence of over a decade of her life on the street, not being able to carry away every item the scavengers had taken out of her home left a flooding feeling of incompetence in her she was unable to stanch. She had tried to collect what was most important, the things that gave her good memories. But how do you decide which things hold more merit than others?

The things more recently acquired could be let go the easiest. Items she had picked up from thrift stores and curbsides on trash day but had been salvageable. Like the turkey fryer someone had put out, or the vintage Barbie collection. The biggest struggle was releasing her husband's clothes; the suits he had worn at his job in Philly as a call center representative, custom made from Today's Man and JC Penny. Baby Boy's outfits by Carter, OshKosh, Stride Rite and Buster Brown Shoes—the outfits he had worn in faded school photographs from first through sixth grades before the accident: the accident that had taken them both away from her.

She peered through the haze of smoke at the dark place across the street. It was a dump as far as Alise was concerned. It wounded her soul to think of moving from her beautiful home to this tiny, dark space. But when Babe had taken her back upstairs, out past the bathroom near the rear entrance, there was a small porch, with just enough room for two chairs, and a tiny patch of grass crouching in the shadows behind a hulking garage along the alley behind the house. That porch was perfect for her. It sealed the deal. This was a place where she and Rueben could retreat, alone and unbothered.

She winced, thinking of how blatantly she had lied, telling Babe what a lovely place the drab apartment was. It wasn't the first, nor the biggest lie she had ever told, and she was sure it wouldn't be the last.

Pretzel nosed through the brush, exploring his surroundings while making sure not to roam far from his master's feet. Alise waved smoke away from her face and squinted at the same white Supra rumbling up into the lot, parking. A lean Black man hopped out and strode across the street, up the steps to 535 Leviticus. The man hammered on the glass window of the door, the force of his knocking echoing across the lot as a muffled echo.

Asleep in his bed on the top floor, Babe didn't hear the knocking. He also didn't hear footsteps padding on the carpeted landing by the vacant lower floor bedroom, nor the more solid footing up the wooden stairs to the uppermost floor. But Babe was a light sleeper, honed from a childhood of constant vigil.

Even though he was in a dreamstate, he sensed the staccato sounds of approaching footfalls beyond the closed door. He sat up in the undulating movements of a Ralph Lauren duvet and climbed out of the waterbed.

He opened the door as Matthew approached the doorway, stopping him short.

"Why are you here?"

Matthew walked forward, speaking in a low rumble. "I'm ready to come home."

Babe could tell from the slight elongation of his vowels he had been drinking. This annoyed him. "I don't think so. We will do better if we can move on with our lives."

The problem for Babe was when Matthew was slightly drunk rather than falling down pissy drunk, Babe found him alluring. The deep rumble of his voice, the slightly dirty smell of his hair, the slightly sticky feeling of his damp skin, and the slick of his absolutely hairless body, all those things still attracted him in spite of thirteen years of cohabitation and familiarity bordering on disgust for the behaviors outside of the bedroom. His rude manner of talking to people, his antisocial, homophobic demeanor, his casual, continual use of beer and drugs were behaviors with which Babe had become increasingly disenfranchised.

As Matthew moved forward and nuzzled his neck, Babe acknowledged the physical part of their relationship had never been an area of struggle for him even though Matthew screwed around—his soft lips and gentle, exploratory kisses, the comfort Babe felt from the heft and weight of his dick. The actual process of seduction, the leisurely preamble before the actual mechanics of sex, was a powerful intoxicant, sometimes impossible to repel.

"I don't got nowhere to go. Darrell's.... I can't stay with that Black motherfucker. I love you, babe. I fucked up. Why can't you accept my apology like a grown man, and let us move on, and do what we got to do? We the only Black couple doing big things. Why you want to mess that up, babe?"

"Are we? Are we doing big things? Big things like what?"

"You know none of these other gay boys out here got they own house. You know we rock shit together."

That amused Babe because he had had to drag Matthew's dead weight every step of the way through the home buying process. Matthew had not had the discipline to put money aside each paycheck for a down payment, devoting more time to buying weed than property. He had not been able to sustain a bank account. He had been unreliable with paying bills: if given the money to do so, he would spend it on anything but the identified bill. Babe conceded he was dependable, despite all his bad habits. Matthew faithfully placed the allotted amount of money Babe asked for each pay period in the red lacquered box on the side table in the entry hall so that their monthly bills could be paid. But left to his own devices, Matthew had not grown to more mature behavior. And thirteen years with no progress had grown monotonous.

"I don't know what other people have or do not have, and I don't really care. You always left me with most of the responsibility. You never did anything with the tenant thing. I always took care of it by myself."

"I leave it to you because that's your shit. You love it."

"I don't."

"Yeah, you do. You love acting some big shot white man, coming in and collecting rents, bossing people around. Acting like Mayor McCheese."

"Why is handling your business acting like a big shot? You think everything about getting your money or trying to attain a certain level has to be credited to white people. That's bullshit."

"Only people I know doing shit like that is white people."

"Then you need to move in different circles. Step away from the folks you've known. And what about your parents? They own their own house. My parents own properties, lots of people we know. We should have been working together, you left me to do the grunt work myself, because you thought it was 'white people shit'. I searched properties, met with agents and bankers, did the research, even got up the down payment because you didn't really take me seriously. So don't act like this is some kind of miracle."

"All those people are old heads. People in our twenties should be out having fun, enjoying life, not putting money in the bank and brown bagging lunch for work, re-using sandwich baggies and shit."

Babe sighed. The discussion would not lead to enlightenment. They had spent thirteen years circling the same stale topics, with no noticeable progress. He was tired of it all, of asking the same inane questions, like why can't you cook some of the time since you went to culinary school, and why don't you do all of our laundry instead of only washing your work uniforms, or why do you spend near every evening in a weed-induced haze of monosyllabic attempts at communication, which usually degenerated into the go-to communication fill-in—mind-blowing sex.

"Listen. I need more time. Time to sort things out. Get a better picture of what I want for my life and for us in this relationship. Can you understand what I mean?"

"But where am I gonna go?"

Babe folded his arms, staring at him through the darkness of the unlit room.

"What about if I stay downstairs in the empty apartment?"

"I already rented it out. She's moving in pretty soon."

Babe heaved an inner sigh of relief. Thank God he had found a tenant, so he could keep Matthew at bay. He now knew he needed to contact her and get her into that apartment immediately.

Chapter Eight

Move in Day

Babe wasn't quite sure what he had expected moving day to be, but he hadn't expected the noisy procession of shouted instructions, disrupting the Saturday afternoon quiet. He finished changing his sheets, always a laborious undertaking, lifting the heavy edges of the waterbed and forcing the fitted sheet around the shifting plastic. He had always imagined a huge hot water bottle. A ridiculous object, really. A concession he had made in response to Matthew's complaints that all decisions concerning furniture had been made without his input.

Babe went down to the landing to discover a lean dishwater-blonde woman with piercing blue eyes, brandishing a smoking cigarette as though she were the maestro at an opera, instructing two Black men, one somewhat middle aged, the other in his twenties, along with a twenty-ish dishwater blonde mirror image of the other woman as they carried various items up and into the room at the back of the landing next to the bathroom. As if on cue, Chance walked out of the back room wiping sweat from his forehead with (Babe noticed) one of the hand towels, which had been hung for purely decorative purposes.

"Oh, hey, great timing. We could use another hand. So, Babe, this is my mom, Ella, my sister Brittney, my mom's old man, Jase, and Brittney's boyfriend, Raheem."

Babe gave a silent greeting. Ella raised an eyebrow in return while the two Black men mumbled a 'what's up.' After they deposited the boxes in the room, they gave Babe a pound. This always made him uncomfortable. He felt like he wasn't doing it right and wondered if somehow the skin-on-skin contact would communicate the level of 'blackness' he imbued, marking him as a fraud. More importantly, he wondered if Chance's comment on his timing meant that he thought Babe intended to help him move his shit.

He smiled facetiously toward Ella, beaming perfectly orthodontia-ed teeth. "Nice to meet everyone. I'm sorry, can you not smoke in here? I've terrific allergies."

Ella glared momentarily, then returned his grin. "Oh! So sorry."

He felt the sense of satisfaction he always felt when he was able to kneecap white people by using the same supercilious facade of politeness they employed whenever they modified his behavior. She turned confusedly, searching for an ashtray.

Babe pointed exaggeratedly toward the bathroom. "You can put it in the toilet. Thanks."

He stared pointedly at his waistband, removing the pager from his belt and walking toward the stairs. "You can handle everything without me, can't you? My pager's been going off like crazy. I was on my way out when you got here. Just make yourself comfortable. I should be back within the hour. Nice to have met everyone."

As he descended the stairs directly into the younger blonde's condescending smirk, he matched her condescension with a withering stare of his own, watching as her expression shifted to grudging respect.

Upon the slamming of the front door, Ella exited the bathroom, barking orders. "Come on, now, y'all. Go get the rest of that stuff. I don't want to be moving shit all damn day."

She fixed her gaze on Chance. "You didn't tell me you was moving in with a Black man."

"Why would I tell you that? How's that matter?"

"It don't matter you moving in with some random stranger you just met? You never mentioned him before, so what is the story?"

He shrugged. "No story. He needs a roommate. I need my own place."

Ella narrowed her eyes. "You two fucking? I wasn't born yesterday."

"Does it matter?"

Chance watched as Ella examined the space—the thickly wefted carpets, the crown molding—moving toward the living room, grunting approvingly at the leather furnishings. He followed her, making his own assessments of the surroundings.

He picked up a heavy gold Durga statue, standing on the fireplace mantel, and read the gold content written on the base. He went over to the CD stand by the shelves of albums, quickly noting a few: Micah Paris, Annie Lennox, Dee-Lite, and Crystal Waters.

"He seems like he's doing okay. Drives a fancy car, got this nice big place. He's not struggling. Got that beeper and everything. What you think?"

She barked out a laugh. "You think maybe he's a doctor? What's a man like that, got all this, need from you? How old's he? He's probably same age as me."

Chance snorted, "I don't think so."

"Well he damn sure closer to my age than he is to yours. All an old ass man like that can possibly want from a boy like you, ain't got shit but what's in his pants, is exactly that. And I'm not saying that's a bad thing. Just telling you to be smart about it. Get what you can, but don't get in no deep shit. These niggers are stupid. Even when you think they're smart, sooner or later they mess up and lose it all. That beeper life catches up to them. So, you better make sure you know where the money gets stashed.

"You be careful. I'm not going to be getting you out of any shit you get caught up in. You been using drugs? I'm not gonna have no kid of mine strung out on crack "

Chance laughed. "That's funny, Ma. Real funny."

"You mark my word, is all I'm telling you. If you get caught up in some shit you can't get out of, you on your own."

He mumbled, "Yeah. Been there for a while now, you know. Don't you worry, Ma. I'm good." Chance felt a little guilty he had lied to Babe about having a job, but he felt like it was a white lie that he could easily take care of. He just knew he had to get out of that house, and when would another opportunity like this just fall into his lap? What had Babe said to him that day at the liquor store? You have to change your mind before you change the way you live. Well he was switching that shit on its head. He would just have to find a job and find one fast.

Chapter Nine

House of Whispers

While Rueben was happy to move into their new home, he did not like waiting until nighttime to do it. Mama had explained it would be better to move at night, so people were not watching their every move, seeing all their stuff. He did not want people judging them the way the white witch had judged them, did he? Folding their arms beneath their breasts and sadly shaking their heads.

As an added measure, Mr. Mitch was able to drive the truck into the alley and move in through the back door. The back porch was tucked away behind the hulking shadow of a garage with chipped wooden doors folded back as though it were praying. Beyond the small patch of grass, there were two back doors at the house on Leviticus Street. Mama explained the first door, the one with no porch, led to the Black king's apartment, and he should never linger there. There was a small porch off to the side, behind the corner of the house, only visible when you walked along the side of the house.

The adults quietly moved furniture from the truck. The house on the right stood silent, a frayed blind unevenly pulled across the lone window as if it were closing an eye. The door stood wide and gaping like a mouth with no teeth. The interior was dark but seemed to murmur like the lull before a storm. Then, the void roared into sound as a hulking calico pit bull lunged from the innards, yelping madly, and threw herself at the chainlink fence in a frenzy of spit and fury.

Rueben recoiled in shock before reaching into his pocket for a strand of licorice. He offered a branch through the links with one hand and brought the branch in his other hand to his own mouth. The dog quieted down, sniffing rapidly at the red coil, tentatively nipping a small piece before gnawing off as much as the chain link barrier allowed.

Alise approached from behind and knelt to peer at the dog.

"Hey there. Isn't she a pretty little thing?" She reached fingers through the fence and rubbed the massive head.

"How you know it's a girl?"

"You've got to start being more observant. Okay, now. We don't have all night. Bring in the things you can carry. And don't make too much noise. It's late. We don't want to disturb people."

They both watched as a window from the house on the right opened, and a dark head lunged out. "What the fuck is all that noise!"

As if on cue, each window of the house on the right illuminated. One by one, as though a tune was being played on a xylophone, each window opened, and a head peeked out. The unidentified heads all began to make a soft, sibilant sound, more a vibration than an actual word, like as 'hsk', over and over, singularly but then merging into one long wave, reaching out across the darkness until it drove the dog back into the pit of the house.

Peggy Ann, Mitch, Alise, and Rueben watched in the darkness, hands on hips, amazed. Rueben smiled.

Over the course of the next few days, Rueben found that even though he did not like his new home as much as his old one, there was something here he did not have before. While Mama did not permit him to go outside too much, when he did, the pit bull would always come tearing noisily out of the house next door until she discovered it was Rueben. Then she would quiet and wait for a treat. Rueben normally did not share his food, but he liked to share with the dog, Mitzi (according to the Chinese man that occasionally came out to drag the dog back inside).

The other thing Rueben found out was the house on Leviticus Street not only hummed but also whispered.

Mister Mitch and Miss Peggy Ann had brought all their belongings into the apartment. And it was his job to bring all the boxes Mama deemed for storage in the basement.

When she had first seen his obstinate expression, Mama had begun to talk in her happy voice, telling him how great the basement would be. She called it 'the lair,' using the singsong voice she used when telling fairytales, replacing all the sockets with red lightbulbs, casting the huge space with a pulsing hue. She pointed to all the shelves, all the pipes hanging from the ceiling from which they would hang curtains and tapestry, making a maze like the knights of King Arthur.

He had no choice; he would have to like the lair. Even though Mama told him he could sleep in bed with her in the bedroom upstairs as he had at the old house, she also told him it would be better if he stayed down in the lair whenever she was not home. It would be safer. They didn't want the Black king to hear Pretzel and Puff Puff, did they? So, it was best for them to stay downstairs. Both animals loved to rest in the comfort of his body heat. Rueben loved it too, patiently waiting for them to step around, maneuvering their paws until they discovered a comfortable position. Rueben spent a lot of time down in the lair with his pets. He wanted to help them get comfortable in their new home. He didn't want them to be homesick, as he was, so he spent a lot of time with them, listening to Mama's footsteps above as she prepared dinner or shifted furniture while listening to Eric B. and Rakim, or Run DMC.

It was during the time he spent in the lair he learned his new house was more than just a house. Here, if he was still enough, the house talked to him.

The first time, he had been stooping down, pouring kibble into Pretzel's bowl. Pretzel came dashing forward, nosing around in the food. Rueben nudged his snout and grabbed a piece of kibble, nibbling inquisitively. It wasn't bad. But he was glad he wasn't a dog. Lucky Charms tasted way better than kibble even though it was hard to tell the two apart.

On the crest of some far-off music, some woman singing in a way that made him think of a lady with big bosoms, long blonde braids, and a hat with horns, a whisper, light as an idea floated on the damp basement air.

"No help. No help."

Chapter Ten

Mitzi

Mama had put sheers on all the windows to help Rueben. The panels wafted on the breeze of an open window as she explained how great they were.

"See. This is like being outside. You can stand behind them, and no one can see you, but you can see out at everything going on outside!"

She was right. He was able to see people coming and going from the bedroom window at the front of the house, and the massive black dog trotting around the neighboring yard from the kitchen window. Mama had told him to be sure he never stood directly in front of the window, but if he stood off to the side, he could hear the people living in the neighborhood. And he could sit on the chair in the kitchen and talk to Mama while she sat on the porch smoking a cigarette or reading a book to him.

That was how he had caught his first glimpse of the Black king. Mama had stood up, flicking the cigarette butt into the grass, and waved away the remnants of smoke as he came out the other door, holding a bulging green bag of trash, which he took to the big black cans in front of the praying garage doors.

He was tall and fast with giant snakes whirling about his head. He had one bushy eyebrow undulated above glaring black eyes like an angry caterpillar. He nodded at Mama, not breaking stride.

Rueben's attention shifted as the vacuous silence from the void next door filled with the sound of scrabbling claws and wet growls, and Mitzi charged out of the door and banged against the gate. The Black king kept walking, cursing under his breath about fucking white trash and their fucking ghetto dogs.

Mitzi ran back toward the house, then sprung again at the gate, leaping over, falling on her thick jaw before standing and running toward the man, now stiff with terror and surprise. Mama screamed, "Mitzi!"

At the same time, the man put out both hands, fingers splayed, in front of him and barked, "No!"

The dog paused at the confluence of voices from different directions. She halted, walked forward, butting her snout against Babe's knees, sniffing absently then taking a nip at his thigh before jumping back over the fence and retreating inside.

"Oh my God. Are you all right?"

Babe dipped a finger into the tear in his cargo pants, gaping at the smear of blood on his nailbed. "I don't believe this shit. That beast tore my goddamn pants. They're Abercrombie!"

Alise moved forward and knelt to examine the damage. Behind the sheers, Rueben also moved forward, watching the snakes on the Black king's head tumble forward angrily.

"Why in the fuck they keep that door open day and night, anyway, is beyond me." Babe began to scream toward the open doorway. "Hey! Hello in there! Can anybody hear me?"

"Thank God it's a surface wound. She could have done a lot more damage. I think she was as scared as you. That's probably the first time she jumped the fence."

Babe huffed in exasperation. "I don't give a shit if it was surface or not. And now that she knows she can jump the fence, that bitch will be doing it all the time! Hey!"

She shushed him. "I'm pretty good with her. Why don't I go knock on the door? You can go clean yourself up, and I will get Drew to come over here by the time you come back down."

Babe was once more incredulous. "Are you insane? That's a pit bull! You think you're pretty good with her, and you go over there and get your throat snatched clean off. Then who's going to pay your rent? No ma'am. I think you'd best knock on the front door like you got some sense."

"Yeah. You might be right. God knows I wouldn't want my sudden death to interfere with your rent payments."

After Babe banged into the house with the slamming of the door, Alise walked around the the latched gate and entered the neighboring yard. She walked cautiously toward the open doorway, grabbing a stray metal trash can lid on her way.

Rueben watched her, listening intently, hoping to hear the house tell him something, but he heard nothing. Alise turned on her heel and headed back toward the apartment.

Rueben's mind began to race. This was his chance, and he wouldn't have much time. Mama reached for the key hanging from a chord on her neck. He stayed quiet, willing her to forget he was there. He retreated, backing toward the counter dividing the kitchen and the living space, waiting as Mama unlocked the padlock on the refrigerator door, and took out the package of liver that had been defrosting for tonight's dinner. His eyes strained to peer into the fridge. He would not have much time if he in fact got any time at all, and it would be helpful to know ahead of time what was there. He would have to move fast.

He peered down toward the floor, afraid if Mama made eye contact, she would read his intention and crash his plan to the ground before he put it in action.

She grabbed the package to her chest and spun back toward the door, not even bothering to close it.

Rueben licked the chaff from his lips. He surged forward and opened the refrigerator with a satisfied grunt as he peered inside. He frowned at the limited contents. Meager cups of Light & Lively, wan bottles of Crystal Light, and packets of mayonnaise. He grabbed a half-filled tub of Country Crock and quickly checked over his shoulder while he tore off the lid, dipped in a fist, and plunged the golden slather toward his waiting mouth. In his haste, he collected a few gobs in his long hair. Feeling the panic of the ticking clock, he didn't waste time inventorying the shelves, grabbing whatever was within arm's reach, despite its value or lack of value, then swallowing it with a satisfied grunt.

Chapter Eleven

The Cypher

The earthy, metallic lure of blood nudged the back of Mitzi's olfactory senses. She hopped up from her perch on the basement landing and trotted forward. The heavy blood scent weighted down the lighter notes of sweat and the merging blend of chemically treated hair and smoky carcinogens from the human carrying meat, but not able to mask the odor of her sex. That smell was always the one most compelling in humans. It was the one Mitzi used to differentiate them. This woman's was slightly peppery, of course, mixed with a metallic sting even more powerful than what emanated from the liver she waved in her hand.

Observing the dog grow calm as she approached, Alise flagged the animal organ back and forth, like a lure, before creeping into the darkened, filthy kitchen and moving past stacks of dirty dishes. She opened a cabinet, found nothing, then opened another, and again found nothing.

Mitzi began to growl irritably. Alise grabbed a plate etched with coagulated yolk from the sink, slapped the piece of liver onto it, and gingerly sat the plate on the basement landing while cooing 'good girl' comfortingly toward the dog's massive head. Mitzi's short tail bobbed in excitement.

Once her head was immersed into the plate, Alise gently closed the basement door and nudged Mitzi's rump as she caught the lip into the frame, and latched the door shut. Mitzi barked with a distracted anger but seemed more concerned with what was before her than what was beyond her.

The house was a darkened, musty doppelganger to her own apartment, and, more than likely all of the other houses on the block. The kitchen was the same design but still had its original counters and cabinets, painted a faded yellow, chipping off at the corners. Where her apartment had a counter dividing the kitchen from the living room, there was elaborate woodworking and columns marking the entry into a dining room. The windows were covered with shades, pulled down so little light fell upon the heavy oak dining table, which was covered with a forest green table runner and boxes of papers and envelopes with an old typewriter facing her.

The mantel was lined with dusty photos. Alise approached and picked one up. A smiling Asian woman with gleaming, blunt cut dark hair held a baby with stout legs aloft from a boat. There were many photos. Many of the same woman at various stages of life. A wedding with a stern faced, lean Asian man, her train pooled around their feet. The same man and woman holding hands with a stubby child. The woman, standing in a younger version of this same kitchen, a hand splayed to block the camera lens, an artful dab of flour on her forehead and a rolling pin in the other hand.

The low static of a television droned from a room toward the front of the house.

She walked toward the illumination. An old Asian woman sat slumped in a tattered Barcalounger. The TV was the only light emanating in the dim caused by the drawn window shades. It sat on an old metal stand with dented legs. The woman was much older now. The once-sleek black bob was now a silver chignon, but it was the same woman in the pictures in the dining room.

"Hello?" Alise tried to ignore the acrid scent of shit permeating the room. The woman did not budge. There was a TV tray beside the chair with a cup of tea and four uneaten wedges of sandwich, a cup of water, and various amber vials of medicine. A box of adult diapers was carelessly tossed beneath.

"Hey. Is anyone else home with you?"

The woman remained unmoved as though there was no one in the room except herself. Alise walked out into the hallway toward the stairway and yelled a loud hello. The only response was a rabid volley of yelps from Mitzi, and she slammed her bulk against the basement door. Alise jumped unexpectedly.

"'Kay. Guess there's nobody here but us, huh?"

While she tried to ignore the disgusting stench coming from the woman, the stench she had first attributed to Mitzi, Alise's years of nursing kicked in, and she fell into beast mode. She shifted the chair into recline, grabbed a pad and hoisted it beneath the woman, removed her soiled diaper and began to clean her up, grabbing the empty wash basin from the floor and putting the mess into it. She was grateful to find premoistened wipes, and she began to explain to the lady what she was doing, so as not to alarm her.

"Now, you're all right. Okay, sweetie? Let me help you get cleaned up a little bit. I know you don't know me, but there doesn't seem to be anybody at home. And I'm sure you don't want to sit around in this for God knows how long, right? Won't take but a second to get you right as rain."

"Hey, man. What the fuck you doing in my crib?"

She had been securing the tabs of a fresh diaper when the voice startled her. She turned to find a thin Asian man wearing outsized Hilfiger jeans, a white Hilfiger shirt with a large yellow pocket, and a baseball cap with a brim shaped into a curve and pulled low over his eyes. He was carrying a bag of groceries, which he sat on the floor and walked toward the woman, doing a quick assessment.

"Hey. Mitzi jumped the fence out back and bit Babe, so I came over to get you, but nobody was home."

"So you walk up in here like you five-oh and shit? That's not cool, man."

"You're right. Sorry about that. I followed Mitzi in. I'm trying to keep the landlord from flipping out. Diffuse the situation before it gets crazy, you know."

He knelt down and smoothed the woman's hair. "You all right, Grandmom? This bitch hurt you?"

Alise put her hands on her hips. "Okay, hold up, Drew. I know you did not just call me a bitch. You better be thanking me for cleaning her off instead of calling me out my name. If you were concerned about your grandmom all like that, she wouldn't be sitting here all by herself in her own mess with only a pit watching over her, and your back door standing wide open."

Alise turned back to the woman and readjusted her housecoat, murmuring assuring sounds to keep her calm. When she turned back to him, he looked at her sheepishly.

"Sorry about that. Didn't mean to diss you like that. I can't be everywhere all at once, you know? I gotta work. Run errands. I can't afford no nurse, or nothing, so I pray, rely on God and Mitzi, and so far, we been fine. Grandmom is okay watching her soaps. I check in during my lunch break. But anyway, thanks."

"It's cool."

"You might want to take a sec to go talk to dude next door about what happened. Smooth things over."

"Yeah, I guess. Listen, you not going to go call Aging and Adult on us and shit, are you? It would kill my Grandmom to be living in some institution with all them decrepit old white people."

Alise shook her head. "I hear you. Who would want that? Maybe I can come check on her during the day. I'm not working right now. I don't have much to do."

"That'd be great. But yo, I don't got a lot of money to be paying you. Grandmom gets stamps. Maybe we can hook you up. Break you off some?"

"Bet."

When they walked out onto the front porch, Babe was already standing there, pacing agitatedly, his arms folded across his chest. Chance lounged against the railing separating the two porches, smoking a clove cigarette. Drew inserted his hands into his pockets and slouched forward, a dip in his walk.

"Yo man, my bad. Sorry about all this. Mitz never jumped the fence before. It's not like her."

"How would you know this? You leave that goddamn door open day and night. As far as you know, she could be jumping that fence all the live long day."

The houses of Leviticus Street grew silent. Normally there was a steady ongoing hum, the hum of activity and life, but now, everything was quiet, except for the two men yelling on the porch of 535.

Drew laughed, brief and oblivious. "True. True. She could be. But she's a puppy, and she don't mean no harm."

Unnoticed by the group on the porch, the white, low-slung Supra rumbled slowly past, turning into the alley.

Alise agreed. "She's not full grown. She wasn't trying to hurt anybody."

Babe seethed, pointing at the tooth marks in his pants. "Be that as it may. She *bit* me."

"Yeah, man. But she was playing. If she was serious, she would have done a whole lot more damage."

"This *is* damage. These are eighty-dollar pants. And I want reimbursement."

Drew barked out a laugh. "Ain't nobody told you to pay eighty dollars for no pants. And to wear them to take out the trash."

The yellow van with Animal Control emblazoned on the side pulled onto the curb, its squealing brakes unheard amidst the raised voices on the porch. A squat, uniformed man struggled from the van with a curse. The group did not notice him, but curtains shifted in windows all along Leviticus Street. The man hooked a hand into his utility belt, thumb resting on a matte black taser as he walked up the steps into the confusion.

"It doesn't matter if I choose to wear a goddamn Balenciaga ball gown to take out my trash. The fact remains your dog jumped the fence and tore a gash out of my leg."

"Okay, come on. She was playing with you. She's a puppy."

"So, if I jump over this bannister right now and kick your ass, but I tell you I'm only playing, it's all good?"

The officer moved forward, all base and authority. "Okay, now. Here, here. We can't have terroristic threats being lobbed about. What seems to be the problem? We got a call about a loose pit?"

Babe spun around facing the officer in surprise. "What? Who called the police?"

"Animal Control, sir. We aren't the police. Now where's the pit?"

Babe said. "You got the wrong address, I think. There's no loose pit here, officer."

The man narrowed his eyes. "No, this is the address called in. No wrong address."

Drew said, "I have a pit."

"But we don't have any problems. We're out here chillin'," Babe added.

Alise agreed. "Yeah. Just enjoying the nice weather."

He spoke to Chance, leaning on the railing. "You live here?"

Chance stood up. "I live here. We all live here."

The officer faced Alise. "Is this your house?"

Alise frowned confusedly.

Babe spoke, "This is my house."

"Why does it matter whose house this is?" Alise demanded. "Can't a group of friends have a discussion?"

"You got ID?"

Alise said, "You don't have to answer that. What the hell is this all about?"

Babe answered in a calm, measured tone, hiding his annoyance. "Well, not on me, I don't. Since I am home. But I can go in and get it for you."

The officer addressed Alise. "Everything all right, ma'am?"

Alise glared at him. "Doesn't everything look all right to you?"

"You sure?"

"Everything except for you, escalating this to something it's not."

He answered while glaring at Babe. "That won't be necessary. Just break it up. Let's not create a scene for the neighbors here. This is a quiet neighborhood. We don't have scenes like this. So, you folks have a good day."

"Thank you, officer," said Babe. "You do the same".

The officer barely got back into his car before Babe spun on all the others standing on the porch. "Who the fuck called the police?"

Drew put up both hands in front of him, as though keeping an army at bay. "Damn sure wasn't me."

Babe glared at Chance. "Only a white person would call the police for minuscule type shit like this. That's definitely some white-people shit."

Chance shrugged his shoulders toward Alise. "Well, how 'bout her? Maybe she called."

"She's not white." He smirked. "She just the color of water."

She frowned. "Hey, hey!"

Babe laughed and glanced toward Drew. "I would have thought it was him. But I know he wouldn't snitch on his own dog. Which leaves only you, Chance. Although I guess anybody on this street might have called. Probably fat ass Miss Imogene across the street. Sitting there acting like she's watching TV."

Everyone craned their necks up the street at the outsized woman straining over in her seat to try to hear what was going on."

Chance sniggered. "It's like the circus side show. Sitting out there in that dirty ass housecoat like the sidewalk's her living room."

Drew shook his head, "But the police come up over here. That's the shit they need to be breaking up."

"You got that right," Babe agreed. "But in case it was you that called, Chance, let me let you know, for future reference... You don't ever call the police. Unless I been shot. And even then, you might want to assess the situation first."

Drew moved the bill of his hat back to show his eyes and forehead. "You really couldn't see under my hat? You didn't know I'm not white?"

Babe smirked. "Trust me when I tell you, you white."

"I'm Japanese."

"If you ain't Black, you white. Where'd you go to school?"

"Villanova."

"Right. Fully indoctrinated and co-opted. Now, you going to pay me for my pants, or what?"

Drew sighed, digging into his pocket and pulling out his wallet. "Since you were cool about keeping five-oh off Mitzi's ass, especially since Mitzi already has one strike, and any more would surely result in her getting put down. I thank you, man. Apologies."

Chapter Twelve

Rueben Steals Food

There was no way around it. He already knew what would happen when Mama discovered what he had done. He didn't need the house to tell him, but it began to whisper.

Stay inside. Help. Who called the police? White people. No help. Who Asian, Japanese to be specific. She don't mean no harm. Help, No Help. Don't call the police, ever.

It seemed like Pretzel always knew. He would become agitated. And his paws would skitter frenetically and he would begin to yip shrilly. Rueben tried to calm him, but the dog remained frantic, intuiting Rueben's mounting agitation.

It was hard for him to think clearly. It was as though his distress was in the back seat, resting there, trying to let him know he had done a bad thing, but it was secondary to the feeling of contentment washing over him in a dark wave. There was a yellow fog of happiness drowning his brain, burnishing to a gold pinpoint, the same mellow hue as the Country Crock he had smeared hungrily into his mouth.

He picked Pretzel up and took him into the basement. Through his haze of contentment, he knew it would be best to try to stay out of sight. Puff Puff followed, skirting around his ankles and darting down the steps.

Rueben moved through the stacked boxes, searching for the darkest spot at the back of the room. He removed the box of mashed potato flakes from his pants and shoved it into a chink in the floor. He was excited, knowing he would have this for later. He tucked down into the corner beside his hiding nook and let Pretzel free, but Pretzel refused to leave his side. Rueben rummaged in his pocket, his fingertips gripping granules of salt he had poured there. He brought the salt to his mouth, placed the crystals at the back, and rubbed until a satisfying soreness began to permeate his tongue. He reached his now-moist fingertips back into the pocket, brought out the salt clinging to it, and rubbed it into his mouth, waiting for the familiar comfort of the inside of his lips beginning to swell, throbbing with soreness, splitting open and releasing the metallic pungency of blood onto his teeth.

He leaned back against the cool damp wall, a steady droning emanating from his wounded mouth. Puff Puff mewled loudly. Rueben scolded her, hunkering lower into his hiding space as he heard hammering footsteps pounding the floorboards above him, raining cascades of dust and motes onto his head. Her expletives were shrill but muffled through the cement walls.

When Rueben did not meet her at the door she knew something was amiss. The silence caused her heart to beat faster. She walked to the kitchen filled with foreboding, cursing under her breath at the refrigerator door standing open, the hasp of the padlock drooping limply.

Empty food containers lay on the floor: depleted banana sheaths, diminished apple cores, and chicken bones. She spun around in fury to see if he was hiding under the table or the bathroom before storming toward the open basement door.

Alise was able to track him by following bits of food that had fallen from the folds of his clothing like bread crumbs marking a trail in the woods. She flung back the basement door and descended, calling to him. Pretzel hopped out, barking in response, wagging furiously. She stumbled through the tumbled debris of newspapers and rolled carpets, tossing boxes from a stack blocking off a corner of the room. He crouched there looking up with terrified eyes.

She hurled the last box back, stepping forward and shaking the collar of his polo shirt.

"What did you do?" she screamed. "What did you do?"

She pulled him to his feet and food debris dropped from the folds of his clothing. Pretzel ran in circles around their feet, barking animatedly.

"You ate all this?"

He began to sob, his voice an unarticulated rush of sound.

He pushed himself free from her grasp and stood with his head down. She swatted at his arm in frustration. "I told you to stay out of there, didn't I? You fat fucker! Didn't I tell you about that? Everything. You ate it all, everything. There's nothing left."

He moved out of reach, wrapping his arms around himself protectively. Alise moved toward him and grasped at his belly through the thick of his shirt, then moved to grab at the flesh of his thighs, but her hands were not able to take hold. She punched his fleshy upper arms. "You see this? Fat! This is nasty. You want to die. Is that what you want? Do you want to die? Leave me like everybody else! I don't care!"

He let out a low guttural, "Noooo."

He screamed, throwing his arms around her in desperation.

"Get off me."

"No, Mama. I don't want to leave you. I don't." He began to rock her in his arms. She stiffened, then began to rock along with him while she cried and hugged him in return.

"I know you don't, baby. I know. I'm sorry for saying that."

"I'm sorry, Mama. I'm sorry."

"I'm sorry too, baby. I didn't mean it."

Chapter Thirteen

Studying Babe

Chance had known he loved Babe from that first night, sitting in the dark at the Lark Bar, smelling remnants of orange blossom on his breath.

Getting to know Babe often happened more in his absence than when Babe was around. At home, Babe spoke to him in short sentences, most times as directives instead of conversation. Sentences like, "Can you wash out the tub when you finish showering?" or "Can you wash your dishes? I don't like dishes left in the sink." So, Chance got to know him by the lingering smell of Ivory soap mixed with bleached cotton towels in the bath after he showered, the waft of Dolce & Gabbana at the door, the curious, peppery sting of sweat in the house at 5 p.m. when Chance arrived home from work to an empty house.

When he had the house to himself, Chance was able to study Babe by reviewing his artifacts. He read the various issues of backlisted fashion magazines, both men and women, home décor magazines, tomes of gay information and imagery he had never seen before: *Advocate* and *Tom of Finland* catalogs. There were reams upon reams of comic books dated from the 1970s to the present. He studied them all, trying to see through Babe's eyes, looking for something he could not name. He thought of ways to initiate conversation by memorizing obscure details from *W* and *Interview*; physically larger and sensorially bigger and more attention grabbing than all the other magazines. This he did so he would have topics of discussion he knew would interest Babe.

Chance was able to immerse himself in those bursting images, symmetrically perfect faces, graphically bold designs, blendings of fashion, nudity, politics, celebrity in a way he hadn't seen before. He read articles about New York runway fashion shows and treks to foreign lands, kept himself abreast of New York style culture and high society. Stories emphasizing a distinctive, surreal American way of life where excitement, activity, hedonism, extravagance were a casual, ubiquitous occurrence, and yet Chance had never experienced any of this himself.

He studied Babe's belongings. He ran his hands over statuettes of ancient Hindu goddesses, crystal globes resting in ornate stands, sleek furniture of Danish design, ringing bowls and incense cones, decanters filled with amber fluids. He snorted at the cornball unexpectedness of a waterbed, and he reclined into its voluptuous envelopment, feeling the soft weft of the bed linens against his cheek.

Most of all, he studied his music. Stacks upon stacks of CDs, nearly as many as Chance had in his own collection, but there were also rows of records from earlier time periods, some encased in plastic sleeves for protection, others with the telltale sign of a gouge in the upper corner, denoting it had been bought from the discount bins, the leftovers.

He placed the dark vinyl disks on the spinning Technics turntable and became familiar with names he hadn't known before; Sarah, Ella, Blossom, Dinah, and Nancy. From there, he grew to relish the prologue of static hiss, the clottal purge of vibration before the beginnings of inarticulate reverberation sounds somehow more earthy, more sensual than the digital precision of CDs.

Unbeknownst to Chance, far below, sitting in his basement lair, eating flakes of dehydrated potato, Rueben learned too. Songs echoed to him while he played with his army men, dragging them through tufts of basement sediment, riding them on Puff Puff's dust matted back.

Chapter Fourteen

The Botanical Shop

Chance was sitting against the railing on the front porch, smoking a Clove when Babe came out, jingling his keys.

"Hey."

"Hey. Where you going?"

Babe folded his arms across his chest, avoiding eye contact. Chance had found communicating with Babe was sometimes a lot like talking to himself.

"I'm about to take Robby from next door, down to Philly. I need some cash for gas, and he has to re-up, so win-win."

Chance stood up, flicked his butt out into the street, and wiped his palms on his baggy pants with a laugh. "Bet."

The door to the house of whispers opened, and a tall, brown skinned male smoking a cigarette stepped onto the porch, his diaphanous top flowing on the breeze. He was wearing deep red lipstick, false eyelashes. and elaborate cornrows curling to his shoulders.

Babe peered out and yelled in excitement. "Ricky Ross? Is that you?"

Babe ran down the stairs and crossed to the adjoining porch, running up the steps to grab the man in an effusive hug. They both laughed giddily.

"Who else would it be, darling, but the one and only?"

"I didn't know you were in town."

Ricky Ross patted at his braids. "Yes, honey. I was staying with that dreadful sister of mine in Atlanta, and honey, they got evicted, Miss Thing. Ran out of town by bill collectors with nary a heads up to the doll about the situation. The doll had to take the next thing smoking back up here to Uncle Lot."

Ricky's mocha-brown skin was covered with foundation at least three chalky shades lighter than his skin.

"But honey, Uncle Lot moved that *dreadful* daughter of his and her three rugrats back in the house, and done *gave them my room*, chale. And you know the doll can't be around all those damn Bebe's kids. No ma'am!"

"So, you staying here, at Miss Rock's? You were able to get in touch with her?"

Ross rolled his eyes. "It was *tortuous*, darling, let me tell you. I had to call a queen, who called a cousin, who called that diesel dyke Sylvia, after which, I had to wait for a phone call telling me to show up at such and such a time, and finally, there she was. Miss Rock, in all her glory. Painted for the gawds, bitch. Not a light on in the house, like we don't know she's one-hundred-and-fifty-seven-point-eight years old, and she can hide the ravages of age by standing in the goddamn shadows."

They both laughed, leaning on each other in pseudo commiseration. "But let me make this perfectly clear, okay, Miss Thing was peeing, you hear me? That bitch was ensconced in vintage Chanel, backed up with Number 19 scent to match, silver head snatched into the chignon *of life*! And still up on nails, girl. But you know she old cause she the only person still rocking the peep-toe pump, cause bitch, that *been* played out. But she gone make it work, and you best believe."

Ross noticed Chance assessing him closely. He again patted his head. "Who's this white queen all up in my Mona like she getting paid to watch it? Hello, baby, who are you? My name is Miss Ricky Ross, and I'm most pleased to make your acquaintance."

Chance nodded at him from the porch, moving closer so that he could better hear their conversation.

"I know my visage is extremely base model today, darling. When they did the swoop down on my sister's belongings, they snatched up all the dolls Flori Roberts, honey, hundreds of dollars of paint, leaving me no choice but to steal my cousin's cheap ass Fashion Fair when I got here, and yes, I know I'm giving you cremation number twelve, but darling I have to make do until I can re-up. A doll has to crawl before she can walk."

Ricky screamed across the expanse of the porch, "Pleased to make your acquaintance."

Chance offered a weak "Hi."

"So, your name is Hi? Come on darling, you're going to have to do better if you plan to run with these circles."

Chance struggled to follow Ross's rapid-fire, deep Southern-inflected basso profundo, rattling along without seeming to need feedback. Babe seemed to just hurl words into the whirlwind of Ross's diatribes, lobbing in a sentence or question rather than waiting for a lull.

"That's Chance. He's staying at my place."

Ross raised a painted-on eyebrow and gave an "Owww."

"No, nothing like that. He's a roommate."

Mascaraed eyes widened. "This is a judgment-free zone, *B*. You know me. Where y'all coming from? Where y'all going? What's the tea, bitch?"

"I'm about to take Robby down the city for her usual excursion, and *you know* that's going to be the undertaking of life."

Drew came out onto the porch on the other side, hat pulled low, lighting up a Newport. He nodded at Chance, who nodded back.

"Who you telling? That bitch ain't never changed huh? You still dragging her mattress ass down to the city so she can get her sheet cake? Chile, bye. Her big ass still call you all girfed at two o'clock in the morning wanting to chat?"

They both laughed. Babe spoke in a high, tight voice, squinting his eyes as if he were high, "That's interesting, that's so interesting."

"And ain't heard a thing you said! Well, this is perfect timing. Why don't you take me with y'all, and make a stop at the botanical shop because I'm in need. That way I can make sure that bitch pays you proper because you know she be trying to shortchange a bitch so she can buy a bit extra!"

"Oh, you want to go downtown? Cool. Robby said he's on his way down now. I'm surprised you didn't pass him in the hall."

Drew perked up, tossed his cigarette over the railing, and stepped forward. "Yo, can I cop a ride down with y'all? I need to re-up too, and I can give you gas money too."

Ross again raised a brow, watching Babe inquisitively, deliberately raking his eyes over Drew from foot to baseball cap, with a noted, exaggerated stop at his crotch. Chance did an assessment right along with him. He took in his smooth olive skin, the thin, finely chiseled nose and full lips. Drew had thick, dark-brows arcing in an elegant slant that followed the line of his large, thinly lashed brown eyes.

Chance grudgingly acknowledged his attractiveness. He wondered if Babe found him attractive.

"No problem. The more the merrier. By more, I mean the more gas money."

Ross said, "Bitch, you hacking? You be keeping up multiple streams of revenue, baby. I ain't mad at you."

Drew asked Chance, "Do you know if homegirl on the first floor is home? Maybe she can check in on my Gran while I'm out."

Chance said, "From the smell in the hallway I would say she's home. Bitch always smell like sweat. Go knock."

When Drew left the porch, Ross again spoke to Babe. "Look at my grandniece, going all diverse and shit. Good for you, chile. I told you staying in the psychological ghetto would get you nowhere. You must have gotten rid of that crazy husband though. Because Gawd knows she would not be sitting still for this! What's the tea, *B*, girl?"

Babe laughed. "Shut up. I'll fill you in on the ride down."

"Oh, girl! Let me get in here and re-beat this face. I cannot be seen in the city looking a travesty!"

"This is a short little trip. We don't have time for all that."

"Oh chile, stop the madness. I'm going to do a light paint. A beat for a rich white woman being driven into the city to troll for trade or some such. No time at all."

And with that, Ross retreated into the house, banging the door in his wake.

Chapter Fifteen

The DL

Chance snickered at the rotund man that flounced out of the house of whispers when he stopped short at all of them arranged in Babe's jeep. Robby walked down the steps with a meaty palm against his chest in mock dismay. He wore loose linen pants and a matching button-down top flowing over his ample belly, and a wide brimmed panama hat—all in white.

"Goodness gracious. What are all these people? This was supposed to be a quick trip down to Broad and Lehigh."

Ross lunged his outsized head out of the back window, his face now a more muted shade of cinnamon in keeping with the time of night, and bellowed, "Miss Thing, if you don't carry your ass in this chariot forthwith, you will get left!"

"Ricky Ross? Is that you?"

"Why bitches act like I crept back from the great beyond around here. Get in bitch. We been waiting all the live long day for you, and here you come, dressed like

Violet Venable to go down in the heart of north. You done bumped your goddamn head!"

Chance sat in the seat beside Babe, watching Robby with a mixture of amazement and amusement.

Robby said. "You move into Miss Rocks? How'd you track her down?"

"It wasn't easy, sis. But I guess I am as resourceful as you, seeing as you are up in there on the uppermost garden level. Woo, chile, I know it's hot as bull's balls way up there, girl. No wonder you are sweating bullets already when all you've done is walk down three flights of stairs. *B*, let's go. Oh, wait. Miss Thing, let's dig in our Maiden Form and get out our lira, right? My god daughter can't drive on all this beauty alone. She needs gas."

Robby irritably reached into his shoulder bag for money as he climbed into the back seat.

Babe honked the horn. "We got one more rider. And he best to have his gas money at the ready too."

As he honked again, Drew came out, wearing head to toe Hilfiger with a bandana beneath his hat.

"Another rider? What is with all this traffic?" Robby huffed. "Where is he going to sit?"

"Right there beside you, bitch. Where you think?" screamed Ross. "Now scoot your cootch down and make room. This is a Jeep. Plenty room."

Babe rolled his eyes. "What is with this dude? What is he trying to prove with all this Hilfiger shit? He looks crazy."

Chance said. "He fly to me. He must got mad loot to be dressing Hilfiger down every day."

"You would think so. He might as well be wearing Garanimals. All that matchy shit."

"Chile, what is going on with that walk? What's he doing?"

Drew walked toward the Jeep with what was not quite swagger but a sort of slouching back of the shoulders and a thrusting forward of the pelvis that showed a certain laissez-faire, a laid-back aura. He hurtled into the back seat and pressed up against Robby, who protested at the proximity to his girth.

"Oh, my! Watch it, girl. Babe! Who is this? What is going on?"

Drew introduced himself, reaching out a fist for a pound. Robby recoiled from the bony hand as if it were infected.

"Yes. Okay."

"Everybody, that's Drew, who lives next door to me. Drew, that's Robby and Ricky Ross, who lives in the rooming house on the other side. You all met Chance already," Babe said as he put the Jeep in gear and zoomed out onto Leviticus.

Chance barely acknowledged them, raising a fist in greeting, a smirk twisting his lips.

Ross said, "Babe, if you are taking folks under wing, you should be properly teaching them. Now I expect Miss Robby to know this, but she an old heifer, and she set in her ways, and she always trying to pull attention. But these young white queens can't be going down the city like this all dragged the fuck out and things."

Babe agreed. "Yeah, I know. Drew, you got on all that gear like some white woman going into the hood with a diamond ring and gold necklaces. You may as well wear a sign, saying 'rob my ass.' You got to be low-key. Your ass is attention grabbing as it is. You don't need no added embellishments."

Drew reached into the big pocket on his chest, drew out a spliff and lit it. "Man, be cool. This is how I rock. It's no embellishment. It's my style."

Someone mumbled what style had to do with it. Chance eyed the joint with glittering eyes. "Yo, can I hit that?"

Robby said, "Don't you worry about me. I've been coming down to Lehigh for years. Those Puerto Rican boys know me. I am a regular customer." He laughed, "I've been down there in jeans, I've been down there in cootchie cutters. I've gone down right after working at my salon all day, smelling like a field hand, and those boys paid it dust."

Drew took a toke and passed the joint up to Chance. "I wish y'all would stop saying I'm white. That's wack."

"Wack? Did she say wack?" said Ross.

Babe laughed. "Yup. He said wack."

Ross flopped back against the seat. "Girl, I can't! *B*! Where you getting these kids from?"

"I'm not trying to find them. Believe me."

Ross leaned forward and ran his hand over Chance's braids. Chance recoiled. "And what's this child's situation. Girl, who did this head? Why everybody trying to get up in this culture? Are these your Bo Derek braids, Miss Thing? Hmmm? Are you a ten?"

Babe burst out laughing, the Jeep skeetering slightly out of the lane. "Ross. Will you shut up before you make me crash!"

"Somebody turn on the radio," Robby demanded.

Ross said, "You are a six, at the most, Miss Thing, with those raggely braids. Somebody did you wrong. But you are in luck. Tell him, *B*!"

As Ross opened his pocketbook and rummaged around inside, Babe turned on the radio and said, "Ross can tighten up a head. The best at doing braids in Norristown."

Ross tut-tutted him. "Let's not get crazy, bitch. Second best. You know can't nobody come for Miss Jan, bitch. That bitch can cornrow you if you bald-headed. She can twist a scalp like you got hair out the back gate!"

"What!" agreed Robby, "You ain't nevah lied, bitch."

"But bitch, those are temporary cornrows. You know Miss Jan will knot your scalp so tight you got to take those girls out the next day."

"Girl, the last time she did my head I had to pop Tylenol for twenty-four hours! I had scabs in my head. You think I'm lying, but I'm dead serious. Bitch, I kid you not!" Ross found his comb and Royal Crown. "Okay, come on back here, child, and let me do that head right. You're never going to be a ten, but you can at least be an eight."

Chance twisted in the seat and climbed over, his butt nudging Babe's head as he passed. "Drew, switch with me. I'm tryna be a ten."

Babe said, "Hey, watch it. I'm driving here."

"Girl, let's not get crazy." Robby smirked. "You can get to a nine if it's dark out. Ten is out. Of. The question."

"I thought the other one was the hairdresser," cracked Drew absently.

"The other one?" Robby screamed, "The other one! Girl, I can't with these young queens."

Once everyone got settled, Drew moving into the front with Chance squeezing between Robby and Ricky, Ross began to unbraid his thin hair. He breathed lazily. "Honey, she's a hairdresser, but Miss Thing works on those old church hags. The wet sets. Press and curls, honey. She don't take no classes to modernize her skill sets."

Babe whispered, "Let's not forget the Jheri curls."

Ross screamed. "The Jheri curls. Bitch! Don't she live and breathe Miss Jheri Curl? You know your mother do them Jheri curls like there's no tomorrow."

Robby fluttered his eyes imperiously. "There's no reason for me to be sitting on the back of somebody's funky ass head all night when I can put a bit of lye, a bit of chemical product on your head, sit you under Miss Dryer and melt away all signifiers of Africa while proceeding to the next paying head! And keep in mind those old church ladies are the ones with the coins, okay? When's the last time one of them young fish with braids paid you a decent tip? These young twats don't know anything about social niceties."

Robby patted at Chance's shoulder. "Not talking about you, sweetie. But y'all know what I'm talking about."

Ross quipped. "They don't tip because they are feeling some type of way after paying one hundred girls from they rent money to get that head tightened up! That's all they got. Now you want them to dip into they beer money too? Well, now bitch, you done bumped your head."

They all laughed.

Ross screamed, "Bitch, slow down!"

Coming out of Lotts Bar, standing at the corner of Lafayette and Dekalb, stood a muscular dark-brown man, wearing a tank shirt and shorts riding up on large hairless thighs. He had a large afro with a comb sticking in it. They all gazed at the muscular spread of his back, sighing.

Chance said, "Man. I see him walking around town all the time. That motherfucker is beautiful."

Ross wound down the window. "That's my husband, Chauncey. *B*, pull up there."

Ricky huffed. "We don't have time for you to be dick hunting, bitch. I need to get to the city."

"He's gay?" Chance asked.

"Don't look it," said Drew. "Looks like he's fresh from cell block *H*."

Babe said, "Yes, and prison does a body good. Shit."

They pulled closer to the curb. Ross said, "Gay? What would I do with a sissy? Bump pocketbooks? That's a man, honey. Hey, Chauncey. What you doing up in my Uncle Lott's bar? They lifted the ban?"

The chocolate man turned angrily. Ross stuck his head out the window. The man's demeanor changed as soon as he saw her. He walked around to Ross's side.

"Hey, chocolate. When'd you get back in town?"

Ross flashed a row of brilliant, impossibly white teeth. "Round about the same time you got out, I'm presuming. You all healthy and things."

The others observed the interplay with reverent awe.

"Yeah. I make do. You not too bad yourself, Ma. Where you headed?"

"We're going down to the city to cop. What you getting into?"

"Whatever you are, if you down. Ain't got nothing going on."

"Well, get on in then. You feel like coming home with me tonight?"

He shrugged. "What the fuck."

Ross hurled open the door. "Come on, Daddy. Make room, girls. This is Chauncey. Chaunce, you know Miss Robby, I know. And my grand niece Babe."

He barely acknowledged them. "What up. Hey, you got some ones for a beer for the trip down?"

Ross nudged Chance's shoulder as he once more dug into his bag. "Let me see. Y'all got money to contribute to this beer?"

Babe continued staring straight ahead as though not hearing.

Drew dug into his pocket and handed over a few crumpled bills. "Can you get Old E, too, my man?"

Chauncey glanced over, amused. "Sure, man. Baby, who the white boy?"

Ross grinned even harder, placing folded bills into his broad palm. "Chile, who you asking? She ain't nobody. Here, you get what you want."

Robby leaned forward, exasperated. "Can you hurry it up though? You putting us behind schedule. With your fine ass."

He laughed, heading into Lotts. "Be right back."

They all watched him walk away.

Robby said, "I am furious about this wrench in the already intervened upon plan. But bitch, that man is absolutely breathtaking. I didn't know you was tagging Chauncey. Although why should I be surprised."

Ross raised a finger. "Let me be clear. He is not trade. Not for the general population. Chauncey is trade exclusively for the doll, you understand? He got one taste of this lily, and he realized he was not going to be able to get gripped like that from mere cunt. Oh, the doll put it the fuck down on that big Black man. And he was fresh out Muncy, too? Oh, bitch, we broke down the beds at the Rosewood Hotel. He beat this box like it had taken his lunch money."

Chance said. "So he's one of those DL brothers?"

"What do you mean by DL?" Babe asked.

"You know. Those brothers that be fucking around with girls and guys too. Closet cases."

"Why you say closet cases?"

"Ashamed about being gay, so they keep a girl or even get married so nobody will think they're gay."

Robby said, "I already told you, he's trade."

Drew asked, "What's trade then?"

"A guy that fucks around."

Chance said, "And doesn't want anyone to know. Because he's in the closet."

"Girl," Ross bellowed, "what happened to the weed? Because I'm going to need it. I did not expect to be the *Reading Rainbow* or *Mister Rogers Neighborhood* up in here this evening, schooling the white girls. No, ma'am."

Chance, who had been hoarding the blunt, passed it back.

Babe asked. "Why do you say closeted? There is a difference between lying to yourself about who you are and being private because what you do is nobody else's business."

Robby said, "DL is the same as saying keep it on the low. It means don't run your mouth. Just like when you say no snitching. You don't be running around letting people all in your sauce."

Drew said, "Sounds like hiding something to me."

Babe said, "That's because white folks only feel comfortable when they are able to categorize and define something. Y'all have this need where you feel like you have to know everything about everything."

"But y'all always get it wrong," said Robby.

"Can you stop calling me white though? It's disrespectful of my Asian heritage."

"Sorry," said Babe. "That wasn't my intention. All I'm saying is you're not Black. And for me everything not Black is white."

Drew and Chance laughed.

Chance said, "Well, I guess Chauncey ain't too concerned about people clocking him since he about to be seen in a carload of fags. And he was coming out of Lotts. Everybody in town be talking about how that's the gay bar for the Blacks, and the white ones go over the bridge to the Lark."

Babe asked, "How's that a gay bar? In what way?"

Chance shrugged. "That's what I heard."

Robby said, "Have you been there?"

His eyes bulged. "You kidding? And get killed? I seen the people standing around outside. They ain't no joke."

"So, you were scared," said Babe. "See that's what kills me about white kids wanting the Black love stick but too scared to go to the places where you can find it. You only feel comfortable with the ones coming into your spaces."

Ross said, "I can assure you this is the last place you can call a gay bar. This small-minded-ass town calls it that because a few of the dolls, like me, Earnie Cat, and Miss Dion are not afraid to crawl in there and claim a spot at the bar when we need a fierce cocktail. Baby, where you going to find a man at? Not at the gay bar, that's for damn sure. If you want the real trade, you go where the real trade goes."

Drew asked, "You're not scared being in there?"

"Scared of what?" Ross screamed. "Bitch, I am the first lady of Norristown. I wish a motherfucker would try some shit."

Robby said, calmly, "What she means is, she's fucked half the men in Norristown, so there's no reason for her to feel threatened."

"Bitch. Only the ones not looking for a payout to give it up. Paying for dick is your area of expertise."

"Honey, I prefer to pay a man. That way they know who's really in charge. Even though they run around acting all butch and tossing this pussy to and fro, we both know this clutch is running the show."

"Screwing men that are supposedly straight," said Drew. "What's the point? There's no future in that."

"Says you." Ross laughed. "Me and Chauncey been messing since I was twenty years old."

Robby said, "Believe me, it's been a looooooong time since she's seen her twenties."

Ross said, "So here's the thing. We all know fish that fools around with other fish, or she fucked around with girls in college but doesn't consider herself as gay, so why does a Black man need to define himself as gay because he likes to fuck around with men if he gets horny? Why can't he just be sexually free? That's trade, darling. The boys that love to have they dick played with. I've known boys like that all my life."

Robby's eyes glossed over with nostalgia. "The streets used to be full of trade, honey. Like Babe's fine ass cousin, Rocco. He used to come to my house when he was drunk and fuck me like he hated my guts, but bitch, he kissed me like he was searching for God. And then he would beat my ass and steal my money. Oh, I was in love with that man!"

"Well, I don't know if getting robbed and beaten is in line with the topic," said Babe, "but I know what you mean about there being a lot of trade back in the day. AIDS killed a lot of that."

Chance said, "Oh, a lot of people died from AIDS back in the day."

"I don't mean a literal death. But guys that were free with their sexuality, that used to be open to fooling around, a lot of that changed when AIDS started killing people. After that, something that used to be fun, spontaneous, or just a lark, turned into Russian roulette. So, a lot of guys that used to fuck around don't do it anymore."

Enjoying the exchange, Chance pondered how to keep the conversation going. He wanted to maintain relevance in the dialogue.

"I guess I get what you mean. Like, I sometimes fuck around with my sister's boyfriends, and it's all good and everything, but I never really thought of them as gay. They just fucked around on the humbug."

Ross glared at him, yanking on his hair.

"Ow! Hey!"

"You fuck your sister's boyfriends?"

"Sometimes."

"For what?" asked Babe.

"What you mean? Bored."

Babe turned to him. "You fuck your sister's boyfriends because you're bored?"

Ross screamed, "Now you know what you dealing with over here, *B*. She one of those messy faggots. You better keep your eye on her. She keeps shit stirred like your mother here. Miss Robby is *renowned* for offering cash to suck the dicks of her clientele's boyfriends and husbands."

Robby huffed. "Listen. You need to have shit to hold over a bitch's head. Cause you never know when cunt going to try you. So when she spews her homophobic shit and says, 'Well, not you, but you know I don't approve of this lifestyle, but I hate the sin, not the sinner,' type shit. I can smile at her, knowing her man was up in my guts last weekend, snorting my coke and laying in my bed."

"Like I said, messy. That ain't nothing but bad karma, there."

Babe said, "And nasty. That's why everybody in this town is working through the same strain of syphilis, and shit. With all the dick that's out here to be screwing your sister's boyfriends is kind of disgusting."

Robby was offended. "I have never had an STD in my life! I practice safe sex, you know. I use condoms. Preferably Magnums."

Chance realized he had miscalculated. Where he had hoped to generate intrigue and awe, he had sparked skepticism. But he had to stick with his story now. "It's not that big a deal. I don't expect anything. It only happened a couple times."

"*Watch her, B.* I don't feature no hungry bitches. And she hungry. Single white female."

Babe replied, "You may not have transmitted anything sexually, but what about what you're transmitting karmically, what you are manifesting out into the world?"

Robby rolled his eyes, "Oh Lord. Here we go with the Miss Cleo psychic network shit. Y'all got that. Running down to the botanical shop to get some roots and weeds to"—he made air quotes—"'cleanse the air or try to snag some man.' I am a Christian, honey. All that manifesting and karma-chameleon shit does not work over here."

Drew shook himself from his weed-induced haze. "Wait a minute. I thought botanical shop was code for picking up weed? You mean we ain't getting no weed?"

"All right, enough." Ross snapped. "Here come my husband out the bar. We will not have this morbid talk interfering with Chauncey's potential erection. Y'all bitches keep it cute. Come on around here, Miss Thing, so I can braid your shit."

"How we going to fit another person in here? There's already capacity seating, and now you want this gigantic Negro to take up what little room is left?" Chance asked.

Ross glared at him firmly. "You peep that dick jumping around in those tiny shorts. Only for a second, bitch, because I don't want you getting any ideas that will get you fucked up. But do you see that? Now do you think I give a fuck if you feel cramped? You about ninety bucks tops. You better make a way out of things, bitch, or get out. Now scootch over! I can sit on that man's motherfucking lap. And ladies, if you see something going on during that time, look the fuck away is all I can say."

Robby said, "Can somebody pass that damn joint? My nerves!"

He sat beneath the lone lamp illuminating the alley behind Leviticus Street, letting the Supra's engine idle at a fierce, foreboding rumble. The windows were down, letting the soft breeze disrupt the smoke from the Newport he ferociously inhaled, flicking its glowing remnants out to the gravel.

He quickly snapped off the radio, hiding in his car while the light-skinned fat bitch that had moved into the lower-level apartment came out the door, trailed by a rotund brown boy with wild cascading hair. She carried a large shoulder bag across her chest, which caused her to cant slightly to one side. He struggled to hear the far-off voices but was unable to. He could only hear distant babblings like a thin brook, and he watched as the woman turned to the boy, put her hands on his shoulders, and mouthed something, shaking him slightly before the boy bowed his head and shuffled back into the house. She tilted her face to the sky, gripped an object hanging from a chain around her neck, and headed around to the house next door, tentatively opening the door and peering inside before disappearing.

He steered the car up along the grass close to the fence, turned off the engine, and climbed out. Seeing no traffic from either end, he crossed into the shadow cast by the garage and entered the gate. He had a small wooden bat tucked in his back pocket, what he called his nigger beater, which he took out and poised before him in case that mutt came charging out of the house next door. He approached the back door to the upper-level apartment. Unlocked. As usual.

He stood in the small landing area of the laundry room, so narrow that if he stretched his arms out, his fingertips would scrape both walls. There was a small stack of clothing folded on the top of the dryer, which hummed with activity. This had always been his favorite room in the house. On cold winter days, it was nice and warm and always smelled of the engineered scent of linen-fragranced fabric softener.

He picked up a sweater and unfolded it, recognizing Babe's favorite Ralph Lauren turtleneck. He held it to his face. Even though freshly washed, he smelled the ephemera of Babe's cologne. He lowered the sweater to his chest, holding the collar with both hands, and wrenched in either direction, his knees buckling with the exertion, until the fabric gave way, emitting the satisfying sound of tearing cotton.

He threw the violated clothing onto the floor and walked to the door leading up to the main landing walking tentatively and listening for activity. Hearing nothing, he gained more confidence and walked at his regular pace. At the main level, he stopped, made note of the area, his hands on his waist.

He approached the room that had previously been used for storage and then nudged the door ajar with two broad fingers. A low metal futon with black rumpled bedding stood against the opposite wall. A sheet tacked to the window darkened the room He looked around at the dark objects decorating the dresser and windowsill. Posters of Janet Jackson and Madonna, torn magazine covers of Toni Braxton, Mary J. Blige, Lil Kim, Foxy Brown, SWV, and TLC lined the walls.

He lifted the black comforter and sniffed. The smell of white boy: a slight dampness, or mildew, mixed with cheap shampoo, was satisfying to him. It indicated that the white boy was sleeping in this room, and that maybe the little fucker wasn't fucking Babe.

"Faggot-ass faggot," he mumbled, walking back into the hall.

The drive down Ridge Ave, meandering along Henry, was peaceful. Chance, angularly arranged between muscle, flesh, and limbs, rested his head back into Ross's lap allowing his hair to be braided, watching the trees flash by through the sunroof, and taking the occasional swig from the proffered bottle of Colt 45. He giggled at Robby's prim refusal of the offered beer and Chauncey's deeply slurred rebuff. It only meant more for him.

He even managed to allow the radio to drown out the constant drone coming from Ross, who did not seem to be able to be quiet. Drew flipped the radio dial, searching, until "Get Money" came on the radio.

"Yeah. That's what I'm talking about." Drew began to bop his head and wave his hands.

"Hey!" That was my shit! How you going to change the station when they playing 'Runaway'?"

Drew laughed. "Don't nobody want to hear no Janet. Big's talking about some real life shit. Fuck bitches, get money."

"No reason to cast aspersions on Miss Janet, honey," said Ross. "She's royalty. You better bow the fuck down. Don't nobody want to hear this rap mess."

"Don't nobody like rap in here?" asked Drew.

"It's all right," said Babe. "I prefer singing. Real singing."

Ross said. "Yes. If it's not being sung by a big Black bitch, it ain't right. Martha Wash, standing her big ass behind a scrim singing the house *down* while an ugly German drag queen is standing center stage perpetrating, yes ma'am."

Robby said, "And the alpha and omega, honey, Miss Diana Ross!"

Babe and Ross groaned. "Not today, bitch. We are not going to discuss Miss Ross today, Miss Robby. I don't have the stamina."

Robby rolled his eyes, laughing. "You bitches can't take it. You know ain't no bitch standing that can take the crown from The Boss."

Ricky contorted his face, bulging his eyes and moving his head grandly, taking the comb from Drew's hair and placing it before his mouth like a mic. "Hello everyone. I want to thank each and every one of you for coming to my show this evening. I want everyone to reach out and touch your neighbor's hand. *Now!* What's that? You want to take my picture? I'm sorry but my eyes are very photosensitive. That would blind me for the night, and I wouldn't be able to perform for these fine people, and I'm sure we wouldn't want that, now would we? Now, what you can do, you can proceed to the lobby where you may purchase the catalog of my photos for the rather reasonable, low low price of seventy-five dollars. Yes, I love you too. Now, wait, first you need to reach out and touch a motherfucker's hand like you were ordered to. Lighting people, can you please turn down the house lights a bit, I am roasting under this moose hair gilda like a suckling pig. This shit weighs a ton. Yes? Oh, yes, I love you too. What? When am I going to sing? Darling, singing is a very minimal part of the Diana Ross experience. You will get a song around about an hour in. *God damn it I said turn down the house lights!* Yes. Yes. I love you too. *Listen, you motherfuckers got two minutes to get this motherfucking lighting right before I make a call in to Berry to send the helicopter to fly my ass back to Connecticut!* Yes, that's much better. Thank you so much."

Babe hunched over the steering wheel, laughing hysterically while Drew shook his head in amazement.

Robby laughed begrudgingly. "Y'all can make fun all you want, but you know Ross is the template, honey. Fuck what you heard. Who else you know that will take a private jet to go down the block for a plate of fried fish and champagne? Bitch better work."

Babe said, "I will say this. It's a wonderful thing, those hip-hop videos. I'm a house head, but there is nothing wrong with watching those men strutting around with no shirts on. That OPP guy? That's a beautiful thing. And who's those little monsters with the bald heads? Those ugly boys giving you very much 'I'm going to rob you after the show? Onyx."

Drew frowned. "They ain't ugly."

Babe said, "Yeah. Matching gremlins. Just how I like them."

"Hey!" Chance protested as Ross knocked his head with his knee, lunging forward and gripping the seat, trying to pull it back toward him.

"And speaking of gremlins, bitch, stop trying to avoid the topic. What the fuck happened between you and your husband? When'd y'all break up?"

Robby said, "Yes. You been with that man since you were a baby. He probably the one that took your lily. Was he your first?"

"He was. I met him when I was eighteen."

"An eighteen-year-old virgin?" said Robby. "That's more rare than an albino rhinoceros, I think."

Drew said, "So you never been with anybody but him?"

He smirked. "I didn't say *that*."

"How long were you with him?" Drew asked.

Ross said, holding the comb in front of him and continuing the Diana Ross persona, "Thirteen crushingly tortuous, brutally long years, and now"— he began to sing—"She's coming out, she wants the world to know, got to let it show..."

Matthew had *not* been Babe's first. But he didn't see the need to tell the crowd.

Ross came out of character and responded with his own voice. "Baby, whatever the reason, I'm sure it was a long time coming. She was crazy, girl. Always drunk, driving around like Mario Andretti in that raggedy Supra. Girl, to this day I'm still traumatized from when he took us down to the city to cop, and he got mad at Miss *B*, driving up on everybody's bumper. Now we are free…"

Robby groaned at the memory. "She had to be going at least one hundred miles per hour. I thought I was going to die that night. Mercy, Jesus."

Robby made the sign of the cross over his chest, while Ross shouted, "Bitch, I thought we were going to crash headlong into the rocks on Miss Schuykhill and mess up this Mona for life. No ma'am!"

Ross began to sing, reverting to imitating Diana Ross with a glassy falsetto. "Set me free, why don't you babe. No, this song is not part of the Diana Ross catalog, so I rarely sing it in public, but you do remember I once fronted a nominal little band called, if memory serves me correctly, The Supremes, or some such, before that bitch Mary somebody or other tried to take the helm. To disastrous results, might I add."

Babe said, "I will not miss that driving, that's for sure. He drove like a latent homosexual."

Drew said, "A what?"

"Like he hated himself. That got to be exhausting over the years, contending with his self-hatred and his shitty behavior because he couldn't accept himself."

Chance said, "You didn't seem like you were, what can I say...? You two didn't seem like you were a couple..."

"Unevenly yoked," screamed Ross.

"Yeah. How'd you meet?"

"The sex. He was good in bed."

Chance shook his head. "You're not that shallow."

He shrugged. "Of course there was more. He was generous, he was kindhearted. He would give me the world if he could. But never underestimate the power of good dick. Don't buy into the hetero mumbo jumbo about soulmates and romance and fate. The power of good ass is important. Besides. He saw me when nobody else did."

"What you mean, *B*?"

"He was interested in me when nobody else was interested in me."

"*B*. Stop. You are absolutely breathtaking. What do you mean by that?"

"I'm absolutely breathtaking, NOW. This shit took work. Do you think I get out of bed like this? This shit is by design. There is a regimen attached to this. Robby, you know. You know I used to be a scraggley little nobody. And nobody even knew I was alive. Not until I started working out, getting a little muscle. That's when niggas started shouting out from car windows, like 'hey shortie.' And I was appalled. I was like, who's short? It must be these pants making me look short." He laughed.

"Not to me, baby. You didn't give this aura of trade-ness you got now, now that you've been co-opted by the gay clones and their desire to be visually acceptable to the heteros. But you were always fierce, you just didn't know it. Which might be the same thing Miss Matthew was feeling. If you weren't comfortable in your own skin when you were younger, maybe that's all it was for him too."

"Maybe. But what's done is done."

Chance said, "And plus, sucking somebody's dick and letting me fuck you in the alley in back of the Lark are sure signs the relationship has reached a standstill."

Babe rolled his eyes, as everyone in the jeep screamed simultaneously, demanding information.

Chapter Sixteen

Alise's Past

Alise attacked straightening up the cluttered bedroom first while Mitzi rested in the corner, licking a wound on her massive paw. Miss Doris sat in a paisley wingback chair, peering out the window overlooking the parking lot across the street. The television was on, but no one paid attention. Alise first removed the damp bedclothes, smelling faintly of sweat and excrement, balled them up and tossed them into a corner. She went searching in the hallway for a closet, found one near the bathroom, and was relieved to find not only fresh-smelling folded sheets and pillowcases but a can of Lysol, which she carried back with her and sprayed the lumpy mattress before tightening the sheets across the corners.

Miss Doris shifted in her chair, watching her short, efficient movements, darting her eyes with every movement Alise made as she picked up odd debris, tossed things into the wastebasket, wiped down furniture with a damp rag, and moved things around to make room to vacuum.

"You approve, huh? Yeah. I always say cleaning out the cobwebs does wonders for clearing out our thoughts. Right?"

The old woman didn't talk. Drew had told her that. But she found just talking, hearing her own voice, helped motivate her to keep moving. She filled a wash basin with warm soapy water and carried it back to clean the woman up in her Barcalounger. Each time she left the room, searching for soap, the vacuum cleaner, or trash bags, Mitzi thumped heavily along at her heels. When she grew bored with Alise, she would nudge up against the old woman's shins, waiting for her to reach out a tendoned hand to rub her stout head. Alise walked over to pet the dog too. She was convinced the old lady was in there somewhere behind those rheumy gray eyes.

"You like old Mitzi, there, huh? Yeah, she's a good girl. Attention seeking sometimes, but she's a good girl. Aren't you, Mitz?" She joined Miss Doris in petting the animal.

"You know, Drew's not so bad. I'm glad to have met him. Taking this time out to take care of you is a break for me. To be able to get out of the house, knowing you can help someone else, that's a good thing. It's funny. I don't know what it is. Maybe that you can't talk, or me not knowing you, but you're easy to talk to. Maybe I'm tired of carrying things around to myself. Drew told me he never knew you growing up. That he was adopted. I guess every family has their own secrets.

"You have the most beautiful eyes. Such an unusual color. And your lashes, even now, are so long, still black. I can see from your pictures you were a great beauty.

"I was never that. I mean I've always been big. You were so tiny you could have been a model. And that beautiful hair?

"I come from a family of big people. My mother and father both were big, so were all my brothers.

She laughed. "I can imagine what they'd say if they saw me right here, washing up an old Chinese woman. Mom would probably understand, but Pop? He'd be fit to be tied.

"I was the only girl child, so everybody's spoiled me. Mother was always in the kitchen cooking. Cakes, pies, and cookies. She would have me help bake from since I was little, so I always equated cooking with love. The kitchen is still the warmest place in the house to me." Alise laughed, warming lotion in her palms before smoothing it into the woman's parchment-thin skin.

"Nobody ever told me I was pretty. I mean, they never said I wasn't pretty or anything like that. My family didn't focus on things like that. We were a practical bunch, I guess you'd say. Getting things done was more important than trying to make a little girl feel pretty. And Daddy and the boys were more fond of hunting, staying out in the shed with the hounds, cleaning up their gear. The only time they were around the house was at mealtimes.

"I sure miss them though. I haven't talked to them for a long time. I hope they think about me sometimes. I don't really miss them all that much, really. Except like now, taking care of you, when thoughts like that come up, you know?"

Alise thought back to her younger self. The rotund girl in grammar school. The names other kids would call her. The snickering.

"Kids can be terrible little monsters, you know? That's why I'm so protective of Rueben. I know what it's like to be the brunt of jokes. How hurtful it is when kids make fun of you. And when you grow up, it doesn't get better. You always hear those names. It follows you into adulthood. Even when I started in nursing, becoming the best at it, I always felt like a fraud. I was still fat-assed Alice Johnson, the one nobody wanted to sit with at lunch, who walked to school by herself. Even the teachers pretended to be sympathetic, but they laughed too. You saw it behind the pity in their eyes, the wavering lines of their mouths, forcing back the laughter. That's why I pulled Rueben out. The moment I understood what was going on with him, I decided to homeschool him. He would not become a shadow of his true potential. He would not have his spirit beaten down the way I did. I would die before I let that happen.

"I didn't know it would turn into something I couldn't control. You never know that, right? How can you ever know all the things we do as parents, it still turns into something beyond our control?"

Chapter Seventeen

The Bundle of Sticks

When Alise walked into the apartment and was greeted only by Pretzel's wet nose against her shin, her heart began to patter rapidly against her ribcage. She quickly walked to the kitchen and checked the lock on the refrigerator. Relieved to find the padlock secured, she checked all the cabinets and the trashcan. Finding nothing, she walked to the basement door and entered the red-hued interior.

Rueben sat on a mattress by the basement window, arranging players on the board of an electronic football game. He turned the power switch, and the green board began to vibrate, shaking the tiny figures across the board in haphazard fashion. Rueben began making breathy, low-pitched roars: his approximation of a cheering crowd.

"Mama, see what I found? This old-fashioned football game."

Alise stooped down. "Ah. Where'd you find this dusty old thing? My brothers used to play like this when I was little."

"It's kind of corny. But it's kind of fun too. Not like Nintendo. You can't control where you want your man to go, but it's kind of funny watching them, seeing if your man makes it to the goal. I didn't know you had brothers, Mama. Why don't they never come visit, or your Mama and Papa?"

"Oh, my folks died long ago. I told you that."

"You said your brothers all live far away."

Alise stood. "Right. We don't talk. Is this why you didn't come say hello when I came from next door, pumpkin? Your new game?"

"Yeah. I'm busy."

"Okay. Well, I'm going to go get dinner started. You want to help?"

Rueben leaped up after switching off the power on the game. "What we having?"

"I don't know. What you want to have?"

"Mac and cheese? Fried chicken?"

"We don't have time to make fried chicken. What about chicken nuggets and mac and cheese?"

"Can I grate the cheese? We can have some nuggets while we wait, don't you think?"

She laughed. "I don't see why not."

They walked up the stairs. "You want to tell me a story while we work on dinner?"

"What you want to hear?"

"I got one. What about the story of The Bundle of Sticks?"

"Okay. Let's see if you remember it."

"There once was a farmer, who had a family that fought all the time. He tried to keep his family together, and to keep them from fighting, but his words always fell on deaf ears.

"After many, many times, his children could not stop from fighting. So he thought maybe leading by example would be better than just his words. So he called his sons and daughters and told them to lay a bundle of sticks in front of him.

"Then they tied them into a faggot, Mama. What's a faggot, again?"

Alise instructed Rueben to fill a pot with water and then unlocked the refrigerator so she could get the cheddar, butter, and cream, keeping a close eye that Rueben not go into the unlocked cabinets while her back was turned. "You know what it is. A bundle of sticks. I know you haven't forgotten from your lesson plans."

"I think that word is something else. Something people say when they don't like somebody. Like a fat ass or a spic."

"Where'd you hear these words, boy? Have you ever heard Mama saying those terrible words?"

He shook his head. "But I heard them, and they didn't sound nice. And they didn't sound like no bundle of sticks."

"Sometimes people use that word for men not following God's plan to find a wife. Some men go against the Bible and pretend another man can take the place of a wife."

"But you said not following the Bible is a sin."

"It is, sweetie. But that's not what the word faggot is supposed to mean in this story. It's a bundle of sticks. Like we said."

"Okay. So do faggots go to hell?"

Alise nodded. "They do."

Rueben laughed. "Maybe that's why those men are called faggots. They will burn up like a bundle of sticks once they get to hell."

Alise turned the water off and moved the pot over to the stove. "Finish with your story."

"So, if those people with the bad names go to hell, Mama, maybe all those people with bad names go to hell."

"What you talking about?"

"The spics. The fat asses. Don't they go to hell too? You told me eating all the food and eating out of the trash makes God frown, so will I go to hell?"

Rueben looked to his mother, waiting for an answer. She kept her back to him, stirring the pot even though he knew it contained only water. Her voice was a whisper. "No, sweetie. You won't go to hell. I know you can't help yourself. That's Mama's fault. Now, finish your story."

"Oh, yeah. So, the farmer, once he gathered the sticks into a faggot—Mama, I think it would be better if we tell this story without that word from now on."

She turned to him, drying her hands on a towel. "I think that's a good idea."

"So, after that, the farmer told his sons and daughters to take up the bundle and break it. They all tried, but they could not do it as hard as they tried. Then, the farmer untied the bundle, and he gave them the sticks to break one by one. This they did with the greatest ease. Then the father said, 'My children, as long as we remain united, we are a match for all our enemies, but different and separate, we are undone.'"

"Okay. That was good, sweetie. And what's the moral to the story?"

Rueben shook his head. "I told the story, Mama. You tell me the moral."

They grew silent as they heard the front door bang open, followed by heavy footsteps and deep voices as Babe and Chance entered the vestibule, walking through to the stairs leading to the apartment above, followed by heavy footsteps thumping across the floorboards above them.

Babe turned on the lamp, removed the large bundle of sage from a bag, and placed it in the large golden container on the coffee table. He shredded a few pages from a magazine. Using them as kindling, he lit the pages beneath the sage stick with a few matches before he blew on it so that the fire would catch.

After removing his shoes, Chance entered the living room in his stockinged feet and sat on the floor in front of the sofa where he leaned his back against it. The smoke loomed thinly, then grew stronger and filled the space with a pungent, slightly skunky scent. Chance ostentatiously leaned forward to cough loudly into his hand.

Ignoring him, Babe concentrated on the direction of the smoke, the shape it took as it meandered through the space. He focused his thoughts on movement, on positivity and clean thoughts.

Chance lolled his head back exaggeratedly, heaving out a breath. "I'm confused. When my moms was helping me move in, you asked her to put out her cigarette because you have allergies. But here you are, filling up this room with this stank ass smell. And when we sparked up in the car, you didn't seem to mind."

"You ever notice how some people take liberties in somebody else's house? How they presume they can do whatever they want to do? Now I don't know if it's because they are older than me or what the thing is. But you can't come up in my house like you run the show. So, I had to chin check yo' mama." Babe laughed.

"She do be trying to run the show though." Chance laughed too. "Man, that trip to Philly was exhausting."

"All you did was ride down to the city. You didn't even do the driving, so how you exhausted?"

"Do you realize dude gave us a Diana Ross concert for the entire drive back? I thought he had had a dissociative episode or something. He refused to come out of character even when we were in that fucking little shop of horrors."

"The botanical shop? I feel like a total dumb ass. I mean I use sage to smudge my place and all that, but I never heard of a botanical shop before. I thought he wanted to go to Bath and Body Works!"

"He bought some roots he's supposed to burn to chase away evil spirits and shit. A grown ass man believing hocus-pocus shit. So, what's this you doing now?"

"This is white sage. I'm cleansing the space of any negative or toxic energies. Burning sage has been used in many cultures to chase away unwanted vibrations. I wouldn't call it was hocus-pocus. This stuff is grounded in religion. It's not evil if that's what you're implying."

Chance laughed. "This is why we laugh at you people. You believe if you burn eye of newt you can make a niggah love you, or you can keep away demons. Like my mom's old man. If you step on the back of his heel, he damn near goes into convulsions about bad luck, throwing salt over his shoulder and all that. It's like them old Abbott and Costello movies with the bug-eyed Negro all scared of 'ghosteses.' You mean to say you buy that mumbo jumbo?"

"I'm not saying I buy all of it. I'm saying if you, and people like you, want to be all in the culture, it would help if you tried to understand things other than music and clothes, like the origin of the culture instead of passing judgement about things you know nothing about. It's not like shit you see on *Gilligan's Island* or *The Brady Bunch*. Voodoo comes from religion just like Christianity. If you believe a stringy-haired, thin, white Anglo-Saxon came back from the dead, how can you find other beliefs funny?"

"Now you're offended. I'm not laughing at you, man. But you people do funny shit."

"I'm not. You young people always think you're the first to know shit. Just like you were making fun of Robby and how much he likes Diana Ross. How is his loving Diana Ross funny, but you got all those posters of Janet on your wall? And you dress like her, I mean, you got one of those bone necklaces same as hers, and when I first met you at the Lark, you had on one of those earrings with a key in it. How come that's cool but doing an imitation of Diana Ross is not? Where do you think Janet comes from?

One thing had to happen so that the next thing is possible. That's history. Just like with buying sage or a candle from the botanical shop."

Chance stood up, waving both his hands over his head. "Okay. Okay. Truce. I hear you. At least Ricky had a good voice. Shit, he sounded as good as Diana Ross herself singing."

Babe laughed. "Right? But that shit was crazy though, right? I was getting perturbed as fuck."

Babe stood up and collected his removed shoes to take upstairs to bed.

Chance said, "I could tell. It was all over your face. Especially when he brought that comb/microphone into the shop and was asking the bitch at the counter questions through the comb like he was interviewing her and shit. Just think, what if she had been a true voodoo high priestess. She could have fucked his best shit up."

"Right? I'll see you in the morning. I'm going to bed."

"What you talking? You never see me in the morning. I'm out of here before you even get up! Night, man."

The cloying trail of sage settled in his hair, his clothes, and followed Babe up the stairs, down the hall, and to his bedroom. The door to his room was closed, which struck him as odd. He didn't usually close his door unless he was sleeping. He entered the room and flicked the light switch.

Nothing.

He guessed the bulb died and figured he'd change it in the morning, not wanting to go back downstairs to the linen closet for a new bulb and not needing to see as he hastily undressed and threw his clothes toward the general vicinity of the hamper in the corner behind the door. He closed the door and clicked on the white-noise machine in the corner before settling on the waterbed.

He immediately sensed the difference. The weight on the mattress was different. When he stretched out, he felt Matthew's heat as much in his senses as his actual physical heat. Matthew moved a sweat-dampened arm over his torso, and Babe sat up with a gasp.

"The fuck! What are you doing here?"

"I missed you."

His voice was a low treble, the slight delay communicated to Babe the degree of intoxication was moderate, which meant his combativeness would not yet be a challenge. Moderate intoxication, and he was still able to reason and not yet at the point Babe would be repulsed. Matthew touched his back, the warmth there sending shockwaves through Babe's synapses.

"I miss you too. You shouldn't be here."

"You moved that white boy in here the minute I was gone. I was giving you space like you asked. How could you move somebody else in here? I fucked up, but I'm human. You did shit in this relationship too."

"I know."

"That don't mean we can't keep doing what we been doing. This was supposed to just be the beginning. We were going to buy more properties, rent them out, and be moguls. How you going to mess all that up?"

Babe thought back over the years to meeting Matthew at the cruising spot at the train station. What had been a one-night stand had turned into a relationship. Casual hookups had turned into conversations, which had turned to dating, then moved to living together and getting to know Matthew's family and changing their hostility to if not love, at least respect. Then buying a house together: the beginning of the end.

But the infidelity had been part and parcel of the relationship the entire time, as had the drinking and drug use.

Babe used to drink with him, hanging out at the park, experimenting with weed and speed, but where Babe's use had continued to be occasional, Matthew's had increased to dependence.

"I know we've done good things as a couple. But listen, I don't want to put anything on you. All my life I've been put in this good-boy roll. I'm always dependable and upstanding and predictable. I'm tired of trying to live up to expectations of people I don't even know. I don't even know why that was ever important to me. Who am I trying to impress?"

"You don't have to impress anybody." Matthew kissed the back of his neck. "We was doing this thing just for us. Can't nobody hold a candle to you."

"But what's that even mean? It's all bullshit. I don't want to live for other people's approval anymore. I want to live for me. Do things I never did before, go to a bathhouse, travel the world, not be tied down by a mortgage. I'm just sick of this prison of mortgage and car notes, going to the supermarket every week to buy the same boring food, going to a job that is killing my soul, going to church, paying tithes. I'm tired of using condoms, of having to think about safe sex every time I see a dick. I want to screw unencumbered."

"You can't put me out of my own house." Matthew's voice had shifted from beseeching to stern.

"You can have the house if that's what you want. I will move out. If you want to be tied to this mortgage payment each month, it doesn't mean shit to me."

"I don't want this house without you in it!"

Babe yelled, "That's not going to happen! You should go, now. You need to understand this is real."

Matthew embraced him, his mouth warm and soothing on his jaw. His hands were soft, reminding him of what he was missing. He reached out and ran his fingers through Matthew's thick, rough hair, pulling him close, smelling the earthy, slightly dirty scent of him, feeling himself become aroused. His throat thickened, his mouth opened, taking Matthew's tongue inside, hastily removing his clothes.

Sex was fast and insistent. He lay back and let Matthew's mouth cover his entire body. His mind raced. This was a bad idea, gave a mixed message.

He whispered, "You can't stay," as a disclaimer, gasping as his shaft was enveloped in wet warmth.

Their words became nonwords. Instructions were communicated with murmurs and groans. Pleasure was shown by an elongation of those groans.

The sounds of their passion became a part of the other sounds of the house. Babe's gasp merged with the sound coming from the white-noise machine. Matthew's groan unfurled into the air, traveling along the stairs, merging with the smoke of white sage, traveling through the walls and the floorboards. Babe put his hand over Matthew's mouth, trying to dampen his groans, afraid the sounds of their passion could be heard below, not wanting Chance to know what was happening, hoping to staunch their angry, desperate reverberations from traveling through the vents and revealing he was weak, as weak as any rutting animal acting on elemental instinct.

When they finished, Babe lay with his head on pillows, staring at the ceiling, listening to Matthew's alcohol clotted snore rumbling beside him.

He thought about how much easier it would be to lie there, sleeping through the night, letting Matthew rise in the morning, and continuing in their old pattern: Matthew working two jobs. Hardly ever seeing each other. Matthew's weekends spent disrupting the monotony of life with beer and smoking with Darrell while Babe's was spent anesthetizing his brain by buying furniture and useless household objects to fill the gaping void in his life. There was always a certain degree of comfort in the familiar. But things would never be better if he continued down the safe path. He didn't even know what 'better' was for him, but he wanted something different.

He nudged Matthew, who rolled over and threw a possessive arm across his chest. Babe nudged him again. "Hey. You gotta go now."

Matthew opened a red, angry eye.

"So, you fuck me, and send me on my way? Is that how it's going with the white boy downstairs too? Call him up to finish you off when I go?"

Babe sat up, got out of the bed, and reached for his clothing, anticipating things might go left of center and fast, based on past experience, preferring to be clothed should he need to defend himself.

"You know me well enough to know that's not true. This is about you and me only."

Matthew stood and yanked pants onto his lean legs. "I don't know shit about you anymore. All this is new. You wake up one day and decide to break up everything because you tired of rubbers and want to fuck raw. You are one stupid bitch."

Babe sighed. "Of course you are going to focus on one minute area of what I told you. That's what you always do. I don't expect you to get it, you don't have to get it."

As Matthew walked past, he bumped Babe's shoulder with his own and hissed. "It's not going to be easy, I promise. You're not getting rid of me like that."

Babe promptly moved back, dodging the punch Matthew aimed at his face so it glanced off his shoulder instead. Babe pushed him, punching at the back of his head as he darted out the door.

"Just go! Go."

Chapter Eighteen

The Disruption of Time

Violence has a funny way of disrupting memory. Sometimes an act of violence delays time; other times it accelerates, changing memory and merging fact with fiction. Babe's perception of the moment when Matthew swung a fist at him was that the resulting chaos took place within a few seconds. He had moved away from the blow and responded to it with what he perceived to be the most passive sort of reaction: he pushed Matthew out the door.

The space between Matthew's initial blow and the pushing out of the door was wider than Babe remembered. There had been several blows after the first one. Many of them coming from Babe as he struck out with the rage of years of unexpressed fury and frustration.

The only part he recalled was being knocked backward onto the bed, Matthew's hands pressing tighter and tighter around his throat and a slight gasp of shock when, in the midst of being strangled, Matthew lowered his head and covered Babe's mouth with his own, pushing his tongue into Babe's mouth. Babe gurgled in amazement, managing to use the weight of his thighs to maneuver himself into the upper position, emitting a high-pitched, muffled sound of incredulous rage as he tightened a belt (he did not recall where the belt came from) around Matthew's neck, using the broad buckle as leverage, which raised discolored welts as Matthew attempted to curse him through his wind-deprived airway.

Through their passion, they both froze as the howl of far-off sirens permeated the air. Babe loosened the belt, letting Matthew violently push him away. Matthew climbed out of the bed and hastily ran into the hallway and down the stairs. Babe promptly followed on his heels to make sure he did not destroy anything along the way. Chance stood in the lower hallway, holding a phone. Chance followed them to the head of the stairs where Matthew raced toward the back stairwell and out the door through the laundry room.

Babe turned around and looked down to fasten his pants, his chest heaving rapidly and damp with sweat. Chance quickly put the phone receiver in his pajama pocket.

"I know you didn't call the cops?"

Chance shook his head. "No. Why, what's up?"

"Not after what I told you, I know you didn't."

"I was sleep, and then I heard all this noise on the stairs. You okay?"

There was a hard rap on the glass front door. Babe eyed Chance warily, passing him and walking downstairs. Alise stood in the entryway, talking to a tall, burly officer, who was shadowed by a thin, younger, white officer. "I didn't see anything."

"We got a 911 call. A fight taking place at this address."

Babe stepped forward. "Sorry, Officer. That was my fault, I think. I had the TV up really loud, watching wrestling, and I knocked over my radio. Someone must have heard the commotion and called it in."

The officer watched him with an assessing eye. "Mind if we come in?"

Babe laughed. "There's really no need. Like I said, I had the TV too loud, but everything's good."

Both officers focused on Alise. The Black one spoke. "Ma'am, if you are in any danger, you need to speak now. The call we got reported a domestic dispute, and we need to ensure a domestic dispute is not taking place."

He clicked on a flashlight in the darkened vestibule, running the light from Alise's face to her foot. "Are you harmed in any way?"

"We don't live together, Officer. I rent the apartment downstairs. I heard the knocking, so I answered."

The other officer entered the vestibule, filling the narrow space with the heat from too many bodies. "Ma'am, if you feel in jeopardy in any way, you need to let us know."

Alise rolled her eyes. "You guys are fucking ridiculous. I didn't make the call. Now, I'm going in my apartment, back to sleep. Where you woke me up banging on the door like that. I have to get to work in the morning!"

She walked back into the dark of her apartment, slamming the door behind her.

Both officers brought their attention to Babe. "We're going to need to take a look around."

He shrugged. "Feel free."

"Inside the apartment."

Once inside, the men did a cursory inventory of the apartment. Seeing no damaged furniture, their demeanor relaxed somewhat, became less guarded. Chance came out of his room, wrapping a robe around his waist before sitting on the sofa with his legs crossed. The officers exchanged a look. "You live here too?"

Chance nodded.

"Are you the individual that placed the call?"

Again, he shook his head.

"Where do you sleep?"

Chance's eyes widened. He pointed. "Where do I sleep? Back there."

"And you?"

Babe was still trembling from his encounter with Matthew. He hoped his agitation did not show. "I sleep upstairs. This is my roommate."

"What is the nature of your relationship?"

"I just told you."

The Black officer smirked at the other officer. "Okay, sir. Is there a domestic situation here we need to be made aware of?"

Chance frowned. "I don't know what you mean?

Babe's voice was clipped, angered. "He means are we boyfriends. *Right, Officer?* If the big, bad blackamoor has been abusing the white waif."

The officers grew red faced, flustered by Babe's forthrightness. They did one last cursory inspection before heading toward the door, reminding them to keep the noise down as disturbances could result in being taken down to the borough hall. Babe followed them, stiff with fury, sharply slamming the door on their cordial good nights.

"Assholes."

The door did not close all the way. A hand pushed back from the other side. Babe tried to place where he had seen the thin blonde girl, who stood in the porchlight, before.

"Hey. It's Brittney, Chance's sister. Can you ask him to come out here real quick? I need his help with something."

Chapter Nineteen

Ella at the Bar

Violence has a funny way of disrupting things. It can make the once strong weak, and it can make the seemingly fragile dominant.

It didn't take Chance and Brittney long to get to Colletti's Bar since it was right around the corner from Leviticus Street. By the time they walked there, both Jason and Raheem, were huddling on the corner beneath the neon sign, sharing a cigarette. They were relieved to see Chance, both walking toward him before he could even get his foot on the curb.

Jason spoke solemnly, embarrassed he needed Chance's help. "Man, glad you got here. Your moms is on a tear. She cussing everybody out, saying she ain't coming the fuck home. They told her she flagged, but she won't go."

"You're her old man," Brittney yelled in exasperation. "You can't get her out?"

Jason shrugged. "You know how she get when she drinks the brown. She don't listen to nobody but you."

Chance entered the dark interior, praying the bartender wouldn't notice him and embarrass him by asking for ID. Ella was singing loudly above the rowdy crowd in an off-key monotone, tucked away at a table in the far corner of the room. The bar was somewhat crowded, giving Chance some cover.

Ella glanced up from her tumbler and snickered drunkenly. Chance glowered down at her, his hand on his hip.

"Well, well. What you come here for? They got you to do their dirty work? Well, I meant what I said. I'm not going nowhere."

Chance stood above her, hands on his hips. "Why is that?"

"'Cause I'm grown!"

Brittney folded her hands across her narrow chest. "You are embarrassing, man. Sitting up here drinking 'till you're shitfaced, and then you want to cuss everybody out."

"Who'd I cuss out? Who? All I said was I'm not ready to go home. And you run out to get him like he runs my house. He don't even live there anymore. I run shit, don't nobody forget that."

They all sat down, hoping if they moved in closer Ella's tendency to yell would be averted. Chance pulled his chair closer. "You're right. And why do you think I moved out of there? Hmm? To get away from this stupid shit."

"Who you calling stupid, boy? You moved out 'cause you got that jungle fever." She laughed, pointing to Jason and Raheem. "I understand it. You get that honestly."

"Knock it off." He hissed. "Stop making a fool of yourself. You are a grown ass woman, so act like it."

He grabbed her upper arm and shook her. "I'm tired of cleaning up your messes, Mom. Calling out sick for you at work, paying your bills when you're too tired to get up and do it yourself, cleaning up your house. I want you to get up from here, shake the dust off, and go the hell home before they bring the cops in here on your ass."

Ella yanked her arm away indignantly before rising shakily to her and feet where she linked her arm in the crook of Brittany's elbow. "Take me home, baby."

The three men sat at the table, watching them stumble toward the door, Brittney struggling to keep Ella erect. They passed the bar, bumping into a man, spilling the mug of beer he held.

"Watch where the fuck you going!" Matthew cursed.

Ella cupped a breast. "Suck my tit, faggot."

Spotting him, Chance swore. "What the fuck is he doing here?"

Raheem asked, "You know him?"

"Yeah, why?"

Jason said, "He's the one got Ella started. He was over at our table, telling us we can make a couple hundred dollars. Alls we got to do is kill some faggot."

Chance shook his head as if to clear his thoughts. "Wait. What are you saying? He's running around in here offering up money to kill somebody?"

"Yeah. Ain't that one called Babe who you live with?"

Chance laughed. "Are you for real? This dumb ass niggah. He's mad because he got that ass beat, so now he wants somebody to kill Babe?"

"Niggah's crazy. Maybe just drunk though."

Matthew was lurched over the counter at the main bar, mumbling into his beer.

"How much?" Chance demanded.

"How much what?" Raheem asked.

Chance rolled his eyes at the rampant stupidity. "What'd he offer you?"

Jason reached into his back pocket and pulled out a roll of bills. "Five hunnit."

Chance was, incredulous. "Five hundred dollars. You gotta be kidding me."

"That's all a faggot's life is worth." Raheem laughed. "He might've offered more for somebody else."

"What the fuck? You took the money? To say nothing about how the fuck he got his crack ass hands on that much without smoking it up."

"Hells yeah, we took it. We ain't going to do nothing though. But what's his dumb ass going to do about getting his money back? Easy money, man. And your moms is crazy mad because Jase wouldn't break her off none."

Chance watched them laughing hysterically, amazed. "All right, I'm out of here."

Chance walked swiftly around the corner. Ross stood on the porch, ringing the doorbell. Ross turned to face him as he stepped up. The heavy makeup was gone, remnants of lipstick stained his mouth, and mascara clotted his lashes. "Oh, hey, chile. I been knocking on this door for a piece, but nobody's answering. Babe forgot to get his shit from Robby, so I got it for him."

Chance glanced at him warily, approaching the door and opening it. "It's late. He's probably in bed."

Ross walked on his heels, entering close behind him. "Yeah. I won't take long. Just didn't want that fat bitch trying to give my grandniece the okey doke."

"I'll see if he's up." Chance's voice was clipped. They walked up the stairs to the landing.

Ross's eyes sparkled with amusement. "What's the tea?"

"The what?"

Ross laughed. "You don't like me, do you? Don't know whether I'm a little too Black for you or too real. Haven't been able to tell which yet. Or both."

"I don't know what you're talking about." Chance walked up the second set of steps toward Babe's room.

"I think you do. You never been around somebody living out loud like me. It's scary, isn't it? You, so comfortable being you, and whatever that entails. But you can't take my loud Black ass, can you? It's okay, darling. You aren't the first to be discombobulated by the fabulosity of Miss Ross."

Hearing the unmistakable braying voice, Babe came out into the hallway, clicking on his bedroom light. "What the hell?"

"Hey, daughter. It's just Miss Ross. As usual, Miss Robby done gooped you out your cut, so your godmother had to make things right." Ross stormed past Chance, walking into Babe's bedroom, extending his hand with a little glassine baggie between two lacquered fingernails. "Chile, when you been promised blow, you know you got to stay on top of that bitch because you know her mattress ass will have inhaled a whole entire complete eight-ball within *seconds*! So, bitch, here you go. I managed to get into that bitch's villa and scoop up a few toots before she descended upon that sheet cake like you know she do."

Babe laughed, taking the baggie from him. "Oh, no big deal. The amount that stingy bitch gives up is barely worth the effort to inhale."

"No, ma'am! An agreement is an agreement. Think of how much time you wasted driving that bitch into the bowels of the city. Now, yes, it is fabulous to drive through and maybe snatch a lovely Puerto Rican daddy, but bitch, it's still out of the way."

"Where's your little date?" Chance asked.

Both of them silently stared at Chance for a beat before Ross responded. "Home in bed where trade belongs. He has been depleted and is now sleeping to restore his energy for round two, darling. If you need to know all my business."

Chance snickered as Ross continued his diatribe.

"When I got into Robby's place, girl, she was already doinked for the gawds, *B*. Hiding her big ass behind a throw pillow, terrified out of her wits. Now, how she think she can hide all that meat behind a goddamn pillow, girl? Who you hidin' from? Honey, if you can't handle coke all like that, why the hell does she do it? The bitch be hallucinating and drooling and farting from that Maalox cut. The room smelled like she shit herself, girl. I thought I was in the toilets at Grand Central Station."

"Let him be." Babe laughed.

"Oh, I'm not judging. I'm just saying! Listen."

Ross crept over to the wall, leaning his ear against it. "Quiet."

Ross began knocking on the wall, a maniacal grin on his face. He kept knocking until they heard a voice, muffled through the wall. "Who's there? What do you want?"

Ross put a hand over his laughing mouth. "We want *you*, bitch."

He knocked again. Chance laughed, moving toward the wall. "Is that Robby? What the fuck?"

The muffled voice came again. "No! Leave me alone."

Ross knocked louder with more insistency. "I'm right here with you."

"No! Stop! Help! Help."

"There's no help for you, bitch."

"Help. No help. No help."

Babe shook his head. "I don't know if it's more sad or fucking scary. If he's hallucinating like that, who knows what he sees, or what he will do."

Chance asked, "All from snorting blow? There's more going on than that, man."

Ross shook his head. "Bitch, if you been inhaling a goddamn eightball every other day for ten motherfucking years, she's going to have eaten-up space in your brain, chile. That bitch is a zombie. Plus, getting her brain fried with all those goddamn hair relaxers and Jheri-curl chemicals, bitch, there ain't nothing there beneath all that gristle and the press and curl. Honey, it's a goddamn travesty."

Babe shook his head, clapping his hands with finality. "Well, there's nothing any of us can do about it but try to be supportive when we can. So, I've got to get to bed. Work in the morning. Thanks, Ricky, for bringing this over."

As Ross and Chance walked toward the door, Chance said, "Shit, based on what I heard, I'm not so sure you should be doing that shit. If you start screaming no help, no help, I'm calling five-oh, and we know how you feel about that!"

"You don't have to worry about me. I'm a professional." The laugh on Babe's lips disappeared as he closed the door.

Chapter Twenty

You Is Dead

The morning brought two unexpected events to Babe's doorstep.

First, he began his daily ritual. Every morning, upon waking, he would go down to the kitchen, turn on the stereo amplifier, and eat a half cup of oatmeal with a raw egg. Depending on his mood, he might play something smooth or else classic house, like "Still in Love with You," or "Beat the Street." He'd go up to the spare room, strip down, and work out with his free weights.

Bench-press three sets.

Dumbbell flys three sets.

Drop the dumbbells to the floor with a grunt, raining down plaster and dust particles to the floors below like dandelion ether.

Down to the kitchen and bang out three sets of ten incline pushups between two kitchen chairs.

Back upstairs in front of the mirror, avoiding the reflection of his crotch.

He'd hit the shower, call in to work to give his ETA, and then out the door.

Depending on the day of the week, he would bring half a turkey on wheat, a piece of fruit, bottled water, and a bag of almonds with him. If it were Thursday or Friday, he would eliminate the bread and pasta, hoping to minimize bloat for weekend exhibitions at the bars.

Prior to Chance moving in, he would do his cleansing rituals on Friday evenings, but now, since he did not like disturbances or inquisitive eyes, he would burn eucalyptus oil Friday morning, play the soundtrack CD of *The Hunger* or something operatic. He would then fill a hot water bottle with warm, freshly brewed coffee, lay upon a towel of pristine Egyptian cotton on the bathroom floor, and give himself a high enema.

He had read in doctor-somebody-or-other's book about the importance of ridding the body of toxins and the remnants of food left trapped by an inefficient waste removal system. While all that was well and good, he conducted this weekly ritual to maintain a flat stomach.

As instructed in doctor-somebody-or-other's book, he attempted, though usually unsuccessfully, to hold an entire bag of fluid inside his body. His stomach would cramp, and his sphincter would pulsate with the effort of holding everything inside. He would concentrate on the soothing chords of the music, trying to distract himself from the pain his body was experiencing.

When he could stand it no longer, he would dash to the toilet, letting loose with a flood of relief.

This particular morning, as he walked down to the entryway, there among the stack of mail tumbled on the floor was the first rental payment from Section 8. He slid a finger into the seam and read the check. He didn't recognize the name, Alice Norwood.

He froze for a moment, wondering if this were a typo. Alise cracked open the door to her apartment and peeked out with a pandering expression etched across her face. "Hey. I saw the check from Section 8 was there. You get it?"

"It says redeemable regarding Alice Norwood?"

"Yeah. You gone question a sister about her government?"

He laughed. "I'm the last one to go in on somebody about their real name. Hell, I go by Babe, so who am I to talk?"

She laughed, closing the door as he continued outside to his car. Walking across the street, he glanced briefly at his Jeep, his brain not registering what his eyes had glimpsed. Slowing down, he approached his vehicle with a sickening sense of dread.

Scrawled across the windshield in huge white letters, it said You Is Dead.

Babe blinked, hoping when he opened his eyes the thing would be gone. But there it was, blazing beneath the morning sun. It didn't take much pondering to know who had done this. Who else did he know stupid enough to write a grammatically incorrect threat on his windshield?

Embarrassed, he quickly unlocked the car and reached in the back for Windex and paper towels. He liberally sprayed the solution, hoping the blue liquid would blur out the thing. He scrubbed hastily, furiously, until the paper towels turned to mush in his hands. The words would not go away. He thought perhaps the paper towels were not strong enough, so he grabbed a chamois from the back and began anew. Nothing. The thing would not go away.

He felt curtains shift. He felt eyes upon him. He heard far off *hsking* and imagined heads shaking disapprovingly.

He walked swiftly back into the house and grabbed a bucket from beneath the kitchen sink, then filled it with scalding soapy water.

Tears of humiliation tumbled from his eyelashes.

Thirteen years of humiliation. Sitting before the mortgage rep being told Matthew's credit score would make homeownership difficult to obtain. Waiting to be picked up so they could shop for furniture for their new home, and Matthew finally arriving, late and intoxicated. Shopping alone for bed linens and dishes. Arguments about the mortgage being in one name instead of two.

Babe blamed himself. It would have been better to continue renting once they discovered Matthew wouldn't be able to secure a loan. All the rest, the cheating and the drug use, all followed on the heels of the mortgage debacle, so he had to take part of the blame.

Outside, across the street, the Latino boy who had provided Babe's nights of unobstructed views of blissful masturbation was standing in front of his Jeep. He was wearing a dirty T-shirt and chinos. His full black curls fell into his eyes as he leaned into the windshield, swiftly swiping away the wording with a razor. He glanced up as Babe approached.

"You gotta use a razor on this shit. You use water, it smears all across the windshield."

Babe was disconcerted. "Thank—"

"Yeah. I seen you and dude over there ever since you moved in. Good move getting him out. He's trouble. This is a punk ass move, definitely."

"Thank you for the help. I'm already late for work. Wasn't expecting this."

He laughed. "You should have. Based on what I've seen, you guys fighting in the street. Him always fucked up. NowI see you moved in new folks. This, or worse, was bound to happen."

He stepped back to admire his handiwork. "That should do it. Just zip through a carwash on your way to the J-O-B, and you should be golden."

Babe reached out a hand. "Thanks, uh?"

He grabbed Babe's hand in his own, thick and warm. "Wilfredo. No problem. You're Babe, yeah?"

He smiled. "Yeah. Let me give you a few dollars. I really appreciate—"

Manny waved him off. "You kidding? A few dollars for that? You think I'm panhandling or some shit?"

They both laughed.

"No. Not at all."

"Tell you what. You can treat me to a beer. Whenever you got time to chill for a few. Just knock on the door. And we'll call it even. Bet?"

Babe smiled. "Bet."

Around then, curtains slid back into place, and windows darkened.

Chapter Twenty-One

Alise & Kendall

As the rain pelted down, hammering against the shingles of the back porch, Rueben quietly opened the door and sat behind the cover offered by the exterior of the building. He knew Alise would come out to enjoy the rain. She liked the peacefulness of rainy days. If he remembered to stay quiet, he could hear her words to the old woman. He had listened to her through the vents between the house next door and theirs, her story-time voice as soothing as always, spinning stories about people he didn't know as she regaled the old woman with tales of faraway places and people.

It reminded him of earlier days when he and Alise would sit outside or tucked together by an open window, reciting fables, laughing and correcting the other when they misremembered a passage.

He heard the door opening from the adjoining house. He peered around the buildings edge watching Alise wheel Miss Doris out onto the back porch. She took the large silver brush from the basket on the back of the chair and brushed through the old woman's lustrous silver hair.

Mama had always said rain was God cleaning off the dirt men brought to the land. He imagined God, with his long white beard, carrying the biggest hose you ever saw and spraying it down on him like a super soaker. The thought made him love the rain even more.

Mama wasn't telling any stories this time. She stood silently, playing the brush through the woman's hair. Rueben wondered why she was silent this day.

He heard mewling and looked across the grass to see the two shabby feral cats that had taken up residence below the house run through the pelting rain up onto the porch in search of something to eat. Rueben prayed Mitzi wouldn't come barreling out and gobble them up.

The patchwork calico and the scrappy tabby looked like wet scraps of lint climbing up to the porch where Rueben stood hidden. Alise had put out a bowl of food for them as she did each morning before she crossed over to clean up Miss Doris for the day. Rueben didn't know where they came from, the two cats that always traveled together like their own private wolf pack, but he was glad they came. He reached to put a bit of food on his fingertip and held it out to them, making sure to keep himself hidden from view.

As the rain increased in ferocity, Rueben heard Alise yelp in surprise. He looked around the wall as she quickly spun the wheelchair around to drag the woman over the threshold back into the house.

Rueben ran inside his own apartment, shaking his head slowly, rain swinging free in a frenzy. He looked at the refrigerator, and even though he saw the lock firmly affixed, he could not help but check, tugging the handle a few times to see if he might get lucky.

He walked over to the far wall and sat beneath the vent to warm himself. He could only hear bits and pieces of her voice, the rain battering the roof, blotting out most of her words.

"The landlord saw my real name today. Alice Norwood. I thought he was going to give me a hassle over it. Most of the people I know use a different name than their birth name. So, I don't see how that would be a big deal. Shit, everybody knows a Lil Bit or a Man Man. I don't think I ever called Baby Boy by his government name. I'm so tired. I don't feel like running anymore. If he had raised a stink about me having a different name, I think I'd have to stand in it. Look my truth straight in the face. I'm tired."

Rueben licked his fingertip, reached into his pocket, and took salt into his mouth, waiting for that comforting numbness.

"We'd always had Black friends when I was a kid. One, Miss Clara, even used to come to the house. She and Ma worked together, doing laundry on the weekends at the Valley Forge Motor Lodge. You remember the Motor Lodge, used to be out on 202 back in the day? Miss Clara was Mama's ride. Mama never did like driving all that much, always preferred others to take her wherever she needed to go.

"So it was a surprise to me how much everybody was taken aback when I married Kendall."

Alise paused. Rueben heard the click of metal, heard the cellophane crinkle.

"He was so beautiful. It was a whirlwind. Unexpected. I mean, we'd seen each other here and there in the halls at school or around town. But I'd never really paid much attention to him. I mean, what would a guy like that want with somebody like me?

"He was tall, well not too tall, but taller than me. And he was muscular. He had the most beautiful hands and feet. So broad and well-shaped, with really notable veins. You know, like you'd picture the hands of God, only they were black, of course. He was dark, like molten chocolate, with perfect, perfect teeth. He wasn't really all that muscular, more stocky, I guess you'd call it. When I was a kid, they called it husky."

She laughed.

"But anyway, why would a guy like that, with his perfect skin, and beautiful wavy hair like Cary Grant, what would he want with a girl like me? I mean, I wasn't as big as I had been in junior high. I'd started to slim down a little once I got my period and sprouting like a weed, so my Mama said, and so I was maybe a size fourteen/sixteen.

"I once asked him. We both were working then, at the nursing home part-time. He approached me out of the blue one day while I was changing Miss Mabelline's pissy sheets. He came in the room and helped me clean her up, and he asked me if I wanted to get lunch with him during our break. I asked him, 'Why do you want to go out with my fat ass?'"

"He flashed that perfect grin with that classic Roman nose, and he said 'That's why. It's all good to me.'"

She laughed. "We dated for like two months. He was like a storybook prince. It was more than somebody like me had ever seen before. He called every day. He'd have cards stuck in my locker at work, real romantic cards.

Nobody had ever held a door open for me, made sure to walk on the outside of the sidewalk beside me. It seemed like his every waking moment was devoted to wanting to spend time with me.

"When he asked me to marry him after only two months, a little voice told me we were rushing things. I wondered if we should take things more slowly. But he was so persistent, so charming, what could I say but yes? Did I think something better would be coming along? I had my one shot, and I took it.

"My folks were livid. My father never hit me before. They said I was an embarrassment. So, I lied. Said I was pregnant. My brothers locked me in a room and fought me like I was a man. But like I said, I was raised with all boys. I gave as good as I got." She laughed bitterly.

"So, the nigger lover was ran out of town. And I didn't regret a moment of it. Being with Kendall was better than anything that had come before him. Even with all the trouble that followed. Kendall was terrible with money. We both were. We moved from house to house every year, getting evicted because we liked nice things, fast cars, and beautiful clothes more than we liked paying rent."

There was the quick succession of the sounds of flint igniting butane, then a pause before sharp inhalation, and then the sound of air expelling.

"Once I got pregnant, everything changed. I had to beg my own husband to be with me. Maybe I'd gotten too fat after having Rueben. Maybe I wasn't attractive to him anymore. I'd starve myself with all those stupid diets you see on TV. None of that mattered.

"Besides, *I was fucking starving*, you know?

"But even the constant moving and Kendall not keeping a job, when Rueben came into the world, nothing—no man, no landlord, no repossession—nothing could darken the bright space he brought to my life. I was in love. This was what I was meant to be, a mother. This was my purpose in this world."

A blaze of lightening introduced a stirring boom of thunder, followed by the rain pouring down with increasing frenzy.

Alise grabbed the dishtowel hanging from a small rail over the sink, using it to dry the damp from the old woman's hair and face, moving down to her neck, tamping down on the gnarled wet hands clasped in her lap. She gingerly reached forward, slipping the diamond ring from the woman's finger, dropping it into her pocket.

She decided she'd wash the dishes. She pushed Doris up to the old metal table and ran water into the sink, blasting a shot of soap. She loved to make a billowing pile of suds when she washed dishes, enveloping the kitchen in the chemical facsimile of lemon scent.

"I don't regret one second of my marriage. Even with all that happened, I was never more alive. Before Kendall, nothing mattered. Nothing happened for me until the moment he came into my life.

"I know that sounds like old-fashioned, patriarchal shit, right? But I don't mean it like I am nothing without a man in my life even though that's how it sounds.

"My family tried to destroy us. Kendall spent a year in jail for statutory rape.

"Nothing could stop him. He found me when he got out, and we moved to another county, hoping that would be the end of it. They would come by our little bungalow at night. Yelling they were going to string him and his little half-breed in the trees out front. Kendall didn't come from no city people; he came from a hunting family. He was as comfortable with guns as my brothers were. He made sure to keep them in the house, loaded and ready. And he taught Rueben to be comfortable with them too. I think Ruebs could hold a gun before he could talk. Problem is Ruebs learned from his Daddy to be too comfortable with them. They learned to shoot when they should have learned to reason."

Chapter Twenty-Two

Flat Tire

Chance noticed Clark giving him the eye from the very first day he began temping in the mailroom at one of the gigantic faceless office parks in Valley Forge. After the first week, he had mustered up the courage to introduce himself. By week two, he made it a point to stop at Chance's workstation each morning, saying hello and smiling languidly. Sometimes he waited at his workstation in the morning before Chance had even clocked in. He'd find him rooting around, picking up framed photos of his family, or glancing at the clippings pinned to his wall of Janet and Madonna.

It was easy to tell when guys like that were interested. There was a certain hangdog gleam in the eye, a lingering of contact when shaking hands, and a tremulous moving of the mouth that communicated a certain sadness. The problem with that is in most cases, those men were far older than he was. Chance guessed Clark to be in his midthirties. His barometer was based on how high on the waist he wore his drab, gray, pleated pants and his reptile shoes from Stacey Adams.

He had a sort of middle-of-the-road attractiveness, nothing attention-grabbing, but nothing that would make you cringe either. He was tall and the color of uncreamed coffee with a conservative length of flat-topped hair. He would normally date someone like Clark two or three times, just to see what they had to offer before dumping them. But he thought it might be to his advantage to make use of him so Babe would know he was viable to other guys.

It had started with Clark sitting with him at lunch in the cafeteria. That moved to a request for dinner, followed by Chance going down on him in his late-model Maxima. He found the smell of Brut emanating from his crotch too strong.

"What's that scent you're wearing?" he'd asked, gagging and picking a stiff pubic hair from his tongue. He'd have to convince him to switch to something less overwhelming, or at least demand that he ease back on the usage in the future if he expected to be getting regular blow jobs.

After week four, he had invited Clark to a home-cooked dinner on Leviticus Street. If Babe didn't see him with someone, he might think he was bullshitting.

Clark had cooked the meal. Chance's area of expertise when it came to cooking ended with pizza rolls, frozen fries, and takeout. He'd been bummed when they arrived to a Babe-less house but pleasantly surprised by Clark's tender chicken parmesan and fragrant asparagus with lemon butter sauce. So pleasantly surprised, they skipped dessert and instead fucked twice on Babe's red leather sofa before moving to the bedroom for round three. He'd left the door to his bedroom open in case Babe came home during their extended fornication.

Sex with Clark was pleasant enough. He was better to look at naked than he was clothed. Even though he was thin and a confessed couch potato, when he was standing in all his glory, his ass was high and dense, his shoulders were broad and defined, and his belly was sloped and tight. As he watched Clark go down on him for the third round, he supposed he liked the contrast. White men were too much like him. And that bored him.

Insistent knocking at the door caused Clark to rise from the bed before Chance put a hand on his chest and pushed him back down. "It's cool. Just somebody at the door. Stay put."

He picked up a towel from the hamper, wrapped it around his waist, and walked down the stairs to the door.

Alise was standing on the other side, holding a clothes basket against her belly. He noticed her pause in discomfort at his bare torso. Barely perceptible, but Chance caught it.

"Hey. I hate to ask. But can I use your dryer to dry my jeans. They take so long hanging in the basement."

He shrugged, holding the door open for her to enter. "No problem."

They climbed the steps to the landing, and Chance held out an arm toward the rear steps leading down to the laundry room. Clark, in his undressed state, lay visible on the rumpled bed before Chance pulled the door partially closed. He pulled it closed, leaving enough space so that the undressed man in his bed was still visible.

"The dryer is down there."

Alise gasped. "Shit. Now I have to go back downstairs after climbing up those to get here?"

He laughed. "It's a bitch, ain't it?"

He walked back into the room and addressed Clark. "You didn't have to get dressed."

"Why didn't you close the door?"

He shrugged. "What's the big deal?"

Standing above him, Chance opened his towel and flashed Clark. He reached down to push Clark's head closer, watching distractedly out the window behind the futon as a rotund Black boy walked out toward the pathway beside the garage. The boy darted out for a brief second before disappearing again.

"I think I'm going to head out in a bit. It's getting late."

"You don't have to go. Do you?"

Chance sat on the futon, hanging his legs over Clark's lap and began nuzzling his ear. Clark groaned, kissing him back. At the sound of footsteps, Clark pushed him off. Alise came back up and tapped on the door to Chance's room. "Hey, thanks. There were a pair of jeans in the dryer."

Chance took them from her. "Okay."

"I wanted to cry, holding up those pants. I never been that size my whole life. I wonder what it would feel like to be that size."

"Hey. You have a kid?"

She shook her head. "What? No... Why?"

"Nothing. I saw some Black kid in the yard through the window."

"Oh. Yeah. I have a little boy. Rueben..."

The sound of Babe's keys jingled as he jogged up the stairs to the landing. He stopped short at the gathering of people standing there, one wearing a towel.

Chance flicked his head in Alise's direction. "She wanted to use the dryer."

She smiled. "Hope that's okay. It's just a one-time thing."

"Okay."

She moved past him, walking down the stairs.

"I'll knock in about a half hour to see if my clothes are done. Thanks again, guys—"

The doorbell sounded loudly, interrupting Alise's sentence.

"Damn. Thirtieth Street Station up in here today, right?" said Chance.

"Since you're going down, can you let in whoever is at the door?" Babe asked.

"No problem."

Tightening the towel on his waist, Chance stretched an arm toward Clark. "Babe, this is Clark. I told you about him. Clark, this is my roommate, Babe."

"Nice to meet you."

Babe nodded dismissively. Chance noticed Clark giving Babe the same hangdog look he had given Chance on his first day of work. It annoyed him. He heard quick, heavy footsteps ascending. He stared over Babe's shoulder as Wilfredo walked up the steps, joining them on the landing.

"Hey. What's up?" Babe asked.

Wilfredo paused, most likely not expecting to see an unclothed man sandwiched between two clothed men.

"Hey, man. You been driving a Honda Accord? I ain't seen your Jeep out there since that thing happened, so I was thinking you been in hiding."

Babe laughed. "I did swap with a car from my job for a little bit 'til things die down some, but I think the girl downstairs has an Accord."

Chance leaned a hip against the door jamb. "Yeah, that's Alise's car. What's up? Bitch's tags expired, or some shit?" He laughed.

Wilfredo ignored Chance, moving closer to Babe, lowering his voice as he said, "I was polishing my car in the lot, and I saw dude standing out there beside the Honda. Then he bent down for a minute before rushing back to his car and peacing out this mug, his tires squealing and all. So, I went over to see what was going on over there, and the tire's flat."

Babe groaned. "Shit."

Chance said, "That's one crazy motherfucker. You must've put that punany on him. He's gone total psycho."

Chance leaned against the jamb with a little more weight, shifting his body animatedly until the towel fell from his hips to the floor. Clark moved forward, then stooped to grab the towel and hand it to Chance.

Seeing Clark's face redden with embarrassment, Chance cleared his throat, then tightened the towel at his waist. "I better hop in the shower."

Clark said, "Yeah, I'm going to head out. Nice to meet you."

Babe continued talking as though nothing had happened. "Can you show me?"

Babe and Wilfredo went out to the car. Babe shook his head in disgust. The small red car stood lopsidedly against the curb, one side brought low by two flattened tires.

"This makes no sense. Why would he do this? He knows this is not my car."

"You talk like this kind of thing is supposed to make sense. All dude cares about is trying to get a reaction from you. And speaking of reaction, seems maybe you replaced one stupid ass for another."

"Chance? Sorry about that. He's young. He wanted to get your attention, I guess."

"He's not that young. And it's not my attention he was trying to get."

"What do you mean? Trust me, just because you aren't gay doesn't mean he wasn't going to give it a try, let you know what's what."

"And just because I'm not gay doesn't mean I can't spot the game coming from the other side. It's the same kind of shit females do. Same shit, different players. You gonna have to file a police report about this. Or it's going to get worse."

He shook his head. "No. I got this. I'll have to pay to replace her tires is all. Let Alise know what's been going on, maybe have her park in the garage for a minute. I don't know. But no police."

"Man, what you got against the police? Sometimes you have to rely on them. That's what they here for. You are a taxpayer. They work for you."

"Yeah, okay. I got this, right?"

Wilfredo shrugged. "It's your decision, man. But I think you need to get an outside party involved before it goes far left."

The man started to cross the street to finish working on his car. "And maybe get that roommate out too. He don't mean you no good."

Babe smirked. "Maybe you should take greater responsibility for encouraging certain behavior."

"What you mean?"

"Maybe you should close your blinds at night. You might be sending mixed messages."

He flashed a gleaming set of teeth back at him. "That's not a mixed message, my man."

Chapter Twenty-Three

Matthew's Rage

He felt like an old cum rag. Matthew's heart ached with abandonment, and his head raged with a sense of gall. He didn't know what to do with himself. His mind raced. He had all this pent-up energy with nowhere to focus it. Except on the house on Leviticus Street that was no longer his.

He thought about it while he worked his dayshift prepping food for arrogant chemists who barely acknowledged him, just like Babe. He thought about it at his night job, making change and pumping gas for rude people preoccupied with their own lives. Couldn't see his heart was aching. Couldn't know the thoughts running through his head. That he was once a man who felt loved. Who used to go to work each day with intention. That intention was now gone. He no longer had a reason to go to work at a job that had no meaning to him.

He drove past the house late at night, watching the light play in various windows. He parked his Supra in the parking lot, watching people come and go. Babe going about his life as if there had been no before, as if he had never existed. Still smiling. Still beautiful. And it darkened Matthew's heart.

He was filled with rage. What made Babe think that he had the right to go on living the life they had built together, while he returned to the tiny bedroom he had shared with two brothers in his youth with the smell of mothballs and mold permeating every surface, delving into his flesh and his hair?

How had everything changed overnight? Sure, he had fucked around. Usually, it was only to let Babe know when something pissed him off. Like when Babe tried to go back to school, or when he hung out with his snotty-ass friends who he had nothing in common with, and the final insult, getting that mortgage without naming him on the deed. It was spiteful, or to use Babe's words, it was passive-aggressive. But fucking around had never been a major issue before. And hell, Babe had done his share of fucking around too, he was sure of it.

Now, he stayed in this cramped room, trying to stay out of sight from the mouthpiece of rotating Bible quotes his parents constantly recited to him as if they had the quotes on a loop. They quoted the Bible when he came home drunk and crying. They told him this was the reason Babe had put him out: he was a wastrel. Was he on that stuff? People talk. They had heard things. They listened in when he was on the phone, when he stumbled in from the bars at three in the morning, ranting to Babe's answering machine.

You can't ignore me. Pick up the phone, fucking piece of shit. Please pick up the phone. What did I do to you? We can fix this, Babe. Babe. Baby. I still love you. I hate you. I will kill you. You don't know who you fucking with.

What hurt the most was that Babe did not respond. He did not answer his calls, leaving him ranting drunkenly into the answering machine.

It shamed him that he spent all his spare time tracking Babe. He hadn't wanted to follow him around; it was like he couldn't control himself. If Babe would have just answered his calls, he wouldn't have to drive around town, hoping to run into him, searching for his Jeep. Or parking behind the Jeep on Main Street and going into every store there until he found him in the back of Chain Mar Furniture Store, absently peering through catalogs as he always did when he was bored, then walking up behind him and hissing in his ear, "Buying new furniture, are we?" His vision had clouded over from the temerity of it— shopping for fucking furniture.

Sometimes, when he didn't see Babe's car on Leviticus, he would drive down Thirteenth and Locust streets in Philly, vowing that if he saw him with somebody else or that white faggot, he'd run his car right into them. Or he would enter the bars, searching, hoping that he would spot him, praying that he would not.

He'd been relieved to know those two guys he'd paid to kill Babe had taken him for a ride. He didn't want Babe killed. He wouldn't want to walk this earth knowing Babe was no longer there.

He had a better idea. He'd knocked on the door to the house next to what had formerly been his house, and when Robby answered, he whispered to him that he needed a conference with Miss Rock. Robby had eyed him amusedly, his mouth curling into a smirk of condescension and mirth. But Matthew knew Robby's love for wreaking havoc superseded any sense of loyalty. Anything he did would be swiftly passed through gossip circles.

He was patient. Miss Rock's delayed response times were, if not legendary, then at least, urban legend. As she grew older, it became increasingly difficult to orchestrate a meeting. Miss Rock did not believe in paper or rental applications. She didn't do leases either. She didn't take checks or money orders. People paid cash. Not directly to Miss Rock though. Tenants would have to drive across town to another one of her properties, far up on Sandy Hill, where they would hand over money to Boy Mary, a surly, full bosomed dark-skinned woman with a soiled, multihued scarf on her head and a dead cigarette jammed between her full lips.

It was said that Miss Rock only rented to men. That she only rented to Black men. That she only rented to gay Black men. That she didn't accept applications because she relied on intuition to perceive whether one would be a worthwhile tenant. She would give you one phone call with a time and date for meeting. If you missed that call, you missed your opportunity. There was always a clamoring, a waitlist to get into one of Miss Rock's buildings. First, because there was a certain degree of unspoken safety in a building that solely housed gay men, but also because her rates were far below market value, and for a population that was often underemployed, unemployed, or working in nonmainstream levels of occupation, be it panhandling, hacking, prostitution, hairstyling, hatmaking, etc., it was a comfort to know rent could be made even when income was sporadic or unreliable.

His complexion was a buttery, copper tone, so he was sure that he would be found light enough for acceptance once Miss Rock met with him. He would sit tight, keeping surveillance until the call came through.

But then he'd seen Babe talking with that Latino from across the street. Seen him going into the house. He'd felt an emptiness so complete he didn't know what to do with it. Later, he'd paced the small space of his room at his parents' house, punching at his head, punching at the walls, and punching his thighs.

He'd waited until his parents were off to their Bible study meeting, went into the space beneath the floorboard under their bed, and removed a stack of money.

This time, he'd gone about it the right way. He went into Philly to one of the last old-school Black gay dives in the north section and passed around word. After a few visits, someone pointed him to the person he needed, a lean golden-colored man of diminutive height, standing with a pack of loud drag queens. Matthew approached him, noticing the eyepatch covering one of his eyes and wondering if he wore it as an affectation or for utility.

He asked to talk to him in private, much to the amusement of the group, who responded with laughter and lascivious sucking noises.

He was glad to discover that he had enough cash to pay for what he wanted. Something to end the aching tightness in his heart. But it saddened him to discover the paltry amount of money required to take a life. He'd seen stories like this on TV, read about it in newspaper articles, but it still horrified him how easy it was to arrange such a thing. He thought there'd be labyrinthine set of steps, an elaborate ceremony of sorts with some gigantic Italian guy with a cauliflower ear, as opposed to this bald, small-boned gay man. He was a little sad knowing it was this simple, but this sadness was nothing compared to the melancholy he hoped to heal.

Chapter Twenty-Four

Rueben in the Trash

Babe thought it would be a good idea to borrow one of the vehicles from his job, leaving his Jeep out of sight for a while until Matthew's initial rage subsided. He figured it would only take a couple of weeks until his ego healed sufficiently so that he would stop the late-night drunken calls, the mindless threats, the tears. He didn't know which he found more annoying. Something about Matthew being teary-eyed, sobbing, and pleading bothered him. He thought maybe it was comparing it to the nights when he had cried, waiting for Matthew to come home from wherever he ended up and Matthew's cavalier response to his agony at that time.

Even though he was using a car that couldn't be identified as his, he thought it was probably a good idea to keep the vehicle out of sight. Based on what had happened to Alise's car, Matthew's rage casted a wide net, intent on destroying everything in its path. He would park the loaner car in the garage.

Pulling into the alley behind the house, the car's low beams reflected off the figure of a rotund boy stooped over a tipped over trash can. The boy rested one hand on a pit bull's massive head. Mitzi flopped down to gnaw on a bone that toppled out of the can. Babe swore to himself. When he pulled up beside them, neither boy nor dog diverted their attention from the contents of the trash can. Rueben lowered himself to sit next to the dog with a grunt, his hands sweeping the contents out onto the sidewalk.

Babe weighed the likelihood of getting his throat ripped out for a minute before cautiously stepping from his car. "Hey. Hey, what's going on here? Did the trash can tip over?"

The dog remained focused on her bone. Rueben kept a guiding hand on her, keeping her calm with low, comforting chirps. He was dressed in a large, soiled T-shirt, pulled taut across his belly, and a pair of SpongeBob pajama bottoms. Seeing Mitzi was more interested in the meal than his presence, Babe moved a little closer.

"Hey. You hungry? You can't be rooting through the trash, man. You could get sick. There's diseases and stuff here. Stuff that could make you really, really sick."

Rueben held his head down, not making eye contact.

"I lost something is all."

"Okay. Well, if you want something to eat, you can come with me; I can make you a grilled cheese or something. How's that sound?"

"That sounds good."

"Where do you live? Are you staying at the house next door?"

Rueben shook his head. "I live right here."

Babe looked in the direction he was pointing a pudgy finger. "Well, you can't live there, buddy, because this is where I live."

"I live downstairs."

"You're Alise's kid? I didn't know she had a kid. What's your name?"

"Rueben."

"Nice to meet you Rueben," he didn't recall Alise mentioning she had a kid. As far as he could recall, her husband had died a long time ago, and she had passed herself off as single. But it wasn't any of his business anyway. What did he care, as long as the rent got paid. "Yeah. Just let me park the car here. If you sit tight, take Mitzi back inside, and we'll see what we can find, yeah?"

By the time Babe had pulled into the garage and swung the doors closed, Rueben had guided Mitzi and her bone back into the house, closed the door, and stood waiting for him to approach.

"What did you say your name was, buddy?"

"Rueben. I know your name already."

"Yeah? You live here?"

Rueben nodded warily.

"Maybe we should check in with your mom, let her know everyth—"

He shook his head vigorously. "No! We can't do that!"

Babe flexed his brows. "We can't?"

"Mama's not home. She went out to do grocery shopping and pay bills and stuff. She told me not to go outside while she's gone. I'll get in trouble."

"Okay. Well, you should have stayed inside like she said. Anything could happen, you know. But anyway, let's go on up."

The laundry room door was unlocked. Rueben followed Babe up the narrow stairwell, his arms grazing the walls. The upper landing to the apartment was unusually bright. The wall sconces were all lit. Animated voices yammered above the excessively loud music. The walls were vibrating so loudly that Babe noticed the bowl on the hallway table where he kept his keys had vibrated from the middle toward the edge. He pushed it back to center and rushed to the living room to turn down the amplifier, then returned to tend to the boy. He walked Rueben into the kitchen and opened the refrigerator before guiding him to a chair in front of the table.

Chance raced into the kitchen, his eyes large in their sockets. Clark followed.

"Where've you been?" he screamed. "There was some shit going on here this evening."

"What?"

"Your dude. Your nigga just ran amok through here! You ain't see him when you was coming in?"

"My dude?" Babe turned on the stove and placed a pan atop the flame. He knew who Chance had to be referring to, but he felt a sense of disconnectedness as though he were standing outside of his body.

"Your crazy-assed ex. He broke in here through the back door."

Clark nodded in affirmation. "We were in here...uh...eating dinner when there was suddenly all this noise and stomping on the stairs."

Babe smiled at Rueben. "Have you ever had grilled cheese with mayonnaise? It's awesome."

Rueben shook his head. "Let's try it."

Chance swung his gaze from Babe to the boy sitting in the chair. "Hey, who's Bigums?"

Babe said, "Don't do that."

"Do what?"

"Don't call him that. I was a big kid too. And shit like that is hurtful."

Chance clicked his tongue. "Oh, pay it. I was only playing."

"Yeah. But it's not funny. I still carry around that shit."

"You was a fatty? Who'd a thought it."

Clark butted in. "So, yeah. We came running out here, and I see this guy I never seen before walking toward the door with the VCR under his arm and pulling the phone out the wall. I'm like what the fuck? I thought you were being robbed."

"And all that commotion, I was thinking it was you, that maybe you'd fallen down the stairs or some shit. Next thing I know, Clark's got the nigga hemmed up against the wall, his forearm across his neck. Matthew's screaming 'This my shit. This my shit.' I'm like, you ain't taking shit out of here unless Babe's here to say you can take it."

"He tried to bum rush me!" Chance jumped in. "We was tussling in here like the dog fights!"

Babe waited until the frying bread was a satisfactory golden hue before he flipped them over. "Did you call the cops?"

Chance shook his head. "Why do I feel like that's a trick question though? But we had to threaten to! He wouldn't stop fighting until we said we was calling five-oh! Then the motherfucker got gone with a quickness."

"I'm sorry about all that. Was anybody hurt?"

"Nah. But damn, you sure living a thrilling life."

"Yeah. Exciting."

"So, for real, you was a fatty?"

Babe stood grim-lipped.

"That's crazy, yo. You got it going on now, so it's the past."

"By the grace of a shitload of self-hatred." Babe brought two saucers of glittering grilled cheese sliced into wedges to the table. By the time he turned from the fridge from where he retrieved a cantaloupe to slice, Rueben had finished his sandwich.

Chance said, "Them chumpies look good as shit. You ain't making none for your guests?"

"Bitch. I already made one for my guest!"

Rueben laughed as he grabbed the slices of cantaloupe and tossed them in his mouth delightedly.

"Aww, okay. I see how you roll. Hey, you're Alise's kid, yeah? Where's your mom at?"

"She's at work."

Babe said, "I thought you said she was running errands."

Rueben shook his head. "I meant to say she's at her job."

"Anyway, Rueben and I have an agreement, now don't we? That whenever you're hungry, you can knock on the door, and I will rustle up something, huh? No more rooting out back, yeah?"

"Yeah."

Chance rolled his eyes. "That's wonderful. You're a regular Mother Theresa, doing good deeds for waifs and queens. Leviticus Street is turning into the Calcutta of Norristown."

Chance walked over to the table and reached for a wedge of Babe's sandwich. Babe swatted irritably at his hand as Chance continued his diatribe.

"What I want to know is if girlfriend is always telling us how she can't do this and can't do that because she's got to get to her job, why's her car always parked outside, day and night. She taking the bus or something?" Chance yammered away as if he did not see Babe's attempts to signal that he should shut up by madly darting his eyes toward the boy sitting at the table. "Anyway, talk to you later, Clark and me got some things to finish that was interrupted by your jawn."

"Yeah, okay." It was Babe's turn to roll his eyes. To Rueben, he asked, "You want lemonade?"

He nodded. As Babe got up to go to the refrigerator, Rueben swiftly reached out and grabbed the fruit slices left on Babe's saucer.

"Hey. Want to hear a story?"

"Huh?"

"Me and my mom tell each other stories. I know lots of stories."

Babe laughed as he joined Rueben at the table and poured lemonade into a short amber-colored tumbler. "Okay, let's hear what you got."

"An old woman found an empty jar that used to be full of wine. It was empty now, but she could still smell the wine that was in there before. So, she got greedy. She placed it to her nose many times, back and forth. Then she said, 'O most delicious! This wine must have been delicious, it smells so sweet!'" Rueben sat back with a satisfied grin.

Babe frowned. "That's it?"

"I didn't want to hit you with too much all at once. I just met you."

He laughed. "Okay. You got me there. So, what's the moral of your story supposed to be?"

"The memory of a good deed lives."

He clasped his hands together on the table. Babe noticed the dirt lodged under the cuticles. He considered offering to clip his nails so that he could clean the dirt caked beneath them but decided that might be a bit too much for a first-time meeting.

"Indeed. Well, I think you'd best be getting home. We don't want your mother thinking she lost you."

At the mention of Alise, Rueben jumped up, ready to go.

Chapter Twenty-Five

Friday Night Ritual

Saturday nights had three different phases. Babe related these phases to the act of intercourse. First came foreplay. This was the part of the start of the revelry when you were still at home, swilling some alcoholic concoction as you prepared your look for the night. Whether you wanted to project B-boy realness, or Iggy grunge, or Bowie Rockglam.

After that came the dickdown. This was the main event, where you rolled up into the clubs and danced to throbbing bass until your clothes were damp with perspiration. This was Chance's favorite part of Saturday night. He was a good dancer, and he knew all eyes would be on him whenever he was on the floor, bending low and jumping high.

Babe's favorite part of night was the afterglow. The afterglow was when the revelers all funneled out from the bars into the street, filling the air with the vibration of thousands of thoughts and desires.

Babe could feel the electricity of afterglow like a living thing. In foreplay, Babe and Chance roamed the streets from Eleventh to Thirteenth, from the sex shops and strip clubs of Arch to the brownstones of Lombard, and the narrow alleyways and streets in between: Camac, Juniper, Drury Lane, commonly called the gayborhood, where transexuals, crossdressers, and hustlers traversed, where residents mixed with vagrants, and homeless men directed cars to open spaces in vacant lots, offering to 'keep an eye out' on your car while you were in the bars for a few dollars, but they were always gone by the end of the night.

Afterglow was full of possibilities. Gay restaurants blared jukebox music out into the streets, suburban husbands skulked swiftly into video shops, and young Puerto Rican entrepreneurs hid their merchandise in well-cologned bikini briefs, resulting in cocaine that smelled of Drakkar, Polo, Grey Flannel.

For him, the electricity of the streets, the potential for anything to happen, far surpassed the rote, repetitive music and banal stilted conversations of the clubs where white boys spoke to him as if he were an exhibit in a zoo.

This night, in the beginning of afterglow, Babe stood against the plate glass window of a shuttered business, absorbing the frenetic energy that palpitated the streets, his mind humming from liquor and pent-up sexual urges. The sidewalks literally shimmered with heat and humidity. It was here he felt a sense of belonging, where he felt part of one large pulsation of power. Here, he didn't feel objectified even though, ironically, it was the random whistles, catcalls, the acknowledgments of his physical comeliness that made him feel beautiful.

Foreplay and afterglow were the reason that he worked out religiously Monday through Friday to the point of vomiting, starved himself on Thursdays and Fridays so he could maintain his status as one of the beautiful ones.

As he pushed himself from the wall and turned to walk toward Walnut Street, Chance approached from the exit of the nearby bar. Babe walked toward him, laughing at the grimace of disgust on Chance's face.

"What's wrong with you?"

"Some bum just asked me 'Want to see this big Black dick?'"

Babe laughed. "Well, what'd it look like?"

"I don't know!" Chance shouted. "He was a bum."

"What do you mean when you say bum? Like a hobo or something?"

"A what? I mean he was a dirty homeless person."

"Okay, first, I know plenty of what you call bums that are not homeless. Second, you don't ever turn down a man that wants to show off his dick. What harm is there in seeing what the motherfucker got to show? More times than not, it's at least worth a second of your time, or he wouldn't be offering to whip it out. Now, where was he? Let's go see."

Chance smirked. "For real? He was back this way. Come on."

"You got to stop being so judgmental. You are young, gay, single, and out for a night in the gay ghetto of Philly. If we can't be loving and accepting here, where can we be? Here we generate our own money, entertain and educate one another. Even though y'all still try to shut out us Black folks. But here we are!"

By that time, they had come upon the shabbily dressed man they were searching for. Chance pointed to the distracted figure wearing a soiled overcoat, dirty painter's pants, and an old T-shirt. He was still lean and muscular. "Hey, you. Understand you got something you want us to see?"

The man turned around, scratching his head. "You got five dollars?"

"To look at your pecker? Give you a dollar."

Chance jumped behind Babe as the man reached into his belt and brought forth his member with aplomb, flashing rather nappy pubic hair along with the previously advertised dick. Chance giggled. Babe reached into his pocket and handed over a dollar.

"Most impressive, sir. Thanks for that."

"You can get more than that for fifteen."

"Oh no. I'm not in the market. What about you, Chance? Are you in the market?"

"What? Fuck no!"

"I think, sir, he means he will consider it at a later date. You have a good night. And kudos on smelling nice too."

By this point, Babe was talking only for Chance's benefit because as soon as his offer had been turned down, the man had stridden further down the street and dodged into the nearest side street, trying to buy a loosie from Boy Mary in front of the Adonis.

"You crazy, man."

He stood in a far corner of the bar, nursing a bottle of beer. He noticed Babe as soon as they entered through the narrow entryway. He would have recognized him from the picture Matthew had given him for identification, but he noticed him before he recognized him.

He was dressed to be seen, he and the white boy who was tugging his waistband lower so that the strap of his thong was visible. There was a singularity about him, standing in the compact space surrounded by sweating bodies of various hues who were also dressed to be seen. Beneath the tumble of black dreads, the light seemed to emanate from him.

The man of diminutive height was easily lost in a crowd of people much taller than he, so Babe didn't see him standing near, silently watching. Chance appeared to notice, considered, then ignored him as he moved his attention to more visually noteworthy options.

He stood behind them when they went up to the second level, the white one dancing a little too exuberantly, watching others watch him; the dark one dancing a little too reservedly as he seemed too aware of being watched. He was close enough to listen to their dialogue and to smell their scent, watching the tendons of Babe's levator scapulae undulate with sweat. He observed the men approach, making note of the way the white boy grinned voraciously, and the dark one politely bowed to hear whispered propositions before shaking his head then returning to observe the bodies on the dance floor. He counted the number of phone numbers hastily scribbled on napkins the white one placed in his pocket, the searching hugs, the dark one shaking a hand here and there.

Max gazed at the white one engaged in a prolonged interaction with a lean, young wraith. Their hands were roaming along each other's bodies, their mouths were lowering close to skin, whispering things he could not hear but did not need to hear to know. Then the white one turned to whisper something in Babe's ear. Babe bobbed his head briefly and whispered agitatedly, before the white one and the wraith walked away.

Max moved closer, compelled by the combination of Ivory soap, perspiration, and vetiver emanating from Babe. He watched the shift in body language now that he stood alone, the transition from regal and confident with his head thrown back and legs spread assertively. Now, he was more reserved. His shoulders gathered in toward his chest while his head moved back and forth, scanning the room as though he had misplaced something. Babe drifted from the perimeter to the darker recesses of the room and leaned against the wall, seeming to find comfort there in the dark away from the shouting bodies.

Max stood so close their shoulders touched: Babe was warm and slightly damp with sweat. Max kept his shoulder there, finding pleasure in the contact. He struggled for something to say.

Babe turned to him and lowered his mouth close to Max's ear to be heard above the music. Max was enveloped in the scent of him. His breath was sweet with alcohol.

"You know what time it is?"

Max moved closer, feigning as if he hadn't heard him, wanting to smell his breath again. Babe motioned toward the gigantic watch on his wrist, reached out and softly took his hand before he lifted the watch closer to better see the time. He mouthed a thank-you.

The lights came up, and the music stopped. It was two o'clock—closing time. Babe flicked a fleeting glance toward Max before he turned to move out into the crush of bodies swarming the door in a rush to get out before gridlock. Max allowed himself to get caught up in the wave of people, making sure to keep him within eyesight, watching as he ignored side-glances as well as overt stares while oblivious of the stares he generated himself.

All the bars in the ghetto were letting out at the same time, and the streets filled with laughter, car horns, and possibilities. Babe stood at a corner across from the bar beneath the canopy of a closed store, greeting casual acquaintances, making eye contact with handsome strangers, doing the erotic tango for a few moments, smiling at catcalls from cars driving by, or stopping to talk. Max could feel the energy generated in these conversations, it pulsated in the air, this palpable power that was part of a larger, universal network.

Time passed swiftly, and the crowds dwindled while the air grew quieter. People quickly paired up and faded away as Babe watched the late-night mating rituals unfold with a forlorn smile on his face.

Max decided to make his move, swiftly walking up to Babe in the shadow of night, looming close as the man turned to face him.

The two men walked out of the darkened alley off Filbert and peered warily for patrol cars before splitting in opposite directions. Chance dismissively saluted the wraith's retreating back and put his hands in his pockets to fight the night chill. He crossed the street, walking stealthily between parked cars through a vacant lot, thinking that it would be a shortcut to getting back to Sansom. Midway through, two Black guys approached from the other side of the lot. He determined from the sway in their walk, the way they stagger-swaggered and swung their arms, they were not gay. But they were in the gay ghetto, so he figured they knew what was up.

The more muscular of the two whispered to his partner as Chance got closer and beckoned him. "What's up, slim?"

Chance was flattered. He had never been called slim before. "Chillin'."

The men laughed. "Chillin', huh? Okay, I see you. What you up to tonight?"

"The usual. Seeing what's out here. What about y'all?"

"Looking to get this dick sucked."

Chance smiled knowingly when one of the two rubbed his crotch with a knowing leer and asked, "What you into?"

"Whatever you into," Chance responded.

"You got a couple dollars?"

Chance paused momentarily, scolding himself for not recognizing corner boys for what they were. "How much you talking? I don't have no big cash on me."

"Nah. Money for a forty, maybe smokes...."

"Y'all got somewhere we can go?"

"We can go right back over there where you came from with dude."

Chance looked back over his shoulder. There was a squat, dark-skinned guy approaching. He had the stature of a boxer, wide shoulders with legs splayed apart, approaching assertively.

"Yo, I got you, little homie. You need to come with me right quick."

"I don't think he is. Y'all got a problem with that, we can handle this right quick." The short guy tensed, flexing muscle, and raised his massive fists.

The men exchanged a look, shook their heads. "Go 'head then. You got it." The two men quickly retreated, rushing off, Chance assumed, to find some other unsuspecting victim. Chance turned to face the interloper.

"Do I know you?" Chance asked confusedly.

"You do now. It's me, Chauncey. Come go with me. We was watching you from the car across the street. You was about to get robbed big time." Chance followed him across the street where Ross sat dabbing a powder puff at his heavily made-up face. A plume of smoke floated out of the open car window.

"Bitch. You don't recognize a stunt when it's unfolding before your very eyes? You was about to be fleeced of your coins and possibly your pussy. Though from what me and Chauncey could see from the interior of this chariot, I'm guessing that the loss of the pussy wouldn't have bothered you that much. You a hungry bitch, ain't you?"

"Ross? Is that you?"

Ross rolled his eyes. "Girl. Now who else would it be, sitting down here in the cut, face beat to the gawds. You know damn well it's Ricky Ross. Get in bitch. But don't get comfortable."

As Chance climbed in the back, he bumped his head on the low-hanging fabric coming loose from the roof of the car.

"Ooh, you'se a tall girl, aren't you? Watch your head, I don't want the rest of the roof on this deathtrap falling down, giving the doll mesothelioma." Ross waved his polished fingernails at the falling interior.

Chance's eyes watered at the acrid smoke circulating the interior, noticing the sharp, slightly sulfuric smell. "Isn't that from asbestos? I don't think they use asbestos in cars."

"Bitch, don't correct me. I know what I'm talking about."

Chauncey paced back and forth agitatedly outside the car, then punched a fist into his open hand, mumbling how he could have taken those weak-ass chumps and would have fed them their teeth.

"I know, Daddy. You would have served those poor trades like the true man you are," Ross screamed animatedly, then spoke in a lower tone to Chance. "Baby, we been watching those Negroes all night, patrolling the strip, looking for some dumb queen to rob, snatch her dollars for a cap, bash her ungodly. And lookie, lookie, here comes the dumb queen."

Chance ignored the jab, the pointed stare.

Ross continued, "So here I am, sitting with my husband, smoking a little rock, surveying the scene, and drinking a little Chablis because, you know, the doll does not go to those clubs. Those white sissies think they are superior to me, and the Black faggots, with their unwashed asses, act like they ain't never seen a bitch up in there with a face painted to send Iman back to her hut in Somolia. You know these Philly queens can't take the Black girls from the suburbs, honey! We sophisticated. So anyway, we out here, relaxing and parlaying, and suddenly, I see those Negroes plotting to do my goddaughter's new daughter grave harm. I says to Chauncey, you know he used to box in the amateurs in south Philly, 'Daddy, let him feel that bicep.'"

"Who's Iman?" Chance jumped as a flexed forearm plunged in through the window, the brown muscle glinting in the moonlight. He tentatively placed his hand on it, feeling a surge in his groin at the heat.

"Who's Iman, indeed. Never mind, girl. Just stay retarded," Ross continued. "I says, 'Daddy, that's that new child living under my goddaughter's tutelage. The gamine. She 'bout to get got, Daddy. We can't let her get beat like a runaway slave down here in the gay ghetto, can we?' So, I asks Chauncey to get your dumb ass before it's too late. And here we are, bitch, so you're welcome."

Chance wasn't sure if he should thank him or let Ross keep talking.

Ross continued, "So bitch, you interrupted our get high. And Chaunccy could have come to great harm coming to be your knight in shining armor."

Chance stuck his head out the window. "Thank you, Chauncey."

Chauncey huffed out breaths of expletives, punching at the air, bobbing and weaving against an imaginary assault.

"Thank you!" Ross gasped. "Well, that's all well and good. That's cute and everything, but bitch, you should give him a couple dollars to show him you appreciate his act of chivalry. How much you got?"

"Well. I spent most of my money at the spot with Babe. I only got maybe twenty, thirty left."

"Oh, you down here with Babe. Well, bitch, you should have *stayed* with Babe, and you'd be safe. In fact, I'm surprised he let you leave. Some shit about feeling responsible or something. That's why the doll does not come down here with Miss Babe. No, ma'am. She, meaning me, is fully grown, and a wet nurse I do not need." He flicked his eyes at Chance. "Apparently, you do."

Chance laughed.

"Okay. Well bitch, cough it up. It's a paltry amount for saving a queen's life when you think of the costs of emergency room visits, but hey, we'll make do." Ross flicked impatient red nails at him, waiting for Chance to give him the money while screaming out the window. "Chauncey, this broke bitch only got thirty dollars. Can you believe? I need to be circulating in a more affluent circle of sissies."

Ross examined the money in his hands and snapped impatiently. "Well, girl? Why are you still here? Thank you, and goodbye! And be careful out there, bitch. It's every *man* for himself on these mean streets."

Chance shook his head, laughing as Ross's laughter followed him as he got out of the car.

"Bye, crazy."

Chauncey nodded at him before climbing back in the car.

Chapter Twenty-Six

Meet Cute

"You all right? You look like you're lost."

Babe first noticed his eye. It was jarring in its singularity, wounded and occluded, only open partially and marked with a diagonal keloidal scar up to the brow. His face nudged long-dormant, pleasant feelings. His asymmetrical eyes—one large, clear and amber colored, the other wounded, shuttered—were like the window on an out-of-season vacation home, whispering memories of Saturday morning Johnny Quest cartoons. His clean-shaven head was smooth and unblemished. The slight point at the top was pleasing to Babe, nudging memories of Ultraman on Saturday morning TV. There was a spray of freckles along his sharp, angular cheekbones. His eyebrows were strong and light brown like the wisps of hair on his jaw, reminding him of the coloring of his maternal family line. He was not imposing in that he was thin, coming no further than Babe's clavicle.

A few people were still milling about, laughing at jokes, setting up meeting times, or finding out about after-parties.

Babe smiled fleetingly. "Looking for my roommate. Shouldn't have let him roam off. No telling if he's okay or not."

"I saw him standing with you inside the club. Kids like him, I'm sure he's okay."

Babe laughed. "Maybe. But now that I let him out of my sight, I got to troll these alleyways, and you know people will be thinking I'm trolling for another reason."

Max laughed too. "I'll walk with you."

"Really?"

"I know what he looks like. Two sets of eyes are better than one. Ha. Make that one-and-a-half sets."

Babe frowned. "A joke, huh. What's your name?"

"Max."

"Max? That's unusual."

He laughed. "What's so unusual about it?"

"It's not a Black name is all I'm saying."

Babe began to walk up Sansom, out through the alley up toward the Wanamaker Building.

Max shadowed.

"I don't know any Black Maxes."

"You were expecting Leroy, I guess? How many Leroys you know?"

Babe chuckled, self-effacing. "Not many. None. Short for Maximilian?"

"No. Just Max. Largo."

"Babe." He reached out his hand.

Max took it, warm and damp. "Fitting." They both laughed.

Babe blushed and asked, "Like from the Bond movie? The guy with the eye patch? So, you're running around giving pseudonyms. What's your real name?"

"Says the boy named Babe. At least you know the reference. These chicken heads running around out here don't know nothing, that name doesn't cause any sort of flicker. They have no sense of irony, nothing. If it don't have nothing to do with Madonna, Lil' Kim, vogueing, or dick, it's not important to them. But that's my name. I use it for business. It's the name of my shop. Might not be my government, but it's going to be, in time."

"What's wrong with Madonna? Or Lil' Kim?"

Max countered, "What's wrong with dick, for that matter?"

They both laughed. "All shade to vogueing? You one of them?"

"Me?" Babe asked. "Rolling around on those filthy-ass floors? When's the last time you think they dragged a mop through that place? Jesus."

As they came out onto Market Street, a woman in tattered clothing loomed, weaving before them with an outstretched hand. Max waved her off and kept walking, then stopped as Babe searched his pocket and dropped coins into the dirty palm.

"Thank you." The woman reached with her free hand, extending it to shake Babe's hand.

Babe hesitated for a moment before he reached out and shook her hand with a smile. She raised her other hand and touched his face. Babe jumped back reflexively; the woman turned and veered out into a blur of headlights and blaring horns.

"You know she's not going to do nothing but buy drugs with that, don't you?"

Babe shrugged. "None of my business, is it? What she decides to do, if it gives her a moment of pleasure, I'm all for it. That's all any of us are looking for, right?"

They walked down past Thirteenth Street and up Twelfth. They passed another alley, reeking with the smell of urine and garbage.

"Gotta piss real quick," said Max. He grabbed Babe's elbow and tugged him toward the dumpsters. "Whyn't you come back here right quick?"

Babe thought to say no, but before the words came, he was already there, staring off into the distance while Max unzipped behind the shadow of the dumpsters. Babe listened to the velocity of his urine as it hit the pavement, counting in Mississippis as time slowed down, waiting for him to finish.

When he finished, Max came back around, grabbed his elbow again and headed back to the street. Babe realized he was trembling slightly and cursed himself, trying to steady his arm.

"You cold?"

"You kidding? It's got to be like ninety degrees out here."

"You're shivering, that's all. Am I scaring you?"

Babe colored in embarrassment. He thought he had been masking his discomfort better. "Nah. I'm just thermogenic."

"You're what?"

"I take fat burners three times a day, so my internal body temp is always high, and shivering is a way that I respond to it."

Max raised an eyebrow, smiling gently. "Thermogenic, huh? So, you're hungry right about now, I bet."

"I'm always fucking hungry." Babe laughed. "I try not to think about it."

"Me too. Fucking starving. I eat once a day. How else can you stay this size at my age? A rat ran past while I was taking a piss, and I was thinking about how it might taste dusted in breadcrumbs and deep fried in Crisco."

"How old are you?"

"Around the same age as you."

"And how old am I? How would you know how old I am?"

Max laughed. "I'm thirty-five."

"Okay, yeah, that's close." *This guy is full of shit.* He watched him. Observed the musculature of his arms, which were lean and bronze, but had a certain slackness, less full than what he thought a man in his thirties would be. He gauged him as midforties for sure.

Max stopped walking as if he had been struck by an idea. "Are you shy?"

"I guess."

He seemed baffled. "How is it someone that looks the way you do is shy? How can being around somebody like me make you feel that way?"

"How do I look?"

"Come on, Babe. You're not going to tell me you aren't aware of what you look like. I'm not going to believe that."

"What does that have to do with whether I'm shy or not?"

"Maybe not how you look so much. But you dress in a way that draws attention to yourself, right? So, how can you be shy, and yet you want to attract attention? It's like you're saying see me, but I don't want to be looked at."

Babe shrugged. "What do you want me to say? I'm an enema."

"A what?"

Babe laughed, embarrassed. "An enigma."

A car roared past, horn blaring at an inebriated woman tripping over the curb, then falling to the pavement with a rain of expletives. Her voice was deep and raspy, indicating to them that she was trans. Max followed Babe, who walked over, stooped down, and tentatively placed a hand on the woman's bare shoulder.

"Hey, you okay?" He struggled to help the woman stand.

"Take your motherfucking hands off me! I don't need your help."

"Bitch drunk out her mind. Let her be, she don't want no help."

The woman struggled to stand, teetered on her rather high heels, and fell back to the pavement. Babe gave a slight yelp, caught her, and eased her back to the sidewalk. The woman moved her hair from her face. Seeing one of her own, her demeanor softened. "Thank you, baby."

"You hurt? Do you need any help?"

She laughed. "No, I'm not hurt. Mother is feeling lovely. Just trying to get home."

"Where you live? You live in the city here?"

"Baby, what would I be doing living amongst all this whiteness, this rabble? I live out west with my own kind."

"You need a ride? Can we get you a cab?" Babe nodded at Max, who began to search for a cab.

"Yeah. I can't ride the rails like this. Might have to use my knife on banjee trade." Babe was glad to know that the woman was drunk and not injured. Max managed to get a taxi to pull over. They helped the woman to the cab. "How'm I supposed to pay for this?"

Hearing that, the driver barked, "Money up front."

Max said, "Bitch, I know you got money. What you down here for if not to get money?"

Max reached into his back pocket, took out a wallet, and took out twenty dollars. Babe saw him again, this time not his physical persona, but his generosity. He handed the twenty to the woman. "Here. If your trip takes more than this, bitch, you better dig into that stash."

She snatched the money from him, flicking her red nails at him dismissively.

"Be gone, one eye motherfucker. You a salty bitch." She reached out, grabbed Babe by the chin and shook him gently. "Thank you, baby. You are a peach." She glared at Max. "Your husband ain't shit! Bye, bitches."

They both laughed as the taxi skirted away from the curb. Chance walked up behind them. "What's all that about?"

"Bitch, where you been? Don't you ever walk off like that from me again."

Chance proffered a hand, shouldering his way in between the two. "Hey. I'm Chance."

"Max." He shook his hand. "MidTown's right down the street if you want to get breakfast."

The MidTown restaurant was the afterhours spot of choice for coming down from whatever substances had been consumed that night and for elongating the night for inhabitants stuck with few late-night options, given Philadelphia's Quaker origin blue laws, which stipulated that no alcohol be sold after 2 a.m.

"Sure," he said hesitantly, worried how long it would take to get seated, eyeing the long line of nightclubbers along the sidewalk. Wandering around was different than standing in one spot. If Matthew were out searching for him, it was a smarter move to be mobile than the stationary target among a gaggle of inebriated diners. He wasn't scared Matthew would do anything violent as much as he was fearful of being the focal point of a big, public display, amusing all the onlookers who thrived on the theatrical.

As they stood outside the steps of the MidTown, Chance leaned an arm on Babe's shoulder and craned his neck to survey the line of at least seven groups before them. "Would you look at all these homos? We'll be out here till sunup!"

"Be right back." Max went inside, presumably to leave a name with the hostess.

Chance turned to Babe, his eyes glittering with interest. "Who that? You slut."

Babe arched a brow. "Says the queen found crawling out of an alley."

"He's not your type. He's kind of scrawny."

"What's my type?"

"You know. Muscle head. Shirtless, white, tina-head, or gym bunny."

Babe laughed. "What happened to the rich old white guy that was keeping me? And why is it always someone white in your imaginarium?"

Max was standing at the door of the restaurant gesturing at them to come forward. They bumped through the crowd of hostile, inquisitive, and curious eyes and followed him inside. The hostess walked them toward the back of the building to a booth across from a wait station and the restrooms.

"Sorry, babe. It's all we got at late notice."

"It's good, Dy. Thanks." Max guided Babe into the booth and slid in beside him.

Chance flopped down across from them and noisily flipped through the selections of the tabletop jukebox. "Wow. A man with pull. How'd you get us bumped up ahead of those other folks?"

"I know people."

"What you do for a living?"

"I'm a hit man."

Babe said, "Can you mind your own business? What's on the jukebox? Thank you."

"Miss Ida is the head waitress here. I do her hair. Every week. Like clockwork. She comes in to get her head bumped."

As if on cue, a dark form loomed above. Babe assumed this was Miss Ida, sturdy and brown, with black polyester pants, vest, and a gleaming white blouse. Her hair was styled in a molded concoction with stiff bangs falling to her painted brows and falling back from a part across her head into a looming, shiny basket of hair that had curlicues sweeping out of it like a fountain of black ink.

"Hey, babies. What you want?" She sat down large, greasy menus with a loud thwack.

Chance requested a cola. Max quietly asked for coffee and then looked at Babe to see what he wanted.

"The water's fine for me. Do you have eggs Benedict?"

Ida laughed. "Eggs Benedict? This ain't the Bellevue Strafford, baby. What the menu say is what we got?"

Max smiled. "Don't the MidTown got everything you could ever want?"

"The only thing here I want is tips. And make sure y'all leave a nice juicy one when you go. I'll be back when y'all decide what y'all want." Miss Ida turned to scream at someone loudly exiting the restroom. "You ain't got to be slamming the doors like you at home, bitch. Damn, ain't you supposed to be a lady—at least tonight?"

"Sorry, Miss Ida."

"Sorry my ass. Get back to your table and tell me what the fuck you want."

Chance slumped down in his seat laughing uproariously.

Babe looked at Max, dazed. "Is she for real? She talks to customers like that?"

"She talks to them the way they understand. She's an old dinosaur. That's Miss Ida. Hey! Miss Ida, come back, you didn't give me time to introduce my friends!"

Standing at another booth halfway down the narrow aisle that made up half of the width of the building, Miss Ida was already jotting down the order for another table. "They all the same to me, honey. I don't need no names. I'm an old woman. Introduce me once y'all get your orders together. How 'bout that?"

"So, you're a hairdresser?"

"Talk about stereotypes." Chance laughed.

"What you mean?" Max asked.

"Gay man equals hairdresser or florist. I'd prefer if you *were* a hitman."

Babe frowned. "How about you shut up? Don't be an ass."

Max shrugged. "He's cool. Don't worry about it. What do you do for a living, whiteness? Let me guess, you stock shelves at your daddy's hardware store, sucking dicks in the back when Pops ain't around."

Chance laughed. "Sounds like a great gig if only I knew my pops. So no, I suck dicks in the mailroom at my temp assignment."

Babe said, "You're doing temp work?"

Chance flounced in his seat. "Well, it was. But they moved me to perm, being that I'm such a good worker."

Max said, "I imagine you lick those envelopes like there's no tomorrow."

Chance glared at him, but there was grudging respect in his eyes. "Fuck you."

Babe looked from one to the other. "What is going on with you two? Do you know each other or something?"

Max said, "I don't know him. But I sure do *know* him."

Quoting Janet, Chance murmured, "You want this? You. Want. This?"

Max turned so that he was facing Babe. "How about you? What do you do?"

Chance bobbed in, "He licks envelopes too."

Babe flagged him to be quiet. "I'm in social work. I supervise homes for people with special needs."

He grinned approvingly. "That explains a lot."

"Like what?"

"Giving that homeless woman money. Helping that other lady get a cab home. It's in your blood."

"I don't know about in my blood…but I like to think that if I'm kind to people, they will be kind to me."

Max nodded at him.

Chance said, "I been meaning to ask this since day one though. No shade, but what would someone doing social work be needing with a beeper? And your beeper be going off at all hours. Like, weekends and late at night, and you have to jump up, and you outtie."

"So, what do you think it is? Do you think I'm a doctor or nurse, maybe? No. You automatically think I'm the weed man, right? You are so narrow-minded."

"Only people I've seen with beepers sell drugs."

Max interjected. "So widen your circle."

"Thank you!" Babe said, tsking. "And anyway, if you know all these folks selling locally, you need to be linking me in, so I don't have to be driving Robby down into the city. Because he is starting to scare me. I don't even like having him in the car for all that time. He gets to hallucinating and chewing on the inside of his cheek."

"That bitch is crazy. Don't you hear him through the walls at night? Shouting 'no help, no help'? She needs to be put in a permanent cell at Building 50, trust and believe."

"You don't know what he's been through."

"And don't want to. So, Max, why's your eye fucked up? What happened?"

Babe gasped, offended. "How is that your business? What the fuck is wrong with you?"

Chance shrugged.

Miss Ida approached, notepad at the ready "I know y'all ready by now. Max don't usually get nothing more than a coffee. That's why you skin and bones. You can't work all them hours and not keep your body fortified."

A young trans woman at the next booth raised a tentative hand. "Miss Ida, can I get another chocolate milk when you done?"

"That's the third one you had, bitch. Why don't I get you a fucking chocolate cow?" the old woman exclaimed. "Max, who comes to a restaurant and orders four goddamn chocolate milks and coconut cake? You know those cakes are for show!"

"I know it. But I guess she don't know it. Know what you want?" he asked.

"Just a grilled cheese. I'm good." Babe yawned.

Miss Ida put her hands on her hips. "Another one that eats like a bird! I hope the tip is bigger than your appetite, baby. And what about you, young man? What you want?"

Chance said, "I'ma get the wingdings, fries, and let me get a short stack, extra butter."

She grunted approvingly. "That's what I like to see. Real eating."

Babe said, "You better have real money to pay for that too. I'm not picking it up."

Max said, "It's okay. I got it."

Ida gnashed her gum. "Y'all in good company. Eat up, I'm telling you, while you got the chance."

"Sorry about him. And that comment about your eye."

"You don't have to apologize for me. I'm grown. Hey man, if I offended you, I'm sorry."

"No offense. If you want to know something, you gotta ask. But I'm thinking you're trying to be shady, and if you are, that's not going to go well for you."

Above the already-noisy atmosphere, there arose an even louder wave of noise, and all heads turned toward the entrance where a short dark-skinned crossdresser emerged from the tiny vestibule. She wore a silver dress of shimmering beads, its décolletage cut low to show a rib cage splashed with glitter, the rest of the dress pulled taut by an outsized rear end. She bellowed Max's name, waving silver-painted talons in case he didn't see her.

Miss Ida barked, "Cut down all that hollering. This is a reputable establishment. You got to wait to be seated like everybody else."

The woman sashayed past, ignoring Miss Ida's admonishments, seeming to concentrate on swaying the bugle beads on her hips for maximum attention. She breezed to the rear of the building on a cloud of Anais Anais, then bumped her hip into Chance's side, scooting him over by force rather than request.

"I got first prize, Max! I tore them white girls down! You hear?"

"Congratulations. Everybody, this is Diamond."

Babe smiled a greeting while Chance glared.

"I gotta thank you. I wouldn't have got this without you. So, I'm here to break you off."

Diamond reached into her manufactured cleavage and brought out a wad of money. She laughed. "You know them bitches was twisted to have to give me the grand prize."

"I told you," said Max. "If you stick to doing Shirley Caesar, sooner or later you were going to make a name for yourself. Nobody else doing these shows is doing gospel. That's your niche. It took a long time, but it's paying off."

Chance's eyes bugged out at the money as Max stuffed it in his pocket. "How much did you win? Drag be banking like that? And why's you giving it to dude?"

Diamond's voice lost its feminine register. "Who's this in my business?"

A shadow fell across the booth. Chauncey stood there, resplendent in his hetero, muscular glory, his wifebeater clinging to his sweat dampened torso, his afro wild and uncombed. "Yo baby, cab's out front."

Diamond went back to her higher register. "Okay, Daddy. I'll be right out."

Diamond leaned out of her booth, watching his tight, well-shaped calves flex with each step. Chauncey exited through a void of sound as every male eye watched his departure. Diamond shook her head. "Well, duty calls. That man is God's own miracle. And I'm going to let him help Mama soothe this painful vaginal itch!"

Chance said, "He was just down the way with Ross. Now he's up here with somebody else?"

Diamond rummaged through her purse. "In my business again. I see I might need to cut a white bitch tonight."

Babe said, "Ross was downtown? Why didn't you tell me?"

He shrugged. "They weren't doing nothing. Just sitting in a car smoking crack."

Babe said, "And how you know that? Did you see them smoking crack?"

"I don't see oxygen either, but I know it's there. I'm not stupid."

Max said, "You sure sound like it."

Diamond jumped up. "I'm fleecing. Okay, Max. See you back at the house."

She reached out a hand toward Babe, who shook it. "Nice to meet *you*."

She flicked Chance a glance, then flounced out.

"So, Chauncey's not gay, you said. But he's not DL. So what's the story? He was getting high with Ross, now he's going off with another drag queen with a bra full of coins. So, is he gay for pay?"

Max laughed. "Why you so interested in what that man is into? If you want to get dicked down, say you want to get dicked down."

"I'm not saying he ain't sexy as fuck, but I'm confused why everybody is so afraid to call a spade a spade: Black guys fucking around with men, and they have girlfriends. They're bisexual, and they are DL, and for real, they are killing women, living in secret and having girlfriends so people won't call them faggots. It's disgusting. Live in your truth! You like fucking trannies, so what? Just do it."

"Diamond?" Max asked. "She's a female illusionist. She does it to make money, and she's an artist. She's worked on her craft for ten fucking years, and yeah, she dresses up and hustles on the street to support herself, but she's not a transexual. You white people can't rest until you categorize and label everything. That's your baggage, man, not anybody else's."

Babe said, "Ross doesn't consider himself to be trans. Ross wears make up, refers to himelf as female, and he loves loves loves the straight boys. But he's got a dick just like you. Being gay has gradations, right? It's not one thing or the other. You know this."

Chance shook his head adamantly. "No. That's a cop out. Those guys are closet cases, and they are cowards. And they are harboring AIDS and spreading disease and destruction. Don't you read? Black people are dying from AIDS at higher and higher rates, and it's because of these DL motherfuckers."

Max said, "So how is the blame on the what you call DL motherfuckers? Why are the women they sleep with not held accountable for not wearing condoms if we are being told that everyone should be wearing condoms? If the men are to blame, so are the women they sleep with."

"So, we're victim blaming?"

"If there are victims, I think it would be both of them."

Babe said, "My thing is, I think racism is the problem here. Racism is criminalizing Black men, like always. And infantilizing them as well. A Black man is too stupid to determine how he wants to define himself? If a man says he's not gay, why is that not enough? Yeah, there are those that are in the closet. I'm not discounting that. But there are also men that like the feeling of sex, regardless of who it is with, and that doesn't necessarily mean they are gay."

Chance laughed. "Y'all tripping. Racism has nothing to do with this. Everybody knows how homophobic the Black community is, and that's why Black men are ashamed to accept what they are, but it still doesn't give them a pass for being untruthful."

Babe huffed in exasperation. "White people are funny. Some five-year-old little white boy can tell his mommy he's a girl, and his parents will let him wear dresses to school and give him a female name, right?"

Chance nodded. "Not always. But it's a good thing that society is moving toward allowing freedom of expression instead of forcing kids to accept a gender that they do not want."

"Right. So, a five-year-old has the mental capacity to determine their gender, but a fully grown Black man is not capable of deciding what their sexuality is? A white majority has to decide that it's this pathology? This DL shit? I don't buy it. Sexuality is a spectrum. But white folks only think that spectrum is possible for themselves. Look, all I'm saying is, there are multiple truths out here. Just because the majority want to call a thing a thing doesn't mean there aren't other truths out there too."

There was a moment of uncomfortable silence. Max looked at Babe with an expression he couldn't read.

Chance clapped his hands as if to clear the air and said to Max. "No shade. You got beautiful eyes. At least the one I can see. What's with your coloring? You mixed?"

Babe rolled his eyes.

"Contacts. You would probably be da' hotness with colored contacts. I get them all the time. People bring them by the shop, all kinds of colors. Even the ones that have no color, I got those. People bring me shit when they don't have money to pay for their hair. I got TVs, radios, clothes, shoes, concert tickets. A bitch will do a lot to keep her head tight. I'll bring some to you next time I see you."

"For reals? Cool. I always wanted to have different colored eyes. I can dye my hair to match my eye color."

Babe said, "You get televisions in exchange for doing hair?"

"You ain't never had the hookup?"

"Hell yeah. But how's a TV even exchange for getting your hair done?"

Max looked incredulous. "You know how much bitches be willing to pay for their hair? Shit. The hair gets paid before the rent. I do. Okay. And I don't even do braids. But I hire out space at my shop for someone that does hair. Fifty-fifty split, so I do good with that too. Diamond? I buy her gowns, do her hair. Because I'm not having that bitch out here representing us in front of all them white sissies in a dress from Easy Pickins. She needs to be on point. So I make sure her shit is as authentic as the white dragons, if not better. We get that out of Nan

Duskin, Bonwits. Because you know how white people think they the shit even without doing shit. Those girls barely know the words to the songs they singing, let alone give a real show. They stand there, all stationary, boring as dogfuck, and still be snagging the grand prizes."

"That's why y'all got the balls though. Can't nobody white snag trophies at those balls, so what's the difference? Speaking of TV...," said Chance. "Why don't we have cable and shit? I can't be missing new music videos. I gotta keep up on my moves. Can we get cable?"

Max said. "The balls are way more inclusive than that white shit. If you come in and you know your shit, you going to get a trophy, Black, white, or purple. But I'm not interested in the balls. I'm interested in snagging award money. And taking that money from a bland-ass white bitch like you."

Babe said, "You know who can afford cable? Rich people and people on welfare because somebody pays it for them. Cable is not in my budget. We've never had cable when I was coming up. That's not a necessity for me."

"Where the hell you hear that kind of thing? I've had cable my whole life. I don't do drag shows."

Max smirked. "But you *are* a bland-ass white bitch. Guess you one of them welfare bitches too. You grew up on the waffle? You got the gubment cheese and the WIC checks? I should have known. I could see a certain broke-ass bitch quality in the way you dress."

Babe shook his head, realizing he could do nothing to change this strange dynamic between the two.

"I dress like your bull, here. So, you saying he's a broke ass too?"

"No. You try to dress like him. On you, it translates a whole different way."

"What way is that?"

"Skank. McNasty. Gutbucket. Guttersnipe. You want me to go on?"

"Nah, I pretty much get it. Like I said earlier," Chance began to sing. "If you want my future, you better work it boy. No it won't come easy. I know you want this…"

"All right. I need to go to the bathroom. You two think you can sit without killing each other?"

The line to get to the bathroom was as long as the line to get a table. By the time Babe's turn came, he could barely hold his urine. He rushed into the bathroom, groaning in disgust as his sneakers splashed in the muck on the floor, covered with water, urine, and toilet paper. He stepped over to the filthy toilet, unbuckled, and let loose. The mirror in front of him was scratched with etchings:

Ida sucks twat.

Louie got the hiv.

Wait here at 4am if you want dick sucked.

He squinted through the etchings to check his face. His eyes were somewhat bloodshot, but other than that, he approved of how well he had held up through the night heat. Sweat gave his cheekbones an impressive sheen. The door banged open. He jumped. He thought he had locked the door.

Max entered the narrow space, frowning at the stench. "Good God. What the fuck. Is that a turd on the floor? Jesus Christ."

"Yeah. I was afraid to take my shit out. Who knows what diseases are floating around in here?"

Max stepped across the filth and brought his mouth to Babe's lips. Max's lips were soft on his own, lushly pressing against his nostrils. His breath smelled earthy, like honey with the taint of coffee beans and sugar. Babe kissed him back, liking how Max's nose felt against his nose. He felt his smooth head, slightly static with new growth.

"I like you, Babe."

Babe whispered, "Like you too."

He began to shimmer with nervousness.

"You want to come with me tonight?"

Babe shook his head. "I can't. Gotta take Chance home."

Max kissed him again, then cupped the back of his neck with his palm to bring him closer and rumbled in his ear. "I can get him a cab home. I want to spend more time with you."

Babe kissed him back and put his hand on his chest to push him away "I can't. But you can give me your number."

"I'm trying to play it cool, but I want you to know how much I like you. I'm going to Chicago for this big hair show. Lots of connections, opportunities to make good money. But I hope I can see you again, soon's I get back."

Babe attempted to match the verbal banter Chance had developed with Max. "Didn't I ask for your number? You think I want my hair done?"

"Asking for my number doesn't mean I'll hear from you again...."

Babe took a pen from his pants pocket, took Max's hand in his own, and scratched his phone number into his palm. "Okay. I'm giving you my number. That way the ball's in your court. Unless I'm really giving you the number to Yellow Cab Company or something."

Max rolled his eyes. "Thanks. Give me ink poisoning at the same time."

Babe rolled his eyes too. "You know that's not a thing, don't you? Besides, the way your hand is sweating, it's more than likely the ink won't stay on long. Hope your memory is good."

He grinned. "Don't worry. I know how to find you."

Driving home, Babe was usually annoyed when an inebriated Chance sat snoring in the passenger seat. He thought it was only befitting that he, as the driver, be kept company to ensure he be entertained and less likely to nod off and plow into the embankment on the side of the expressway. This night, however, he was relieved to have the time to himself, alone with his thoughts, reveling in the remnants of his pleasurable night without the caustic commentary that he was certain Chance would offer.

He still felt a certain fuzzy warmth in his chest, thinking about Max walking along with him, his piercing stare, his seeming sincerity when he had asked him to spend the night. He was sure Max was lying about his age, and while he wasn't outright lying about his name, Babe thought it was odd he gave a name from a movie character instead of his own. It made him wonder if Max was trying to run game on him. He thought back about the many times he and his friends had given assumed names to guys that did not meet their criteria. Bad breath, church queens, high-waters, outdated haircuts, too feminine, too masculine, too fat, too thin, the wrong kind of white: read not a b-boy or without that Mediterranean swagger. He could still feel the heat from Max pulling him close in the squalor of that urine-soaked bathroom.

When they pulled up in front of the house, Babe deliberately slammed on the brakes and laughed to himself when Chance lunged to wakefulness as he was hurled against the restraint of the seatbelt. "What's going on?"

Babe said, "Home. Go on in. I'm going to drive around back to park in the garage." Chance staggered up the stairs, mumbling about why a bitch had to slam on the brakes like that, and if he had gone through the windshield, he would have sued the fuck out of Babe.

He pulled back out, drove down to the traffic light, and down across the Markley Street railroad tracks, and up to the alley behind Barbadoes Street. He parked, got out, and walked down between two narrow row houses until he faced the rear of his destination. All the lights were out. He searched the ground, found a few stones, and tossed lightly toward the second-floor window.

The window sliding in its housing interrupted the drone of chirping crickets. Babe stood slightly swaying under the sycamore tree, just as he used to when they were both seventeen, sneaking into Matthew's parents' house in the midnight quiet. Babe looked up through his alcohol infused haze and made eye contact with him when his head emerged. Babe couldn't read his expression from the distance, but he thought he saw Matthew's shoulders lilt forward when he recognized him standing there. Babe. Babe waited for him at the back door, standing in shadow out of habit, his mind hurtling back to those early years, when he was thin and murky with desire, restless to feel the heat of another body.

The door opened with a soft sigh. Matthew stood in the darkness, the light of the moon falling on the angular planes of his face. The sight of his bare feet sent a charge through Babe's synapses. He moved close and nuzzled his neck. Matthew stepped back, caught unaware, but then reached for him, pulling him close, bringing his mouth closer and leaning against him as they both stumbled back toward the door. Babe felt the heat of his mouth. The familiarity was comforting.

Matthew closed the door and drew back, watching him through narrowed eyes.

"You're drunk," Matthew's accusation was light as air, murmured against his ear. He pushed Babe against the kitchen counter. Babe pulled him closer, although their bodies were already locked tightly together. He pushed Matthew's head back and nuzzled the hollow at the base of his neck, tasting the salt of him, taking in the smell of his pheromones.

The dogs began to yip. Matthew angrily shushed them, whispering so that his parents wouldn't hear as he tugged Babe by the hand. They were on the stairs, ascending quietly, Babe remembered his teenage years, sneaking into this house, how he kept his weight on the outer edges lest the stairs creak, signaling their presence. The familiar scent of mothballs and mold tugged at his memory. This visit was different from the late-night hushed visits of his younger years, that familiar sweat-funk that used to hit him upon entering the room Matthew had shared with two brothers. It was now replaced with a slight residual reek of marijuana.

The marijuana smell lingered on Matthew's clothes. It tugged his olfactory senses as he pulled Matthew's shirt over his head and yanked at his belt as he breathed heavily. Matthew grabbed his hands, pushed them from his waistband. He bumped Babe back onto the narrow bed, pushing him prone with his hips. Babe felt his arousal. He fell back, ignoring the slight jolt of pain as his head hit the sloping ceiling on his way down. Then, Matthew was on him, his weight a familiar, comforting thing.

"I love you," they both murmured, and the bass in their voices reverberated across the low-lying ceiling.

Babe again reached for Matthew's buckle.

Matthew smacked his hands away. Babe knew he was angry about the audacity, coming by in the middle of the night for sexing.

Babe propped himself up on his elbows, his vision diffused by need. "What?"

Matthew rose above him and straddled his hips. He reached for his own buckle and loosened his pants under Babe's hungry stare.

Babe's eyes narrowed at the coiled spring of pubic hair rising from his unzipped pants. He wore no underwear. As his zipper growled a slow reveal, Babe smelled the familiarity of him, dark and murky like mushrooms, and reached again for him.

Matthew pulled back, not allowing him to touch him.

Babe's frustrated grunt was an unspoken question. Matthew grinned, but the grin did not hide the haunted expression Babe tried not to see in his eyes. He tugged at Babe's clothes, insistent, brusque. Babe helped him.

Their breathing was fast and urgent. So was their lovemaking. Aroused by the knowledge that they had to be quiet, they let their bodies communicate the fury their voices were unable to. Their gestures melded hatred with fury. They reveled in their innate awareness, their familiarity with the other's body, confident in what brought the other pleasure, what did not. They were comfortable in the knowledge that whatever slights or wrongs they had committed against the other, in this act, in this ritual, they had always found common ground.

After, they lay spent, the sheets damp with their semen and sweat. Matthew lay in a deep sleep, nestled against Babe's side, his arm taking the usual, possessive space across his abdomen, cupping his pelvic bone.

Babe allowed a small moment of comfort, feeling the familiar sense of contentment from Matthew's hot breathing on his neck, from the weight of Matthew's dick resting heavily along his hip, before closing off that small, vulnerable path to accepting things as they had always been. He closed his eyes, reveling in that feeling for a moment more, before stealthily sliding from beneath and retrieving his clothes making as little noise as possible.

It began to rain lightly as he drove home. He parked in the lot and sat on the stairs in front of the house, letting the drops pelt his head, cooling him down. All the lights along Leviticus Street were dark, its residents fast asleep as the light of predawn began to arch across the pitched roofs and widow walks of the cavernous buildings.

Wilfredo's low-pitched Toyota crept into the lot. He waved to Babe as he got out of the vehicle. Babe waved back, watching him walk, bowlegged and catlike, wearing a T-shirt and cargo shorts.

"You all right, man? What you doing sitting out here at four in the morning?"

"What you doing getting in at four in the morning?" Babe pointed amusedly at his shorts. "I know you weren't on no date in those cargoes, were you?"

Wilfredo preened, doing a slight muscleman flex, both arms raised. "I know you ain't clowning my shorts. What you got on there? A belly shirt and some shit?"

"You know what it is." Babe laughed. "No. Your shorts aren't bad. You got nice little legs on you."

He sat next to Babe. "Little? Niggah, you ain't see these calves? Little...ha."

"Yeah. Yeah. You were on a little date?"

"Oh, I see what you doing. You keep using that word 'little.' That's like a shot, right? I was on a date, yeah. If you want to call it that. Getting a little pussy." He laughed.

"Okay. TMI. I get you."

Wilfredo raised his nose, sniffing the air and moving his head around exaggeratedly.

"What's wrong with you?" Babe asked.

"I see I ain't the only one out sexing this night."

Babe laughed, short and staccato, and blushed. "What you talking about?"

Wilfredo arched a brow. "You don't know? I know what sex smell like."

"Oh? You're familiar with the scent of gay sex?"

He shrugged. "Sex is sex, man. Ain't no difference. I know the smell of spunk. And you reek of it."

Babe's voice rose an octave. "What about you! You said you just got done fucking. You smell like spunk too?"

He raised his arm and leaned toward him. The small tufts of hair sprouting from the cave of his underarm aroused Babe.

"I don't know. Smell me."

Babe laughed. "Stupid."

"I would hope you can smell some pussy up in there though. You know what that smell like?"

"Fuck you."

Wilfredo's smile left, and he peered at Babe. "Ho. Ho, there. You was with dude, wasn't you?"

Babe blushed. "Dude who?"

"You know what I'm talking about. What you do that for? You want him to keep up his bullshit or something? You get off on a niggah chasing you around town, popping tires and defacing your shit? That's not cool, man."

"It was stupid. I know."

"If you needed to get your shit off, man, I know this gay dude around the way. I could have hooked you up with my boy, Manny."

"Manuel that lives on Main? With the long hair and the pocketbooks?"

"Oh, you already know him."

"*You* know him? What's up with that?"

He shrugged. "I know lots of people."

Babe laughed. "See, you straight people think everybody that's gay is willing to screw anybody else who's gay. What makes you think I would want to screw around with Manny? He's so out there."

"I don't get it. Out where?"

"He's a sissy!"

"If he's a sissy, how come you're not?"

"He's just not my type. No shade on him, just that every gay guy isn't compatible with all other gay guys. It's kind of insulting. My female friends are always pulling that same shit, trying to be Miss Matchmaker with some brick. Okay, so what if I tried to hook you up with Miss Imogene? I mean, I assume she's straight, right? How would you feel about that?"

Wilfredo grinned. "Well, I wouldn't want to marry her or nothing. But she got a pussy, don't she? I'd fuck her once or twice."

Babe stood up, grimacing. "Okay, I've heard enough. That's gross."

"Pussy don't got no face. How you gonna know that wasn't the best pussy in your life unless you willing to hit it to find out. Don't limit yourself, that's all I'm saying."

They both laughed, then looked around to be sure they had not disturbed the peace. Wilfredo stood, waved at him, and walked back across the street, then let himself into his house.

Babe sighed. He had been satisfied by Matthew, so he didn't understand this feeling, watching the broad spread of Wilfredo's shoulders, his burnished muscular arms, and his dark wavy hair. He thought of the word *covet*. He wanted to own Wilfredo's beauty like he owned his car or the artwork that lined his living room walls.

Chapter Twenty-Seven

Alise's PFA

She wondered if Rueben's reticence was her imagination. Maybe it was her guilt for leaving him alone in the house more and more frequently than she had before. For her, it was a comforting feeling, being able to get away from the constant responsibility of parenthood for a child with such pervasive needs but still being close enough to respond to an emergency. She found that she was able to let her thoughts rest on things other than her son. When she was washing up the old woman or cleaning up the simple single male detritus Drew left in his wake, she was able to think about her life and the person she had been before becoming a parent.

When she was home, she found herself preoccupied with thinking of ways to keep Rueben engaged, what games he might like, how to tweak a fable to make it interesting in its umpteenth iteration, or how to keep him away from food.

Ever since she had started what she called her 'job,' Rueben wasn't as dependent on her attention. He no longer sat by the door waiting for her when she left the apartment to take care of errands, he rarely asked her for a story, and he often preferred to sleep on the cot in the basement.

She missed him sleeping beside her in bed, the heat of his body keeping her warm, the rhythm of his breathing a source of calm.

She now often found him silently contemplating, staring off into space. When she was preparing a meal, or cleaning up, stacking newfound items from her searches on trash day, she'd look up to find him gazing absently.

"What is it, pumpkin? You want a story?" she'd ask, and he'd shake his head.

"I'm too big for stories," he'd say.

One day, after reciting a story to him, he blurted, "Mama. Did your Mama used to tell you stories?"

She genuflected. "Not so much fables, like you and I do, where you can learn life lessons. But we would bake pies and cookies while my Dad and brothers were out, and she'd tell me about Cinderella, and Rapunzel, all the fairytale princesses."

"Don't fairytales got lessons too?"

She shrugged as she sat on the floor beside a towering stack of yellowed newspapers. "I guess. But they're not as easy to figure out. Why don't you come help me bundle up these papers I found? Twine's right here."

He flopped down next to her with a grunt. "Was you your mama's favorite?"

"I don't think my mama had favorites. My folks weren't like me. They gave us lots of chores, and you had to get them all done, lest you get the switch. My mama used to tell me that I was going to have a child just like me, that I was a stubborn little girl, always wanted to do things my way, and that one day the Lord would bless me with a child that was stubborn like I was, and that would be my lesson to learn in life."

"What's stubborn?"

"You know. Bullheaded."

"Am I bullheaded?"

Alise kissed his forehead, thinking back.

When she had first come across Kendall's gun, tucked beneath shredded newspaper in a Florsheim shoe box, she had been cleaning, straightening out his closet, full of double-breasted suits and dry-cleaned white shirts encased in thin, clingy plastic. Seeing a gun had not surprised her, in and of itself. She was accustomed to them, had grown up with them. Seeing it in her house and not having been aware of its presence is what had taken her aback.

When he came home from his job as a call center rep, his shoulders sloped, his footsteps heavy, she had asked him about it.

He brushed past her, flopped on the recliner, and clicked on the remote. "Your people been threatening us ever since I been home. More so now since having the baby. Threatening to kill the baby too. What you asking me about that for?"

"That's just talk, Kendall. They wouldn't ever hurt no baby. And they haven't done nothing to you either."

He sputtered in amazement. "I spent a year in jail because of them. I'd say they've done something. It's *you* who didn't do anything."

"What could I do? What am I able to do about threats over the phone that we can't even prove?"

So, she had gone to the county courthouse to inquire about filing a protection from abuse order.

The clerk at the office had droned blearily. "How have you been threatened?"

"Well, it's my husband that's being threatened."

"Your husband needs to come in and file. We can't take a third-party account of events. And a protection from abuse order can only be filed in the event that a family member or spouse is the perpetrator."

Kendall refused to file.

After Rueben was born and grew older, the late-night phone calls with no response diminished. They moved from city to city as Kendall searched for a job that would bring contentment. They usually moved under the cloak of night, skipping out on landlords and bill collectors, leaving behind fully furnished homes, hoping that newly acquired accoutrements would divest them of the negativity attached to their old lives.

While the magic of their courting days was long past, Alise was able to find fulfillment in the joy she found with her son. She poured all that she had into making her child feel the love she had not felt when she was a child. She showered him with clothing and toys, maxing out credit already stretched to the limit. When Kendall bought a new suit, she bought Rueben a new outfit. When Kendall leased a new car, trying to stay one step ahead of the repossession of an old one, Alise bought new toys, got Rueben's ears pierced with gold studs from Tiffany &

Company. Each night, while he lay in bed, she tenderly brushed out his locks while regaling him with stories of pixies, magical horses, and mad queens.

She ignored his delays. When he was slow to potty train, she ignored Kendall's admonishments that she needed a stricter regimen, cursed him when he attempted to force Rueben to sit on the potty for hours, forcing him to void, demonstrating that one action led to another action. When he took longer to make words than what magazines stipulated, she told herself that it didn't matter because she and her son had developed a nonverbal communication even more effective than words. She ignored Kendall's instructions on vaccination schedules, telling herself those criteria had been designed for Caucasian children, and therefore, not applicable to her child. When he was slow to eat solid foods, she let him continue to suckle, cooing to him as he rested within her warmth.

After weeks of unsuccessful feeding attempts as their child became less and less alert, they took him to a hospital where he was deemed malnourished and connected to a feeding tube.

Those interfering doctors, with their knowledge of textbook theories and anecdotal case studies. They forced her to see her child in a different light. What had been a special child growing within a space of love and individuality at his own pace became a defect. Head shape and facial features that had been distinctive were identified as deformation. Behaviors that had communicated hunger, frustration, desire, and need now communicated aberration. He was called something that was not his given name. Instead he became identified as a biological malady, and clinical diagnosis. And she was given a strict set of instructions about how to interact with him for optimum future development.

He was taken from them and placed behind observation glass where they watched him, attached to his feeding tube, growing ever more large, and angrier and angrier, missing her touch, her constant voice, her scent of lilac and milk, the taste of her on his tongue, the drone of his father's baritone, or his scent of fresh soap and talc.

Their maternal connection lost its immediacy, diffused as it became through the separation of space and observation room glass. The paternal connection all but vanished. Kendall stopped coming to the hospital to visit, too heartbroken, he said, to see his son in that sterile, clinical environment.

When he was finally permitted to return home, he was a different person. They no longer knew one another. Alise labored diligently to restore what had been there before the interference of white men, told herself that the original seed of what he had been could be restored. Kendall pretended he wasn't there, unable to accept responsibility for bringing something defective into the world. He wondered aloud if they were being punished for ignoring society's rules lying down beside what had been forbidden as Adam had ignored what had been forbidden to him.

She had to leave Rueben in the care of a specialized day care center paid for with a grant by the benevolent society of nuns affiliated with the hospital, who also gave her a job so she would be able to pay for the seemingly never-ending medical expenses.

During her breaks, Alise would find herself sitting in the maternity ward, listening to the muted cries behind smudged glass, smiling sadly at new mothers, fathers, grandparents, and searching for the missing piece of the broken child she had left there.

Chapter Twenty-Eight

Matthew's Interview

Miss Rock did not call him herself. Matthew had been lying amongst the soiled sheets of his bed when his mother knocked on the door. "Phone call."

He yanked on a pair of pants and ran downstairs to answer. Robby was on the other end of the line. Miss Rock would be available to talk to him about the vacancy. He needed to be at the property on Leviticus Street in an hour. And he should bring cash, his deposit, down payment, in case he was approved.

An hour later, he zoomed into a parking spot behind a beige Mercedes-Benz W116, reeking of Speed Stick deodorant and Royal Crown pomade, waving away the smoke from his freshly extinguished cigarette. His mother had hastily ironed a white shirt borrowed from his father. He had ignored his mother's suggestion that he wear a tie, thinking that his pleated pants, trim belt made from good-quality leather, and black sneakers would suffice. He thought briefly of Babe, always telling him that he should invest in a pair of good dress shoes for unforeseen events and acknowledged this would have been such an occasion.

A flurry of motion caught his eye. Robby was standing at the doorway waving to him anxiously. He ran a hand over his hair, walking up the stairs.

"Hurry up!" Robby hissed. "Don't keep her waiting!"

He walked into the hallway. "She here yet?"

Robby gave an eye roll. "What you think? I'm standing at the door waiting on you? The room is on the top floor across from mine. She's up there, so go on!"

As he ascended the creaking stairs, each floor was notably hotter, the air cloying and damp. The landing of the top floor was smaller than the other landings with a patch of old carpet in need of vacuuming. There was a faint scent that tugged the edge of his memory. He identified it as the trace of cocaine. He made a note to himself that Robby, as a neighbor, might offer an avenue of access to add to his list.

The door, painted a faded green, stood slightly ajar. Dust motes danced along a thin stream of sunlight falling from within. Matthew pushed the door open with a broad finger.

The room was large, made to seem even more so by the high, steeply pitched ceiling and ornate moldings along its many curves and corners. A skylight stood open, bringing a struggling light onto the bare wood floors in need of buffing and a new stain.

Miss Rock stood at the far end of the room, running a gloved finger along the fireplace mantel. She turned to face him with an officious grin. She was a handsome woman with silver hair pulled back tightly, held in place with an ornate bone comb. Her deeply hooded eyes beneath arched, penciled brows, were cool and observant.

She was so dark, Matthew struggled to see her features in the dim room. He walked forward, hand outstretched.

"Miss Rock. Sorry I'm late."

She pulled herself erect, her shoulders thrust back in perfect posture stretching to her full, intimidating height, ignoring his hand. "You are not late. You are right on time."

There was a lone chair, an old Hepplewhite with faded brocade seating. She lowered herself to the chair and crossed her black stockinged legs. She slowly tugged at the fingers of a gloved hand, her eyes dark and fathomless.

"I understand you are in need of housing?"

He gulped, feeling awkward. "Yes."

She appeared to wait.

"Uh. Yes, ma'am." He chastised himself for his lapse in social etiquette.

She looked at the paper in her hand, which was only the name and phone number Matthew had written out and given to Robby so he could be notified when Miss Rock was available to see him.

"Tell me about yourself."

He tried to guess what she might want to hear. What might impress her.

"I have two jobs. Won't be no problem paying my rent."

She remained silent.

"I'm quiet. I know how to fix things. The floors here could use buffing and a new stain. I can do that. Make sure the trash is on the curb every Tuesday. A lot of times people here forget to take the trash out on time."

"Are you familiar with people here?"

He shook his head. "I used to live next door, so I know."

"Who are your people? Where are you from?"

"I'm from here. My folks live on the East Side. I got three brothers. We all went to Norristown High School."

"Did you all graduate?"

"Uh. Yes, ma'am. We all of us graduated."

"College."

"No ma'am. We didn't go to college."

Her stillness was discomforting.

"If you had been able to afford it, would you have gone?"

He thought about that and blushed. "Probably not, ma'am."

"How about your parents?"

"Ma'am?"

"Did your parents finish high school?"

"No, ma'am. They didn't. My father had to drop out to take care of his family. My mom too. They married young."

He could see her taking inventory of him, assessing his nervousness. He knew she knew who he was. She was toying with him.

"Why are you in need of a place to live, Mr. Minter?"

Matthew laughed, shifted his feet. "I'm at my folks place, right now, and I'd like to be out on my own. So I won't be underfoot, you know?"

She bobbed her head regally. "Why do you no longer live next door?"

She was imperious as she waited, expectant of an answer. It somehow reminded him of the look Babe had given him that night in the alley at the confrontation that had ended it all.

He didn't know how to answer her.

He thought back through thirteen years of memory, trying to find the moment, the thing he could find that would allow him to say to himself, ah, that must be the reason, but he could not find it.

He didn't think the infidelities were the reason. He had been able to keep those to a minimum and had also been able to keep them mostly to himself.

He thought about his drug use. He wasn't a tragic story of addiction with a horrific childhood that had driven him to drugs. He used them like all the people he knew had used them—'recreationally,' as the doctors and volunteers at HIV testing centers called it. He had smoked weed since seventh grade, as had most of his cohorts. He had experimented with cocaine, hash, opium, Quaaludes, and crank in high school. All the parties that had been held back then usually had one form or other of a substance to experiment with.

When crack had been introduced, it was no big deal. It was another accompaniment to the weed, which by then was being soaked in embalming fluid and other substances to enhance its potency. He wasn't an addict.

Addicts ran around scrounging for money, set themselves on fire. They'd all made fun of Richard Pryor, freebasing and setting himself on fire. That's what addiction looked like. He didn't make enough money to be a cocaine addict.

"I don't know why, ma'am."

She pointed to the closet door. "There is another chair inside. Bring it and have a seat.

He pulled the chair before her, leaned forward expectantly.

"Do you know that boys who like boys live here?"

He nodded.

"Do you like boys?"

"Sometimes."

"So, you would like me to rent to boys that sometimes like boys? Did you love the boy next door?"

He held his head down in desolation.

"Have you loved girls the same way?"

He spoke into his lap. "I never loved anybody like I loved him."

"Why are you no longer there? Everyone knows what they've done when it ends. What did you do?"

"I couldn't fill the hole in his heart that his mother tore out. No matter what I did, it wasn't enough."

She stood, smoothing the pleats of her silk skirt. "Thank you for coming out to meet with me. We will give you a call to update you."

This time, she took his hand when he extended it, smiling remotely.

Clark pulled on his pants, releasing postcoital pheromones of their completed sex. Chance lay on the futon, his arms crossed in a sulking pose.

"You're always in a rush to leave. We barely hang out at all anymore."

Clark huffed in exasperation. "You know I have responsibilities."

Chance was growing weary of Clark's 'responsibilities.' Every evening and weekend hour was filled with obligations to his ailing mother or church duties, leaving little time for Chance. Clark would call, say he's in the area or stop by after work before going home. They'd have a rushed bout of sex, and Clark would mumble some declaration about needing to be somewhere as he hastily dressed.

At work, he no longer stopped at Chance's desk, saying it would appear inappropriate to coworkers.

Chance didn't understand why this bothered him. He was aware that he had only shown interest in Clark with the intention of letting Babe know that he, too, was viable, desired. But Babe barely acknowledged Chance was in a relationship, smirked as though entertained by a private joke at any mention of Clark's name.

Clark bent down to give him a preoccupied peck, and then he was gone.

Matthew exited the room into the hallway, noticing Robby's door still stood open. As he passed, Robby called from inside. Matthew stood at the threshold.

"How'd it go?"

He shrugged. "It's probably a no. I didn't read faggy enough. That's one strange lady."

Robby crossed his legs, sitting among the many pillows on his tufted bedspread. "You can always stay here if you need a spot. I know it would be kind of weird with Babe being so close and all, but fuck it. He made a choice, so let him deal with the repercussions of that choice."

Matthew rested his fists on his hips. "Live with you? I don't even know you like that. How would that work?"

"Look, why don't you come in, and let's talk it out. See if we can make it work?"

Matthew sucked his teeth. "You think I would do some foul shit like that?"

"Foul? It's a resolution to your dilemma."

"Well, everybody knows that you foul, so it's not so surprising. But I wouldn't lie down with your disgusting ass, so you can run around town telling all your bitches like you do with everybody."

Robby laughed, rolling back and grabbing a pillow, clutching it in his arms. "Whatever."

He ducked behind the pillow as if trying to hide and whispered, "No help. No help. No help."

Matthew walked away, baffled, and ran down the stairs, his heart racing.

Out on the porch, he paused, his hand still on the doorknob. He looked around at the vacant street, unaware of the shifting blinds in the windows along Leviticus Street. He did not hear the whispers floating on a breeze: Robby's mantra was pounding in his brain. He descended the stairs, then walked along the side of the house into the laundry room of what had once been his home. He could smell him. The confined space was redolent with his scent, mixed with Neutrogena sesame body oil. It overwhelmed him. He rested a hand on the dryer, mumbled to himself as a comfort to slow his breathing.

He was not aware of his actions. The heat of the room drew perspiration to his head. He wiped it away, hot. He unbuckled his borrowed belt and his no longer freshly ironed pants and let them fall to the floor around his ankles. He removed his underwear. He yanked at the lapel of his father's shirt, the buttons pinging against the metal of the washer like pebbles on a beach. Sweat meandered down the concave of his chest.

He grabbed his limp member and tugged jerkily, grunting between sharp intakes of breath as he felt himself grow florid. He arched back against the wall, allowing his upper back to rasp along the flowered wallpaper. His narrow hips leaned away as fluid burst in a wild arc across the far wall with a stifled grunt. The force of his ejaculation caused his knees to buckle, made him lean forward to rest his forehead on the machine, waiting for his breathing to become less ragged.

When he was able to stand, he stepped out of the pool his pants left at his feet, walked up the stairway to the landing of the apartment, damp with his expenditure. A ripple of color tugged at his periphery.

He stood there as if he had lost direction. He turned toward the open door on his right and saw Chance there, lying on a futon with a thin blanket covering his bare chest. Matthew gave a start, then stopped as Chance made eye contact with him. Matthew was surprised that the boy was not startled by either his appearance or his nudity, but rather cocked his head slightly and lowered the coverlet to show he was also unclothed.

Matthew smelled the murky funk of sex. He felt himself respond to it, the familiar tightness in his groin. He approached, pushing the door closed as he entered.

"Leave it open."

Chapter Twenty-Nine

Babe's PFA

The Montgomery county courthouse stood majestically at the apex of Swede and Airy Streets. It was built in 1854, an impressive representation of Georgian style with broad steps leading up to a portico of ornate columns, all made from resplendent King of Prussia blue marble. The monolith was the perfect representation of the trajectory of the town itself. In the eighteenth century, King of Prussia blue was renowned for its fine quality and accessibility. It was used for many public building projects up through the nineteenth century when it became known that the marble was not as grand as it had been thought. It was discovered to be a poor performer, cumbersome, and prone to decay, unable to adapt to change: its large-grained majesty resistant to carving and other attempts of adaptation.

As styles and tastes shifted, the courthouse continued to stand, still impressive in its cool, stylized hauteur, but like an aging beauty in a bar, often more appreciated for what it once had been rather than what it now was.

Despite its physical appearance, the building was still an effective apparatus in imparting the message that had been part of the original intention when it had first been built. Walking through the wide doors, Babe felt diminutive, despite being over six feet tall. He asked the guard for directions for filing a protection from abuse order. The guard politely instructed him to empty his pockets, remove his belt, take off his watch, and pass slowly through the metal detector, flashing a red strobe.

He tugged his belt free from its loops, depositing it into the grey plastic bin, then held his pants up by the waistband. He walked through the detector, flinched slightly at the responding beeps. He was told to go back through and asked if he had anything else in his pockets. They also had him remove his jacket and placed it in another plastic bin. Babe walked through the detector and sighed in relief when the detector did not beep. Then, he spread his arms and legs as instructed and waited while a wand swiped alongside his torso. Nodded in response to the guard nodding. Removed his belongings from the bin. Searched the floor to be sure none of his money had fallen during the ride on the conveyor belt. Clasped his watch on his wrist. Drew his belt through the loops and fastened it.

Babe tamped down on the mounting surge of annoyance causing acid to burn in his stomach. This process seemed so convoluted. It reminded him of the clerk at the liquor store holding his ID up to the light for an in depth look or holding his money up to verify that it was legal tender, or even the delayed response of bartenders at the bars. All these behaviors that seemed designed to remind him that he was not the same as them. They all made him hypervigilant, this constant reminder that other people seemed to think he needed to remind him he was Black.

They asked for his ID. He drew his license from his wallet. Stood spread legged while it was reviewed. The guard politely instructed him where he should go. He walked out into a grand hallway. His footsteps echoed on smooth marble, voices also echoed, bouncing off the towering ceilings. The hallways were broad, expansive, making him feel vulnerable even though he was not aware that that was what he was feeling. He walked downstairs to more hallways and rooms closed off by gleaming mahogany doors.

A middle-aged white lady at the prothonotary desk listened politely before handing him papers to complete.

Of course he would need to provide his name and his address, but cataloging the specifics of the relationship, putting a pen to a document, writing down his name, affiliating himself in this way to Matthew's name and address, brought up a feeling of vulnerability. Warning bells rang in his head. As his reticence grew, his senses grew more attuned. He could hear the scratch of the pen running along the paper. Time seemed to slow down, move in reverse. He became a little boy, listening to his parents instruct him about the importance of staying away from the police, of how to behave when unable to avoid police contact.

Time ceased moving, all the moments of his life careening in on one another. Every police interaction melded into one large cacophony of experience.

He had been pulled over driving along the back road, running perpendicular to the Reading Railroad line, heading to Philly.

"Can you turn it down, homes?" asked through a mocking laugh.

Driving his father's BMW, newly licensed. "Is this your car? Do you live at the address on this license?"

Hopping in the car, barefoot, shirtless, a pair of basketball shorts, a quick jaunt down the street to Wawa. "Where you headed?"

"Wawa."

"You mean 7-Eleven?" asked in an attempt to create discordance.

"No, I mean Wawa."

The time he had picked up his cousin and his four female friends in University City. He'd rushed them to get into the Jeep, so he could catch the light, veering through the yellow as it turned to red. The resultant pull over with three squad cars.

"Turn off the car! Put the keys on the roof! Now!" all the cops yelled at once. Questions came from all directions. "Why did you run that light? Who are these people in the car?"

The girls in the back, screaming about police injustice, indignant in all their ivy-league, newly learned, civics-class glory, demanding fair treatment. "This is the water buffalo shit all over again."

"You mad? Niggers ain't supposed to be at Penn?"

"Don't get mad. Get your money up and your SAT scores, and you, too, can be parlaying at the U of P."

"Why did you run that light?"

"Everybody runs that light, Babe!"

"Why'd you run that light?"

"We go Rodney King up in this piece, and you best believe Johnnie Cochran will be getting us a checkup in here."

Babe remained silent. His parents had trained him. He answered no questions other than name and address. His silence infuriated them, and he took a modicum of pleasure from that. He whispered to the girls in the back to shut the fuck up because if there was a "Rodney King up in here," it would be his ass, not theirs, spread-eagled on the pavement, spraying blood and brain.

Then he was twelve years old, riding in the back of his mother's W116. He watched the back of her silver chignon, fastened with its bone comb, the car slowing down as they approached flashing lights with a roaring crowd.

"Stay inside," she instructed. Her silk skirt fanned a voluminous plume as it caught the wind from the opened door.

He hadn't been able to see much through the Black bodies standing around, shouting. But he did see the body at the center, crouched on its knees, hands over the back of its head, and the bodies of the men in blue uniforms, waving black sticks, demanding they stand down. One of the men in blue was Father. Babe waved his hand, smiling broadly, but Father didn't see him.

There was a body at the center of blue, screaming in confusion. Mother came through, walking to the body, holding up her hands to defend him. The man in blue that was not Father approached her, his black stick raised high.

Babe shook his head. He didn't know where that recollection had come from. Had he merged footage from the Rodney King chase with another memory?

He attempted to focus on the PFA petition. He shook his head at all the superfluous words and pseudo-Latin insertions. He was always amazed at the way white people would use a seven-syllable word when a one-syllable one would be as effective when creating legal documents. This, just like the cumbersome edifice in which he now sat, was another attempt at psychological and psychic domination by people in authority, a way to generate feelings of inferiority, so the person on the receiving end of the onslaught would feel small, out of sorts.

> *The Petitioner respectfully requests that this Court issue an Order of Protection from Abuse against the Respondent, as provided for in 10 .... C. , S 1041 et seq. In support of this request, the Petitioner states that...*

> *Petitioner's relationship to Respondent is:*

> *Current or former spouseLiving togetherCurrent or former substantive dating relationshipChild in commonFamily member (specify relationship)Custodian of Children*

> *The Respondent has committed the following acts of abuse against the Petitioner (Please describe all the acts of abuse you wish the Court to consider including dates if known*

Babe thought back over the years. He couldn't think of incidents that would qualify as 'acts of abuse.' Matthew certainly didn't have a firearm. He wrote down the dates and locations for the time when Matthew had broken in on Chance and Clark, the time Wilfredo had told him about Matthew flattening Alise's tires, and the time the police had come to the house when he had found Matthew in his bed.

He hadn't been witness to Matthew breaking in, though. Nor had he seen him slashing Alise's tires. Also, Alise hadn't filed a police report because Babe had reimbursed her for the tires. He also didn't know if Wilfredo would be okay with having his name and address written down as a contact for a legal document. Shit, now he wondered if Wilfredo was undocumented. That could stir up an entire shitstorm of events.

He needed to do something. He didn't want Matthew to think he could continue to act out—tracking his car, following him into the city, destroying property—but were these things abuse? He hadn't taken anything out of the house that night since Chance and Clark had been able to head him off. He'd written that embarrassing shit on the windshield, too, but Babe didn't see how that could be considered abuse. And no one had seen him do it.

When he was done, he took the paperwork back to the prothonotary desk where he was directed to go down the hallway, through another vast passageway, to speak to a family advocate. He knocked on the door and was taken aback when it was opened by Mitzi the pit's owner, Drew.

"What are you doing here?"

"Working. What do you think?" Drew sniffed the air, smelling Babe's Neutrogena body oil. "Coming up here smelling like a bowl of sesame chicken rice."

He laughed. "Well you should be feeling right at home then. Fuck you."

"You here about a PFA?"

Babe nodded.

Drew ushered him into the small space, barely able to accommodate the table and two chairs. Drew wore a pair of baggy chinos with a striped Hilfiger shirt tucked into his trim waist and a baseball cap with a large *H* emblazoned on the front.

"They let you work like that?"

"Like what?"

"I've been written up two times for wearing a hat to work. And we can't wear chinos unless it's Friday. To say nothing about how twisted they get about my dreads."

Drew shrugged as he sat in a chair. "I'm an advocate. So it's kind of less formal."

"If you were Black, I bet it wouldn't be *less formal*."

"Shit. Here we go again with the Malcolm X shit. You got to stop trying to use race for everything that you think is unfair. Sometimes shit is not fair because that's the way life is."

"That's what white people say so they can keep on doing their shit."

"If you keep using race as a weapon, how do you think you are ever going to rise above the problems you think you have? All you're going to do is use it as the excuse when you don't."

"All I know is being me, being Black, is a joyous thing. I enjoy the music in our talk, the sex in our walk, the wisdom in our world view, everything. How we stink when we work hard, how we smell better than brand new money when we clean up. It only becomes heavy when white people are around."

Drew smirked. "That's real poetic. Look, I'd like to sit here and talk to you about what I think is the problem as it relates to the Black man in America and all that, but I'm here as a representative for the county, so how about you sit down and let me tell you about how the protection from abuse process works."

Babe sat. "I don't think this thing is applicable to me. The form states that you need to be either related to the perpetrator or a paramour."

"You're sort of right. This process is not designed to address gay relationships, per se. But you can still file as you two used to live together. The PFA process is meant to address domestic violence. To keep women safe, particularly after they've made the decision to leave the perpetrator, which takes a lot of bravery and many times leads the partner to further acts of intimidation and violence."

"Well, he's been doing crazy shit. Breaking in the house, defacing property. But I'm not a victim of abuse."

"Do you know what abuse is? How can you say you're not a victim of abuse?"

"Do I look like I've been abused?"

"How would you look? You know, you don't necessarily have to be Farrah Fawcett in *The Burning Bed*. And for gay people, men in particular, sometimes people don't realize when they're in an abusive relationship."

Babe shifted uncomfortably.

"I've been your neighbor for quite a while. I've seen him coming home drunk, I've heard you two fighting. The vents carry sound from your house, all day long, back and forth, sounds moving from one house to the next like a schizophrenic hearing voices. Probably everybody on the street has heard you guys. You know Miss Imogene be pulling her Barcalounger out on the sidewalk so she can hear better."

Drew laughed but Babe was mortified at the thought of everyone hearing what he had thought had been private. Drew sensed his discomfort, softened his voice. "You might not be getting your ass kicked, but did you ever think that you can be a victim of abuse even if you are able to defend yourself?"

Babe wasn't able to talk, disabled by disparate scenes of violence from his past. His cheeks flushed red.

Drew inhaled, appearing somewhat embarrassed. "That being said...between me and you, this system isn't designed to acknowledge gay relationships as worthy of granting a protection from abuse order. If you have a couple of police reports you can provide that support the abuse where police have documented that they have witnessed physical contact, it would work in your favor."

"So, I'm supposed to have called the cops, right? Get him to kick my ass when they get there? Where they do that at?"

Drew shrugged. "I'm just telling you. Shit, the cops say that to the hetero couples too. If they don't see the man in action, many times they make dude stay away one night so everybody can cool off."

"How'd you get a job here if they're antigay?"

"I didn't say they were antigay. It's not something that's acknowledged as worthy of a PFA. And anyway, it's not like I came in here flouncing around screaming 'Hey, I'm gay. Now give me a job.' It's nobody's fucking business. We don't go around pouring out personal information. That's what you Americans do."

"Now who's being racist?"

"Just facts. So, what I'd suggest you do is rather than focus on the gay thing, you say that he used to live with you. Now, they might try to delve more deeply about the extent of what was entailed in 'living together,' but you wait and see. Don't volunteer any information until they ask specifically. You have any questions?"

He had no questions. He needed to do it, stop thinking about it, like ripping off a Band-Aid.

The courtrooms were on the upper levels. Drew walked him out of the bowels of the building. The elevator took him into the sunlight of the more expansive rooms, boasting wide windows with picturesque views of the town he had never seen before.

He entered a room filled with people milling about and talking at loud volumes. He had expected that there would be hushed tones, given his high school classes about how one conducted oneself in settings like these. Scanning the room, Babe was reminded of the motto attached to the statue of liberty; the crowd of mostly Black- and brown-hued people were tired, poor, huddled masses, teeming with disparate scents. He smelled old cigarettes and damp clothes, mixed with underarm perspiration and hair grease. Children screamed and cried while mothers jostled them on hips or in strollers. The only disruption of color were the attorneys attired in drab Brooks Brothers suits, and court staff, who were all white, excluding the massive bailiff and the security team. The courthouse staff were cordoned off from general population by a wooden bannister, which also created a psychic differentiation where those wearing street clothes were on one side and those wearing suits were on the other.

A uniformed man wearing a badge strolled the length of the banister, glaring sternly at the assembly, a smirk etched on his face.

A gavel banged, and the uniformed man demanded silence.

The crowd grew silent.

Babe sat confusedly.

A name was called, and a woman rose and walked through the gate into the suited side. She approached the judge, who asked her to describe the incidents of violence he read loudly from her petition.

Babe was horrified, listening to this woman talk about the many ways her husband had caused harm to her. People around him were immersed in private conversations, talking to counsel, and others were listening to the woman enumerating her husband's drunken assaults. Babe would have to stand up there, in front of all these people, and tell someone he did not know—this old white man—that he was gay, and that his boyfriend was a perpetrator of domestic abuse. He imagined all those eyes focused on him. The snickering that would erupt. The questions the judge would ask.

He stood up, passed stumblingly by jutting knees and feet, and exited the room.

He turned to head toward the elevators and was brought up short by Drew, who was standing along the wall talking with someone. Drew walked over.

"What's up?"

"All those people in there. That's not what I was expecting."

"What were you expecting?"

He shrugged. "I don't know. I guess that it would be me and a judge or something. I didn't expect that all those people would be there. Airing out our personal shit like some kind of zoo in front of everybody else."

"I understand what you mean. But this process, like other legal proceedings, is a community process. So, like trials, hearings, town hall meetings, and stuff like that, many of these things are open to the public. We, as community members, have the right to know what is going on where we live, and even more importantly, we have the power to educate ourselves to how these things work and how everything is interconnected."

"That sounds great when you say it—court appointed designee—but what I saw in there is a bunch of busybodies and gossips sitting around like they're at the *Jerry Springer Show*. I wouldn't go on there, and I damn sure won't be airing out my personal shit for general entertainment." Babe walked toward the elevators.

Drew followed him on. "You are not that important that everybody in there wants to know your shit. They have their own shit that they are concerned about."

"Let you tell it. Believe me, as soon as I let it be known that I was living with a man, and he was kicking my ass, the word would hit the street before I even exited the building."

"So, is that it? Are you ashamed about being in a gay relationship?"

Babe was angry. "No. I'm not. It's like what you said earlier, I don't run around airing my personal business, just like you Asians."

"Did you ever come out to your family?"

"Come out? I didn't need to come out. Black folks don't run around making announcements about what's going on behind closed doors. White gays do that to feel validated. I already know my value."

"Do you? You've been involved with an abusive partner for over a decade, right? How is that knowing your value?"

The elevator dinged to a stop. Babe rushed off. "Fuck you."

The men in uniform looked over, silently placing palms over their weapons.

Drew grabbed Babe's elbow and spoke in a lower tone so as not to be overheard. "I'm not judging you or any of the choices you've made in your life. But I think you need to do some soul searching. Ask yourself if the real reason you don't want to file this PFA might be related a little bit to shame. I mean, it's understandable. I know how people in positions of authority treat us. I see it every day working here, how people that should receive the same considerations under the law are seen as objects of derision for their sexuality.

"Hell, we all know how it's set up in here to deal with nonwhite people as criminals before any evidence to show it. And think about how women are dealt with in domestic relations, and that the father is seldom given equanimity—assumed to be a dead beat—and poor people are the life blood that feeds this whole system, pouring their limited funds back through bails, fines, lawyers, and all that.

"But you have a chance to put a chink in the armor of this monster. It might feel like your story is insignificant, but it's important. Until more people in same-sex relationships step up and let people know this is a problem, we'll never be able to move toward a place where laws change and start recognizing us."

Babe nodded, gently pulling his elbow free. "Thanks for your time. When I get the desire to be Captain Save-the-Fags, you'll be first to know."

Drew shook his head as Babe turned to leave.

Babe drove back toward home at breakneck speed, expressing his fury at Drew's condescending remarks by mashing the accelerator to the floor aggressively. To accuse him of being some sad closeted homo because he didn't want to yammer details of his sex life to the whole world was ridiculous! He had been raised to be wary of outsiders, to show manners and reticence when in the company of those you did not know. He felt that standing up there talking about what were honestly embarrassing events was counter to every instruction he had been given in childhood.

A beige Mercedes W116 sat parked at the curb in front of the house on Leviticus Street. The fury that had been burning in his chest at the courthouse turned to a burn of dread, lodging heavily, leaving an acid sting in his mouth.

He turned down the engine, leaned his head forward to rest on the steering wheel for a moment, and whispered a quick mantra, fortifying himself before getting out to confront his mother.

.

Chapter Thirty

Mother

He heard the quiet voices as he stepped up to the hallway landing. That sunken feeling grew heavier as he walked toward the voices.

He walked through the meandering of L'Air duTemps in the hallway and approached the doorway. She sat regally in the leather lounge chair by the bay window, her stockinged legs folded at the knee. Her hands rested on the arms of the chair, gleaming nail lacquer that was a shining echo of her silver silk skirt and twinset.

Chance sat opposite her on the sofa. So intent was he in her aura and the nervous yammering that aura compelled from him, he did not notice that while she gave the illusion of bestowing her undivided attention, she did not give it. She fixed Babe with a piercing stare the moment he appeared. Her eyes were always dark but became darker when she was vexed, melding into her luminous skin, seeming to disappear.

Chance continued talking, seemingly unaware of Babe's entrance. She cut him off with a smooth erudite voice. "There you are, my dear. Your friend said that you'd be back soon. That you'd gone off to file papers at the... courthouse."

The slight pause before she pronounced the word courthouse was imperceptible to Chance, but Babe caught it. If a soul was able to wince, his did.

Chance stood, smiling broadly. "Babe, you didn't tell me you had a mom."

Babe put his keys on the mantel before he stooped to kiss her upraised cheek. The smell of expensive pressed powder tugged his memory. "I didn't know I needed to announce having a mother."

He laughed. "You know what I mean."

He bowed slightly then backed out of the room. "It was such a pleasure meeting you, ma'am. So classy. You have to come join us for dinner some time. Let me drive that benzo."

She applied a sedate smile, impermeable as the *Mona Lisa*. "It was a pleasure, my dear. I may take you up on your offer one of these days."

They were silent as the sound of Chance's boots thumped down the stairs, followed by the slam of the door. Babe took a seat across from her on the sofa. His eyes looked down at the table rather than at her. He knew she remained silent to increase his discomfort. The more discomforted Babe was, the more prone he would be to tell what she wanted to know. He tamped down on his agitation.

She seldom came to his house. Once, to give a cursory inspection shortly after they had moved in while Matthew was at work, communicating her displeasure with an expression and a finger dragged through imaginary dust.

He knew why she was here.

"Your...friend...tells me you had business to take care of at the courthouse."

This was an easy one. He could lie about this one since he had not filed the PFA. "Just applying for my parking-permit sticker."

She seemed momentarily satisfied with that answer. She was familiar with parking-permit stickers since she owned the house next door and had once lived on this street. He identified her next sentence for what it was—a bomb lobbed to put him off kilter.

"You look as though you've gained a bit." She watched him through fathomless eyes.

He was not able to remain unaffected by her remark. Despite knowing what she was trying to do, the feelings still came; childhood memories of scoldings, being told he was too fat, hands grabbing at his flesh, squeezing, and threats of fat camp.

"You think so? My body fat percentage is five. Any less would require that I be dead." A small victory, but he grudgingly conceded first round to her.

"So. You are renting to white people. Have you gotten that desperate?"

He winced. He had known that was coming. "I needed help with the mortgage. Matthew and me aren't together anymore. I couldn't swing it by myself."

She shook her head. "Matthew and *me*? Has your new tenant's presence been so deleterious so soon? There were no dependable colored persons in need of housing? You have always been so hasty, unwilling to exercise patience. You would have been better served to pass the word at a good church. Waited for inquiry by a nice, hardworking, colored young man. But not you. Rush. Rush. Always rushing."

He scolded himself for the grammatical error. That had been a sloppy mistake. One he could have saved for later. He wouldn't be given many concessions during the course of this interaction: he needed to use them astutely.

"Chance is okay. It's not a long-term arrangement. I needed to make sure I could make my note until I locate a more suitable option."

"You are renting out the apartment below. You did not arrange that the rental income for that unit would suffice without you needing to bring in a roommate? Where is your business sense?" Juanita hissed, low and seething, "And she is white too."

Minor victory, so he savored it silently. "She is Black."

He knew how much merit she placed on lighter gradations of color. He saw her pause, restrategize.

"On welfare, no doubt. Sitting outside. In the middle of the day." She shivered, a look of distaste etched on her darkly rouged face, "Smoking a cigarette."

"She has a little one. She's lost her husband. She's getting back on her feet. She's a nurse though. Yeah, she gets public assistance to help with her rent. All that matters to me is that the rent is paid on time. All the rest is none of my business."

Unlike Alise, Chance's payments were always late, and it was causing him financial stress. He made a mental note to have an in-depth discussion with him when he returned.

"It's like disease, my dear. If you surround yourself with undesirables, it infiltrates. You will become undesirable. You would think that it works the other way. That people become energized when exposed to those of a better caliber, but it doesn't. The undesirables infect you, tear down your property values, and infest everything you work hard for. You're going to find yourself in a bad way, and your father and I are not in a position to help you."

Mentioning his father made him angry.

"Just because people might be at a place where they aren't able to do what they had before doesn't make them undesirable. Like me, for instance. I'm at a crossroads right now. Newly single. I don't have the financial security that I had before. But I'm finding a way out. Learning to do things differently than what I did before. That's all that's happening with those people you say are undesirable."

Juanita laughed—slight, belittling. She stood, looking out the window to the street below. "Do you know how hard it is to struggle out of a difficult situation? You won't be able to do it if you think bringing in people you don't even know is the solution."

"How's Chance an undesirable? He's got a job, goes to it every day. Just like I do."

She kept looking out the window even though he knew she wanted to see the impact her words were having on him.

"Do you think I haven't seen that sort before? With his nigger-friendly hair and his nigger-friendly clothes, wanting to take the 'Benz' out for a drive. That sort is one generation removed from the trailer park. He is no friend to you. That sort thinks everything you have should belong to them. That you took it with government incentives and diversity initiatives."

Babe leaned forward, watching her sharp shoulder blades through the fabric of her twinset. He had always admired her erect posture. He laughed. "I don't have anything he could possibly want, believe me."

She turned to him and walked close. "They don't see things the same way you do. What you see as having little value, they long for because they don't think we should have anything at all."

"Come on, Mother. When you were coming up, things were different. People aren't like that anymore."

"They take everything. Your great grandmother's restaurant. The first one by a Black woman on the Main Line. Doing well. Too well. And they ran her out. Made her too scared to keep going."

He spoke tersely, dismissively, "You told me all about it."

She continued, undeterred, "Took our land. Gave us land nobody else wanted. My daddy worked and slaved his whole life, gave his life savings for that land, and when they decided that land was now valuable, decided they could make money turning it to resort property, the land was deemed 'eminent domain.' Dragged him off his own property and threw him in jail for refusing to leave it."

He took her hand. "I know this. But we can't change what happened in the past. You want me to go around thinking every white person is my enemy, like they're going to do me harm?"

She took her arm back. "If you're smart."

"Well, I can't do that, Mother. I can't live walking around with all that hatred. You know how heavy it is to carry that kind of hatred?"

"Yes. I carry it every day. And my load weighs far more than yours."

"We don't even know if all those stories are true. Nobody ever shows any property records, land deeds. All we have is Granddaddy's say-so. And he died in an insane asylum. He was always sick since I can remember."

She backed off, appearing stung. "I never thought I'd hear this nonsense from my own child. When you give birth to a baby, a son, no less, and you first look into his eyes, you never know how they turn on you."

His laugh was like a bark. "What are you saying? You didn't give birth to me. Your sister did."

Swift and furious, she slapped him across his face with wrath and precision. He felt his teeth tear into the interior of his mouth, tasted the iron of blood. She stepped back with a sweep of silk, her perfume growing heavy as rage mixed into her sweat glands.

The scent nudged him, shifted his memory, reminded him of something he could not quite form into a concrete thought.

Juanita took a kerchief from her handbag, dabbed her forehead. "I apologize for that. But I will not be disrespected. Not after all I've done for you."

Babe felt the sting left from her rings on the bones of his face. He spoke into his lap. "It was not my intention to disrespect you, Mother."

She strode again to the window, her hands clasped behind her back. "It has been brought to our attention that you have had some interaction with the police here."

Ah, the true reason for this visit. Fear that he might be tarnishing the family reputation. "There was a minor skirmish about the dog next door jumping the fence. You know they have that pit bull next door."

She tsked, murmured about the influx of undesireables taking over the neighborhood. "Still in all. Your name was tied to these calls. You know this sort of thing does not reflect on your father in a positive light. We have a responsibility."

"It will not happen again."

"Your father was the first colored man to work for the force. We do not expect you to bring embarrassment to him. To us."

"Father retired many years ago. He doesn't even interact with the force. He's tucked away in a home"— Babe deliberated on whether he would get away with adding to his statement, took the leap, lightening the impact by replacing his original instinct to say *just like my mom*—"too."

Juanita turned, her urge to lash out was evident. Babe took satisfaction in that.

"We will always have the obligation to uphold your father's good name and give honor to what he had to sacrifice by taking that position. Do you understand what it means to be first? What you have to endure in this world, where we have to be twice as good to get half as much? You have no idea what your father suffered. How he was disrespected every day when all he wanted to do was protect and serve like all his colleagues."

He stood still. "Yes, ma'am."

She tucked her kerchief back into her handbag and gathered herself to leave.

"This world is not easy for our kind. We have to compete for every advantage, and even then, they let you know that you don't measure up. If you drop your guard, they will look at it as weakness. Goodbye, son."

The cloud of scent left in her wake repulsed him, made his stomach turn in knots. He stood, rushed to the kitchen, and stood over the sink, breathing heavily.

Babe turned from the sink in a fog of distraction, then walked over to the table and slumped heavily into a chair. Absently, he reached for the saltshaker, then poured the crystals into his hand, admiring the way they captured and refracted the light from the sun shining through the window. He brought his hand to his mouth and licked, feeling the salt meld into his tongue. He poured more salt and brought it to his mouth. It wasn't enough. He removed the cap on the shaker, poured a small tuft into his saliva-slicked palm, and rubbed it hard into the back of his mouth, and waited for that satisfying feeling of abrasion, the tearing of flesh as numbness, finally began to swell his tongue and he could feel his lips began to split, spreading an elemental taste of earth and iron through his nasal and his buccal cavity.

Chapter Thirty-One

Rueben's Bullying

Alise had gotten by with three to four hours of sleep for many years. As a nurse, sleep deprivation was as common as sixteen-hour shifts, usually a package set. But it was creeping through her bones as a constant weariness. She continued going through the motions of her self-imposed schedule, but there was a minute of reluctance at the periphery of her consciousness when she rose each morning at four.

She would watch her son sleeping beside her, or if he had decided to sleep downstairs, she'd go down there and pull the comforters back up from where they had been tossed during the night. Pretzel would stir and rise from Rueben's heat to follow at her heels as she scooped Puff Puff up into her arms to rub her soft fur.

They'd all go to the kitchen, and she'd set the coffeemaker to brew. The trio'd sit on the back porch for a smoke while waiting. Pretzel and Puff Puff would forage in the outside pet bowls, nibbling at whatever remains were there, knowing they would have to wait for Rueben to wake before they were fed fresh food and water.

She'd finish her cigarette, flick the butt into the grass, and go back inside to the bathroom right inside the door to wash her face and underarms. She loved the smell of fresh-milled soap. This small indulgence she didn't share with Rueben. She had to stand on the toilet seat to reach it way up there, tucked behind rolls of extra toilet paper. Hiding soap was silly, but she got a selfish satisfaction when she used it. The irony of hiding soap was that the deodorant soap, sitting in plain view in the soap dish, intended for Rueben's use, wasn't being used either.

Alise raised her arms to dab on deodorant. She ignored electric jabs of weariness intermittently flashing, paid no heed to what her bones were trying to tell her. She gazed in the mirror, dabbed on liner and lipstick. Flinging back her braids, she thanked Ricky for simpler hair maintenance since she had let him give her micros.

Back in her room, she pulled on a pair of tights while sitting on the chair followed by one of Rueben's T-shirts. She liked the roominess, plus she liked to smell him while on her morning errands.

She slipped into a jacket and grabbed her large duffel bag and folding cart. As she walked through the hall to the front porch, she looked out at Leviticus Street, cast in the gray of a blue moon. Birds were beginning to sing. She had at least an hour and a half before most people would be out on the streets heading to work. She liked to do her morning walk before everyone was out. She didn't like the thought of being gawked at while she walked briskly, raising her arms, swinging them in wide arcs so that her heart rate would be properly elevated.

She had been taking morning walks for several months but had yet to see results in her waist size. She would probably need to pick up the pace, move up to jogging. Each month she told herself she would add running the following month.

According to *Shape Magazine*, she needed to change her diet and add more vegetables and lean proteins. But she felt guilty when she didn't make the foods Rueben enjoyed. He was so happy when she prepared macaroni and cheese or potato salad. His happiness was the only reward she needed.

Not that Alise always prepared such things for him. There were dangers in doing that. Most times she didn't feel like going through the ritual of preparing an elaborate meal. Many times, she didn't make it to the supermarket to get all the ingredients for the meal she had in mind and didn't have the energy to go pick them up last minute. Rueben was just as satisfied with microwave bacon or chicken nuggets. So, she'd cut cheddar cheese into cubes, pour a glass of Juicy Juice, and go back to bed.

Alise had wanted to do everything different this time. She had thought this time might be better without Kendall there, interfering in the way she wanted to do things. But she was losing control. Things were falling into the same pattern as before where dreadful things had happened.

She had been aware kids were making fun of Rueben far before they had gotten the phone call from the school. Of course she knew. Rueben used to tell her everything.

She would wake him each morning, peeking her head through the door, in a singsong voice, "Sweetie, don't you feel like getting up now?"

He acted differently now. He used to fling back the coverlet at her voice, ready to find his breakfast. That had changed. He would stay in bed, making her come to sit on the edge to rub his shoulder.

"I don't want to go to school, Mama. I don't feel good."

She'd take his temperature or switch his breakfast to crackers and broth and let him lie in bed all day, informing the superintendent that Rueben would not be in for a few days. But those sick days began to accumulate, absent days became weeks.

"Sweetie, don't you like school? You used to like school so much, learning about numbers and learning to write."

And he had told her about the names. About the snickering and pointing. They'd even made up a nursery rhyme about smelling like onions. They called him Funyuns. People in the neighborhood had seen him outside playing in only his underpants. The kids called him SpongeBob Shitpants.

Kendall had scolded, saying he had told her over and over about letting a boy his age run around in his skivvies. Her eyes saw him as a baby. Her baby. But he told her she needed to see him through the world's eyes. Especially as a Black boy. He told her she had no idea of what she had wrought, no idea what he would have to navigate as he moved toward adulthood, and the scaffolding for what adulthood would be like had started from the moment Rueben took his first breath.

She should have known that, seen that, when the doctors had first swarmed in and changed him from darling baby boy to developmentally impaired. But she had ignored the warnings, determined to make the world right.

Kendall had been furious to discover she continued to let Rueben outside in his underwear. Furious she had kept him home from school. She'd told him that it was the best choice, safer than her first, primal instinct: to go to the school and put her hands on every cruelhearted, mean-spirited little monster and hurt them the way they had hurt Rueben.

Kendall had had his own solution. Each evening when he came home from work, he'd take Rueben out back to the garage and teach him how to fight. Showed him how to stand with his feet spread, how to balance his weight so he could move swiftly. Taught him how to arrange his hands into a fist and how to hold them in front of his face for protection.

"You're a big boy. Use your size to your advantage. And if the boxing isn't working, bite a motherfucker. We know you like to eat. Pretend it ain't nothing but a Quarter Pounder with cheese."

Alise had been horrified. The idea of her child getting into fights worried her. What if he got injured? She was much more comfortable with the thought of fighting them herself but realized if she were thrown in jail there'd be no one to take care of Rueben.

She'd been even more terrified when she walked out to the garage one day, to tell them that dinner was ready, and Kendall stood behind Rueben, showing him how to pull back the trigger on a gun.

"He's a baby!" she had wailed.

"How old were your brothers when they learned to shoot? What'd you tell me?"

"That's beside the point. This is a different world than that. We are in a different place."

"Oh yeah? We still live in cracker territory. And all you crackers learn to shoot while you're still in diapers. Meanwhile, all the niggers living in the city know nothing about this. They running around listening to gangsta rap, watching videos where niggers pretend to be down, but nobody knows shit about really being able to protect yourself. We're all sitting out here like fish in a barrel."

Alise had not heard anything he had said. He had called her a cracker. That was what he thought of her. Her heart grew heavy with it. Despite everything they had endured together, what they had shared, despite bringing a child into the world together, he saw her as the enemy.

She'd reminded him the taunts made no mention of race. Not everything had to do with race. She told him he carried his race around his shoulders like an albatross, standing at the ready to use it for every negative event in his life. He stared at her, incredulous at her stupidity.

She had known her marriage was gasping its last breath.

It was what followed—the calls from the superintendent about Rueben's stealing of food— that brought her marriage to an end.

Alise had memorized which streets corresponded with which days and proceeded in the proper direction accordingly. This was collection day for Marshall Street. She unfolded her cart and rolled it through the alley behind Marshall, keeping an eye out for things of value. She spotted an old Mr. Coffee sitting on the ground beside a can where a stray cat foraged for food. She cooed soothingly at the cat, nudged its head with a finger carefully, lest she try to scratch in self-defense.

The coffee machine was shot, but the carafe attached was in good shape and had no nicks. She placed it gingerly inside the shredded paper in her duffle bag and moved on to the next pile where she spotted an old perambulator. It was a little worse for wear. The fabric on the sunshade was tattered and torn. But she could see the beauty beneath its faded exterior. She appreciated the majesty of craftsmanship from an era long gone in the old curves and bespoke wheels. She pushed it to see if it still rolled.

Alise glanced at her watch. She needed to get back home before Rueben awoke, so they could go over his lesson plans. She had about an hour.

It always gave her a comforting feeling, this morning ritual. It soothed her to know that she might be able to find a space for things people had thrown away. She placed the bag with the coffeemaker into the carriage and moved along, searching for other things that had been cast aside by foolish people.

Chapter Thirty-Two

Diana Ross Tubman

The baseline from Bjork singing "Big Time Sensuality" rattled the windows of not just Babe's house but shook foundations of several connected buildings, communicating to observant neighbors that the inhabitants of 535 Leviticus were preparing for a night on the town. Just as worshippers of Islam visit Mecca to realign their spiritual vibrations, each year, in celebration of his birthday, Robby conducted an annual visit to his Mecca: Diana Ross.

Babe peered at his reflection with satisfaction. He wore trim, navy silk pants, the wide waistband sharply nipping his waist, and a low-cut gauze Gautier shirt of deep burgundy. He resisted the urge to straighten the hem of his pants, which fell sloppily around black croc ankle boots, Max's advice on how to properly wear boots ringing in his ear. His hair was wrapped in a black band that towered in a sloppy pillage above his head.

As if on cue, Chance came out of his bedroom, wearing a midriff leather vest and baggy jeans and spun around for Babe to admire.

Babe rolled his eyes, screaming over the music, "What the hell are you doing? Go back and change."

Chance stopped midspin. "What for? This shit is poppin'! Why are you dressed like an undertaker?"

"We aren't going trolling for dick. We're going to a concert. You don't dress like a slutbucket to go see Diana Ross. Show some couth."

"I don't know why I'm going to see Diana False anyway. She ain't had a poppin' tune since 'I'm Coming Out.'"

"You going because the ticket was free, bitch. You can stay the fuck home, you know. Don't nobody care if you do. But if you're going, go back and change!"

"Free tickets because don't nobody want to go. Why she get all these tickets before she checked to see if people wanted to go?"

Babe shrugged, then ran into the living room to turn down the music. "Robby does this every year. Gets tickets and rents a limo to go to the Diana Ross concert at the Music Fair. It's how he celebrates his birthday."

Chance went into his room, leaving the door open as he rummaged through trunks to find something suitable. "And does his boyfriend bail every year? Or just this time? I don't see why I'm changing. I spent a grip on that gear."

"You spent a grip when you haven't paid me rent for this month? I need you to pay me on time. I don't like to do late payments. I never pay my mortgage late. That's the first thing I make sure to take care of."

"You know you'll get it. It's not like you're hurting for the money."

"How do you know if I'm hurting or not? I brought you in here so that I wouldn't fall behind on my mortgage, and you are supposed to be making things easier. Instead, you are causing me stress, worrying about when you're going to pay me each month."

"I'll get it to you next pay, promise."

There was a knock at the door. Babe turned to answer. "Hurry up. That must be the limo."

At the landing, Babe opened the door to find Rueben on the other side.

"Hey. Everything all right? Where's your mom?"

"She's at work. You got something to eat?"

"We're about to head out. I don't have time to fix you anything. Come on up, get some fruit or something."

A search of the kitchen revealed that there was little food available: container of Quaker Oats, containers of whey protein, and skim milk. Rueben was crestfallen. "This don't look good."

He laughed. "It is kinda pitiful, right? Hey. Why don't you come with us to the concert? We can pick up something to eat there. What time's your mom get off?"

Rueben's eyes brightened. "She'll be gone all night."

"You have her work number? Maybe you can call her and ask. Where's she work?"

"I don't have her number. She can't get calls while she's on the floor."

"I can write a letter explaining where we are. You think she'll be okay with that?"

Rueben shook his head excitedly. "I never been to a concert before. What's a concert?"

"It's where somebody sings songs or performs music. Do you know who Diana Ross is?"

"I seen her on the radio?"

He was wearing an old T-shirt and basketball shorts. "Okay. Well. First, we need to find something for you to wear. Come upstairs with me. I probably have something that can fit you. It won't be the best, but it will do."

Rueben followed Babe upstairs. Chance came out into the hallway wearing a pair of chinos and a button-down checked shirt. "How's this? Am I sufficiently devoid of all individuality to your satisfaction? What's this?"

"I'm Rueben."

He snorted. "No shit. What's he doing here? We got to get going."

"He's coming with. Do you have anything that might fit him?"

Chance's eyes bugged out. "What are we running here? A convoy? A shelter? How many tickets did that cokehead buy where you be inviting people all willy-nilly?"

"I like Coke," Rueben informed them.

"You got something he can wear or not?"

"Let me see. I'm sure I stole some trade clothes from Jase and Raheem when I moved out." Chance turned back to his room to hunt for suitable clothing.

Babe pushed Rueben into the bathroom.

"Listen, buddy. You smell. You are too old to be running around smelly like this. Plus, you are bigger, so you have to wash up every day, especially get your underarms and your feet. And your crotch." Babe handed him a washcloth and bar of soap.

"Plus, we are men. Men stink. You use deodorant?"

Rueben shook his head. Babe held a stick of deodorant in front of him, held Rueben's wrist, and lifted his arm over his head to show him how to apply it. "After you wash up, you swipe this under your arms so it can help you to stay nice smelling. Got it?"

The smell burst from the container, clear and brilliant like fruit, unfurling pleasantly into the room like a newly peeled orange.

"So, I'm going to give you a second to wash up here and go see what we can find for you to wear. Here's a towel. Let me know when you're finished. And hurry up. We can't be late!"

Rueben took off his shirt and then turned on the tap. As the water gurgled noisily over the drain, he contemplated his reflection in the mirror. His flesh was generous and brown with folds beneath his chest where it gathered near his underarms. He raised his arm and moved his nose to sniff his armpit. He was murky and astringent. He was accustomed to this smell. It had not been notable to him before now. Now, Babe had identified this smell as something that stunk and was undesirable.

He rubbed the deodorant under his arm, feeling it drag at his flesh, smelling the notes released as it moved across his skin. He put his shirt back on as Chance flung open the door, holding a large red shirt.

"Hey. This should fit you. Put this on."

Rueben took the shirt from him and held it to his chest. Chance eyed him suspiciously, sniffing. "Did you wash?"

Rueben shook his head in rapid succession.

Chance moved closer, sniffing.

"Nah, my man. You didn't wash. You still ripe."

Babe walked to the doorway. "All done?"

Chance said, "No. He perpetrating. He ain't wash. He bird bathed it."

Babe entered the room, holding a pair of pants.

"Listen. You need to wash up for real. Now you can do it on your own if you are able to be trusted to do that, or you need me to do it for you? You can't be going in front of all these white people smelling like a runaway slave. Making me look bad."

"Here we go with the white/Black shit again."

"What if Diana wants to reach out and touch somebody's hand, and that hand turns out to be yours, and you stinking like an onion patch? You screwed up your chance to be in the presence of greatness."

Chance rolled his eyes. "I don't think Miss False will be touching down anywhere near this group."

"Shut up. So, Rueben. What's it going to be? Can I trust you, or do you need me to do it for you?"

"You can trust me."

He seemed to swell with pride at Babe's approval.

Babe took the washcloth from him, ran it beneath the hot water, scrubbed the soap onto the cloth until a frothy lather developed, then handed it back to him. "Get under them arms now."

Chance shook his head, walked to the tub, and turned on the water. "Listen. I know we don't have much time. But that funk needs to get immersed under some water. A whore's bath is not going to cut it."

Babe scanned the boy in his entirety. "You right. You gonna need to take a quick shower, hit your privates, wash your ass."

Chance took the deodorant from him. "And what's this girly deodorant? You know his Black ass needs Mitchum. This is a full-grown niggah."

Chance went back to his room to get the deodorant, and Babe closed the door behind him.

Once Rueben cleaned up and changed into fresh clothes, he took the three-sentence note Babe had scribbled onto a scrap of paper downstairs and hastily threw it onto the low coffee table in the living room. As he rushed back outside, the note was swept up on the breeze created by his movement and drifted onto the floor. Rueben heard the footsteps descending the stairs and excitedly joined Babe and Chance as they walked out to the gleaming, black Town Car idling at the curb. Miss Imogene rose from her lawn chair to stare down the street as they climbed inside.

Rueben and Chance ogled the interior in awe. It was like a living room on wheels with a wet bar, a television with amplifier, and tufted seats like a sectional sofa. Chance flung himself on the far side and slid down to the shag carpet on the floor.

"Whoa, man. We ballin' or what? I feel like Lil' Kim about to get a train run on her or some shit!"

"You would. Settle down, would you? It's a Lincoln. It's not like we in an Escalade or something."

Rueben discovered a panel behind which was a tray of nuts, cookies, and a minifridge stocked with water, sodas, mixers, and juices. "Wow. Can I take some nuts?"

"Sure." Babe leaned over, "What they got in there? Any candy? I want some chocolate."

Ricky glided down from the porch. He wore a backless, black, sequin top and tight black denim pants. Oversized sunglasses covered his heavily mascaraed eyes and a demure matte, berry color stained his lips. His hair was a tight cap of fingerwaves around his perfectly shaped head. Small diamonds gleamed from his ear.

"Look at you," Babe said as he entered the car.

"Are those real diamonds?" Chance asked.

"Miss Thing, everything the doll do is real." Ricky perched beside Babe, casting a sunglass-shaded glance at Rueben. "What have we here? White girl trolling schoolyards for her dates?"

"This is Rueben. Y'all had all these extra tix, and Alise is at work, so I invited him along."

Ricky shook his head. "That's a lot of bacon, honey. What she feeding the boy? Hog maws and fatback?"

"Ain't he healthy? We'll be back in a few hours, so I figure we'll make it back before his mom gets off work, so we should be fine."

Ricky shook his head. "You know you asking for trouble. You gone take girlfriend's son out with a gaggle of faggots. To see Diana Ross, no less. You know they always thinking we trying to recruit. This is messy to me, *B*. Is this bitch a shit starter? Cause if she is, you are lighting the fuse for some shit."

"She's a quiet girl. Never hear a peep from her."

Ricky laughed, peering out the window as Robby walked to the car. "Would you take a gander at this mattress-ass bitch. Is she giving you a Dominique Devereux, Detroit edition? And sweating already when all she done did was pump down three flights of stairs. Looking like a furnace in spring."

Robby was resplendent in white. He was a pilgrim dressed to symbolize purity in preparation of his personal hajj. He wore a wide brimmed hat, and a voluminous top fell to his knees with large, cloth-covered buttons. His palazzo pants were the same shade and fabric as his top, and he wore white silk espadrilles. He breezed into the car like a movie star.

"Well, look at you," Babe repeated.

"You better work, bitch!" Ricky screamed, and he and Robby began laughing, leaning against each other and high-fiving. "You make me sick. Always trying to outdo the doll. No, ma'am. I won't have it!"

"Darling, this is my night. It's all about Robby and the fabulosity attached to being Robby this evening. And don't you motherfucking forget it..."

Robby stopped short as he spotted Rueben sitting next to Babe. "What the devil?"

"Hi, Mister. I'm Rueben. Thank you for letting me ride in your nice car. Are you famous or something?"

"He's with me," said Babe.

"Is he famous?" Ricky quipped, "Darling, you don't know the half of it."

"Very well," Robby sighed. Then, toward the uniformed driver at the head of the car he shouted, "Driver! Onward! We must first fleece down Miss Marshall Street and we absolutely cannot be late for the grand dame, so let's make haste!"

"Bitch, why we going down Marshall?" Ricky demanded. "You trying to flex for the masses?"

"I have to make a stop at Anna Julia's."

"You going to cop? Now?" Babe asked.

"Chile, we don't need to be going to Animal Julia's. You are going to ruin your night before it even starts."

"Listen. This is my birthday, and nobody's is going to tell me how to celebrate it. Anybody that has a problem can hop on out."

"So you think you're going to carry that on in through security at the Music Fair? Are you retarded?"

"I know how to be subdued. Everybody chill. Damn."

As they rode up Dekalb, Robby stared out the window, gasping melodramatically. "Oh, I hate driving on this street. It's so treacherous, all this traffic."

Ricky said, "Bitch, ain't this where you crashed up your car one week after you got it?"

He leaned back against the upholstery, bringing the back of his hand to his forehead with an anguished groan. "I never drove again after that! My head went through the windshield! I could have been maimed forever!"

"Whyn't you stop over dramatizing, Miss One? You had three stitches on your forehead."

Rueben was wide-eyed. "I'm glad you're okay, Mister."

Robby grimaced distractedly. "A child that has compassion. How droll."

Ricky continued, loudly, "Mister? Now *that's* a kee kee. The only thing that was maimed was perhaps your cognitive fortitude, help, no help."

"Shut the fuck up," Robby snapped. "My first salon was on this street. One time this homeless woman had passed out right in the middle of the street! And you know how cars be cutting through Dekalb. Well, Miss Rock, that was back when she used to come to me to bump her head. She had her regular Friday 9 a.m. set up. I wouldn't open that early for anybody else, but Miss Rock needed her head bumped *early*, bitch, cause she had shit to do, m'kay.

"So anyway, she sees this bum sprawled on the street. She parks her car in the middle of the street, right in front of the woman..."

Ricky asked, "Did she have her Mer? You know that skunk *lives* to be behind the wheel of Miss Mercedes. Like rich white cunt."

"You *know* she was Mercedes *down,* bitch. And bitch, she crawled out of that Benz in this motherfucking full-length black sable coat, and she goes over to this woman in the street, and she helps her to the curb."

Babe frowned, this story refracting differently in his memory, flashing an image from the back seat of the car. "I don't think that's how that happened..."

"Now mind you, she's dead center on Dekalb. Traffic is backed all the fuck up, cars hooting, Negroes screaming. Miss Rock pays them dust! She brings this skunk *into my shop*. And orders her something to eat before sending her on her way."

By this time, they were in front of Anna Julia's house. Robby bounced out and into the house while Ricky flicked nails at her from the window. "Hi, Animal. You looking fab, girl."

Anna Julia was a dark-skinned Haitian woman wearing braids with brightly colored beads swinging around her head. She had a stooped posture and broad features.

Babe said, "Animal Julia, is right. That bitch look like a silverback go-rilla."

Chance and Rueben laughed. Chance said, "She does!"

Ricky said, "So you saying Black people look like monkeys? *B*, you hear this racist-ass shit?"

Chance said, "I'm saying what y'all were saying!"

Babe said, "We can say it, you can't. What if we said your mom looked like a pelican? That wouldn't be right to say because white bitches look like pelicans."

"What the hell are you talking about? So y'all think white women look like pelicans?"

Ricky laughed. "You know you wrong, right? Pelican-ass bitches!"

Rueben said, "Does my mom look like a pelican? What's a pelican?"

"Your argument makes no sense, Babe. Because by that logic, you're saying *you* think Black people look like monkeys. But that I'm racist if I say that, but you can say it,"

"I don't make the rules."

Ricky said, "Animal Julia is not representative of the entire race. But, by happenstance, she so happens to resemble a trope that has historically been used as a way to denigrate Black people."

"I don't know what the hell you're saying."

"I'm saying Animal Julia looks like a goddamn ape."

Rueben thought of how he might change the atmosphere in the suddenly overheated vehicle, "Does everybody want to hear a story?"

"What do you want to tell us?"

"I know about the sleeping princess. How she slept for years and years, waiting for her knight on his white horse to come and save her."

"Sleeping Beauty?"

He nodded, "She was the fairest damsel in the land. With long yellow hair and beautiful white skin..."

Ricky said, "You ever seen a bitch like that around here? Because I sure haven't."

Babe cut an angry glance at Ricky, who was oblivious. "Language."

"No. Because she's a princess. She's not like you and me. And besides, it's a fairytale. It's not real life."

Ricky said, "Well, what do you think fairytales are supposed to be, sweetie? They are stories that explain our life or teach us about who we are as human beings. What's the story about some woman high off her ass on Ativan tell us about life?"

Chance cracked, "That it's better to sell your scripts than to take them?"

Babe interjected. "I have a story for you, Rueben. About a Black woman that used to fall asleep, like your Sleeping Beauty did, but she would fall asleep in the middle of the day like while she was doing her chores; sweeping, gathering firewood... And like Sleeping Beauty, she lived under a curse, but instead of waiting for a man to come to her rescue, she rescued herself and came back and rescued other people that were also living under a curse. The only thing is, this isn't a fairytale. This was a real woman that lived long ago. She was Black, like you and me. Have you ever heard of Harriet Tubman?"

"She was a real person?" Rueben was perplexed. "I read in my history lessons how people came here so they could worship God. And I read about immigrants came here and some of them had to work to pay for getting here, but I never heard about a real-life woman."

Ricky squawked, and Babe shushed him with a wave of his hand. "Yes, some people, called indentured servants, usually Irish or German, had to work to pay back what someone paid for their passage on ships to travel from their lands to get here. Those people had to work for maybe seven years to pay off their debts. After that though, they were free."

Ricky said, "But people like us, Black people, they were stolen from their homes in Africa and forced to come here in chains. They didn't get to work off any debt. Those people weren't immigrants. They were slaves. They were forced to work every day from sunup to sundown. Very hard work, work that sometimes killed them. And they were forced to do that for the rest of their lives."

Rueben remembered that word, slave, from when he was pretending to wash himself at the sink, and Babe had said he didn't want to smell like a runaway slave, so he knew it was not a good thing.

Babe said, "So anyway, there was a slave woman called Harriet. She had this thing called narcolepsy where she would suddenly fall asleep in the middle of doing something. They say this happened because the White man that owned her hit her in the head with a hot iron because she wasn't working fast enough. Slaves used to be beaten when they didn't listen or when they didn't work fast enough."

While they waited for Robby to complete his business, Babe and Ricky told the story of the runaway slave that ran to freedom under cover of night, using the moss on the north sides of trees to guide her. Although they were telling the story to Rueben, Chance seemed to be just as spellbound sitting beside him with wide eyes.

Rueben learned there were real live princesses. And they weren't white women with yellow flowing hair, but they were brown like he was. He listened in awe about the unassuming Black woman of small stature coming back to the South after her escape, a gun tucked into her clothing for protection and to discourage any fellow runners from turning back.

Rueben sat silent during the rest of the drive, immersed in imaginings of a Black woman hiding from 'paddy-rollers', running from state to state.

Rueben didn't hear the loud voices arguing when Robby returned to the limo. Or Babe urging Robby to wait until later, so that Rueben wouldn't be witness. Or even Babe ordering the driver to stop the car, stepping out to guide him to the seat beside the man in the front seat, wearing the big black cap. He anxiously waited for Babe to lower the partition window so he could hear the rest of the tale of the outlaw runaway.

Trees and billboards jettisoned past the window as the limo shuttled across the bridge into King of Prussia. Rueben imagined Black Moses, walking across this bridge one hundred times over, on her way to freedom with her life in danger every step, with wanted posters offering hundreds of dollars for her capture, dead or alive. He imagined what she might have looked like. Maybe she looked like Mama.

When he saw the beautiful woman in a shining red gown with arms spread wide like an exotic bird, sequins gleaming, he imagined Black Moses was a beautiful cocoa brown with hair flowing long and full to her waist, with large doe eyes and eyelashes like blinking tarantulas; a smile beaming from gleaming red lips, walking through the crowd of worshipful people as she supervised their hand-holding and sang about love and unity. He wondered if Diana Ross had a gun hidden in the folds of her gown.

Chapter Thirty-Three

Rueben Missing

It was sundown when Alise got the old woman into bed and went back home to get dinner together for Rueben. She should have run over to prepare his meal sooner: she had become so immersed in the ritual of caring for the woman and with regaling her with stories from her past that she had ignored her parental obligation in favor of her own personal desires.

Her heart only pattered lightly in her chest when she opened the door upon a darkened interior. She did not fully panic at that time. She figured Rueben had fallen asleep before the sun had gone down. He was frightened of the dark, but if he had gone to sleep first, she was glad she had arrived before he awoke to darkness. She flipped on the light switch and walked through the light nudge Puff Puff made at her feet.

She descended to the lower level and walked past the mounds of accumulated detritus, then circled the stacks of books, newspapers, and recovered items, whispering his name. When she came upon the mattress in the furthest corner with only Pretzel snoozing at its center, her whisper turned to a scream.

She spun around, arms outstretched and toppled piles of magazines. She slipped as she ran through glossy pages, flinging clothing from drooping clotheslines, then ran back upstairs with the dog at her heels.

She threw open the back door, revealing an empty porch. Mitzi barreled from the open doorway next door and stood on her back paws to lean upon the fence, and Alise patted the giant skull absently, trying to calm herself. Panic would not help. She walked through the back gate, down the alleyway running perpendicular to Leviticus Street. Trash cans stood like sentries at the back of each gate. None had been disturbed. There was no sign Rueben had come through this alley. She walked down its length, looking in both directions, sweat beading her brow.

Alise scolded herself for leaving him alone. For not putting padlocks on the doors. For being so foolish, so careless.

She ran back inside and out the front door to the hallway then banged on Babe's door. Perhaps they had seen him. They had seen him before out in the backyard.

Alise should have known then, when they had seen him outside, she needed to be more vigilant. She was so tired. All the years of keeping everything to herself. Her tiredness had led to carelessness. And now she might have lost him, the only thing she had left after her life had fallen apart.

A sob escaped her throat, wet with mourning.

She sat on the porch. Told herself he would come back. She needed to be patient. Sit there and wait for him to return. Kids wandered off all the time. Maybe he had gone to the store around the corner in search of something to eat.

What if he was wandering and was found by the police? She thought about what she'd say to them. How she'd explain herself. He wouldn't go to the police of his own volition. She had taught him the folly of getting attention from the police.

Maybe she should call the police. Report him missing. They would be able to find him much quicker than she could.

No. She couldn't do that. She'd have to wait. He would come home. It was the only thing he knew. She was all he had. She had made sure of that.

Chapter Thirty-Four

After the Concert

The early evening crowd at the Midtown was slightly less debaucherous than the late night crew. Medical students and doctors from the university across the street interspersed with the transexuals and ballroom kids. Geriatric loners perused daily newspapers over a cup of tepid coffee, and families took a break from visiting hospitalized relatives while forlornly flipping the pages of greasy bifold menus.

Rueben and Babe sat at a corner booth. Rueben was eating a stack of french toast with gusto while the early evening crowd meandered through. Ever vigilant, Babe kept a wary eye on the plate-glass window in case of a Matthew sighting, always prepared to handle the unexpected. The rest of the group were in the ladies' room where they had been for at least fifteen minutes, sampling Anna Julia's coke.

A woman breezed past to the ladies' room door, jiggled the handle, and banged furiously. "Come on outta there, bitch!"

Rueben giggled as he wiped syrup from his lips. "This is a funny place."

Babe rolled his eyes, sipping his soda. "Yeah. It's a riot."

There was a loud wave of greetings as Miss Ida entered through the front door with a flimsy trench coat over her uniform. Max was behind her, holding a flowered bag Babe assumed was for her.

"Pipe down. I'm not on the clock yet." She yelled at the room. She bustled through toward the back of the building.

Babe caught Max's eye and nodded as Max approached and then sat down with an expansive grin.

"Hey. What you doing here on a Friday night?" Babe asked.

"Miss Ida was my last customer of the night, so I drove her in to work."

"It's like you're her son or something."

"She's too old to be taking the bus down here. Hell, she's too old to be working here. But what you going to do?" Max glanced across the table. "This your little brother?"

"Neighbor's kid. We took him to the Diana Ross concert."

"Hello, man." Max reached out a hand and Ruben shook it.

"I wish I was his brother," Rueben managed to say between gusty slurps of soda.

"We? You on a date?"

Babe laughed. "Jealous? Chance and some friends are with us. They're in the toilet."

"What if I am jealous?"

"I've been to your house twice. Both times you've had some young boy there—not the same one either—just laying around."

"I told you, Babe. Those are my slaves. I am a busy person. I have little time to do errands. I'm always working, and when I'm not, I'm taking care of my mom. These chickenheads all out here trying to land a sugar daddy 'cause they don't want to work. So, I have slaves that clean my house, cook for me, and give me some pleasure. I give them money, buy them a bag of socks, or new Adidas; they give me what I need, no muss no fuss. They aren't like you."

Rueben frowned. That word again. "Slaves was from olden days."

Max laughed.

"And how am I?"

"You get your ass up every day and go to work. You might not like it, but you do it. You aren't running around trying to find a payout because you nice to look at. You're polite. You care about people." Max laughed again. "You're here with your neighbor kid that you took to see Diana Ross. Them slaves don't mean nothing. They know their position."

A shadow fell over the table, Chance swaying above them. "Oh, shit. I didn't know we was going to be picking up strays."

Max narrowed his golden eyes. "I know you ain't talking about strays, Smutbucket..."

Chance sat beside Babe, speaking sotto voice, "I think you better go check on your peeps. They look like they need help."

Babe glanced apologetically at Max as he stood.

Max said, "Need help?"

"No, I got it."

Babe's first response upon walking into the ladies' room was fury. The restroom was neat and clean, smelling of lavender. The floors were dry. There was a small purple lounge chair tucked in a corner where Ricky sat with his legs crossed, one foot kicking agitatedly.

"Why the fuck do the women get to have a nice toilet while the men's room is covered with piss and shit and hypodermic needles!"

Ricky said, "Because, darling, we are ladies, and we know how to take care of our shit! We don't crap on the floor and fling excrement on the walls like the trades be doing. That's why I use this facility because, girl, I do not intend to catch lock jaw off the doorknobs of the men's room. Miss Robby is girfed for points, girl. Girfed. Miss Thing! Come on out!"

A low murmur rumbled behind the stall. Babe pushed at the door with a gingerly applied finger. Robby was sitting on the toilet lid, his back facing Babe, his shoulders hunched. As the door opened, Babe could hear what sounded like Robby humming through his nose. He had a large mound of cocaine on the back of the toilet, scooping piles up to his nose with his concert program.

Babe's stomach recoiled at the image as he pushed his way in, speaking low. "Hey, Robby, we got to get going. I need to get that boy home before his mom gets off work and calls the police on me."

Robby stood and swiftly repackaged his drugs in a glassine baggie in two motions. "Not a problem. We sure don't want any interactions with Maggie, do we?"

Babe said, "I want to thank you for keeping things out of sight for the kid. I know this was your night. I appreciate it."

"Darling, do you think I'm a savage?"

Robby walked to the door, flung it open. "Never underestimate me. Let's be going. I can take my shit home and call a lovely piece of trade to come spend the night and beat my ass."

Babe and Ricky laughed, shaking their heads. Ricky took a compact out of his bag and began to apply pressed powder to his face in the mirror.

"This was a fun night, but the doll is tired. I don't have the stamina of my youth."

"Robby told me you had gone down south to your folks because you were sick."

Ricky glanced at him through the mirror. "Yeah. I supposed you heard about me having to get radiation treatments. I needed my family by my side."

Babe let out a relieved breath. "Oh. Robby told me you had AIDS and you had gone home to die. I was hurt you never said bye to me. Whatever you had, or have, I was hurt that I didn't get the chance to tell you how much I love you."

Ricky dropped the compact, rested his hands on the sink, looked down, and shook his head. Babe strained to hear his whisper. "They didn't want anything to do with me. My own mother said this is God's punishment. Wouldn't even let me eat from the same plates as them.

Do you know how hard it is to eat homemade macaroni and cheese on a paper plate? That shit is heavy, *B*." Ricky laughed.

Babe was confused but laughed hesitantly along with him.

"It pissed me off. Had me sleeping out on the back porch like the goddamn dog. Using the old outhouse."

"Wh—?"

"So, when they were all out, I would go inside and get a glass from the cabinet, drink me a nice cool glass of water. Go take a good long shit on the toilet. Lay on Mama's bed, roll around on that motherfucker. On her prized patchwork quilt. Only they came home too soon." Ricky's laugh was not mirthful. "Kicked my ass. But I gave it back to them good. Until they got my uncle to jump in. They threw me out without a fucking red cent. Left me to get back up here on my own steam."

Babe took his hand, squeezed.

"I'd rather be up here waiting to die than down there killing my soul. Any day. At least I know I'm loved here."

Babe nodded, blinking back the stinging in his eyes. "Why are you talking crazy? There's meds out her now. Treatments so you don't have to die."

Ricky let go of his hand, smiled tremulously. "We're all still waiting to die. Aren't we? Robby working twelve hour days doing bitches heads so he can pulverize his brain cells all night. You, yu spent all those years with somebody that can't really love you because he hates himself so much. The cheating, the fights. At least now I see some fight in you, finally. You're making the moves to get away from that relationship Because you were dying trying to maintain some gay version of a marriage. I mean, what is that if not self-hatred? Trying to ape the straights." Ricky shuddered with exaggerated revulsion.

"That's what you think of me? That I hate myself so much I'm pretending to be straight?"

"Well, what would you call it?"

"Trying to make a relationship work isn't self-hatred. It's what you're supposed to do. If you've made a commitment to share your life with someone, you don't just throw it away on a whim, or when something isn't perfect. You try to work through the bad spots."

"Bad spots. That's what we're calling ass kickings now. You're a very smart person, B. But it seems yu don't know what abuse is. Or you don't think you deserve better."

Ricky took one last look at his reflection, thrust back his shoulders and headed to the door. "Let's fleece, *B*! The doll does not exist to spend time in tavern toilets!"

They exited the ladies room and headed back to their table. As they passed, a broad shouldered, slightly overweight woman with brilliant blue hair brushed past, pumping into Ricky and leaning down to talk to a group of people at a booth. "Damn. These big boned girls really can't take us suburban girls, can they, B? You can't tell me that bitch couldn't get by without damn near dislocating my shoulder. They know us girls from the outlying districts come to town and pee, honey, and they just can't take it."

Babe laughed and sat down beside Rueben. "You okay?"

Rueben's eyes were large as saucers, tracking the blue haired woman's movement with awe. Ricky was sitting silent in the corner, lost in his own reverie.

Chance loudly slurped a hot chocolate, oblivious to the whipped cream sticking to his upper lip. "Thanks for inviting me, Ricky. That was a really nice show. I was surprised."

Ricky shook his head as if trying to clear his thoughts. "First, I didn't invite your white ass. And second, why you surprised? Miss Thing, Miss Ross is the ultimate showman. She gives a grand show. Cant' none of these new gyrating cutns come for Ross, bitch."

"Let's not get crazy. She was cool and all. I was shocked she could carry a tune. But she ain't no Janet or Madonna. She stood as still as a post. Why didn't she have some choreography to break things up?

"You don't need choreography when you are the goddamn grande dame, bitch!

Robby yelled. "You get good show. You don't have to be twisting and pussy popping begging for attention. See you young sissies are so desperate to be looked at you don't realize the bitch standing 'still as a post' beside you is the one that be snatching all the dick."

Babe nodded. "It's like art. Grace Jones doesn't move around all manic and animated. You bring the viewer to the art, not the art to the viewer."

Ricky said, "Besides, where you think them heifers got their inspiration? Ain't no Black skunk was giving you sequins and lashes and wigs out the back gate until Ross did it."

Chance laughed. "All that hair. What's up with that?"

"Bitch, you gots to give the public weave for the gawds. And fishtail gowns so no other skunk can try to share your spotlight. Janet's cute and all, but come on, No competition."

"What about Celine Dion. Barbra Streisand."

Max said, "You white kids always want to pull Celine and Barbra out y'all ass when the discussion comes to divas. Do you hear either one of them bitches get play in the clubs? You sound like them old head white girls that drag Judy Garland out the crypt."

"I ain't heard Ross getting no play in the clubs, neither. Their time is past."

"Nevah!" screamed Robby. Rueben laughed.

Babe said, "I love all those singers. And let's stop acting like there was nothing but gas and fog and then the Lord said 'let there be Diana Ross'. There was Josephine Baker, Sarah Vaughn, Dinah Washington, Bessie Smith...Stop the madness. You two are just as narrow minded as Chance if you think nobody existed before Diana Ross. She just happened to have timing that coincided with television, so she was seen by larger groups. And white people."

The blue haired woman walked past the table, bumping Robby's shoulder.

"What about Cher, then? She still gets play in the clubs And she was seen by TV audiences back in the day."

Robby slurped his soda, gurgling through his straw. "Oh, Chere don't count as white cunt, honey."

"How you figure?" Chance asked.

"Any bitch that jumps in and out of wigs like they change they draws has got to be part coon."

Max smiled, "Babe, I like your friends."

Ricky clenched his teeth, "That blue haired dragon got one more time to bump me with them concrete titties and I'm going to knock her the fuck out. I'm trying to be civil in this bitch, but she is testing me big time."

Rueben looked, once more in awe. "She's a movie star. I seen her on TV."

Babe shook his head disapprovingly. "Rueben, telling stories to entertain people is one thing, but telling lies is something else. You know she's not no movie star."

He was adamant. "I seen her on TV. On Jerry Springer."

Max nodded, laughed. "He's right. And that sissy he's sitting with was on the show with him."

Rueben smiled, "She was on the show and she told her boyfriend she had a secret to tell him. Then she told him she was a man, and then the boyfriend threw flowers oer her head and she splashed a cup of water at him. Then the other lady sitting at the table with them said she was the boyfriend's mother and then she started fighting the blue haired lady. And then they all started dancing on a pole."

The table was silent. Everyone stared at Rueben.

Babe said, "And that's what it's all come down to. Back in the dayTV sent out images of Nat King Cole ad Ella Fitzgerald so the masses would understand that Black people weren't something to be feared or made fun of. Now we got Jerry Springer."

Max said, "Don't you know these ballroom kids all go on these talk shows with some made up story. One pretends he's straight and is dating tranny and doesn't know the tranny's a tranny. Now who the fuck believes this guy is straight is the bigger gag. She practically has daisies coming out of her ass."

Rueben laughed.

"So the Springer show is fake?" Babe wrinkled his brow in consternation.

"I don't know if it's a hoax or not. Maybe the producers believe that crap. It's a way for some kids with no money to make a little bit of chance."

Ricky laughed, "Well shit, I need to give them a call and get me some extra coins. Robby, you can be my unsuspecting straight husband. But bitch, if you throw hands you going to get dealt with."

"That's so fucking embarrassing." Babe frowned. "So these people go on national TV, making a mockery of not only being gay but cooing for the white folks. For a couple hundred dollars. More entertainment and perpetuation of stereotypes for the white man."

Chance said, "Don't you think Black people watch the show too? How is this a white/black thing? I'd be more concerned about what messages it sounds out to kids like Rueben."

Ricky said, "Fuck white people. Why should we care what they think or don't think? If a queen can make some change to pay her rent without breaking the law or risking her life, who cares about the respectability police? Our folks spent decades trying to impress white people with decent behavior and what has that gotten us?"

"True that." Babe stood up, brushing imaginary crumbs from his pants. "I'm ready to go. Can we get the check?"

- 328 - | David Jackson Ambrose

Chance peered at him. "It's really weird. Why do you haate white people?"

Ricky huffed in exasperation. "Here she go, placing herself at the center of the conversation again. Girl, this is not your show."

Babe looked at him. "I really try not to think of them, to tell you the truth. White people are a burden. They make it hard to love myself."

"What's that mean?" Chance asked.

"For me, being Black is a celebration. When I'm in a store where there are only us shopping, or at church, or with family, listening to our cadences, they way we move, how we speak to each other in this kind of short hand that you all think is broken English, the way we smell, little girls with their hair freshly braided and greased, brothers wearing Muslim oils, old ladies with perfumed scarves on the bus, it's comforting, you know? You slow down the pace of everyday living, and just allow yourself to be comforted by that feeling, that familiar. You immerse yourself in it. It's a joyous thing, like your being enveloped in a hug by a big Black woman with nice big breasts smelling like baby powder. It's only when y'all come around that it becomes heavy. With your arbitrary rules and constant vigilance like it's your job to make sure we don't 'get out of line'. I only have to think about being Black as something that is secondary to my essential self when I see how white people see me."

Max slid out of the booth and help Rueben as he sidled out, lightly grabbing his upper arm to make sure he stood straight.

Max said, "I don't dislike white people. They just don't matter to me. And that's probably more insulting to y'all than being disliked."

Ricky stood, rubbing his hands together before clapping them. "So what B's saying, to sum it all up, it's not all about y'all. Now let's fleece!"

Chapter Thirty-Five

Confrontation

The drive home was quiet, each person lost in their own thoughts. Rueben sat immersed in excitement from his night. From being outside and the concert full of strange smiling faces, to eating all the french toast he wanted at the restaurant with the foul-mouthed old lady.

The only blip in the silence came from the constant low drone coming from Robby's throat as he sat tucked in the corner of the car seat. He pulled his feet up on the upholstery, wrapped his arms around his knees, and tucked his head down as though trying to hide, burrowing into the corner, making himself small.

Babe shook his head with a disgusted look on his face.

"Miss Robby, bitch. Get a grip on yourself, chile. You okay?" Ricky screamed.

"I'm fine," Robby said in a monotone drone. His tongue pushed against the interior of his cheek, pushed out, reminding Rueben of a gerbil.

Ricky said, "I see why Nancy says just say no, ma'am."

"It's just not cute," Chance scorned. "Not cute at all."

"What he on? Blow?" Max asked. He had agreed to go along with Babe, who promised to drive him back to pick up his car before sunup when tow trucks would pick it up for him.

Babe said, "I never saw it do like this to anybody but him. But I'm not familiar with Nancy's Just-Say-No-Ma'am campaign."

When the limo pulled up to the curb, Babe asked Rueben to wait for him to return from helping Ricky get Robby to his room. To Rueben, Robby didn't appear to need help. Robby hopped up from the seats and flounced from the car on a cloud of perfume with tail notes of something less pleasant. Chance showed Max up the stairs to the house, and Rueben walked behind them, too excited to wait.

He burst through the door of the apartment, yelling for Alise through the darkened rooms. He was so excited he began telling Alise about his night even though he didn't see her. When the upstairs door banged open Rueben jumped, startled at the sudden noise. Puff Puff screamed loudly as Alise stepped on her tail when she crossed the room.

Rueben was so animated, so thrilled, he didn't notice her demeanor, did not register the wet glottal sob that erupted from her throat as she neared him. She switched on the lamp near the door and lunged toward him. She hugged him violently, pressing him to her like a lifejacket on a plummeting jet. Puff Puff darted past, running out into the hallway. Pretzel stood at the doorway, yipping angrily at her.

"Mama. It was awesome. I went to see Diana Ross. She's this beautiful lady, like the fairytale princesses, with long flowing hair and brown skin just like mine. She sang nice songs like you hear on the radio. She's way better than fairy tales. Did you know Harriet Tubman was a real live soldier on the Underground Railroad? And that she guided our people to freedom like Moses in the bible? Babe and Chance took me to this restaurant to eat, and there was TV stars there like this lady that used to be a man with blue hair, that dances on a pole and fights her boyfriend because he didn't know she was a man. It was the best!"

While he talked, Alise held him at arm's length, stood him up, turned him around, checked his body for signs of damage. She grabbed his face and peered into his eyes, searched his skin for indications of tampering. Oblivious, Rueben continued telling her about his experience, his eyes large and bright.

Babe tapped tentatively at the partially opened door. "Hey, sorry about it being so late. We didn't mean to keep him out so long."

Alise spun to him and pushed Rueben behind her as though she were hiding him, and then stood closer as if trying to shield the mounds of discarded papers and items collected from her morning excursions. Rueben looked up at her confusedly.

"You had my kid with you? How dare you!" she screamed. "How dare you take my kid out of here without letting me know. What right do you have?"

"I'm sorry. Didn't you get my note? I thought we'd be back before you got home from work. I didn't mean to scare you."

"I thought he was dead out there. You can't just walk off with people's property like that."

"You didn't get the letter? Ruebs, didn't you leave the note like I told you?"

Rueben moved from the shadow behind his mother. He put his hands in his pockets and looked down guiltily. Alise looked at him, wild-eyed. "And what's this shit you have on? Take that off. Those aren't your clothes."

She lunged toward him and animatedly pulled at the shirt, popping buttons. Rueben pushed her hands away.

"Stop it, Mama. These are my going out clothes. Babe and Chance give them to me."

"You take them off. They aren't yours. I take care of you, not them."

Babe spoke soothingly, looking at Rueben with commiserating eyes. "I'm so sorry about this. We wanted to take him for a nice night out. He was totally safe. Robby from next door had extra tickets, so I thought it might be a nice thing for Rueben to experience. He enjoyed the show."

"Fuck the show. You took my kid out with you and those, those, fucking freaks. God knows what y'all did to him. You all right, baby?" She again searched his body for signs of damage.

Babe stiffened at the word, his entire demeanor moved from convivial to something Rueben could not identify. The word reverberated along the walls through the vents.

Chance appeared over Babe's shoulder, his face was twisted into a mask of contempt as he shouted over Babe's shoulder. "Freaks, huh? So, you think we did something with that kid? Are you crazy?"

Babe looked from Rueben to the mother. "I can assure you, your child is unsullied. Despite popular notions, we are not on the hunt for children to molest. I also promise you that I'll never take your kid again. It was a big mistake, and I'm sorry about that."

Rueben pushed Alise's hands from him. "They're my friends, Mama, and we had fun."

Alise whispered, "Or do you not know that the unrighteous will not inherit the kingdom of God? Do not be deceived: neither the sexually immoral, nor idolaters, nor men who practice homosexuality, nor thieves, nor drunkards...."

Babe spoke loudly over her voice, "Nor revilers, nor swindlers will inherit the kingdom of God. You're not the only one able to spout Bible verses. And I'd guess that deceiving the department of welfare, using Section 8 to pay your rent and having a job on the side might be included in that swindling and thievery piece, don't you?"

"Fucking hypocrite," Chance muttered.

Rueben reached inside his pocket, pinched clusters of salt, and brought them to his mouth. Babe saw the boy move his fingers to his mouth.

"Fucking hypocrite is right," Babe said. "Hiding your fear behind a Bible quote. Just like you used religion to help get you in here, talking about how you liked that the church is right down the street. When's the last time you went to that church, or any other for that matter? And look at this place. Did you not get to the quote about cleanliness yet?"

He pushed the door wide, sweeping his arm jerkily. "Don't you want to spit any biblical quote about God's vision of cleanliness?"

"Disgusting!" Chance hissed.

"Stop it." Rueben said, "Don't talk bad about my mom."

Babe looked at him and clamped his mouth shut.

Alise said, "I don't care about what you or anybody else does behind closed doors. I only care about me and mine."

Chance said, "Yours? You make it sound like your kid is a piece of furniture, a possession. And judging from the junk in this villa, you don't care all that much about your property any fucking way."

"You could have killed him! He could have died."

Babe rolled his eyes. "Okay. Now we are not merely pedophiles, we eat children or something? Do we do some sort of sacrifice or something?"

"You ever hear of Prader-Willi syndrome? It's a birth defect, and my kid has it."

Babe said, "I've heard of it, yeah. Where children are born missing a chromosome, right? And they have feeding problems."

"Kid's got no problem feeding, trust." Chance laughed.

"Feeding problems that turn into an eating disorder. Where they eat uncontrollably. They'll eat everything they can, and literally will eat until they kill themselves. You took my kid to a restaurant. He's not like normal kids where he can just go to a restaurant or the grocery store.

Without me to supervise him, he could kill himself. I should call the fucking police and report a kidnapping."

Babe looked around at the padlocks on the cabinets and the refrigerator.

"That's where we're going now? Threats to call the cops? That's the strategy? You're going to act like some sheltered white bitch and use the police instead of resolving matters on your own? What you going to tell them, the big Black nigger threatened you? I don't think that one's going to work for *you*, so I guess you have to go to the thing about faggots bringing their abhorrent lifestyle to your doorway, huh?"

Rueben yelled, "No I'm not. I'm not that Willy person. I'm Rueben!"

Alise turned to him. "Hush up, Rueben."

"I won't. You're lying! I'm not your fucking Willy! You're fucking Willy!"

She lashed out with her hand and struck him across his face. It was loud, jarring in its immediacy, causing Chance and Babe to flinch in response.

Rueben didn't cry. His fists were clenched at his side as he stared at her. He reached into his pocket, took out a pinch of salt, and brought it to his mouth. He rubbed until he felt the satisfying burn, the sting of his lip tearing.

Chance said, "I see how shit gets handled in the houses of the holy. Praise Him!"

Alise grabbed the doorknob and flung the door shut with a bang.

Chapter Thirty-Seven

Robby

Robby sat by the window, gazing at the skyline through the sheers. He had turned on the radio so that he wouldn't feel alone. Being alone was frightening, brought voices from out of nowhere. Luther Vandross, Marvin Gaye, Teena Marie, and even the smooth drone of DJ Butterball introducing the songs: those voices had soothed him on many occasions. Tonight, he turned up the volume, hoping to drown out the angry voices and the words that fell in disjointed, accusatory pinpoints around his head.

Freak crazy unsullied molester.

Fun unrighteous kingdom of God.

Immoral idolater thief.

Property, kill him, die, kill him let him die, doesn't deserve to live die.

No help no help...

He had been so proud. He had worked so hard. Worked a full-time job cleaning out plasma bags at SmithKline while going to beauty school, learning his craft. After graduation, getting a second job, doing heads at a salon on the Main Line, learning how to do hair for the blue-haired set that attended the cotillions and horse shows. If he got in the good graces of a few women of means, ingratiated himself, it would be a connection that led to better opportunities, better tips, invites to use summer homes, cosignatories on bank loans...

Those better opportunities never panned out, but Robby had made his own opportunities. He managed to save enough money so when his boyfriend, Eric, spotted the old, dilapidated salon sitting back from the road when he was driving home through Valley Forge Park, Robby was able to locate an agent and make an offer.

The place needed a lot of work, but the bones were still there. The old salon hadn't been used for over a decade. As a child, his mother used to visit this place every week. It had been one of the first salons in the area catering to both white and colored patrons. The old hood dryers, rust-spattered shampoo sinks, and tattered vinyl swivel chairs would have to be replaced. Everything would need to be replaced, but with elbow grease, energy, and hard cash, he could be up and running within six months.

Eric had taken out a second mortgage on his house, much to his wife's dismay, telling her he needed it for health expenses. She pretended to believe him. But it was for Robby. Everything Eric ever did had been for Robby.

They used that money to make the salon gleam with multiple mirrors, black porcelain wash basins, chrome fixtures, and chairs upholstered with real leather. Ricky, fresh out of Parsons, had curated the huge plate-glass frontispiece even though the building sat so far from Valley Forge Road that passersby could not see it. The first display, Ricky had used one of the mannequins he had bought from a fire sale at a defunct department store (he had named her Pompeii). He dressed her in an old Dior New Look of gleaming white lace, bought from the Village Thrift, with a tiny, nipped waist and billowing peplumed skirt. Her wig was a blonde chignon spray-painted Day-Glo red, black, and green à la Stephen Sprouse. An Afro pick with a clenched fist was jammed into the knot at the crown. Not satisfied the message was blatant enough, Ricky splashed her alabaster skin with streaks of shinning obsidian and painted her lips Groovy Grape by Wet'n'Wild. He threw little Fisher-Price figurines all about her feet, along with an intricate Lego village—making her a post-war Gulliver among a village of white Lilliputians.

The first calls had come before Robby was even officially open for business. He used to like to go to the salon to clean up after sundown. He loved the traffic zipping past the huge plate-glass window out front while he listened to soft jazz on the radio. Sundown was the only time he had available to work on the place since he had not yet stopped working his temp job, trying to stack as much money as possible before his grand opening.

"I got it!" he'd yelled to Eric, who was lining up product in the storage room, when the phone rang.

Robby had thought it was a joke. The voice was so ludicrous, low and scratchy like the bad guy in a Barbara Stanwyck melodrama. Homos were a macabre bunch. He knew many of his friends would think making a call like that was funny.

"We don't want your kind around here. Go back where you came from."

So, he had quoted a Barbara Stanwyck line. "Sorry, wrong number."

But the calls had continued. Nothing alarming, at first. Just one call every few days. But after the first few, when none of his friends came forward to confess, he realized someone didn't want him in the neighborhood.

He opened the salon for business with no fear. Hell, he was accustomed to threats. He had been one of the first Black students to attend Upper Merion High, and certainly the first openly gay one, wearing flouncy blouses and freshly wet set hair (before he had moved on to the popular Jheri curl). He had gotten verbal threats all through his first year of high school, along with death threats scrawled on bits of composition paper pushed through the vents of his locker. A group of sneering white boys had even promised if he returned to school in anything but "regular" clothes, they would run him up the flagpole out front of the administrative building.

That had all stopped by his second year. Eric had taken off from work, come up to the school, and had had Robby identify the group that had threatened to run him up the pole. He had kicked each and every one of their asses with a methodical efficiency that was terrifying to others but thrilling to Robby.

By his third year, he had even managed to make a few friends. Robby'd been invited to join the Black Student Union, and even though he was still considered an outcast, it was a sort of accepted outcast status. Liberals pointed out that they had an African American homosexual at the school, and he was assimilating just fine. He would never be invited into their homes, but he would be included in many social clubs and photo ops for the newspaper and yearbook so everyone could feel great about their open-mindedness. And Eric kept constant vigil, at the ready should any threats be made to Robby's person.

The white patrons never showed. Their absence was a scream in Robby's head, but that scream was muted by the quiet, steady appearance of Black church ladies, who showed up from Phoenixville, Devon, Wayne, Pottstown, Spring City, faithfully, every Thursday and Friday to get their hair washed, pressed, and curled for socially obligated weekends.

The late-night phone calls continued, accelerated. The calls were supported by inane, mundane events: dead birds on the step; squirrels, or possum. Nothing overt, especially considering the heavily wooded surroundings, but these events were more than happenstance, he was certain. The knot in the pit of his belly confirmed it for him.

Eric told him not to involve the police, said they wouldn't do anything, to let him handle things. Robby wasn't able to heed that advice. He called the police, demanding that they come out and survey the area.

Police responded dutifully, if wearily, as visit after visit provided no evidence of harassment. Dead animals were as regular in these parts as traffic tickets. They were hardly proof of criminal activity. Police courtesy gradually turned to apathy. They came to view the rotund, sweating, brown man with his wild gesticulating and flouncing clothes as histrionic; they watched with derision as he stormed at them from the meticulous interior of his salon, referring to misdeeds without supporting evidence. He became known as a crackpot. His calls were taken with a grain of salt. Onsite response to his calls grew less frequent.

Eric sternly told him that he was to never be alone in the shop. If there were no other beauticians working, he should call Eric before finishing with the last patron so Eric could drive out to the location, drive him home, and keep him safe. Robby secretly liked this directive. It gave him more time with Eric than he usually had. Before, they would see each other once or twice through the week. Now, they were together most days, excluding Sundays and Mondays, even if only for the duration of a drive home.

That last night, he hadn't called Eric. Mrs. Jones, his last customer for the day, had promised to drive him home. When snow had first begun to fall, it had not raised any alarm. It was beautiful, in fact, had become picturesque as the light fall turned heavy, blotted vision. Sound muted beneath the onslaught. The few cars still on the road moved silently, cautiously through the relentlessly falling sheets of snow. Icy high beams refracted light into opaque cataracts on the plate-glass window.

Robby hurried through the process, hoping the less than pristine curls he created would pass muster, wanting to get on the road before it got too bad. When they were finally ready, and he had closed down, shutting off all but the solo lamp that illuminated the display window, he rushed to the storage room to make sure the back door was latched while Mrs. Jones went out to warm the car.

When he had made his way out, his boots slipping perilously on the slickened walkway, Mrs. Jones met him and requested to use his phone. Her car would not start.

She called home to her husband, lamenting ole Betsey's unreliability in inclement weather. When she hung up, she ruefully apologized. She would not be able to take him home. Mr. Jones did not tolerate his kind. She had to be upfront with him, instead of beating around the bush, creating another excuse. DeForest Jones was a devout Pentecostal. He refused to have Robby in his car, chastised his wife for having offered to take him in hers.

Robby had replied curtly, re-evaluating their relationship. She needn't worry. He'd make a call.

Eric exploded. He was furious Robby had allowed himself to depend on one of those "devout" churchgoers. He told Robby to keep the doors locked and the lights out and to wait in the storage room until he got there.

The problem was that Robby, in his independence, in his zeal as sole proprietor of his own business, had not given Eric a key to the salon. So, when the brief, terse knock at the rear came, he had opened it without asking who was on the other side, assuming it was Eric.

The violence had been brief. He'd never seen a gun before, but he knew what it was when the stark, sulfuric, metal odor flashed as the butt struck him in the temple. He fell back against the shelving in the tiny room with a low groan. The moonlight from the open door fell into the room behind two dark forms. They merged into one mass of violence, yanking him up— *faggot*—shaking him and pushing him against the wall as bottles of solution toppled onto the floor—*nigger*.

Robby struggled to recollect the specifics of that night, but it only came to him as flashes of pain and words like ephemera, hitting his medulla in intermittent punches. The beam of a flashlight had blinded his sight as he was tied to his prized red leather chair, his wrists bound by cords from his own equipment.

Where's the money, faggot?

Do you want to die bringing perversion to our town?

Nigger, faggot, nigger.

Burn this place to the ground and you with it, porch bunny.

He didn't know when Eric showed up. He only knew that he heard his voice, and then he didn't hear his voice anymore. After that he only heard him scream. Then Robby's hands were untied, and they were dragging him, dragging Eric out back through the snow where their screams were dampened, silenced by the falling whiteness.

They made him watch, would not let him look away, while he begged them, swore to them that he would never come back, that they could take the money, there was more hidden under a floorboard in the storeroom. They laughed and made him watch anyway. Watch Eric, once tall and proud, with shoulders broad and muscular, with a physicality so immediate Robby used to hear opera whenever he entered a room, now diminished. They strapped him to the fence post. His eyes struggled to see through the dark, but also tried to not see the blurred forms swinging, hitting him, melting his beautiful face to mush, deconstructing sharp cheekbones to blood-smeared abstraction before turning and descending on him.

He screamed into the pelting powder.

Help? There's nobody here to help you, faggot.

No help, no help, no help.

Snow had never kept her off the road. She had business to take care of, and the old Mercedes was a reliable business partner, keeping her safe and insulated in any weather. Ten-year-old Balthazar sat in the back, strapped in, reading a Nancy Drew mystery. She thought he should be reading more scholarly work, something that encouraged learning, but her husband had convinced her that a child should not spend 100 percent of their time learning; learning could be encouraged along with healthy doses of pure entertainment in between.

At first, she thought the dark form tumbling in her high beams was pure imagination, a trick played by the falling snow. Then, she thought it was an animal, perhaps a deer that had been hit by a passing vehicle. Deer were as common as grass in Valley Forge Park. People familiar with Valley Forge Park were also familiar with ubiquitous roadkill. As she approached, however, she realized the shadow at the lip of the road was something other than an animal.

She slammed on her brakes, an automatic response, causing the car to fishtail along a patch of ice. Balthazar yelped in the back seat, his hands gripping the seat on either side of him. She gritted her teeth, praying the wheels would make purchase, eased her boot off the brake, steered into the trajectory, and thanked God as the tail end began to straighten.

She stopped the car and told Balthazar to stay seated, to keep his seatbelt fastened. She reached beneath the seat to find the jack she kept there for unexpected occurrences, bundled her scarf about her neck, then opened the door.

Her heart thumped loudly in her ears. She couldn't identify his face, covered in blood and pulp, but she saw his hands were Black, grasping at the sleeves of her Black glama coat. The salon hulking darkly in the distance told her who he was. She shushed his mumbling, and the blood burbling forth instead of words caused her stomach to lurch. The woman told him everything would be fine.

"Help, no help," he told her. His desperation threatened to drag her down to the snow with him.

She steadied her posture in the snow, wondered if blood was able to be cleaned from fox. Assumed it had to be; after all, weren't the foxes bloodied when they were bludgeoned to make coats?

She weighed the affects dragging a bloodied man, mumbling "Help, no help" would have on the twelve-year-old in the car. She removed his hands from her coat, ignored his beseeching her not to leave, went back to her car, and issued stern instructions to Balthazar.

"Take off your seat belt. I want you to lie on the floor, small as you can. Stay hidden. And don't come out for anything until I come back to this car. Do you understand me?"

His eyes were large as saucers as he nodded solemnly and slipped down from the seat to the floor of the sedan, Nancy Drew tucked under his chin.

Coaxing the bloodied form to help her, she dragged, pulled him back from the road, back toward the salon, ignoring his pleas not to go back there. She followed streaks of blood that ran in two directions and followed the one that led to the back entrance of the building. The lug wrench from her car was lodged into her waistband, heavy and assuring even as it made their maneuvering more labored. The cold metal digging into the flesh on her hip was a comfort.

He screamed as though being struck when they entered the building. She ignored him as she felt her way around. She clicked on a light switch, and he screamed again, demanded she turn it off. She sat him in a blood-streaked chair, consoled him, and asked for the phone. She followed the direction of his pointed finger, called her husband, who was working a double shift, as usual. He dispatched squad cars and told her to clear out.

She told him help was on the way. "No help," he said.

She tried again to turn on the lights, again he screamed like a wounded animal, throwing himself beneath furniture. She turned on the television. Diana Ross flickered onto the screen, chipper and enigmatic as she welcomed viewers to her show. She sang to him, hunkered beneath the shelving against the wall, resting in a pool of blood. While he was distracted by the movement and sound coming from the TV, she walked back out into the night.

She sat locked in her car, waiting for the sirens and throbbing red lights; her eyes poised on the road and her foot resting above the accelerator lest something untoward appeared before the police arrived.

When help arrived, they surmised from the message from dispatch, from the blood-streaked snow, and from the form hiding in the salon that a robbery had taken place. The officers dragged the screaming form from beneath the counter, demanded answers, then pulled him to the road. When Robby began to resist, telling them there was somebody else, they raised batons, angered by his resistance.

She jumped from her car, told them what had happened, explaining that the bloodied form was not the perpetrator of a crime. She saw her son peering at the scene through the cold-fogged windows and worried about how this would affect him.

The police once more raised batons, angered by *her* resistance, and struck at her. She stumbled back, her coat pelting open on a breeze as she raised a hand, loudly identifying herself and her husband as one of them.

The ambulance loomed. She looked through the bloom of blood clouding her vision back at her car to make sure Balthazar had not seen the police strike her with the baton. She worried so about how this thing would affect her child, her baby, her Balthazar, Babe. She locked eyes with him peering through the fog-steamed windows and her heart dropped. They wouldn't listen to the blubbering bloodied figure. They blurted words that seemed to be germane to the scene, shock, hysteria, hospital. They left her to fend for herself as the ambulance loomed in light and sound.

Robby turned off the radio and went back to the sofa. The voices weren't helping. They were only adding to the muck in his head, making it harder to think. He hugged the pillow to himself then covered his head with it as he ducked down onto his knees. Robby chewed the inside of his cheek, finding solace in the sting of his teeth cutting into flesh.

Finding out that Eric was dead had been the beginning of the end for him. By the time the police had been able to understand his fractured sentences, it was too late for Eric. Hypothermia was the official cause of death. Injury by blunt force trauma was secondary.

Hearing that there hadn't been any suspects hadn't surprised him. Detectives were suspicious when he was unable to describe his assailants. They'd worked with him, patiently trying to give him cues to catalyze his memory. Did he see a watch? Did he recall the timbre of a voice? Perhaps he saw a scar or a tattoo. Even in the dark, the eyes adjust, become able to see. Robby remembered nothing. Nothing but his cries for help and Eric's crumbling face.

There were the visits from Eric's wife. Her requests were delivered in the dull monotone of the grieving widow. The subdued delivery did not lessen the impact of her words. She begged that he not reveal the true nature of their relationship. It would crush Eric's children to find out their father was gay, the victim of a hate crime. Gay bashing, they called it. He owed it to Eric's memory and to his children, she said, to keep his mouth shut.

Requests for money followed. Eric didn't have life insurance. He was young. He hadn't expected to need life insurance so soon. How were they going to pay all that money to bury him?

Robby paid what money he could. Closed the salon, closed out all his accounts. He'd wanted Eric to have a sendoff that showed how much he had been loved. It also helped to assuage his guilt. Eric's family was left destitute. They would lose their home, unable to pay the second mortgage he had taken out to help Robby open the salon. It was the least he could do.

One last favor: Could he not show up at the funeral? It would be humiliating to his children, to his memory. He at least owed them that.

Chapter Thirty-Seven

Laundry Room

The effects of his recent run in with Alise still trembled through his body. Not wanting to hear Chance raging about "homophobic Black bitches," Babe took Max up to his room. He felt Max's eyes on him as he lit a cleansing candle and burned a quick smudge, which rapidly clouded the room with smoke and the scent of peppermint. He smiled uncomfortably before he walked over to the bed where Max sat, shifting like an amoeba. He reached both hands down and placed them on Max's smooth head, then kissed the slight peak at the top. Max wrapped his arms around Babe's waist and pressed his head into his abdomen. He pulled him backward and lay back on the bed. Babe enjoyed the warmth of their shared heat. They both shifted around and entwined their legs.

"You're shaking. That woman honest to God got you shooketh."

"No. I'm good. It was my fault, for real, taking that kid out and not letting her know."

Max moved his hands down from Babe's chest to his flat belly. Babe turned away from him and shifted his rear up close to Max's pelvis. Babe felt Max's groin grow warm against his back.

"I like you, Babe."

He covered the hand Max held on his chest with his own and whispered, "I like you too, Max." Babe was embarrassed. He didn't know what to say.

He jumped reflexively when Max slipped his hand beneath his shirt. After he got past his discomfort, Babe enjoyed the warm feeling, the tactile pleasure, but a feeling of dread rumbled through him. "Would you mind if we just lay like this? Without doing anything?"

Max sighed. "Sure, Babe. I'm not just trying to sex you. Whatever you want me to do for you, I'll do it."

He laughed briefly. "I'll bet."

Max was quiet for a moment.

Babe sensed his discomfort, so he turned around and faced him. Babe kissed his forehead, then moved his mouth to kiss the smooth shaved head. "Sorry. I believe what you say. Hell, you don't need to wait around for me, I know. We already talked about your harem."

"And what I said to you at the MidTown is the truth. They play their position. If they want to suck my dick real quick, who am I to deny them? But we ain't doing anything beside that and a little slap and tickle. When you walked past me that first time, I knew you were the one. You walked past me, and I smelled your crotch."

"Huh?" Babe laughed softly as he drowsily started coming down from the adrenaline high of the earlier incident.

"You smelled as fresh as newborn colt. Everybody in that place smelled like day-old sweat and desperation. You smelled like Ivory soap."

Max's voice was slurred. He was drowsy too. He had told Babe about working fifteen-hour days for the past week. Sleep descended upon him rapidly much to Babe's relief. He lay there, listening to Max snore like a buzz saw. He moved back a bit so he could look at him. The slight asymmetry created by his wounded eye only made him more beautiful to Babe. Sometimes, when he was excited, both his eyes would widen, and Babe could see the cataracted cornea. It was a filmy opaque color, the lightest blue he had ever seen. It sent an erotic charge whenever he saw it. It flashed a sense of familiar touchstones from his youth: Helen Keller, Johnny Quest, Laura Ingalls, Little Stevie Wonder, and Jose Feliciano. The familiarity made him feel safe.

Max treated Babe with a sort of respectful deference he had never experienced before, and while it felt great to him, it also left him hesitant.

He was also hesitant for physical reasons. Max was lean and trim, but there was a certain dearth of muscularity that made Babe leery. He was used to the uncultivated physicality that most Black men in his experience brought to the table. Most Black men he had been with had a natural symmetry and muscularity honed from genetic disposition, and Max's lack thereof made him suspicious.

Max had to be older than he admitted. He wasn't opposed to an older man. He was more bothered about why he would be dishonest about his age. If he was dishonest about something so innocuous, how honest was he in general? He didn't even know Max's real name.

His hands played over Max's sleeping form, moving down to his legs, his ass, firm, but with a bit of slack, and he thought of Matthew's ass, hard and so firm that it sometimes hurt.

He quietly extricated himself and stood a moment, staring to be sure he was still sleeping, and then he stepped into a pair of sweatpants and tied the sash. He squinted around in the dark for the keys and wallet Max had put on the dresser, quietly picking up the wallet and taking it with him downstairs.

In the light of the living room lamp, he opened the billfold and took out the ID card. First, he looked at the name and nodded in acknowledgement before looking at the date of birth and comparing to his own. At least he had been honest about his age. He was only thirty-five years old. Babe stood in the quiet of night, staring out the bay window. Another possibility, one he could not shake, was Max could be HIV positive. The disease had raged through the community a decade ago before new medications had been discovered. Black men he had worshipped, idolized, adored, morphed into skeletal wraiths, whispers of their former selves. He thought of Ricky, hiding behind voluminous clothing and Flori Roberts maquillage. He shivered, told himself it was not revulsion but rather caution. He didn't want to be that person. Judgmental, fearmongering, stigmatizing. He knew it was wrong, but the feeling came anyway. The thought of illness and unhealthiness had turned his stomach from the time he was an adolescent, watching the disapproval in his mother's eyes as she sized up his weight and the gradation of his skin color, deeming him unacceptable.

Babe's thoughts turned to the boy downstairs. Prader-Willi. He thought of the photos in the medical dictionary. The fat bodies with tiny, pointed heads and small hands and feet, reminding him of torpedoes. He remembered the fascinated revulsion he had felt paging through the pictures.

Yes, the boy was overweight, but not like the pictures in the medical dictionary. In the restaurant, he had eaten his food like any regular person would eat, not like the descriptions of voracious appetites and details veering toward the animalistic Alise had said as she hysterically gestured toward the padlocks on their kitchen cabinets.

The phone rang, snapping him back to the present. He knew who it was. Who else would call at this hour of the morning? He promptly picked up, hoping it hadn't awakened Max. He didn't speak into the receiver, just heard heavy breathing.

"Babe."

Matthew spoke with languid, deliberate annunciation as he always did when he had been drinking.

And Babe responded the way he had learned over the years, gauging his level of inebriation. "What?"

"How are you?"

"I'm good. What about you?"

"Okay. Listen, I called to give you my new number in case you needed to reach me for anything."

"At four in the morning?"

Babe listened to the number. It tugged at his memory. "Where do I know that number from?"

"I'm staying at Linda's."

"It's that desperate?"

"I couldn't stay with my folks another minute. You know how they can be."

Babe laughed. "Did you have to memorize Bible quotes each morning for breakfast?"

He laughed too. "Just about."

"I thought she said she'd never talk to you again after you 'turned gay.'"

Matthew laughed that low rumble that had always turned Babe on. "Yeah. Well. That was a long time ago."

"So, did you tell her you're not gay now?"

"She's lonely. I'm tired of being by myself. We know each other."

Babe sighed. "I know what you mean."

"I'm still waiting on you, Babe. I'll always be waiting on you."

Babe was silent. He didn't want to be with Matthew, he knew that now. But he couldn't help but feel a slight sense of power hearing those words.

"I'm on foot, for now. The car needs a lot of work. I'll be out of commission for a minute. Unless you got a couple thousand you can lend me."

Babe laughed. "Shit. I need to get some money *from you*. This mortgage is kicking my ass."

"Isn't that what you moved that boy in for? He ain't paying?

"It's a lot more than I thought. His contribution, the rent from the tenant, it's still a struggle."

"I can still come back home."

"What about Linda?"

"Fuck Linda. She know what time it is." The bass of his voice rippled through Babe's groin.

"Is your car out of commission? Or did you get impounded for drinking?"

"I never could get away with lying to you."

Babe thought, in fact, there had been many lies he had gotten away with. "Remember our first car? That Mustang?"

Matthew laughed. "Ole Lana. Cost us four hundred dollars."

"Oh. My. God. How you loved that heap."

"She got us everywhere. Rehoboth Beach. Baltimore. New York."

"That thing was a death trap! You had a piece of wood holding the front seat up! I hated that car."

"I loved that car. That was the beginning of us. I miss her. I miss you too. Can I see you?"

Babe stiffened even though he willed himself not to. "It's not a good idea."

"Why not?"

"The way you showed your ass in here? Breaking in and trying to walk out with shit? How am I supposed to explain you in here to Chance after he and his boyfriend had to fight to get you out of here?"

Matthew breathed heavily in response. Babe thought he heard sobbing. "So he tells you what to do in your house, now?"

Babe paused, vacillating between good sense and desire. He breathed out exasperatedly. "Come in the laundry room. The door's unlocked. Just wait there. I'll come down. But don't turn on the light."

Matthew hung up.

Babe wasn't sure if that meant he would do it or that he was insulted. The thought of it aroused him. His dick throbbed.

Max had likened his hesitancy to some ethereal quality, being a standout from other people, whatever that meant. Babe felt like a sham. It had nothing to do with that.

Matthew was the familiar. A comfort. The respite of his body, his mouth, his dick, his ass, smell of his balls, and his breath. He was able to revel in the immediacy of coital experience without thinking about playing a role: top or bottom, butch or femme. What role did he have to play this night?

When Babe walked into the laundry room, Matthew's hunger in the darkness was full and urgent. He smelled the dirt in his hair. The funk of his desire emanated from his armpits like a loud angry thing. Babe moved toward him with anxious, urgent movements. His want was dire and demanding. He brought his mouth to Matthew's full lips, their teeth clicked together at the impact of their collision, he could taste the salt of Matthew's perspiration, reminding him of salt, reminding him of something he could not name.

Chapter Thirty-Eight

Rueben's Change

The change in her son terrified her. His silence was deafening. Since that night, that moment when she had struck him in an uncontrollable rage, he was much quieter than he had been before. Now, he would rise each morning, walk up from the lower level, go into the bathroom with a towel and washcloth, and take a shower. Alise watched him, baffled.

She would rush to the kitchen, hearing the water from the shower hissing in the room beyond, and rustle together his favorites. Scrambled eggs with cheddar cheese, french toast, and a big glass of orange juice. She'd have everything sitting on the table, waiting for him to exit the bathroom. He'd sit before the aromatic display, move bits of food around with his fork, take a few disinterested bites, drink his juice, and push away from the table, shaking his head.

"You want anything else, honey? How about pancakes and sausage? You know it's not good to leave food uneaten, not with children going hungry all over the world. It's a sin."

He'd shake his head again and tell her in a clipped voice he wasn't hungry.

"You know what this reminds me of? The story of *The Little Red Hen*? How does it go again?"

"What about Black Moses?" he asked with doleful eyes. "She set her people free just like the Moses on TV at Easter time."

"Black Moses? I don't know any tale like that. Why don't you tell that one to me?"

He shook his head. "No. I don't want to tell you a story. Don't you know any stories about people like me? About slaves?"

She thought about it, mined the depths of her brain, scrambling for a story. "You're not a slave, Pumpkin. You're a little boy, Mama's little boy."

"How come you never say my name? Why do you call me Pumpkin? Or Prader-Willi."

"Did you know, sweetie, that Aesop was a slave? He lived long, long ago, and he told many of the same stories I tell to you."

He frowned. "He came from Africa like me and like Babe and like Mr. Ricky and Robby?"

"No, he came from another far away land. But he was a lot like you too. He was very smart, making up these stories. And he was disabled too."

He stood up abruptly, his hands on the table. "I'm not dis—able. I'm not that word!"

"Sweetie, it's nothing to be ashamed of. All God's children are beautiful in His eyes, always remember that."

"Is Babe and Chance beautiful in God's eyes, or is they going to burn in hell like you said?"

Alise's temple throbbed with agitation. She tried to calm her quickly rising fury. She did not want a repeat of her reaction from the previous occasion. "You are too young to understand some things, sweetie. Some things in this world you won't understand until you are bigger."

"I don't want to be bigger. I understand things right now, Mama, I know what you did."

"What do you know?" she whispered, her voice light as gas. "Tell me."

"I know you let Puff Puff get away. And he's gone forever. And you lost him. And now we only got Pretzel."

Alise heard nothing other than *lost lost lost lost lost* over and over from a void of blackness in her heart. She pushed herself away from the table, stumbled to her room, and slammed the door shut. She had to get away from him, from his accusing words, his eyes telling her somehow, he knew more. This wasn't just about Puff Puff. He knew more. Somehow, he knew.

Chapter Thirty-Nine

Breakdown

It happened on the night Babe decided he needed to return the vehicle to his employer and bring his Jeep home. He was taking advantage of their benevolence, and if he continued using the company car, they might decide he was taking advantage and can him.

He and Chance were in the Suburban, driving along Route 202, on the way out to Frazer. The light at the intersection of 202 and Gulph Road was notoriously long, so Babe stomped the accelerator, trying to make the green as it blinked to yellow. He cursed as he missed it, jerkily slamming the brake.

Chance stiffened outstretched arms against the dash as he hurled forward. "Damn. Trying to kill me?"

"Buckle up for safety, motherfucker."

Chance reached exaggeratedly for the seatbelt and clicked it loudly. They both laughed, then sat in silence, waiting for the light to change.

Babe heard the opening chords of a song on the radio. Low horns signified something ominous, something on the horizon. He shushed Chance and turned up the volume.

"What the fuck is this? You heard this before?"

Chance listened as a woman sang/warned in a throaty but strident, heavy with mucus voice.

....

Chance shook his head. "Never heard this bef—"

Babe shushed him, listening.

He felt that shiver in his core. The one that made the hairs on the nape of his neck go up with goose bumps raising on his flesh. Of course he knew this song. He'd heard this song before, many times in his childhood, sung by The Delfonics, playing on his parents' turntable or on the car radio during outings. Sang in the falsetto popular during the seventies. Part of the reason the song in this revised rendition was both comfortably familiar and new. He had never heard it like this before. Sung with emotion that could only be conveyed through the vocal pyrokinetics of a woman's voice. This song spoke to him. Told him that something new, revised, like this song, like a phoenix from the ashes, was on the horizon.

A male began to rap, low and hypnotic.

"Is that the Fugees?"

Babe shushed him again.

They both screamed. Feeling as if they had discovered something new.

"Who the fuck is this!"

They turned up the music, heads bobbing, eyes closed, ecstatic.

The light changed to green. Babe stomped the gas. The car shot forward, went through the intersection, wobbled, and veered toward the left. Chance grabbed the roof strap just as sparks flared up on the driver's side window. A loud metallic screech ripped through the cabin. Babe hit the brake, but the car was already immobile.

Babe opened the door and hopped from the truck. Chance, not knowing what to do, sat in the cabin. The large tire on the driver's side had torn from the bolts, leaning against the underbelly of the wheel casing of the Suburban.

He looked over as Chance jumped out and circled the vehicle.

"What the fuck?" Chance's voice was incredulous.

"Tire came loose. Looks like the bolts holding it on rusted loose."

"But this is a new car. How the fuck that happen?"

Babe got the jack from the back, placed it under the vehicle, and attempted to loosen the other lug nuts.

"I feel totally useless. How can I help you fix this? You can't change this tire by yourself. You see how big this car is? It's liable to fall over and crush you."

"I'm not by myself." Babe glared at him, then renewed his attention on loosening the lug nuts."

"I don't know nothing 'bout birthing no babies, Miss Scarlett. You on your own."

After a few failed attempts to loosen the oversized hardware, Babe conceded Chance might be right. "Go check to see if that gas station has a pay phone."

"What you want me to do that for?"

"Call yourself a cab. You might as well go home. You're no use to me out here. And it's getting cold, anyway."

He could call Matthew. Even if he had to walk there, Matthew would make a way to him if he told him he needed him. But if he got Matthew involved, it would create expectations of getting back together.

There was also the possibility Matthew was responsible for this. If that were the case, calling him would be letting him know his attempts to create havoc hit the mark. He also did not want that.

Once Chance was safely tucked away in a yellow cab, Babe made another call. He waited in the darkness, watching cars zip past, listening to the radio while he waited, wanting to hear that song, hear that voice again.

Once they had gotten the tire placed back on the wheel, Wilfredo followed him back to his job where he parked the vehicle on the lot. He climbed into Wilfredo's Toyota and pointed across the lot toward the rear of the garage, where his Jeep was parked.

Babe listened to the Toyota idle like an angry lion across the blacktop, feeling Wilfredo's stare in the dark of the vehicle.

"Why are you staring at me?"

"Who's staring at you? I'm driving."

More silence.

"Those lug nuts weren't rusty. They were loosened."

"Okay."

"Okay, what?"

"What you want me to say? Lug nuts get loose sometimes."

"You don't think they were loosened on purpose."

"Could have been. There's no way of knowing."

"I'm just going to say this. I been in many relationships, right. The ones that didn't want to let go, it was because I was giving them a reason to think that they shouldn't."

"What reason? If you were with crazy bitches that don't accept when it's over, you're saying it was your fault? This is my fault?"

"I thought me still coming around, fucking them, lightened the blow. That's pure ego. I was sending a mixed message. If you loved this guy, ever, you owe it to him to leave him the fuck alone."

"I am leaving him alone."

"You know don't nothing go down on Leviticus Street that somebody don't know about. That's all I'm saying to you."

"I appreciate all your help. I do. But you should mind your own business."

Wilfredo stared at him. "Bet."

Babe sighed. "Sorry. I'm not used to people knowing the things I do. I don't like it."

He laughed. "You serious? Shit you do is not private. That younghead you live with is an open book. And he might look up to you, think you are the bee's knees and shit, but youngheads don't know how to show that in the right way. He is mucking you all up, and you don't even see it."

"Okay. Somebody else that's trying to 'warn' me about the crazy white boy living in my house. That boy can't do shit to me, even if what everyone is saying is true, because he don't have anything I want or need."

"You should know white people well enough to know they ain't got to have shit for them to fuck shit up for you, and you ain't got to have shit either. It's what they *think* you have that creates problems."

"The racist ones may be like that. Chance isn't one of those." Babe laughed. "He's blacker than me. He wants to be Black so bad it makes him hate his own people."

"Once they get tired of digging around in the dirt, they always know they can fall back on their own culture. When they get themselves into shit they can't get out of on they own. That white privilege comes back with a vengeance. They don't ever hate their own kind so bad as to totally throw them away. They're just on the back burner waiting for an emergency."

Babe had given thought to the possibility Matthew had something to do with his car trouble. He had avoided the thought, told himself it couldn't be.

"Okay, you want me to make a big confession? I been screwing around with my ex. Are you happy?"

"You don't have to confess shit to me, man. I already know! Shit, do you. As long as you're ready to handle the repercussions."

"It felt kind of good. You know? Knowing you have this kind of control over another person. Even when they know you don't want them anymore. It feels kind of powerful. And I thought about all the times I sat up waiting for him to come home. All the lies and shit. The times he made me feel like shit. And now I have the upper hand."

"Yeah. I know. I felt like I was the shit too. Till a bitch busted out the windows in my car."

"This is a whole different thing though. The stuff he did before. The writing on the windows, trying to take a VCR. Those were like temper tantrums, trying to make himself seen. This...this...what if I was on 202 when that wheel gave out? Going seventy miles an hour. I could have been hurt. He seriously wants to hurt me. Or he's too dumb to think through everything that might have happened."

Wilfredo laughed. "I'm totally willing to believe any dude that writes 'You is dead' on a windshield is dumb as a bag of nickels, but he knew what he was doing. He didn't give a fuck if you lived or died. If you keep ignoring that you're even dumber than he is."

The insult stung. But he knew Wilfredo was right.

He also knew when he stopped seeing Matthew altogether and Matthew realized what was happening, his attempts to gain Babe's attention might grow worse, could become even more overt than the mere loosening of a lug nut. He climbed out of the car and headed toward his Jeep, imagining he could still feel Wilfredo's eyes peering at him intently.

Chapter Forty

Changed Locks

The next day, Babe bought three new locks from Home Depot, along with the instruction manual, praying at checkout that his credit card would process the payment. He was close to his spending limit, having made use of it for small incidentals: extra groceries, gas, soap and toilet paper—something he would normally never do. He found that even though his net worth was technically at the same place as it had been when he and Matthew were together, if he considered the added income from Chance and the rental unit, his on-hand funds were still on the brink of zero.

Curtains and blinds of nearby houses blinked and shivered as he knelt at the door with his (Matthew's) toolbox, removed the old hardware, and replaced it with the new. It empowered him when he had successfully changed his first lock. This had been a task which normally fell to Matthew.

He moved around to the backyard, focusing on the door to the laundry room.

While he was concentrating on dislodging the old screws, a shadow fell across his shoulder. Thinking it was Matthew, he jumped, stood up, defensive. Alise stood there, clutching a jacket closed in front of her chest. Her eyes were red rimmed, and her hair was knotted and disheveled.

"I changed the lock on the front door. I'll get a key to you before the day is out," he said tersely.

She lit a cigarette and inhaled strongly. "I wanted to apologize to you. For that night. I was out of my mind with fright, and I said things that I shouldn't have."

"Don't worry about it. I was out of line, taking your kid."

"You going to kick me out? I can't afford another place."

"I'm not kicking you out. You pay your rent on time. That's all I care about. But you need to take care of that place. It's a pit. If the borough did visits, I'd be screwed."

She flicked the cigarette, then burst into tears. He wanted to console her, but he couldn't forget the sting of her words, the angrily hurled Bible quotes.

"You all right?"

"He hates me."

"Who...? He doesn't hate you. He got caught up in the moment like the rest of us did."

"He won't talk to me. I lost the cat. I lost control of everything."

"He's a kid. He'll be fine, sooner or later. Kids sulk. You buy him a new game, new sneaks, he'll be good. We've all lost control of everything. I think that's the first commandment of adulthood. Your life is shit, and you can't do anything about it."

She smiled grimly, nearly a grimace. "I tried so hard to do it all. To make this thing work. But the older he gets, the less I know what to do for him. His hair. I can't even take care of his hair."

"He has beautiful hair. So long and curly. You don't even have to do anything to hair like that but wash and condition it now and then, and maybe grease his scalp."

"Grease his scalp? My husband used to grease his scalp, but I never paid attention. He had beautiful hair. Soft and wavy. Like a Roman sculpture."

Babe snorted. "Why not a Nubian Warrior? I mean, was your husband Black, or is Rueben biracial?

"He was Black, yeah. And Rueben is biracial."

"Wh—? Is he adopted?"

She stiffened at the question. She drew herself up taller, tugged the collar of her jacket firm to her face. "He's my child."

Babe frowned, not understanding.

"Sometimes, you tell a little white lie, you know, to make things better. When he was a little boy, he thought he was different than me. He hated himself. Said he didn't want to be Black. He wanted to be like me. And the kids...children can be so despicable. They'd call him vile, ugly names, made fun of him all the time. I mean, he wasn't just Black, he had this problem too, PWS. They were just monstrous.

"So, I said I was Black too, that I had biracial parents. I wanted him to learn to accept himself. I didn't think about how heavy it would become to have to live with that lie year after year. How I would have to deny part of who I am to keep the lie going."

"You're not Black."

"One lie told to your kid turns into a repetition of the lie. I've had to tell it to everybody I meet, pretend to be what I'm not. I feel like a big fraud. Then, you come along, and I can see how useless my lie is for him. He can see himself in you, and it was that simple. I couldn't even get him to take baths, and now, he's taking baths every day, brushing his teeth, talking about Harriet Tubman, things I couldn't do for him. Everything I do for him is a waste. I can't do those other things for him. Teach him about his history. How to be a young man. He looks up to you."

"A one to one, man to man talk about stinking is a blip on the screen compared to years of mothering and sacrifice. You think everything you've done as a parent doesn't matter just because you couldn't get him to wash his ass. That's crazy."

"No, I know you're right in my head. But in my heart, I feel like I failed. I tried so hard. I promised God I would be perfect this time if He let me have another chance, but I wasn't perfect."

"How the hell did you expect that you would be? And you mean to tell me you can't read up on Black history? Brush up on your Phyllis Wheatley and your Frederick Douglass. You can get that knowledge at the local library. Hell, you owe it to him to know where he comes from as much as you do to teach it to him. How can you have thought he would be able to have a sense of pride by you pretending to be something that you're not? You want him to be proud of a lie. I mean, you have an advantage over a lot of Black parents. You homeschool so you can teach the things that the public schools gloss over. Like the transatlantic slave trade that has been whitewashed and revised in those textbooks to be an immigration story instead of kidnapping, slaughter, and rape. What the fuck?"

"There's a specific curriculum that has to be followed. I was hesitant when I saw that shit. But I figured these books are created by experts far smarter than me, so maybe they know something that I don't. I thought maybe peer review had decided it was too traumatic for kids to know the truth about the ways men hurt and destroy other men."

"Just like you not being honest about who you are. Kids are stronger than we give them credit for. How can a lie be less traumatic than the truth? That textbook version is a lie."

She used the sleeve of her jacket to wipe at the tears on her face. Babe leaned forward, gave her a brief hug. "You'll be all right. He's going to be fine. Just be patient with him. And tell him the truth. He deserves that. Once he knows you're being up front with him, I think he'll stop the old silent treatment. Hell, that's the only thing I've done. I'm up front with him. He respects that."

She smiled at him through bleary eyes, nodding in gratitude.

Chapter Forty-One

Restraint

She would have kept him home every day. Every morning when he told her the kids said terrible, dreadful things. Laughing, pointing at him. She wanted to protect him. Kendall wanted him to be tough, resilient.

"He's got to learn that living in this world with Black skin as your calling card doesn't give you the privilege of hiding, staying home when it gets tough out there. This...this *syndrome* ain't no harder than being born Black."

Kendall said that, but his behavior showed that the problem was more than a desire to have his son stand strong in his identity. He was ashamed of his son. He treated his child as an embarrassment, an aversion: the same way those elementary school children, whose mouths hurled vile, hateful things, and the faculty, who pretended not to hear the hate assaulting her child day after day.

She learned to become someone else. She became Rueben's warrior but masked it behind the facade of a solicitous suburban mother. She wore flowered, pleated dresses with a bowed collar, paired with white hosiery and tied her drab blonde hair with a ribbon, coiled it above her head and brushed out feathered bangs. She wanted the faculty to like her. Didn't want them to see her as trailer trash with the Black husband. She baked cookies and cakes and purchased gifts for new teachers. She conducted introductory orientations each new school year where she instructed people on the specifics of Prader-Willi Syndrome and the special needs Rueben might require.

She grew tired of the repetitiveness. Of praying each year the new teacher would be understanding, might have experience with special education and Individual Evaluation Plans. She knew better than to hope that anyone would have knowledge of PWS. But if they at least had familiarity with teaching kids with other special needs, at least they might be more predisposed to the extra work that would be involved.

By Rueben's last year of elementary school, her script had become rote.

> *Hi. I'd like to introduce you to my child. He has PWS. He loves school and loves the attention of his teachers. Praise goes a long way in keeping him focused. He really loves English and story time—math, not so much. He can become easily frustrated. He used to have behavioral outbursts but not so much now, but we must be vigilant in keeping him away from food. It could kill him or at least make him very sick. In fact, I will be willing to come to the school each day at lunch time to ensure that he is safe during a time that could be very dangerous to him if left*

unsupervised. He will be given a TSS worker, but let's be honest. Those people are not very reliable, and there is high turnover for the position, so there will be many days where they are no-shows. You must call me immediately when that happens, so I can try to give you, and Rueben, the support you need so as not to disrupt the classroom. He has been bullied. Terribly. And that has changed his demeanor. He used to be an outgoing child. Now he is surly and withdrawn and needs to feel the love and support of his teacher to draw out his loving nature. I know love is not a word that is customarily used in a school setting, can in fact lead to legal complications, but I feel stressing the importance of love is the most effective word in demonstrating what my child's needs will be for the coming school year. He has been specifically targeted by student _____. We have been in contact with both his parents and the police, but there has been very little intervention. Both parties seem to think 'boys will be boys' is sufficient explanation for the terrorism my child has endured year after year at the hands of this boy and his group of bullies. You are to keep my child away from _____ at all costs. I have a video of Rueben, and I have prepared where he introduces himself to you and I'd like to play it for you now before you actually meet him in person when classes begin.

She was there every afternoon with Rueben's meticulously packed lunch in hand, calories calculated with scientific precision. She pretended she didn't see the judgement in their eyes, what they thought of her: overprotective, slovenly, and bearer of defective children.

She told herself that the IEP created by the school, with its focus on behavior modification and the creation of a restraint plan, implemented when Rueben's frustration with being denied food escalated to a physical manifestation, had not been created because the faculty felt that addressing the needs of a Black child required a more hands-on intervention than it would had he been a white child. But given that Rueben was the only Black child with special needs at the school and the only child of any race that had a restraint plan in place while the other children who displayed physical aggression utilized the seclusion/de-escalation room where sensory boards and light therapy strategies were used as part of an evidence-based modality of crisis management instead of the basket hold and two-man supine restraint, it was difficult for her to convince herself otherwise.

But they had never contacted her. The school board, with their IEP's, their assigned therapeutic support staff, their behavioral specialist, all felt they were most equipped in dealing with the challenges presented by her child.

Oh, sure, they had listened to her, valued her insight, documented everything she relayed at the "team" meetings, but eventually, they began to see her as overly involved, one of those helicopter parents, with her daily appearances and refusal to let her child ride to school on the short yellow bus that pulled up to her house each day. She was ashamed of that bus. The message it screamed with its loud, tacky color and lack of length. She would walk right past that bus, droning with the stilted communication efforts of its inhabitants, hustle Rueben into the Galant, and drive him to the school herself.

When they finally deigned to phone her, it was to tell her of a dreadful mistake.

That was the word that rang in her ears long after she ended the call.

dreadful dreadful dreadful

The word droned in her head like a demon.

She was working a short shift at the hospital when the call had come.

They had taken Rueben to a seclusion room. He had been "out of control," they said. A child of his size, his girth, had required two staff to escort him to a safer place, so other children would not be harmed, traumatized by the violent display of anger he had erupted in when confronted with stealing food from his classmates.

She had warned them, told them the most effective strategy would be that they not demand he return the food, not confront him in such a vigilante sort of way. Making a deal with him, requesting that he trade half of what he had taken in exchange for something else of value—like five minutes free time on a video game or quiet time with his favorite book—was the better strategy to de-escalate her child.

The behavior management plan designed by their PhD level expert instructed otherwise. A two-person facedown restraint had been deemed the most effective way of controlling Rueben in the event of a crisis. She had screamed at that word. *Control.* What did they mean by *control*? She had been told the physical restraint would only be utilized as the method of last resort in crisis intervention. "This was not crisis intervention. It was treatment failure," she had yelled at them.

Why did her child need to be controlled, and the other children were given the tools by which they could regain control of themselves?

Positional asphyxiation.

She heard the despair in his voice beneath the veneer of professional courtesy. The dread.

An unfortunate mishap.

Those were the words he used to tell her he was dead. During the scuffle to get him to the ground where he would be safer, where he would be less likely to harm himself. During the scuffle, somehow legs had gotten tangled. Staff had fallen on him during the *transition* from upright to prone.

As he had continued to struggle, staff continued to apply the IEP approved restraint. After thirty minutes, they turned him over to adjust his pants. Why had they needed to adjust his pants? How had this been deemed important?

He was not breathing. His heart had stopped. He was en route to the E.R.

She dropped the phone, then ran to the bank of elevators. Prayed to God. If He saved her baby, she'd never let him leave her sight again.

But she had broken that promise to God. She had been selfish. And now he hated her.

Chapter Forty-Two

Chance & Matthew

Babe was a little drunk. Nothing major, a little buzz from one Grand Marnier rocks too many at Paradise Alley where he had stood off in a darkened corner on the second floor listening to vintage house and gospel remixes. The second floor tended to skew slightly older than the first level where hip-hop music attracted the B-boy wannabes and DL crowd, but ballroom voguers would dance upstairs, flailing arms and diving on floors in reckless abandon amidst the older househeads and church queens, and then reining it in, they'd troll the first level, trying to appear straight acting in search of those B-boy wannabes and DL men.

He had been surprised when Chance had pleaded out from Saturday Night Ritual, copping to a headache. Paradise Alley was one of the only gay venues left with a Black crowd, and Chance leaped at any opportunity to go there, afraid of going alone, claiming that he didn't feel safe unless he went with a Black person as his calling card.

Babe had been skeptical. They had both gone out all weekend long in the past, headaches be damned. They'd toss back a few Advil, chase it with a shot of vodka until they could score some coke to numb the pain. It was more likely Chance had foregone going out in favor of an opportunity for sex, more likely than not with someone other than his boyfriend.

The windows at the back of the house were dark. He pulled up to the garage and parked adjacent to the bay to allow other cars passage. Even Chance's bedroom window was dark. Completely dark, which was unusual. When he had company, he usually kept a purple light burning. "For ambiance," he'd said. While that struck Babe as odd, it didn't hit him as particularly alarming.

When he entered the apartment, the quiet was deafening. Unsettling. Chance always kept music playing, even when he was sleeping.

He stood on the darkened landing, goose bumps raising on his flesh. The air was damp with the smell of soap from the open bathroom door. He moved closer. A towel lay bunched in the corner beside the hamper. Babe could smell his body spray and deodorant, but beneath that, along with those overpowering, heavy notes, he smelled something more familiar, something he had a more carnal knowledge of.

He clicked on the light in the hall and walked toward that familiar scent, toward Chance's bedroom, toward the door standing slightly ajar. The smell grew stronger. The lightbulb cast a weak light on the empty futon and tousled bed linens. Babe moved closer, lifted the bedspread, and stood awash in the smell of sweat, the funk of spunk-smeared bed linens. He smelled him like an ephemera: the strong burn of sweat mixed with the dirt of his tightly coiled hair, pheromones Babe identified immediately. It was as familiar as his own scent, as familiar as his upraised legs or bending low. The odor of his coital breath. The mothballs that permeated his clothing, his flesh. The particular murk that unfurled from his underarms when he ejaculated. Matthew's scent.

Babe's stomach lurched with certainty. He threw the blanket back on the bed, his eyes burning with surprise and his olfactory senses ablaze with the familiar.

Chapter Forty-Three

Chance

The first day Babe didn't come home raised no panic. Chance assumed that he had gotten sidetracked by Max or maybe even some other possibility. Particularly since it was still the weekend. But when day two passed, then day three, a slight rumbling of discomfort began to loom. He went through his day, going to work, joking with his coworkers, going out to lunch with Clark, but all day long, he worried about where Babe might be, if he would be home when Chance got there.

By midweek, when he walked up to the house from the bus stop, stopping to chat with Miss Imogene, who sat bundled in a coat at her open window, he began to panic.

"Where's that other one?" Miss Imogene asked, jerking her head in the direction the house with darkened windows. "Haven't seen him come or go all week now."

Chance flicked his finished cigarette into the street, hugged his arms around his torso, and shook his head. "Yeah, this isn't like him. I guess he had things to do."

"You call his family, his friends? See what's going on."

"I met his moms, but I don't know how to get in touch with her. I don't know any of his friends neither."

"What do you mean you don't know his friends? You been living with him all this time, and you don't know nobody he knows? You know those other two that stay next door, don't ya? What you call them if they ain't his friends."

He was reluctant to approach Ricky or Robby, wanting to respect Babe's privacy, which he valued. But by the time the weekend came and went with still no word from him he gave in, fearing something might be wrong.

He tentatively walked up the stairs and entered Babe's bedroom. He rummaged through his closets, went through his personal items, his bills stored in a flowered box hidden atop an armoire. He read the past due notices from utility companies, repossession notices from auto loan companies, the foreclosure notices, the letters from law offices on professional letterhead. He remembered their conversations where Babe had stressed that he needed to be paid promptly, that he had financial obligations, that Chance's lax payment commitments made it hard for him to stay on top of things.

Robby didn't answer his door. Chance heard him, though, behind the heavy oak door. Low, pealing droning, plaintive and repetitive. *No help, no help, no help.*

"You got that motherfucking right." He grumbled, walking down to the next level, then banged on Ricky's door.

Ricky was there. After knocking, he heard him on the other side of the door, talking on the phone. A shadow moved beneath the crack of the door. Ricky stood there for a good minute or two before opening the door, acting surprised to see him.

Chance stood there, not comfortable with a silent Ricky.

"Did you come here to stare at me? To what do I owe this unexpected pleasure?"

"You heard from Babe? He's been gone all week, and I'm getting panicked."

Ricky leaned lazily on the doorframe. "Why would you panic? Babe is grown. She'll come home when she wants to come home."

"Yeah. But it's not like him not to show for a week—"

Ricky spoke, interrupting his sentence. "You don't know anything about Babe. How do you know what's like him and what's not?"

Chance laughed, quick and uncomfortable. "I know him good enough to know this ain't regular behavior."

"You listen to his records, pillage his books and magazines, ape his looks, make yourself comfortable with everything that belongs to him, and that makes you think you know him? It takes more than pissing all over shit like a rabid dog to know somebody. You got to be observant about the things beneath the surface."

Chance frowned. "What the fuck are you even saying?"

"What I'm saying, Miss thing, is that when a bitch wants to come for somebody's throne, she's going to have to do more than bathe in her dirty bath water. But anyway, no ma'am. It's not the doll's job to track any sissy's whereabouts. Even the ones I love. Fear not! She shall return!"

Ricky slammed the door shut.

Chapter Forty-Four

Baby Trade

Alise had changed locks too. She had installed a deadbolt on the back and front doors. Deadbolts that required a key to lock and unlock them, which she kept on a chain around her neck. She told Rueben she only wanted to keep him safe. She had risked too much to let him be harmed, she said.

She only used the deadbolts when she had to leave the house for groceries, visits to the welfare office, or other errands, so Rueben wouldn't leave the house. Wouldn't be exposed to "undue influences," she said.

But she seldom left the house anymore. Terrified Rueben would go missing, she had stopped caretaking for the old woman next door. Instead, she contented herself by popping a Valium and sitting before the soothing drone of reruns of old television programs, cajoling Rueben to go spend time down in the cellar with Pretzel. That way, there was an added layer between him and access to the outside world.

She wasn't stupid: she knew the Valium were addictive, but it helped her. It was like a cashmere blanket for her thoughts, allowing her to forget her guilt. She sat in front of June, Ward, and Wally, immersing herself in banal, manufactured intricacies, resolved within a half hour, unlike the problems she had created for herself. For thirty minutes, she ignored the loud, accusing voice in her head, telling her she let Puff Puff get away, and how much longer would it be before Pretzel, and then Rueben, got away too. How much longer before she lost everything all over again? All her carefully collected possessions, gathered during the past year living on Leviticus Street would fade away, too, as they had before. Just as she had lost the house. And lost Kendall.

Valium allowed her to think of nothing, instead of everything. It kept the other voice at bay, the voice that told her she had to do something, take back control.

It was the same voice that had screamed in her head since that day when Rueben died. It was there while she listened to the hollow, empty explanations. The meaningless apologies. It was there when she held her child's lifeless body in her arms, howling like a lost, wounded thing. It had been there through the funeral while she listened to benevolent words but saw judgement in their eyes.

During Kendall's whispers of lawsuits, and meetings with attorneys. Through court proceedings and Kendall's constant talk of how good it would be to get out of debt, to get a second chance at things.

While they waited for their windfall, the voices grew louder. The only time she didn't hear the accusing voice was in the quiet solace of maternity wards, sitting amongst the voices of cooing new mothers and white nurse's scrubs. The structure and rigor of maternity wards was a comfort. It belied the chaos that loomed outside. She'd take the Galant and drive, sometimes for hours, until she spotted a hospital that seemed safe and secure. She'd pull into the parking lot and search for the maternity unit where she'd sit until sundown, running down to the cafeteria where she'd order coconut custard pie, or some other trifle that reminded her of the simpler days of her youth.

When the money came, she was barely aware of it. It meant nothing to her. No dollar amount would fill the ache in her arms, the void left by her missing child. She didn't even care when she came home one night from a day at a hospital in another state to find Kendall gone. She was relieved. He was only a reminder of how abysmally she had failed. When he depleted their bank account and absconded with all the settlement money, she had not been surprised. She expected nothing less from him.

The fact that he took the money was a reassurance he'd leave her alone for good. The money filled a void for him, but it didn't fill her void. She asked God to take away the ache she carried with her every day, she promised she would be a better mother if He would only give her another chance.

The lone Black baby in the maternity ward had been a sign from God. She had known God placed him there to answer her prayers.

Rueben stood in the shadow of the cellar doorway, watching his mother succumbing to the little white tablet she had tapped into her hand from the amber vial on the table in front of her and taken with a gulp of water. She held a cracker in one hand. He watched her hand rise languidly from her lap, as she tried to aim the cracker toward her open mouth. Drool dribbled down her chin. The cracker never made it to her mouth, instead she battered it against her sallow cheek, as she softly listed to the side, her head moving closer and closer toward the armrest as though in slow motion. He stood there, waiting.

Once she sank into slumber, Rueben drifted forward, stepped in front of her to be sure she was sleep. The deadbolts on the doors did not bother him. He knew all he had to do was wait for the pills to make her sleepy, and then he climbed out the window and leisurely explored his neighborhood.

At first, he would only drift as far as the porch, then to the sidewalk, and then to the parking lot across the street, always fearful he would not make it back before she awakened. But as he became accustomed, as Alise became accustomed, to the frequency of her pill taking, he learned there were long stretches of time before she would come around. Even when she finally woke from her stupor, she would still languish unaware under the lingering effects, allowing him to slip back inside without her being aware of anything.

This time, he had a specific purpose for slipping from the house. He didn't plan to go far. Each day, he stood hidden behind the sheers, waiting for Babe, listening for the roar of his Jeep pulling up. He saw Chance drift out to the porch, looking up and down Leviticus Street, wringing his hands anxiously. Rueben was worried too. When many days passed with no sighting of Babe, he began to think of bad things, things that happened in fairytales: Babe being pushed into an oven by a cackling crone with a hairy mole, being baked in a pie by an evil gremlin, or being stolen by a jealous queen.

Now he knew those were only fairytales, made up stories. "You ever seen a bitch like that around here?" Ricky had asked. The people in those stories didn't look like him. Things like that didn't happen in real life. In real life, Harriet Tubman saved herself. She didn't wait around for a prince on a white horse because there was no prince to save her.

Those stories were fairytales, but he was locked in a house like Rapunzel. But he was a real person, like Harriet, and it was up to him to save himself.

When Chance came out of the house next door and walked back onto the porch, Rueben made his way outside, meeting him on the landing.

Chance stopped short at the boy in front of him.

"What do you want? I'm busy here."

"I want to know where Babe's at."

"So do I." Chance laughed, short, staccato.

"I want to talk to Babe."

"Listen kid. He's not home, all right? I don't have time to fuck around with you. All you want from him is to stuff your fat face, and you can't 'cause he's not here. And I'm damn sure not feeding you, so your fat ass moms can come at my neck like I'm trying to suck your little unformed dick. Just get out of here."

Chance walked inside the house, slamming the door behind him.

Rueben looked at the door as he reached a hand into his pocket for a pinch of salt.

He did not like Chance. He was not a nice person.

Chapter Forty-Five

Babe & Max

Max lived in a small apartment complex in a small town on the Philadelphia city limits. Despite its proximity to the city, the town had a suburban feel that Babe found peaceful. He could roam small side streets, roam the shops along Sixty-Ninth Street alone in his thoughts. He was first startled when passersby would nod or say a friendly hello, but as week one turned to a second week, then a third, Babe grew accustomed to, even enjoyed, the casual friendliness of the area. He'd nod back with a fleeting smile as he entered Sound of Market, sorting through the tremendous racks of vinyl records, or perusing the tiny thrift stores, smelling of mold and ancient perfume. The smell of mothballs would hit him, reminding him of Matthew, and he would head back to the fresh air of the sidewalks.

Max arose most mornings at seven. Babe would get up with him, and they'd prepare breakfast. Max didn't eat much. He'd brew coffee and read the paper. Babe would have half a cup of oatmeal with a raw egg, and they'd have small talk until both would leave around eight: Max headed to his shop in North Philly, Babe headed to his gym in King of Prussia where he'd workout for an hour and a half, shower, and head to work from there.

He had given Babe a key to his apartment. When Babe had shown up at his door that night, his eyes red and bleary, asking if he could crash for a day or two, Max had asked no questions. He had taken his tiny gym bag and guided him inside. Babe usually had the place to himself after work at five. Max usually worked until nine or ten, so Babe would sometimes clean up the apartment, full of antiques that quickly accumulated dust along with various pieces of ornately designed furniture. Or he'd prepare dinner and drive it down to the salon where he'd coax Max into taking a half hour away from making money to actually sit down and take a minute for himself, to eat a full meal for a change.

Just as he had been struck by the friendliness of the people in Max's neighborhood, he was amazed that all Max's clients knew him, treating his entrance with his arms full of bags of steaming dinner aloft, with a sort of deference. They would cluck like protective hens or say "So this is Babe, huh? I'm glad you came down here to make this boy eat. He ain't nothing but skin and bones."

The shop was a mishmash of collected fixtures and styles. Max had acquired objects from closed salons and fire sales around the state, then filled his store with them. He was frugal with money. But he also spent a lot of money on hair products and gave lavishly; be it providing gowns for friends to do drag shows, buying clothing for the young boys (who he called his slaves) that traipsed in and out of the apartment and the salon, or doing hair for women that were unable to pay.

When Babe had asked how he could afford to give so freely to so many, Max had shrugged. "If you don't give money, you don't get money. Scared money don't make money."

"That may be so. But I need all my shit. I'm barely staying afloat as it is. If I were to give my money away, I'd be in the poorhouse."

"You give your time away. That's as vital as money, maybe more so. You're doing the same thing I'm doing."

"How so?"

"You gave Chance a place to stay. You giving that little fat kid and his mom a place to stay, and that bitch disrespected you under your own roof. You do things for people too. And that's why good things come back to you."

That night, Babe stayed with Max at the Salon until closing. He helped him close up the shop after the last customer left: disinfecting furniture, dusting fixtures, and sweeping errant tufts of hair, both human and manmade. Max stopped him. "You don't gotta do that. We can lock up. I pay the slaves to do that."

"I wish you wouldn't call them that."

"When they respect themselves, stop dick hopping, I'll give them more respect." Babe frowned at him. "All right. I'm sorry, Babe. I'll call the slaves li'l chicken heads from now on."

"Thanks." Babe laughed. As Babe headed to the door, Max stood stock still in the center of the shop, hands on his hips. "What?"

"You know your hairline's receding?"

Babe sighed. "I know. Another sign of my impending descent to old age. It's thinning on top too."

"Getting old is a bitch. You'll soon be a wizened thirty-five."

"You think I'm being dramatic. It's not me, it's my fellow gay brethren that are the problem. You know I was at a party last summer, and some queen said to me, "Leather pants? You won't be able to get away with that much longer."

Max laughed. "And she probably looked like the McDonald's Grimace, right?"

Babe laughed, short and cruel. "Bitch, if Lionel Ritchie is still getting rashes in his crotch from leather chafe, I think I got a few good years left on the leather."

"But you should let me cut your hair. Holding on to those dreads doesn't make sense when everybody can see that new growth isn't coming in like that."

He shook his head. "No way. I'm not ready for that."

Max shrugged, clicked the lights dark, and followed him outside.

When they got back to the apartment, the smell of lemon furniture polish and disinfectant signaled the recent departure of one of Max's slaves. Babe changed into his sweats while Max was in the bathroom. He clicked on the TV while Max went across the hall to check on his mother, who had her own apartment where she was assisted by an attendant while Max was working.

After an hour, Babe turned off the TV, went into the bedroom, and hunkered down under the thin blankets. Max came into the room and shuffled through the darkness, removing his clothes. He turned on the TV.

Babe pulled a pillow over his head. He couldn't sleep unless there was complete silence. Max couldn't sleep unless there was a TV or radio going. Max walked toward the bed in his loose boxers. He was terribly thin. The weeks Babe had spent with him showed Max focused on work and making money with little attention to eating. He worked twelve-hour days and ate one quick meal while drinking cups of coffee to keep him going.

Max stopped short, standing in front of the bed with his hands on his hips. Babe looked out from the pillows.

"What?"

"I like you, Babe."

"Thanks. I'm thankful for everything you're doing for me. I appreciate you."

"I don't want you to be thankful. Babe, sometimes you do things that show you want to make a break from the way things have been, but then you turn around and do the same shit you've always been doing."

"You want me to go back home now?"

Max sat on the bed and turned to face Babe. "You can stay with me the rest of your life, if you want to. Being with you has been...nice.... It's a joy. But you have a house. Filled with people. Filled with financial responsibilities you aren't addressing. You can only avoid things for so long. If you don't shut it down, or take the reins, how can you expect things to be different?"

"So, you want me to go back home."

Max laughed. "I want you to cut them ridiculous dreads."

Babe was terrified. And he was angry that he would be terrified about something as banal as hair. He was trembling nervously, sitting in the chair in the kitchen biting his nails, while Max circled him, eyeing his head like a falcon about to descend upon a rabbit in the snow.

Max leaned forward, kneaded through Babe's dreads, searching for lumps and bumps. "Okay, you got a good-shaped head. You should be good."

He leaned forward so Max could get at the back. Babe watched thick tufts of his hair fall to the linoleum like inert, slaughtered things. He listened to the labored metallic snip as the thin shears struggled through the length of each hank of hair. Babe wanted to tell Max to stop, that he'd changed his mind. Maybe he could get him to use bonding glue from his salon to reattach the severed pieces.

The apartment was silent, save for the distant drone from the TV in the bedroom, and Max's concentrated breathing as he focused on his work.

After the locks were removed, Max splashed orange blossom oil on his hands, rubbed them together, and rubbed it through Babe's hair. The smell was bright like a burst of sunshine. Max powered up a set of clippers and moved close.

Babe smelled his breath, mixed with cola from the dinner they had eaten earlier. It was pleasant. He peeked through slitted lids at Max's mouth; the color of burnt sienna, full beneath his trim mustache. His amber eye glowed like a feral cat. He moved behind Babe and gently cupped his neck as he guided his head down to apply the warm clippers to his nape. Max's body, lean and warm, leaned against Babe as he removed the shadow of hair from his well-formed head. Max's erection pushed against the small of Babe's back. Like a woman syncing up during a menstrual cycle, Babe stiffened as well.

Max spoke slow and languid, "New look. New start."

Max rubbed the contours of his head. It was pleasing, comforting, and safe.

"You have to put that boy out your house, Babe. You have to learn to be more assertive about what you deserve. You don't have to be afraid about being pissed off. You have a right to be pissed off and to tell a motherfucker you're pissed off."

"But I'm not pissed off. I'm hurt."

"You're pissed off. What's happened to you? What kind of childhood did you have that you are afraid to even admit you're pissed off about shit? What Black man doesn't have the right to be pissed the fuck off all the fucking time? I'm pissed off right now, Babe. I'm pissed off that I'm sitting here cutting the hair off this beautiful fucking Negro, and my dick is hard as a baseball bat, and I'm pressing my shit all up in his back, and he acting like he don't feel it."

Babe blushed as he laughed.

He thought about the night of the Diana Ross concert. That night when Alise had slapped Rueben. It had sparked something in him. He had been angry. He had wanted to jump on that woman and make her feel the pain that she'd made her son feel. That anger had scared him. He could not understand how that one incident had elicited such strong feelings.

Babe remembered Rueben, thinking no one was watching, shoving his hand in his pocket, then slipping salt to his mouth. And he thought about himself as a little boy, slipping salt into his own pockets. For some reason, the feeling of the weight of salt in his pockets had reassured him. He could rub salt into his own tongue, creating his own pain. That way, his mother was no longer in charge, no longer the one able to bring him pain. He could control his pain instead of giving someone else that power.

He remembered telling his mother, reminding her she was not his mother, and her swift, violent response. It echoed in his mind. It merged with remembrances of Rueben, screaming, "I'm not that Willy! I'm not that." He, Babe, was Rueben.

"I was an abused kid. And I didn't even know it until that night of the concert, seeing that woman hit her kid just because he expressed himself, showed her his anger. That's the kind of thing my mother would do. All through my childhood. Just cruel words, you know, like 'you're getting fat,' or 'you're acting like a girl,' you know, if I was watching Julia Childs or a cooking show. Stuff I never considered abuse. I mean, she didn't lock me in the basement or beat me with a hotcomb, you know, so I never felt like I was a victim."

"A lot of us think only women can be victims. But what about gay bashing?"

"Well, yeah. That's different. I mean me and Matthew had fights all the time. But I wasn't a victim of domestic abuse because he couldn't kick my ass." Babe laughed.

"So, you can only be a victim if you lose the fight?"

Babe shrugged. "I don't know. It's confusing to me."

Babe felt Max's warm lips on his head. Max kissed him before pushing him off the stool. "All done."

Babe grabbed the mirror Max held out to him. He examined his reflection. "Great. I'm Mr. Fucking Potato Head."

Max folded his arms across his bare chest as his dick began to lower in his boxers. "You're beautiful."

Babe crossed to him and enfolded him in his arms. He kissed Max's bald head after leaning down a full foot. "Thank you."

Max breathed heavily into Babe's chest. "You know what it sounds like to me? It sounds like you are so accustomed to being treated badly that you don't even recognize when it's happening."

"That's bullshit."

"You've been raised to accept shitty treatment, or you're so enmeshed in it that you can't see it from a different perspective, Babe. You lived with a woman that regularly hit you and your dad. You watched her hit your father, who explained it away as high-strung behavior. And he was too much of a man to strike back, so he accepted it. Then when you move away from your folks, you live with a man that gets fucked up, fucks around right under your nose, and fights you on the regular. And you know it's not right. Your head tells you that this is not the way life is supposed to be, so you leave him, but you don't change the locks on your house because you don't want to hurt his feelings. You open your house to this young boy and he fucks your ex. *In. Your. House.* You let a homophobic bitch continue to stay in your house. And she's loony tunes. You say the bitch got padlocks on the fridge. Whatever. She disrespected you. They all disrespecting you, but you still in this sort of purgatory place where you are still willing to give everybody the benefit of the doubt. Maybe you think you deserve to be treated like crap."

Babe listened while he swept up the hair on the floor.

"You don't have to sweep that up," Max said. "I told you, the sla—I mean, the chicken heads will take care of it."

Babe collected the hair into a plastic grocery bag. "I think not. You think I want them bitches collecting my hair to craft into voodoo dolls? I got enough problems."

"I'm telling you. Once you clean house, your problems will go away."

They walked back to the bedroom and climbed into the narrow bed, enjoying each other's warmth. Babe hugged Max, hunkering up on his butt. Max shifted uncomfortably and bumped Babe off so he could turn around and shift Babe to face away from him.

"Oh, it's like that, huh?"

"Like what?"

"Nothing." Babe laughed. He thought the discussion was over. It had grown late, and they both needed to get up early.

As Babe drifted off, Max spoke again. "Do you want me to get the white boy out for you?"

"Hmmm?"

"You can't leave him having run of your house while you hide away like a wounded animal."

Babe was insulted. "I'm not a wounded animal. I needed time to get my thoughts together. We live in a real world. You can't clap your hands and take care of everything that bothers you."

"Yeah, Babe, you can. If you have money problems, and you can't pay your car note, you can make that go away. If somebody won't leave you alone, you make them go away."

Babe sat up. "What are you talking about? Max, you just called me an animal. You're the one that sounds like an animal. We don't handle our problems like that. Sometimes people do terrible things because they are hurting, they're in pain. But how is responding to shitty things with shitty things of your own going to make things better?"

Max sighed as he ran a hand along Babe's spine. "That's why I like you, Babe. I knew it the first time I saw you in that filthy hole in the wall, standing among all that trash, smelling like a fresh young thing."

Babe was silent.

"Everybody was in there looking for something, somebody to save their life from this big yawning void of boredom. But you weren't looking for anything or anybody."

"What about you, Max? What were you looking for?"

"This world is full of ugly, hateful, pathetic people, Babe. You can call them wounded souls and talk about how everybody's in pain all you want. But that doesn't take away from the fact that those people do horrible things to everybody in their path."

"If you stay away from those people, they can't affect you..."

"How can you stay away from a motherfucker that won't let you be? Did white boy tell you about your ex going around the bars offering to pay somebody to get rid of you?"

"What are you saying?"

"Horrible people do horrible things. Stupid people do stupid things. They don't stop to think about anybody other than themselves. And it's people like you, Babe, that end up on the wrong end of their bad intentions."

Babe stood up, looking around for his pants, his keys. "Stop this. I don't want to hear this."

"I was looking for you, Babe, because I was sent for you. You spent thirteen years with someone that thinks your life isn't worth five hundred dollars."

Babe stopped listening, jerked at his clothing and tugged it on. Max got out of the bed, tried to touch him. Babe shook him off.

"Who are you? You're somebody that can do these things? You make cars disappear? People?"

His amber eye glowed in the light of the picture tube. Babe shook his head in disbelief, grabbing his gym bag. He abruptly left the room.

Chapter Forty-Six

Chance & Ricky

That last day, when Chance turned onto Leviticus Street from the bus stop, nothing struck him out of the norm. Curtains shifted in windows. People gathered on porches. Conversations drifted to silence as he walked by. But these weren't things that would not happen on any other day.

Wilfredo and his brothers sat on the stoop smoking a blunt, passing around a bottle of beer, their voices rumbling like car engines revving at their mark. That struck him as unusual. Especially when he nodded a hello toward Wilfredo, and he stared through him, lifting the bottle to his mouth with the flex of a golden bicep.

As he stepped up onto the porch of 535, Rueben stood in the window, staring out at him with vacant eyes. Chance lifted a hand to wave, but the curtain fell, leaving only his dark silhouette behind the dirty glass.

The door to the apartment stood ajar, held open with two filled trash bags.

Chance hastened his pace, thinking Babe had finally come home.

When he walked up to the apartment landing, he saw boxes stacked on one another, sealed with masking tape, labeled with various headings in black marker; towels, clothing, and bric-a-brac. His bedroom door stood wide. Chauncey walked out, carrying a box labeled CDs with Ricky supervising at his shoulder, giving instruction in a deliberately loud voice.

"Be careful with that shit. We don't want to damage anything." Ricky pretended to notice Chance by happenstance. "Oh, hey."

"What the fuck are you doing with my shit?"

Chauncey unceremoniously dropped the box in the hall and headed back into the bedroom for another. Ricky put his hands on his hips as he faced him. "Babe called me. He is indisposed at the moment, so he asked if I could help to facilitate you moving out."

"Moving out? What's wrong with him? Is he okay?"

"Oh, he's fine. But he will be better when he gets this situation taken care of. So, I knew you were busy at work, and working is great and everything, you know, because we all need money. So, I thought I could make this more efficient by packing up your things for you, so you could be all set to make arrangements when you got here."

"I'm not moving out. When's Babe coming home?"

"Oh, but you are." As if on cue, Chauncey dropped another box with a loud thud.

"Bullshit. I know my rights. You can't put me out without giving me notice."

"This is your notice."

"We'll see about that." Chance stormed into the living room and swiped magazines off the tables, his head swiveling about.

Ricky held up the receiver of the phone. "You looking for this?"

Chance snatched it out of his hand.

Ricky laughed. "I wondered how long it would take before you tried to bring the police into this. You ain't paid rent for the past two months. Going on three if you count the past few weeks when Babe hasn't been here. You think you have rights? What are they, squatter's rights?"

"Fuck you."

"You think they going to come in here and treat you like some white bitch? You sitting here trying to perpetrate like you down with the culture, but like all you wiggers, you want to run back to your privilege when it suits you. But you forget, you're just a faggot, and the police don't give a shit about faggots. Dick suckers don't get to rely on their race unless they hide being gay, and you can't, honey. It's written all over you; your walk, the way you talk, your clothes, and your stupid ass hair. When them cops come up in here and see your gay ass, you won't be nothing but a joke. Especially when they run up in here and see the doll, in all her fabulosity. We're all a joke to them. So yeah, give them a call. Let's see what happens."

The next few hours were a haze for him. He called Ella, told her he needed help bringing his clothes back home. Brushed aside her questions. Snapped at her, "Just come!"

Ricky and Chauncey sat in the living room, ostensibly watching TV while seeming to keep watch, making sure Ella, Jason, and Raheem didn't pack up items other than those owned by Chance. He looked at Jason and Raheem when they first entered, sizing them up, speculating whether they were the sort that would try to test Chauncey, who nearly vibrated with the desire for a brawl. He stood glaring at them, grimacing menacingly.

They nodded wanly, and Ricky sat back. There would be no dust up this day.

Chapter Forty-Seven

Since Babe was on a budget and his funds were low, he engaged the okey doke. He removed the locks from his doors, put them in a bag, returned to the hardware store with his receipts, and exchanged them for new locks: one for the front door, the apartment door, and the laundry room.

Rueben's heart soared when he spotted Babe walking from the parking lot, carrying a bag. He had to wait a while as Alise had not yet drifted off, so he sat in the bedroom, listening to Babe's laborings in the hall.

Later, he climbed through the window onto the porch and rang the doorbell.

Babe was surprised. "What are you doing out here?"

Reuben was surprised too. "Where's your snakes?"

"My sn—?" He rubbed his head. "Oh. Yeah. I got a haircut. I needed to get rid of the old to make way for the new. You like it?"

"I had to climb through the window. Mama's sleep."

"I saw the deadbolt on the door. I'll have to talk to her about that. That's dangerous. What if there's a fire when she's not here, you wouldn't be able to get out. Then I'd have to kick in the door."

Rueben pictured superheroes with capes and face masks. "Cool."

"Not cool. I can't afford new doors."

"You got something to eat?"

Babe paused. "I don't know if that's a good idea, Ruebs. I didn't know before that you have a problem when it comes to that—"

"No, I don't. I'm not willy."

Babe knelt to sit on the cement portal of the doorway. He patted the spot beside him. Rueben squeezed his bulk into the space he'd left. "Look buddy. There's no shame in having what you have. The things we have that sometimes a lot of other people don't have, those are the things that make us special. Those are the things that God gave to you that make you stand out from other people. You know how some people have green eyes, and other people are tall, and others are small?"

"Or some people like boys and not girls."

Babe paused uncomfortably. "Yeah. Yeah, I guess you're right. That too. That first time I saw you out back, going through the trash cans. That shows me that you have a problem, right? And I don't want you to be ashamed about that. But I want you to understand that you shouldn't be going through the trash can for food. It's unhealthy. You could get sick eating rotten food."

"But I wasn't doing that because of Willy. I was doing that because of Mitzi. She wanted something to eat. That Willy person is the other Rueben. The one that died."

Babe grew annoyed. "Listen. I know you make up stories to entertain yourself. When I was a kid, I made up stories too. But there's a difference between lying and telling a tale—"

Rueben cut him off. He told him the story he had learned by listening to the whispers coming through the vents. The story that had come to him in the middle of the day when he was lying on the soiled mattress in the basement back when Puff Puff was still here. The story of the first Rueben, and how he had died. He remembered when the whispers began to sound more and more like his mama, the same high-keening moan when she cried, how sad she was, all alone, visiting maternity wards where newborn babies sat in glass boxes waiting for new mommies to take them home and love them. How mama had said she took the brown baby all alone, the baby with no mommy of his own. How she had taken him and hidden him in her house. How she named him Rueben to replace the one that went to live with God. How she told the new Rueben that he was just like the other one, that he had Willy, and she had to keep him safe, so she locked up all the food, and she locked up the new Rueben, too, so that he would not die like the other one. And it was good. It was just new Rueben and Mama. And nobody would take him away from her.

Babe listened. Incredulous. Could this story possibly be true? Or was this kid creative enough to make this story up such a story? Rueben had a penchant for telling stories. Was this one of those?

He contemplated how things would pan out if he called the police. He needed to keep the boy safe. No child should be living in the squalor and filth in that apartment with locks on the cabinets. Padlocks on the refrigerator. The boy that was "homeschooled." Meaning no one knew he even existed.

He worried about how involving the police could blow this thing up into something beyond control. He thought of all the years where he had been taught not to involve the police. But he now knew those were his parents' issues, borne of generations of negative interactions. He told himself his parents' issues were not his own.

"Why don't you come upstairs with me? We'll get something to eat. Something healthy, right?"

Rueben folded his arms across his generous chest. "Right. How about orange slices?"

The fragrant smell of sliced oranges permeated the kitchen. It helped to clear the muck in Babe's brain, left there by the sordid tale Rueben had told him. He went to the living room to get the phone. He was still uncertain whether he should call or not.

By the time he went back to the kitchen, Rueben had finished the oranges and was standing at the refrigerator looking inside.

"What are you doing? We agreed on orange slices."

"I want more."

Downstairs, Alise rose confusedly from her fog. Her hair had come undone from the braids, and she raked her fingers through it, tugging it into a sloppy knot as she rose unsteadily. She looked around the empty room and called for him. Pretzel sat by the door. He ran over to her and jumped into her lap. She brushed him off, curious about him being on this level if Rueben were on the sublevel.

The cold breeze blowing the blinds through the wide-open window caused her heart to race, her breath coming in short gasps. She grabbed the phone as she shouted his name and ran downstairs to the cellar, which was cluttered with debris. She stumbled over piles of cast-aside garbage, not finding him anywhere. She didn't want to call the police, but she didn't know what else she should do.

She ran out to the porch and screamed his name, loud and full of anguish. She was not on the porch on Leviticus Street; she was in that hospital room, all those years ago, listening to those words again.

an unfortunate mishap mishap mishap....

Miss Imogene heard the shout, sitting, as she was, at the window inside her tiny apartment. She pushed herself up from her recliner and lumbered out to the sidewalk with her hands on her broad hips.

Babe and Rueben heard her too. Rueben jumped up from his chair and scrambled beneath the table in Babe's kitchen.

"I don't want to go back there," he whispered. "I want to stay with you, Babe."

Babe told him to stay there. He walked down the stairs and out to the porch and grasped the yelling woman by the shoulders to turn her around.

"Hush!" he hissed. "Stop making a fool of yourself. He's okay. He's safe."

She was wild-eyed. "What are you doing to him, you fucking pervert. He belongs to me."

Across the street, Wilfredo must have heard a commotion, like a murder of crows, so he came out to the stoop to see what was going on. The woman across the street was holding the phone out at Babe as if it were a weapon, a gun.

"You can't get away with this. I'll fix you good."

"Will you? Go on and call them. He's told me what's going on in there. Does he 'belong' to you? You think you can take whatever you want to take? That your need is more important than anybody else? Maybe I already called them. Or maybe I called Child Protective Services."

She stared at him with a sinking feeling in the pit of her gut. "You don't know anything about me."

Next door, the house of whispers began to shift. Curtains wafted on an unseen breeze. Window sashes hissed as they rose in their casings. Ricky came out onto the porch.

"What is happening out here?" he demanded.

"I know more than I care to," said Babe. "I know you did what you always do. Grabbing at everything after you fucked up your own life. Fill your continent with disease and perversion, and go somewhere else to get a fresh start where you fill that one with disease and perversion too."

"Who are you to talk about perversion? You, laying with other men, taking drugs into your body."

"Drugs?" Ricky asked. "Miss Thing, you can barely stand straight. What are you talking drugs?"

Wilfredo spotted Chance, walking up along the sidewalk. He gave a brief shout, nodding toward him to warn Babe.

Babe said, "Now is not a good time, Chance. You need to leave here."

Robby drifted downstairs, stood in the shadows behind the open door, observing the scene in amusement. The white Supra coasted past on the farside of the parking lot across the street. Wilfredo eyed the car warily.

Chance came onto the porch, oblivious to Babe's request. "You can't throw me out like the trash. You didn't even give me the courtesy of talking to me face-to-face."

Ricky said, "The courtesy was that he didn't kick your ass. Fucking his man, not paying rent. Take your ass away from here before we make due on that ass whipping."

Chance said, "You don't even care about that dude. You treat him like he's a piece of shit. Fucking him in the laundry room in the dark, on the floor, like an animal. All I wanted to be was your friend. I wanted to be a part of your life, and you acted like I was a joke because I'm not Black like you."

Ricky said, "You *are* a joke, wigger."

Babe said, "Treat you like a joke? I let you in my house. Took you around my friends. Let you in my life. How much more did you need? I trusted you in my house, around my things, that you rifled through, put your hands all over, took my clothes. You pissed all over my hospitality. I got nothing more to give to you."

Upstairs, beneath the table, Rueben heard the voices. He heard Babe's voice, full of anguish. He climbed up from under the table, wanting to help him. Was Mama hurting him?

No one noticed the squad cars pull up, not until the officers, full of authority, hands resting on batons and holstered guns, meandered onto the porch.

"What's going on here, folks?"

The question was a valid one. It was a question any passerby might have asked. It was the uniform, the stance of the officer asking the question that gave it a different heft, turned the question into a threat. It was the backup squad car and the other three officers in uniforms, dark like birds of prey, descending onto the property that turned that valid question into one of menace.

The lead officer assessed the scene as he had been trained to do, determining who was the most threatening based upon his years of experience in de-escalation of domestic violence scenes. He focused on the African American male, over six feet, muscular stature, bald, dressed in jeans and T-shirt. He decided to move him from the rest of the individuals.

Hearing the commotion, Drew walked out onto his porch, pulling his hat lower over his face. "What's going on?"

One of the officers barked at him, "Go back inside, sir."

Alise screamed, "These people are trying to take what belongs to me."

No one noticed the overweight Black boy standing in the doorway.

Until he reached into his pocket, grabbed something, and began to take his hand out of his pocket.

Backup spotted sudden movements. Someone, maybe everyone, shouted.

"Gun!"

Mitzi, reclining in a dark corner, resting on her massive paws, caught notes of a manufactured strawberry scent wafting on the air, notes she had come to associate with Rueben and licorice ropes. Notes she had come to associate with a treat especially for her. She pushed herself up and trotted toward the open door.

Babe looked in the direction they all turned. Heard the warning. Lunged forward, rushing to push Rueben back inside the hallway.

"No!" Babe shouted. "There's no gun here! No!"

Mitzi smelled the bodies, dark like splatters of ink, descending upon Rueben. She tore out of the doorway, roaring with fury, lunging toward them, her jaws spread wide, her aim low and true.

Robby tucked himself into a ball, biting his tongue.

No help, no help, no help.

Acknowledgements

Once upon a time, a boy lived in a space that was rampant with rage. Whose existence endured ugliness and deliberate, curated violence. He was a gentle boy. The hatred around him confused him, caused him to withdraw into a world of his own creation, where he created sisters and cousins that protected him from abusers, bullies and psychic destruction. In the midst of this apocalypse, on a small t. v. screen, a woman appeared. She was beautiful and talented, smiling, glamorous, and kind. More important than that, she was brown. Her spirit shined bright. It pushed aside the darkness. The boy learned the power of dreams. This was not a miracle. The world around him did not suddenly grow bright with promise, but the boy learned how to hope, and he held tight to his dreams, he learned strategies to strengthen his spirit, music, books, art, nature... And the world that sought to destroy his spirit failed its mission.

Maria Milligan, you always believed in me, you were my first fan, always excited to see the next page, always positive and full of ideas. Your light has shined and saved many people. I am one of them.

Ann Green, Tenaya Darlington, Paul Patterson and JoAlyson Parker at Saint Joseph's University for all you have done to support turning the dream to reality.

Sarah Varlack (Aunt Poodles), Marie Collins (Aunt Pat), my mother's spirit lives within you. Thank you for allowing me to channel her.

Cecil Varlack (Uncle Tony), the kindest, most generous spirit I have known. To have known you was a gift from God. You showed me that masculinity does not have to be toxic.

My siblings Teresa Matthews and Robert Jackson, thanks for always being in my corner.

Simone Richardson, Maddie Owens, David Barnes, Shawn Hooker, Brian Bazemore, Curtis Thomas, Candy Bazemore, my BFFs for life.

The many untold beautiful spirits of those no longer here that continue to inspire me. Those who really did bang the walls and shout the house down to "Goddess of Love" and "Somebody Save the Night".

There are many people I have never met, no longer here, whose loss I feel with an ache that is heavy and palpable, too many to name.

Thank you to Lambda Literary. Without your acknowledgement that my words meant something to someone, I might have given up in the face of so much disregard.

Thank you to Ashley and the NineStar Press team for seeing the dream and giving it power to release into the world.

Adam Oliver: You are a beautiful spirit. You make me believe the world can be a beautiful place. You live life fearlessly. You terrify and exhilarate me. I love you.

Always: Carolann Ambrose. The world is an empty place without you.

About David Jackson Ambrose

David Jackson Ambrose is a graduate of the University of Pennsylvania. He has an M.A. from Saint Joseph's University and an M.F.A. in Creative Writing from Temple University. He has presented at the National Conference for Teachers of English. His exploration of race and the mental health field was selected for honorable mention for AWP's 2016 Intro Journals Project. Ambrose was selected as a 2018 Lambda Literary Award finalist for his debut novel, State of the Nation. He describes his work as "a focus on marginalized people and the ways identities are shaped by a confluence of the prison industrial complex, the mental health factory, (both of which he refers to as neo-plantations) and police state apparatus as it collides with gender, sexuality and the construct of race to impose disability and hierarchy as part of the design of American capitalism."

Email
djac@sas.upenn.edu

Facebook
www.facebook.com/davidjrhd

Twitter
@DJacksonambrose

Website
www.davidjacksonambrose.com

Also from NineStar Press

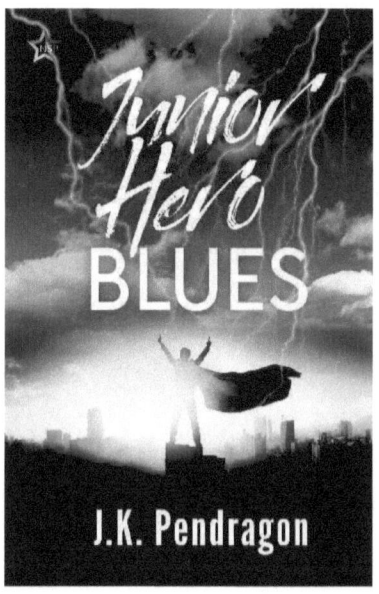

Junior Hero Blues by J.K. Pendragon

Last year, Javier Medina was your average socially awkward gay high schooler with a chip on his shoulder. This year, he's...well, pretty much the same, but with bonus superpowers, a costume with an ab window to show off his new goods, and a secret identity as the high-flying, wise-cracking superhero Blue Spark.

But being a Junior Hero means that Javier gets all the responsibility and none of the cool gadgets. It's hard enough working for the Legion of Liberty and fighting against the evil Organization, all while trying to keep on top of school work and suspicious parents. Add in a hunky boyfriend who's way out of Javier's league, and an even hunkier villain who keeps appearing every time said boyfriend mysteriously disappears, and Blue Spark is in for one big dollop of teenage angst. All while engaging in some epic superhero action and, oh yeah, an all-out battle to protect Liberty City from the forces of evil.

Welcome to the 100% true and totally unbiased account of life as a teenage superhero.

The Q by Rick R. Reed

Step out for a Saturday night at *The Q*—the small town gay bar in Appalachia where the locals congregate. Whose secret love is revealed? What long-term relationship comes to a crossroad? What revelations come to light? The DJ mixes a soundtrack to inspire dancing, drinking, singing, and falling in (or out) of love.

This pivotal Saturday night at *The Q* is one its regulars will never forget. Lives irrevocably change. Laugh, shed a tear, and root for folks you'll come to love and remember long after the last page.

The Boss by J. Calamy

Nicholas Erickson is happy to be the smallest cog at the US Embassy in Singapore, a big step up from prison. Nick lives with a terrible secret: he killed a family of three in a traffic accident, for which he was imprisoned and became a pariah back home. The only threat to his second chance is the truth—and Nelson Graves.

Shipping Magnate Lord Nelson Graves is secretly the head of crime syndicate Red Sky, making him the biggest arms dealer and drug boss in Southeast Asia. Graves is tired, lonely, addicted to opium, and trying to get his imploding crime syndicate back to business. There is a traitor in his organization and an old enemy is back on his tail.

A romance builds between hot-headed, reckless Nick and unhappy, ruthless Graves. But nothing is that easy. Shoot-outs, bombings, and vindictive exes prove Nick's past and Graves's present may be a lethal combination.

Connect with NineStar Press

www.ninestarpress.com

www.facebook.com/ninestarpress

www.facebook.com/groups/NineStarNiche

www.twitter.com/ninestarpress

www.instagram.com/ninestarpress

www.ingramcontent.com/pod-product-compliance
Lightning Source LLC
Chambersburg PA
CBHW050611110726
47899CB00001B/60

*9 7 8 1 6 4 8 9 0 2 4 8 2 *